Formerly a lecturer at Loughborough University, Roger Hubank's previous book *Hazard's Way* won the Grand Prix at Banff Mountain Festival 2001 and also the Boardman-Tasker Award 2001. His first novel, *North Wall*, was favourably reviewed by Al Alvarez and has featured in two anthologies. Of *Hazard's Way* Jim Perrin wrote. '...[it is] quite simply a masterpiece – the finest piece of fictional writing around the subject of mountaineering ever to have been published in this country...' Roger Hubank still climbs at a modest level. He is married and lives in Loughborough.

NORTH

A novel

ROGER HUBANK

PHOENIX

In memory
of the officers and men
of the Lady Franklin Bay Expedition
1881–1884

With respect

A PHOENIX PAPERBACK
First published in Great Britain in 2002
by The Ernest Press
This paperback edition published in 2004
by Phoenix
an imprint of Orion Books Ltd,
Orion House, 5 Upper St Martin's Lane,
London WC2H 9EA

Copyright © Roger Hubank 2002

The right of Roger Hubank to be identified as the author of
this work has been asserted by him in accordance with the
Copyright, Designs and Patents Act 1988.

A CIP catalogue record for this book
is available from the British Library.

ISBN 0 75381 769 1

Printed and bound in Great Britain by
Clays Ltd, St Ives plc

'And for the season, it was winter, and they that know the winters of that country know them to be sharp and violent, and subject to cruel and fierce storms, dangerous to travel to known places, much more to search an unknown coast.'

WILLIAM BRADFORD, *Of Plymouth Plantation*

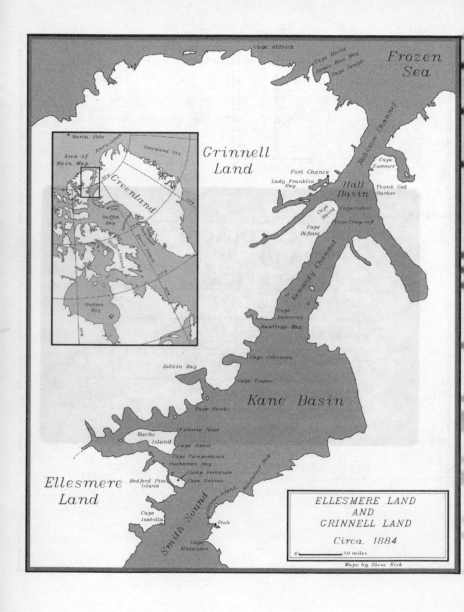

Cape Aldrich

Cape Hecla
James Ross Bay
Cape Joseph

Frozen Sea

Grinnell Land

Robeson Channel

Cape Sumner

Fort Chance
Lady Franklin Bay

Hall Basin

Thank God Harbor

Cape Lupton
Cape Baird
Cape Defosse
Cape Craycroft

Kennedy Channel

Cape Lawrence
Rawlings Bay

Cape Collinson

Dobbin Bay

Cape Frazer

Kane Basin

Cape Hawks

Victoria Head
Bache Island
Cape Albert
Cape Camperdown
Buchanan Bay
Camp Fortitude
Bedford Pim Island
Cape Sabine

Ellesmere Land

Rosse Bay
Littleton Island

Cape Isabella

Etah

Smith Sound

Cape Alexander

Inset map:
North Pole
Arctic Ocean
Greenland Sea
Area of Main Map
Greenland
Baffin Bay
Davis Strait
Baffin Island
Hudson Bay

Legend box:
*ELLESMERE LAND
AND
GRINNELL LAND*

Circa. 1884

0 ——————— 30 miles

Maps by Steve Kirk

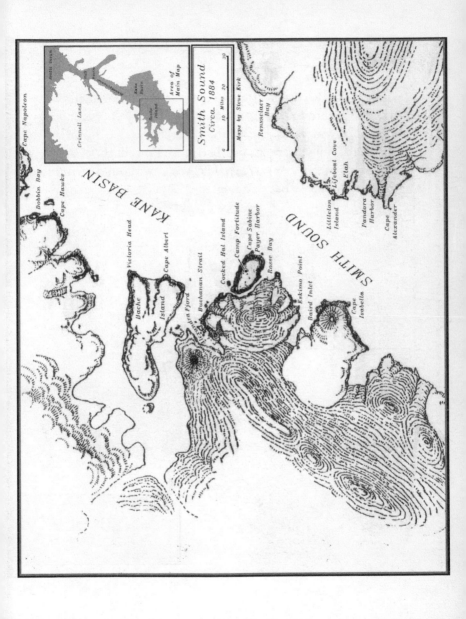

Smith Sound
Circa 1884

Maps by Steve Kirk

0   10 Miles 20   30

Area of
Main Map

Grinnell Land

Cape Napoleon

KANE BASIN

Dobbin Bay

Cape Hawks

Victoria Head

Bache
Island

Cape Albert

Buchanan Strait

Cocked Hat Island

Camp Fortitude

Cape Sabine

Payer Harbor

Rosse Bay

Eskimo Point

Baird Inlet

Cape Isabella

SMITH SOUND

Rensselaer Bay

Lifeboat Cove

Littleton Island

Etah

Pandora Harbor

Cape Alexander

ACKNOWLEDGEMENTS

I wish to acknowledge my debt to the work of the Polar etholo-gists and anthropologists, Franz Boas, Barry Lopez, Jean Malaurie, Alwin Pederson; to the biographers and historians A. L. Todd, Wally Herbert and Theodore Powell; above all, to the journals of Lt A. W. Greely, US Army, without which this novel could not have been attempted.

ONE

In Washington, towards the end of the nineteenth century, in one of the fine town houses that lined three sides of an elegant square, six men were sitting down to dinner. They were, with one exception, powerful men. The previous day, gathering at the death-bed of an expiring administration, they had secured a modest appropriation for the furtherance of a carefully nurtured project. Though all had contributed in some measure towards that success, it would be short of the truth to suggest that all shared a common interest. Amos Potwine, Chairman of the House Committee on Appropriations, was repaying a favour. Henry Clarke, editor of the *New York Sentinel* had wielded his pen in the expectation of favours to come. In those days there was nothing out of the ordinary in such accommodations. One way or another, everything came down to politics. And politics, as their host might have put it, was mostly favours.

There were times – they came round every four years – when the Honourable Lucius Clay felt a cynical contempt for his profession. He was an old man, apple-cheeked, with that thatch of soft white hair constituents admire to see in their elder statesmen. A black patch covered one eye, the result, it was rumoured, of a duel fought while a student at the University of Virginia. The other, twinkling genially in its socket, surveyed his fellow Americans with a blue, avuncular gaze that belied the senator's reputation as a savage wit.

Amos Potwine was nursing a stiff neck. He'd spent an uncomfortable morning standing in an icy wind, while the new president delivered his inaugural address.

'One thing's for sure,' he remarked, savouring his champagne. 'From now on we won't be drinking this stuff in the White House.'

A ripple of laughter went round the table. The new president's wife was as steadfast in her convictions as her husband had so far proved unpredictable in his. He was a man nobody knew, and nobody wanted. At the national convention, after a great many ballots failed to resolve a deadlock brought about by the implacable hostility of rival factions, he had been nominated for no other purpose than that of detaching his state's delegation from the candidate favoured by Senator Conkey of New York.

Already he was being written off as a national disaster. The *New York Sentinel,* a staunch upholder of the previous administration, was unequivocal in its scorn.

> Never before has there been such woeful confirmation of our proudest boast: that the highest office in the land is open to the humblest citizen. Indeed, the new Chief Magistrate might be exchanged for another just as good in any corner grocery from Tallahassee to Tuckernuck Island.

'I wonder what old Abe would have said,' continued the congressman.

'Oh, I can tell you that.' A Virginian whose sympathies lay with the South, Senator Clay had stuck with Lincoln and the Union, though at great cost to himself. 'Old Abe would have said, "No one's going to shoot this fellow, with Tyler Greig next in line."'

The laughter which greeted this sally was not shared by one man present. Lieutenant Parish was conscious of his rank. Or lack of it. He gazed awkwardly at the gilt clock on the mantelpiece. French, he guessed. He was not quite at home among fashionable people.

'Well,' said Potwine, picking at his lobster, 'the president may be safe enough, but I reckon Senator Conkey would sure as hell like to take a shot at Ty.'

There was another burst of laughter. William Parish shifted his gaze from the clock to the painting over the fireplace. A long lean man, even at table he sat a good half head taller than his fellow guests. Extravagant black whiskers, jutting to a point, concealed the scars of a jaw shattered twenty years before in the fighting at Antietam Bridge. So far he had said very little. He was here to be inspected, and was conscious of the fact: conscious, too, of his new white waistcoat, and the white kid gloves bought on Pennsylvania Avenue. He was wishing he hadn't worn the gloves.

'Poor old Ty couldn't believe his ears,' spluttered Potwine. "Drop it," Conkey told him. "Drop it as you would drop a red-hot shoe from the forge." "But Ithamor," quavers Ty, "this is a greater office than I ever dreamed of attaining."'

This time a drumming of hands on the table boosted the merriment. The new vice president's reputation as a seeker after spoils was legendary.

Then, as the laughter died away, the conversation resumed on a tentative note.

'Will the new president look favourably on our expedition?' Rufus Chance was himself a man for whom others were usually glad to do favours. He was a youngish man, shadowy under his sallow, clean-shaven skin. Thick ebony hair brushed back over his skull emphasised the pallor of his brow.

'I doubt he's aware of its existence,' smiled the senator. 'What have the good folks of Iowa to do with the North Pole?'

'I don't suppose your new chief will approve,' remarked the editor to General Sweetsir.

'He doesn't. He told me so.' The general, a civil war veteran with sweeping moustaches, put on the bearish growl of the new Secretary for War. ' "The business of the Army, sir, is to account for every dollar, and to protect settlers from the attacks of savages. Not to go squandering public money on fool projects in some God-forsaken wilderness."'

Parish's lip curled in his beard. He came from a stony, hilly country where the winters were prolonged and hard. And yet actual landscapes were of less importance than the landscape of the spirit.

As the meal progressed the senator's gaze turned curiously from time to time towards the Yankee lieutenant. He was recalling Sweetsir's words of recommendation: *This man is the real thing. He has that inward call. What's more, he's a sticker.* Severe whiskers, together with a gaze slightly magnified by the thick lenses of his spectacles, gave him a studious look. Lucius Clay guessed he'd got himself an education at one of those New England country colleges.

Certainly the Lieutenant had read everything he could get his hands on. When not occupied with his duties at the Signal Office, he had devoted many hours in the Library of Congress poring over books and journals. He had prepared himself as thoroughly as study and reflection could ever hope to qualify a man for an arduous and dangerous undertaking. And yet his part in this venture (should he prove to have one) would rest, he knew, on the say-so of mere know-nothings.

General Sweetsir, though, had the bit between his teeth.

'Just think of it, gentlemen. For the first time in history the countries of the world will be joined together in scientific enquiry. The first systematic examination of Arctic phenomena. Tides, currents, winds, temperature, ice conditions, precipitation, magnetic phenomena, barometric pressure, earth currents, solar radiation. Just think what that would mean. A collection of basic information about one of the great unknown regions of the world.'

The general was a man of huge enthusiasms.

So, with the drawing of the cloth and the arrival of Madeira on a silver tray, the talk turned again to the polar seas, and the lure of the Farthest North.

'Didn't the British extend the record a few years back?' Clarke turned to his neighbour.

'That is so, sir,' returned the whiskery man. 'And three men paid with their lives.'

He left it at that. Though his eyes loomed owlishly in their bottle lenses. Lt Parish might have been reflecting, with pitying disapproval, on the English sailors lugging their boats north over the Frozen Sea, hauling away like the slaves they were to

4

their old remorseless gods. His expedition (the lieutenant regarded it as destined for himself) would achieve something more durable than a few quickly withered laurels of fame.

'So you have no mind to improve on the British record?'

Rufus Chance entertained vague memories of another Army lieutenant who'd sailed off to the polar region a few years back, and not returned. He had no wish to be associated with another disaster.

Sweetsir chuckled.

'We're interested in rather more than setting records for endurance. Isn't that so, Lieutenant?'

Parish cleared his throat.

'I believe serious scientific exploration is to be preferred to mere striving after distance.'

He lived at such an intensity of purpose other people sometimes felt belittled by it, without knowing why. They held it against him, nonetheless.

But General Sweetsir was for setting minds at rest. He spoke of the dangers of one-season dashes. Of wintering in the ice. That was the mistake. Relying on a ship that could so easily be crushed and sunk.

'Our guess is that's what's happened to De Long.'

He glanced at Parish, who nodded slightly as if in confirmation, but said nothing.

'Now what we have in mind,' Sweetsir continued, 'is a substantial frame building, carried in sections on shipboard, put together after reaching Lady Franklin Bay. It would be the first step towards the setting up of a permanent Polar colony. What's more, there's coal in Grinnell Land. Coal, gentlemen, only five hundred miles from the Pole.'

The general could not resist a glance at Rufus Chance, whose great fortune was derived from the anthracite mines of Pennsylvania.

'There is still so much we do not know,' he went on. 'We don't yet know for certain whether Greenland is an island. There's good reason to believe there's open water north of Kane

Basin. Maybe even a great polar sea ...'

The general paused to put a light to his cigar.

The coal king would have been hard put to locate Kane Basin on the large globe that stood to one side of the fireplace. Nor had he any opinion as to whether Greenland was or was not an island. Rufus Chance had no conception of the Arctic, except as an immense prospect, an infinite horizon.

'I understand, Lieutenant,' he said, turning his dark-lidded eyes on William Parish, 'this is to be entirely an Army operation?'

'That is so, sir.' He said nothing more, though Mr Chance was looking expectant.

Senator Clay slid tactfully into the vacant space.

'If the Army is to bear responsibility for the expedition, then the Army must be in command. Isn't that so, Lieutenant?'

'I consider it essential,' said Parish tersely. 'A civilian mentality would be quite unfitted for an expedition of this kind.'

'Besides, the Army's record speaks for itself,' put in the general hastily. 'It was the Corps of Topographical Engineers who carried out the exploration west of the Mississippi. The railroad surveys too.'

'Beautiful volumes,' the senator murmured softly. 'A joy to behold.'

'It cost a million dollars to publish them.' Amos Potwine might have been recalling an old wound. 'It cost more to publish them than to fund the expeditions.'

'Do you think you'll have funds enough to meet the expense?' he added. There were limits to what he could be expected to pull off, especially at the start of a new administration.

'One must do the best one can,' replied Parish cautiously. His appointment had yet to be confirmed. 'Though the hire of the vessel alone,' he had to add, 'will use up most of the appropriation.'

'Is that a tactful "No"?'

The Lieutenant might have believed himself accused of some mealy-mouthed evasion, for he brought the double barrels of his lenses to bear directly at the questioner.

'Since you raise the matter, sir, I may say that there was a time when the federal government placed a greater value on what could be learned from scientific exploration.'

'I suspect the Lieutenant is afflicted with that terrible New England conscience,' said the senator slyly. 'He has the temerity to believe that some of our surplus wealth should be used for the common good.'

'What I believe, sir,' replied Parish stiffly, suspecting he was being teased, 'is that we as a nation have been singled out to do great work. And there is work to be done, real work, in Grinnel Land.'

A reserved man, yet his spirit was most roused when the dark Puritan blood surged in his veins.

'There! Didn't I say so?' crowed Senator Clay delightedly. 'The New England conscience.'

Not long afterwards the party broke up. Refusing the offer of Chance's carriage, the lieutenant was the first to leave. He liked, he said, to walk. He was not accustomed to dining on fresh lobster, and was half expecting to have to pay for his indulgence.

Snow, which had threatened all evening, was falling as he set off across the square.

Senator Clay stood in the hall bidding farewell to his guests.

'Well, do we have our man?'

'You know my opinion.' General Sweetsir was shrugging his bulky torso into a topcoat. 'I believe he's head and shoulders above all other candidates.'

Lucius Clay stood at the open door to bid farewell to his guests. A hush lay over the square. No sound carried through the muffled air. Beyond the roofs of the houses the pale dome of the Capitol stood fast, though the sky seemed to be descending.

The senator's eye dwelt momentarily on the rangy figure already receding into the snow.

Yes, he was thinking. Cautious, ambitious, thrifty, pertinacious ... A thorough Yankee.

TWO

In a country town in western Massachusetts a young woman sat alone in the back parlour of an old brick house on Willow Street. It was a somewhat boxy room overshadowed by its furniture, which was dark and heavy. Though the walnut clock on the mantelpiece had not yet struck four o'clock, the day was dying fast. The young woman too was overshadowed. She sat slumped in a chair drawn a little way back from a brown secretary desk where pen and paper lay ready to hand. Her arms rested limply in her lap, one hand clutching a letter. Glaring light from a single lamp cast into gaunt relief a small plain face, compact as a fist, whose customary gaze of lively intelligence was clouded by the certainty that her last resort had gone. The light betrayed, with cruel emphasis, the sunken chest, the narrow sloping shoulders, the dark rings under her red-rimmed eyes. She had not slept for several nights.

Martha Stevens was used to thinking her own thoughts, with no one to hinder.

For once, though, she might have been glad of another soul to confide in. A sympathetic silence would have sufficed. But family and friends are nothing if not predictable. *A man will follow his own star. If he don't go looking for it, it generally comes looking for him.*

Poor Mother, she thought, had never gotten over the war.

Her gaze rose to the photograph above the desk in which a dreamy-looking man in uniform sat with folded hands clasping a bible, eyes distant. At his side stood a tall straight-backed young woman, her tense fingers clasping his shoulder. She might have been trying to hold him back.

Martha Stevens had to admit she'd been clinging to the hope that William might not, after all, be appointed as commander.

8

He'd said himself there would be plenty of men pushing for the post. And she felt ashamed, the more so for him wanting it so badly. The command alone, he'd said, would mean a certain degree of fame. She felt a qualm, recalling the excitement in his voice.

A red setter slumbering at her side sighed deeply, as if in sympathy with her mood.

From the start she'd been deeply unhappy about him going. Oh, she admired his determination: that dogged drive to get on, not just for himself, for her too. Yet she felt he was too driven by pride and ambition. And something more: a hunger for something that excluded her, that went beyond her. And it made no sense. It made no sense for a man to go down on his knees and tell a woman he could have no other for his wife, when all the time there was something that mattered more.

She'd suggested a period of waiting. If there was a likelihood of his going to the Arctic, it might be wiser to put off marriage until he returned. It would, in any case, be a test of their feelings for one another. He'd agreed. Now, with his command confirmed and a two-year absence looming, he was begging her to reconsider.

She looked again at what he'd written: *There can be no question of my going without we are married first. Something would be missing from my life without which I fear I could not do my duty as I would wish to do it. All my thoughts would be with you. I should be afraid to lose you, and the strain would be unendurable ...*

Oh, she knew what it meant, his passionate declaration. If it came to it, he would go. He would go, and he would suffer all the more. And she would be to blame.

Yet what if she were to stop him going: stifled his dream? Some day, for sure, it would rise up again. It would come between them. She knew it would. No, she wanted him to go.

Somewhere in the house a clock began to chime. A low, dolorous lament, it seemed to be tolling the months of separation.

It would be hard, he'd said: hard, but patience and fortitude would see them through.

Now the silvery chimes of the walnut clock were taking up the count.

Well, no doubt she could bear up.

The setter raised its head, eyes fixed on the figure in the chair, and thumped its tail.

Martha Stevens sighed again. She was, she thought, a very weak woman.

*

He had turned up the year before, a tall, stiff, figure in his uniform.

'There is a man at the door,' announced the little maid, at a loss. 'An army lieutenant.'

She was new to her duties, which were still inclined to fluster.

'A man.' Miss Matty looked grave. 'What shall we do with him?'

But the girl only stared, and waited to be told.

'A *man*,' repeated Miss Matty thoughtfully.

The lumpy girl nodded, eyes fixed on the mistress.

'Then he had better be shown into the front parlour. It is impolite to leave him standing at the door.'

Though the visitor seemed in no way put out, left at the porch, hearing the breeze stirring the branches of the white pine overhead, looking over the brick house, painted a warm yellow, with its white trimmings, its green shades.

The hall clock was striking the hour as Martha Stevens, having waited some moments, entered the room, to be startled by an immensely tall figure turning towards her. Her first impression was of a long narrow face peering at her through a thicket of whiskers.

She saw from the yellow straps he was a cavalryman, like father.

'Lieutenant William Parish, ma'am. Fifth United States Cavalry.'

His eyes loomed at her through thick spectacles.

He saw a young woman, her face with its broad curved forehead framed by two smooth bands of chestnut hair, regarding him with a steady gaze. With one hand she clutched a blue worsted shawl about the shoulders of a dress of white piqué. It was, he saw, exquisitely clean.

Somewhere in the house another bell began a deep bass booming.

Miss Stevens had begun to explain that her mother, the late colonel's widow, rarely saw visitors – indeed, she rarely left her room – when the door opened to admit a black figure, gliding in with a stiff *swish, swish* of bombazine.

The Lieutenant rose to his feet.

'Lieutenant Parish has called to pay his respects, Mother.'

The widow inclined her head.

'My husband would, I know, wish me to thank you, sir. He cannot thank you himself. But will do so, no doubt.'

'The Lieutenant was with Father's regiment in the Wilderness,' murmured Martha Stevens.

Thus prompted, the visitor cleared his throat.

'The colonel was a fine man, ma'am. I was grieved to hear of his death.'

His condolence was acknowledged with another gracious inclination of the head.

'Yes ma'am,' affirmed Lt Parish, after a pause.

'It was a blessing, sir. My husband suffered constantly.'

After years of pain Professor Stevens had finally succumbed to the ball which struck him down that day in the Wilderness.

The Lieutenant cleared his throat again: stared hard at his hat. Frugal in all things, his habit of thrift extended to speech.

They sat in silence in the little parlour, a room whose knife-edged furniture and impenetrable surfaces suggested a place set aside for strained encounters.

A shaft of sunlight lay across the widow's dusty bombazine.

'I do not care to go out much,' she observed, *á propos* of nothing, 'lest my husband might return and miss me.'

She was having one of her days.

The angular man sat on the edge of his hard chair, holding on to his hat. His spiky knees stuck up most noticeably.

From another part of the house came a soft silvery chiming. The Lieutenant thought he counted eight.

'My father was fond of clocks,' the young woman ventured apologetically. 'We have a great many, as you see.'

Wound up regimentally every Saturday night, by Wednesday or Thursday they had deteriorated to an undisciplined rabble. Now it was the little parlour clock firing off an irritable falsetto.

The Lieutenant resisted a temptation to take out his watch.

'My father always knew which to take notice of, and which to disregard.'

'I dare say it's easily remedied,' offered the visitor. 'A matter of regulation.' And might have stood up to put things right, given any encouragement.

But the young woman only smiled. Her mother would have nothing changed.

So he sat remained stuck to his chair, shifting his gaze to the open piano.

Nor could Matty Stephens be of any assistance. She had quite run out of things to say.

So there they were. And might have remained, stiffening irrecoverably, had it not been for Lizzie Boot's blunt intervention.

'Will the Lieutenant be staying for supper?' she wanted to know.

'There is new custard pie,' she thought to remind.

Supper, served on the kitchen table, brought about that restoration a meal will sometimes furnish.

'Such a rare pleasure these days,' sighed Mrs Stevens over the pie. 'Matty's chickens are so difficult.'

'No more so, I'm sure, ma'am, than most chickens,' said the lieutenant gravely.

'Though they are temperamental birds, certainly,' he thought to add.

In the homely warmth of the kitchen, he was beginning to thaw a little. On the stone hearth a red dog was setting about its supper.

The visitor spoke warmly of the colonel, his late commander. All he would say of the conflict, though, was that if it were possible for war to engender any virtue it would consist in this: that it taught a man what things really mattered, and what did not.

'I began to see there might be more to soldiering, ma'am, than simply striving to kill one's fellow men. So I took up my books again.'

'I am not a great believer in books,' observed the widow, taking a knife to the pie. 'I fear they joggle the mind.'

Martha Stevens poured her mother a glass of water.

'You went back to your Bible, Lieutenant?' she enquired, to restore order.

'No, ma'am. I studied telegraphy.'

Mrs Stevens paused in her slicing.

'It is the new method of communication, mama.' Miss Stevens was glad father had afforded her a good English education. The female mind, he used to say, should not be neglected, God having designed nothing in vain.

'Ah yes, the lanterns.' Mrs Stevens might have been entertaining some vague notion of lights ducked in and out of barrels.

'The Lieutenant is travelling to New Hampshire on war department business. Inspecting the Signal Service station on Mount Washington.'

The visitor took this as his cue.

'Meteorology affords many fascinating problems, ma'am,' he informed respectfully, 'the solution of which will bring outstanding benefits. Think how useful it would be if we could bring you advance warning of your winter storms.'

The widow poked nervously at her custard. The man was

peering at her again through his bottle ends.

'You are joining the Weather Service, Lieutenant?' she managed to get out.

'No ma'am. It is my ambition to command a scientific expedition to the Polar region.'

Such unpredictable shifts proved too much for Mrs Stevens.

'Ah, science ...' she murmured vaguely, and turned her attention to a preserved peach.

Thus launched, the visitor embarked on a brief account of Arctic exploration, to which he firmly expected to graduate when he had finished criss-crossing the West with telegraph stations. A certain liveliness animating his narrative, as he spoke of Kane, Hall and Franklin and the search for the North West Passage, could have been capital letters jostling together. Martha Stevens was subject to her late father's satiric flashes.

Then, of course, there was the race for the Farthest North – not to mention the Pole itself.

Supper, though, was icing over. Mother, she saw, had burrowed into another peach.

Shortly afterwards the visitor took his leave.

'I hope I may be allowed to call on you again,' he remarked at the door. 'On my return from Mount Washington.'

She could scarcely forbid it.

✳

For the last hour the train had run south following the river valley. At last the railroad swung away from the river to run for several miles beside a road bordered with elms. Not far off now, the town nestled comfortably within a circle of hills, one bald top, higher than the rest, overlooking wooded bluffs stretching to the horizon. The Lieutenant sat gazing out at fields of rich red earth. Deep too, he guessed. Not like the till and hardpan of his native hills.

Now, sliding past the window were scattered homesteads,

each with its own wood lot: horses, cows, chickens, vegetable gardens, orchards, with the dome of the observatory showing through the trees. Leaving his bag at the depot Parish went up the hill on foot. A few folk out and about gazed at the lean, long-boned army lieutenant wondering which folks he belonged to. But the rangy man, a stranger in this place, walked past them up the hill, past trees, churches, a livery stable, a school, a joiner's shop, *Zebulon Snell, Boots and Shoes*, hearing, if only remotely, the greetings of neighbours, yet feeling the tug of settled life. A place to put down roots. If only because home was the place you started from. But no: home, he corrected himself, was at the end of the road. Remembering his vocation. Which was awfully high, if awfully lonesome. The indicators of his destiny were too austere to allow for anything less.

Rounding a bend between the willows, he was overtaken by a wagon drawn by a plodding mule. He nodded briefly to the man on the cart who removed his pipe, spat, and nodded back.

So, recalled to himself, the Lieutenant turned in at the iron gate, his boots dusty from the tar walk, and went on past the hollyhocks and up the gravel path to the brick house, shady beneath its pines, a bird of passage still.

And was received with the best china, the dark blue with the Landing of Lafayette.

The meal started badly, on account of a contretemps over some broth.

'That girl will never do,' declared the widow darkly.

The Lieutenant was mopping a sleeve.

'Mother still pines for Doris,' the young woman soothed. Doris being a former domestic of ancestral pedigree, recently removed to become a Mrs Lawlor.

'No, not pine,' the mother took pains to distinguish. 'But I was in the habit of Doris, and do not care for Lizzie Boot.'

The Lieutenant brooded amid masses of dark mahogany as Miss Stevens hacked at the roast fowl. A slant sun threw yellow bars across the polished table. It lavished over the portrait of his late commander a pure golden glow that made luminous all Parish most admired of fortitude and cool composure. He had followed that good man from Massachusetts through Washington to Balls Bluff, then the Peninsular Campaign, Antietam, Fredericksburg, and so to the awful carnage in the Wilderness and the Minié ball that tumbled the colonel from his horse.

'As to that colonelcy,' said the widow firmly, 'my husband had no qualifications for the post. None whatsoever. Though a gentleman of the highest literary and moral worth.'

'He was certainly that, ma'am.' Parish laid down his fork. 'Also the colonel had something very rare. A gift for inspiring men.'

Something in the visitor's voice suggested it might be a gift he aspired to himself. Martha Stevens was a prey to sudden intimations. At the same time she began to wonder about a person known only as 'father'.

'The college refused him leave of absence to enlist,' the widow was complaining, 'so he took study leave, then volunteered.'

She had not forgiven him that.

'He used to say the war changed everything,' the late colonel's daughter remarked uncertainly. No more than a child when it started, in all her life she had never travelled more than ten miles from her home.

'Well, by the time it finished I knew I had a country,' said the visitor, dabbing his whiskers with a napkin. 'I'd been there. I'd tramped its hills, slept in its forests. I came back to find I had no family, no home. So I guess I found a change.'

It could have been an invasion of birch and maple, spreading again over land cleared with so much sweat and toil. Or else it was a memory of tumbled walls marking abandoned fields and pastures that brought a certain bleakness to the visitor's voice.

The young woman caught a glimpse of marks not visible to a naked eye. It was another of her lightning-like apprehensions.

'Ah, we were all changed,' said the widow simply. 'None of us are the same.'

After dinner, the widow retiring to her room, they sat out on the back porch, the tall Lieutenant and the slight young woman, who had pinned a shawl about her narrow shoulders.

He took the rocker. Since she insisted. Her father, she was saying, used to rock her on his knee when she was fretful. She had been a fretful child.

The Lieutenant was afflicted by the painful hollows of her throat.

'When I was restless,' he remarked, 'my mother used to put me in the woodbox and give me an onion. So I was told,' he added truthfully. His mother not being in a position to confirm.

So they sat looking out across a meadow, where the hay had been raked into heaps.

She pointed out the bare isolated top rising above an outline of unbroken forest. Mount Famine, so-called in settler times. Cattle pastured there never thrived. Up on the hill was the pine wood where she used to walk with Father. And over there were the roofs and gables of the college.

'He taught every subject in the curriculum at one time or another,' she went on. 'Excepting mathematics.'

'I should like to have gone to college,' remarked the visitor.

At sixteen young William Parish had led his class at high school, and delivered the valedictory address in Latin. But was too proud to say so now.

'But with no funds …' He raised a hand as if to indicate that a man must play the cards he's dealt. 'So I had to educate myself the best I could.'

She guessed he was not a man to give up easily.

So, by degrees, he came to tendering something approaching a *curriculum vitae*, though whether he was applying for a position, the Lieutenant could not then have said for certain.

After high school he had been tutoring some cousins who were behind in their books when he heard of the shelling of Fort

Sumter. He left to join the Union Army. A truthful boy, he gave his age when asked. *Take a walk around the block, son*, the sergeant said. *See if you can get any older.* He was old enough when he got back.

'That lie,' he confessed wryly, 'was my first taste of the iniquity of war.'

She sensed some puzzling contradiction at work in him. Something unresolved.

'And yet the slaves were freed,' she prompted gently. 'The Union was saved.' Out of loyalty. For she knew her father had taken up arms on behalf of justice and the right. Though they had always seemed oblique things to her. Somehow at an angle to life.

'For a long time afterwards,' continued the Lieutenant, not appearing to have heard, 'I did not feel I was living in the same country as the one I was born in. Then I was fortunate enough to have the privilege of serving under General Sweetsir. He introduced me to the Arctic.'

Martha Stevens thought of the Arctic, when she thought of it at all, as a kind of zero into which men plunged incomprehensibly. Even so, she looked with misgiving on yearnings for escape. She had an unsparing conscience.

And yet a man, Mother said, will always want a life apart.

Pussy, though, had jumped up into his lap, and was rubbing her head against his fingers.

Absently, the Lieutenant began to stroke the cat. His gaze was distant, fixed on the horizon, where Mt Famine raised a barren crest above the forest.

She saw, with a pang, that he was vulnerable to dreams.

So began a courtship carried on largely by correspondence, a circumstance that suited, since they were both of them adjusted to their own company, and could get by on a diet of ink and paper, being nourished since childhood on the written word.

He was a painstaking correspondent, leaving out nothing that might be instructive, or of use. Letters arriving from all over the South and West told of interesting methods of construction, and the difficulties of obtaining supplies.

She wrote of a late spring frost that had ruined the apple crop. Or else it was bread: her rye and Indian bread won second prize at the agricultural fair. She sealed them, her letters, not quite believing, as she wrote in her looping hand, the addresses of exotic destinations: Ft Benton … Fort Missoula … Ft Apache, Arizona …

Now he was in the Dakota Badlands; now in Montana Territory. Then weather so cold, a blizzard so unrelenting, he nearly froze to death before he reached the Powder River and the safety of a cavalry escort. Of its commander, he wrote: … *a good fellow, and an enthusiast for Arctic exploration. Rainbird would make a capital companion.*

She was so glad he'd found a friend.

Separation seemed to draw them closer. Or else it was an affinity of longings. She, in her New England kitchen amid the smell of baking, imagined supper by a campfire; sleeping on the ground. For him, all journeys ended along a road lined with willows. Desert and mountain intervened. But that was no more than a schooling for the undoubted trials and achievements that lay ahead. At times, though, the Lieutenant was troubled by a fear that he might be no good.

One morning Lizzie Boot came out to the orchard, bearing a letter.

Miss Martha was collecting eggs. And had to transfer them to the uncertain security of Lizzie's apron before sitting down on a tree stump.

Clutching the letter to her she waited patiently for Lizzie to withdraw.

After a paragraph regarding the problems of securing timber for poles … *needless to say, the whole region is entirely devoid of trees* … came a declaration of unexpected vehemence. He would have her and no other for his wife. Taken aback, she wondered if he was proposing marriage, it not having occurred to her that anyone would want to.

It was an unsettling moment in a life that had known little intimacy with others.

Though his courtship was of the plainest. He believed her to be kind and good: patient in adversity, persevering, able to endure. He did not doubt but that she would deprive herself of comfort and repose to render assistance to a friend in need.

She was perplexed, for she was not conscious, herself, of any such qualities.

He was equally frank about what he referred to as his 'disposition': *I am determined in accomplishing whatever I undertake, hard to be persuaded that I am wrong when I have once formed my opinion upon reflection, so sometimes obstinate and unyielding, and rather particular, liking to have everything in the right place and done at the right time. I have a little personal irritability in my constitution* ...

As to his character, he would like to have suggested the names of some clergymen she might consult, but, lacking the advantages a more settled life might have brought him, was unable to do so. Instead, he urged her to apply to Judge Tyrrel in Jackson, New Hampshire, who would furnish details of his family antecedents, and to General Sweetsir, of the US Signal Corps.

So the Lieutenant put his cards on the table, believing absolute honesty to be essential. He wished her to be under no illusion as to their life together. It would be one of industry, frugality, and application.

He could be quite insufferable, she saw. But she would put up with that.

✳

All the relatives agreed it was a most unsuitable season for a wedding. A biting wind. The byroads choked with snow. Aunts and cousins, trudging over from Heathy Lea and Westhampton to witness what had always been considered an improbable event, would have set forth for nothing less than family duty.

Not only the unseemly haste, but then to marry an outsider. A man no one knew. A man, moreover, whose imminent departure on some fool mission was beyond all figuring in Hartfield, Mass., where folks tended to shake their heads at journeyings hither and yon.

'When Thankful marries,' Aunt Babbit was heard to declare, 'I'm sure it won't be to astonish the family.' The Babbitts regarded themselves as pure stock, without even a wife in seven generations that wasn't from New England.

The ceremony was performed in the library by Reverend Dwight, with the relatives as witnesses, though less interested in one known from infancy, than in the stranger who had so staggered them all. Who turned out every bit as satisfying an oddity as they could have wished for, so long and skinny, with that disconcerting loom of eyes magnified by spectacles. The black beard jutting to a point.

'He don't look like no Indian fighter to me,' Cousin Thankful had to whisper.

She'd been expecting something more like the coloured prints. But a husband is a husband. And the uniform was real enough. She consoled herself by feeling sorry again for poor Matty's flat chest.

Afterwards, the guests stood talking of crops and stock, and cases of sickness likely to prove fatal, with an air of a thing concluded, all but the consuming of a small cake and a little ice cream. For the bride, though, there was, as always, unfinished business calling for her attention. In the wash room Lizzie Boot was bursting into floods, declaring she wouldn't stay, not if Miss Matty was leaving home she wouldn't.

'But who will look after my chickens?' Matty did her best to console, though the red-rimmed eyes seemed close to overflowing.

Mother, too, was as provoking as ever.

'Your father went away a fine strong man ...' She left the rest unsaid.

21

To General Sweetser, hovering in case of need, it was a cue for intervention.

'There is no danger, dear lady,' he assured. 'Why, taken man for man, the mortality is greater *here* than it is among Arctic explorers. It has been so these past twenty years.'

But the widow was adamant for disaster. Breaking off abruptly, she retired to her room.

Matty would have followed mother had it not been for the general, who was now addressing her.

'Were I not quite certain of him returning safe and sound, I should not let him go.'

He was looking at her most earnestly. It was, besides, a golden opportunity. Especially for a young officer denied the usual advantages. The general himself was a graduate of West Point.

'Believe me, Miss Stevens – Mrs Parish, ma'am – it will make him a famous man.'

She inclined her head, while summoning an expression that might be taken to reflect some semblance of the fortitude looked for in an army wife.

'I think I should go after Mother,' she stammered.

Mother, though, had resumed the face that suited a widow best. And would not be comforted.

So, descending the stairs again, the young wife spotted the tall figure of her husband through the open door: saw, with a pang, that he was standing apart, a lonesome pine silhouetted against the icy panes of the library window. Though the tall Lieutenant, by no means ill-at-ease, was looking out at the dead land with a kind of bleak satisfaction. To outstrip the crowd he had long since learnt to soar. He was, in any case, expecting soon to be entering his own wilderness.

But Reverend Dwight was wanting to present a Bible. When she looked again, she was comforted to see William deep in conversation, no doubt on some matter of polar geography with Professor Cousins, who had been Father's friend. Soon everyone was wanting to wish her well. She found herself sucked back among the aunts and cousins. Then it was Professor Cousins taking her by the elbow.

'Matty,' he told her gravely, 'I do believe you may have married a remarkable man.'

Soon a solemn little procession was forming up in the hall.

Then Tom threw open the door, the guests flinching as they filed out to be battered by a blustery wind, the Lieutenant holding his hat clamped firmly to his head, while hanging on to his bride. So they all teetered down the path where Tom had scattered cinders over the frozen snow. Though she turned back at the gate to embrace again good Aunt Buffum who'd agreed to stay on for a week or two, and Lizzie Boot, who promised faithfully to take no notice of Mother. Then fell to kissing the shivering aunts and cousins. Only Mother, unrelenting, wouldn't come down. She wouldn't watch them leave.

But Tom was lifting the bags into the shining buggy. She had to go.

So Martha Parish, as she must be now, allowed herself to be assisted up into the buggy, settling next to the stranger she had married. Though Tom, clicking his tongue at the sorrel horse, felt more like kin – or was it perhaps the waistcoat where she had buried her face when Father died? It was the kindest place.

'Goodbye … goodbye,' waved the aunts and cousins, 'Goodbye …' spilling beyond the gate and taking up defensive positions behind a parapet of snow, Cousin Thankful fluttering her kerchief.

'Goodbye …'

Already their shrill cries of farewell were fading on the frigid air. The cold had laid its hand on everything.

To the Lieutenant, buffeted by the wind, the air seemed to vibrate with vast currents of energy flowing and driving everywhere. At the same time small things took on a terrific intensity: slender grasses the frost had thickened: beads of water threaded on a stalk and frozen there. A slant, prismatic light, splintering from icy trees and bushes, opened an Aladdin's cave ablaze with splendours, now a gem of sapphire blue, now one of amethystine purple, now intense topaz yellow, now sea-green beryl changing by degrees, as the buggy passed along the road, to rich emerald green: hundreds on a single branch, so large, so intense, they seemed to burn like Sirius in the summer sky.

They trotted on, with a clink of harness, past the livery stables, and the joiner's shop, that might not have existed for the Lieutenant, who was gazing on a landscape unimaginable, except to an eye that could see. But Matty's eyes were only for her childhood that was jogging past: the pine wood up on the hill, and Thundery Meadow that brought memories of the time the wind and darkness came, and Father had covered her face under his cloak. Little Miss Larkin came bobbing again from the little school room, now forlorn and unpainted, and Lettie Kellog was calling at the gate, *The bell's gone ... the bell's gone ...*

All her life, she saw, was laid out around her. Places which, now that she was leaving, were only just becoming irreplaceable. The frog pond. The blueberry pasture. Now slipping away. Slipping past with the leafless trees. And she was powerless to call them back. Suddenly things all around and things that were far off down the years came swimming so close together as to bring on a kind of double vision. For Martha Parish. For whom old Mr Snell could have been waving from the door of his shop to remind of a new shoe lost in the mud. Mother had been so vexed.

Now mother was up in her room stitching, and wouldn't look.

After that she had to keep her eyes fixed on the tips of the sorrel's quivering ears, otherwise she would have burst. Then she felt a gloved hand clasping hers under the rug. Glancing up at the remarkable man her husband staring resolutely ahead, she saw he was ready, now, to set forth on his great adventure.

So she put her arm through his, and sat clutching her bible, submissive to the greater ordering.

THREE

So the Parishes, as they must be now, left Hartfield on that afternoon of winter bareness, with Matty Stevens still clinging to the
shrill cries of farewell that might have been forever fading on the
frigid air. Though everyone had long since hurried back inside.
Her last sight, looking back, was of the overarching trees at the
top of Shady Hill, where the road ran down to the passenger
station. It brought a lump to her throat.

Meanwhile, a country she had never seen was beginning to
unwind remorselessly beyond the glass, the western sky turning
more and more to a pure polar pink as the train rattled through
the miles towards Boston.

The Lieutenant too sat in a dream. His satisfaction, now he'd
achieved his purpose, rendered him impervious to anything
outside himself. Only he was conscious of his wife's weight
against his shoulder, rocking with the motion of the carriage.

The next evening saw them finally delivered at the Washington depot of the Baltimore and Potomac railroad. A hansom
hurried them through enormous empty streets.

They were to reside, it appeared, in Foggy Bottom: a gaunt
boarding house with peeling shutters and a scrappy patch of
uncared-for grass. He led the way upstairs to a landing lined
with boxes and packing cases, then a dreary room with high
bare walls. There was a strong smell of cooking.

'Well, this is it,' he said, looking round. 'A bachelor's apartment, as you can see.' What was of no consequence before
suddenly an embarrassment. 'I guess it needs a woman's hand.'

She saw he was apologizing for what he'd brought her to.
Before she could say anything to reassure he was clumping
down again to fetch up the bags.

She sat down on the horsehair sofa. Looked round at what

she'd taken on: iron stove, oilcloth carpet, piles of books stacked against the walls. A life lived out of bags and boxes. A life spent in rented rooms.

Stability, she knew, did not rest in external circumstances, but had to be laboured at. Yet the task seemed daunting. Making up her mind to buy a rug for the floor, she went across the landing to inspect the kitchen.

To start with it was all strangeness. Summery gleams, slipping between clouds of sleet and snow, brought days that could have been June, when the blood flowed through her veins like rills of sparkling water. Across the Potomac, over Arlington, a delicate haze coloured the hills. From her open window Martha Parish found she could see for miles down the wide, shining river. Above all, the strangeness of a husband. Maybe married life, she had been tempted to believe, wouldn't properly begin until he came back from the Arctic. Supposing marriage a kind of heading out West. A territory that had to be settled, with crops to raise and stock to keep alive. Only to find, a thing she'd never expected, a flowering of her own wilderness.

On sultry spring days the Lieutenant hired a village cart, and took his bride on excursions out through the metropolis of Georgetown and into the quiet shadows of Rock Creek. They drove by still lanes through the leafless woods: so still the young woman could sense the moist shoots pushing through the earth, pushing against their covering of leaves.

The husband too might have stumbled across what he was intended for. As if he held between his arms the actual wonder of the world.

Each morning, though, after his porridge of split groats with cream, the Lieutenant sat down to his preparations. All his thought was of Arctic footgear and buffalo sleeping bags, fur hats and mittens. Now he was drafting letters to Greenland for the commissioning of sleds and dogs, now it was to the Secretary of the Navy regarding the chartering of a vessel.

He was in the grip of expedition fever, a wholly consuming

condition that seized the mind to the exclusion of all else. He was going to Grinnell Land.

'*Ooming-mannuna,*' he informed his wife. That was what the Eskimos called it. 'Where the musk oxen have their country.'

A region, he went on to explain, of extraordinary interest, only indifferently explored, and rich in every form of life. There would be meteorological data to be collected, maps and surveys to be made, animals and plants to be observed and studied. There was probably no area in the whole circumpolar project which would so well reward expeditionary work.

Then the Lieutenant's wife, still languorous from the warmth of the bed, reverted by degrees to scrawny, flat-chested Martha Stevens, recalling her mother's bitter warning that men were different. They led different lives.

'I expect there will be terrible blizzards,' she ventured once.

'Snowfall over most of the Arctic is quite light,' replied the Lieutenant, emerging from the back of beyond to which he was so often withdrawn.

He welcomed questions from members of the public.

'Actual snowstorms, as you know them in New England, are quite rare. Though I expect we shall encounter frequent ground blizzards of lying snow whipped about by the high winds. They can go on for days.'

Most days he went out, to the offices of the Signal Corps, or further afield, inspecting tents, stove pipes, windproof lanterns, cookers, estimating the quality of fur and woollen clothing, seeking tenders from food processors and other suppliers.

Evenings, after the supper things were cleared away, he spent poring over maps whose compelling vacancies a man might conceivably grow to occupy. Or else he sat bent over the table, drawing up lists of stores, covering page after page in his cramped, angular hand.

'If I remember rightly, Kane urges the advisability of taking a liberal supply of tinned brown sugar,' he observed, to no one in particular, before reverting to his usual distance.

Sometimes his eyes were set still further, fixed on things that were far off. Then Martha Parish suffered the opening up of strange internal vistas: an icy waste stretching away.

Meanwhile her needles continued to click, as if of their own volition, knitting an afghan to comfort the solitary bunk of Lieutenant Parish, polar explorer.

One evening there was another step on the stair.

Martha Parish put down her work, and stood, prepared to greet a visitor.

'Rainbird,' said the Lieutenant, stooping slightly as he entered the room, 'may I present my wife?'

How very unlike William, was her first thought, for the newcomer seemed so stocky, muscular, beside the suddenly lath-like figure of her husband.

'You will recall my letter from this gentleman, Martha,' he reminded.

She did indeed recall it. And William's exclamation of delight: *This is wonderful news. Rainbird is the real thing. A real rough-and-tumble frontiersman* ... She looked into a leathery face, with coarse straw-pale hair spilling about a network of fine lines. Lieutenant Rainbird could have been in his early thirties.

'Mrs Parish, ma'am,' he saluted, with a bob of the head. His blue eyes rested on her a moment, then slipped away with the indifference Matty Stevens had grown up with. She withdrew to her duties in the kitchen, leaving her husband declaring with great earnestness:

'May I say, Rainbird, how gratified I was to have your acceptance. To tell the truth, it was more than I dared hope for.' His eyes behind the thick lenses gleamed with enthusiasm. Lt Parish was occasionally disposed to admire such powers as he had not himself been granted, though proud to have done without them.

'I guess I surprised myself,' said the visitor wryly. Impulsive in his longings, Lt Rainbird was sometimes a stranger to himself.

'Believe me, Rainbird, in the long run this mission must be to our advantage.'

'I trust it will,' said the visitor, who had begun to suffer from a sense that he was getting nowhere.

Martha Parish, though, was bringing in the fowl pie she had prepared for supper.

'I tell you frankly, Rainbird, we're very much on our own,' she heard her husband saying briskly, while putting an edge on the carver. He was confiding in a brother-officer. 'Neither the President nor the Secretary for War has the slightest interest in our doings. I fear the War Department has very little conception of what we're taking on.'

The visitor smiled cautiously. He had very little idea himself.

'We have no friendly board of Arctic experts to assist us with counsel and advice,' his host continued, slicing up the pie. 'No lavish funds at our command. When we've paid for the hire of our ship, we shall have less than six thousand dollars for the rest of our requirements.'

'But it is to be an Army operation?'

'Most certainly.' Parish paused, a segment of pie poised between fork and carver. 'Had it been otherwise I should not have accepted the command.'

He deposited the pie on a convenient plate.

'Even our civilian specialists will be required to enlist for the duration of the expedition.'

'Specialists?'

'An astronomer and a photographer. And of course our surgeon, Dr Fabius. An interesting fellow, by all accounts. Though not acquainted personally, I am corresponding with him over the purchase of dogs. A native of Baton Rouge, I believe. But he has lived in France for many years.'

Rainbird nodded amiably. He had no particular objection to a Frenchman.

'He is a graduate of the University of Paris,' the Lieutenant thought to add, evidently gratified by a prize capture. 'We pick him up in Greenland. Foxer, our second lieutenant, is, like yourself, a frontiersman with an outstanding record. Our first sergeant, Emmons, is also an excellent man.'

Martha Parish looked lovingly at her husband, who was bubbling with enthusiasm. She would have liked to caress his face with her finger-tips, but did not dare.

'May I ask, Lieutenant,' she enquired, 'what leads you to volunteer for this expedition?'

'I guess every man feels the need once in a while, ma'am, to get into the wilderness,' smiled the straw-haired man, for whom there was always somewhere else he was trying to reach.

Martha Parish smiled. She was hoping to hear something of their guest's experiences of the frontier. She had a sense of an illimitable land, incomprehensibly rich and full of wonders.

'Mr Dwight, our minister, has called it "the face of God".'

For a moment the visitor seemed to hesitate, sipping at his coffee, before replacing the cup carefully in its saucer.

'Well, you know, the West can be pretty ugly at times.'

His blue eyes glinted sharply, as if he spoke of brutalities not fit for a lady's ears. Then the tanned face twisted into a tight half smile. Revelation had gone far enough.

Though she sought to draw him out. His chief impression? Oh, fatigue. What did he remember? Being hungry, mostly. Certainly he had eaten handsomely of the fowl. It was as well William ate so little. But the visitor's conversation was confined largely to rowing, which he had practised as a youth in Philadelphia.

'A wholesome pastime, Mrs Parish ma'am. Though I had no great skill,' the visitor added modestly.

'I'm sure you were extremely proficient, Lieutenant,' she said dryly.

'Well … perhaps I was,' smiled the former champion of the Schuylkill river, to whom candour sometimes came easily. Especially with ladies.

Supper ended, and the dishes cleared away, the table was spread with maps and papers. The men fell to discussing the business of the expedition. She took up the slippers she was embroidering for William, wondering if the lieutenant had rowed without his shirt. The semi-nude state of oarsmen on the

Hartfield River was a constant irritant to respectable ladies who lived along the banks. *It is a total mystery to me,* good Aunt Buffem was given to agitating, *why the sons of gentlemen will persist in rowing with nude bodies. Why do they do it? I can't believe there is any advantage in rowing without a shirt.*

Fingers slipping into the soothing motions of her embroidery, she let her mind glide with the scullers, still heads bent, skimming like pond skaters over the surface of the river, only marginally conscious of the voices at a distance, now and then picking up snatches of conversation to do with lime juice or dog food.

The expedition leader, running his finger down a list, had begun to delegate certain matters to his second-in-command.

Glancing up she noticed Lt Rainbird standing over the bent figure of her husband. He was stifling a yawn.

No, she thought. He did not strike her as a man who listened closely.

One day in late March Lieutenant Parish took his wife to call on Senator Clay.

It was an afternoon of blue and gold. In the square the buckeyes were already greening with the first flush of life. The Lieutenant paused a moment to point out the great bronze statue of Andrew Jackson mounted on his horse. Martha Parish wore the richly textured lavender dress her husband had deemed suitable for social occasions. For Washington, he pointed out, was not Massachusetts. Expectations in the nation's capital were very different from those in a small New England village. Matty Stevens did not doubt it. Now, as they approached a handsome, wide-fronted house of quince-yellow brick, she was conscious of the *swish, swish* of her skirts. She wished the bodice fitted better.

A black manservant showed them into a long salon richly furnished, where two men sat at a window. General Sweetsir she already knew. The other, an old man leaning on a cane, rose with difficulty to greet her.

Martha Parish had been expecting to meet a tragic figure, for she knew the senator had lost his wife in childbirth, and that his only son had been killed fighting for the South. Certainly it was a face of savage character, with its black eye patch, and hooked, hawkish nose. A raking shaft of light fell on a tangle of snow white hair springing up around the great dome of his skull.

Then a booming voice tumbled words at her like rocks.

'My dear Mrs Parish.'

But she would not be afraid. All the same, she was conscious of her large hands that she never knew what to do with. Washington ways still left her at a loss. So she stood uncertainly in the same raking light, trying not to appear nervous, though the seams of her ill-fitting bodice were standing up in ridges. William, moreover, was already disembarking on a farther shore. She heard his voice, very brisk and pertinacious as he tackled General Sweetsir on an urgent matter to do with tinned brown sugar.

But Senator Clay was ushering her to a seat on a spindle-legged sofa, before resuming his high-backed chair.

'How do you like Washington?' he enquired, benevolently enough to be sure. 'You must find it very colourful after the winter vegetation of New England.'

His single eye regarded her quizzically. Geranium and mignonette, spilling over the sill behind his craggy head, seemed to chide the barren wastes of Massachusetts.

'I guess New England folk are more absorbed in the severities of living than in its gaieties,' she replied with spirit. 'But we have our colour too, senator. You should visit us in the Fall.'

He was conscious of two dark eyes, set wide apart in the small compact face, regarding him uncertainly.

'I fear you'll find us rather dull dogs, Mrs Parish,' he went on. 'Here, no one talks of anything but politics.'

'My father,' she replied unthinkingly, 'used to say that the best men do not stoop to politics.'

The senator seemed slightly startled.

'Oh!' she gasped. But the remark was out. She could not call it back.

'Your father was quite right,' said Lucius Clay gravely. 'It is a dreadful thing to govern others, Mrs Parish. Keep well away from it.'

He suppressed a smile as he rang for tea. She was exactly the wife he would have predicted for the Yankee lieutenant.

Though Martha Parish was sinking through the sofa at having spoken so.

But Senator Clay did not ask if she danced, or played cards, or, indeed did any of the things which, in the national capital, seemed to be expected of a lady. And for that she was grateful.

The same silent manservant was placing a tea tray on a low claw-footed table.

Yes, she said, fishing with tongues for a lump of sugar, she had visited the White House.

Not long after her arrival in Washington they had taken a car down Pennsylvania Avenue to look at the Executive Mansion which was indeed quite white, not overlarge, with the prettiest front garden of trees and flowering magnolias, and a green lawn with slim park railings separating it from the road.

Most remarkable, though, were two long lines of men snaking along the drive to the front entrance, one going in, the other coming out.

'William did explain that they were seeking office under the new administration. Surely they can't all expect employment?'

Across the room the business meeting had struck a rock.

'I can't just walk down Pennsylvania Avenue and buy these things,' she heard her husband say.

'I'm afraid that rests with the Secretary for War.'

The general's voice was regretful, but what more could he do?

Meanwhile, Senator Clay was explaining that after every election the new president and the Senate had the power to re-appoint to every post in the government's employ.

'It's called rotation of office. And a necessary precaution. Government posts must be passed around as often as possible. Think of the enormity of people holding their positions for life, possibly even passing them on to the children.'

They exchanged smiles, but not yet of recognition. Martha Parish suspected she was being teased. Yet it was, she saw, a humorous mouth.

Meanwhile the Lieutenant's mule was plodding on its dogged errand.

'It's not simply a question of obstructing me. It is Congress itself that is being thwarted.'

'Do you know, I envy your husband, Mrs Parish.'

The young woman fell to examining a scalloped detail of her sleeve.

'In this town,' the senator went on,' there are men as grasping, as devious and dissembling as any prince of the Renaissance. Among such men your husband goes about like a latter-day Natty Bumppo. A true American. And I admire him for it. *Lighting out for the Territory* ... Are you acquainted with Mr Twain's Huck Finn?'

Mrs Parish could not be sure this man was not now laughing at her husband with his talk of Natty Bumppo.

'No – I envy him,' he assured her. The sea-grey eye, she saw, was truly wistful.

'If I were a younger man I should go with him.'

'Then you would have to join the army, Senator,' was her swift rejoinder.

Then, laughing together, they were both gilded in the same shaft of light.

As the days went by the nation's capital became increasingly pre-occupied with the absorbing business of government. The town was agog with the warfare that had already broken out between the new president and Senator Conkey. Newspapers and magazines, drawing on an alleged youthful addiction to boxing clubs and the company of prize fighters, were printing the grossest caricatures depicting the new Chief Magistrate knocking seven bells out of the Senator from New York. Or else it was a tippy-toed travesty of Ithamor Conkey waltzing his hippopotamus bulk beyond the reach of a bemused and baffled opponent.

Entranced, all Washington looked on. It was the only show in town.

All this was of no interest to Lt Parish. He cared no more for politics than for the indifference of the ignorant populace. He had matters far more pressing to occupy his mind.

He sat one morning in his office in the War Department, leafing through a portfolio of photographic portraits. In front of him sat a stocky, well set-up young man, with hair of a good dark brown and a thick moustache. He had travelled down from Pittsburgh.

Parish could see from the sitters, the families of steel men and other notables, that this George Reade was well thought of.

'You are seeking a change from photographic portraiture?'

'Yes, sir,' said the young man firmly, who had begun to suffer from a certain hollowness of heart. He had not seen much of the world, and was hoping to find some truth that had not so far manifested itself in Pittsburgh.

'And why do you wish to go to the Arctic?'

'I guess,' the young fellow laughed nervously 'to see what I'm made of.' He might have been embarrassed by his own temerity.

'I see from your letter that you have worked as an artist.'

'I was a painter once,' the young man admitted frankly.

Fate had saddled him with an honest simplicity of expression, and a gaze seemingly prepared for any eventuality, having learnt early how the worst can happen. At the age of twelve he had seen his father run over by a coal wagon. It proved a turning point in the life of one who might otherwise have grown true to type. But had turned out a sturdy wastrel, in the eyes of his uncles. They were industrious, deep-lunged men who'd thrived on smoke and furnaces, and scorned a man who owed his daily bread to the toil and sweat of others.

'I take it you received a proper training?'

'At the Pennsylvania Academy of the Fine Arts.'

For this, and later extravagances, the uncles blamed the mother, who'd paid his fees, and continued to support him in his idleness.

'This expedition will afford a rich opportunity for a young artist such as yourself. Mirages, and so forth, and of course the Aurora Borealis.'

It might have been a hunger for light the Lieutenant saw leaping across the young man's face.

'Yes indeed,' he went on thoughtfully, 'there will be many striking phenomena.'

There were also certain intimations, disclosed to the Lieutenant alone, of a more heroic theme. Mindful of the painted walls and ceilings of the War Department, he had begun to envisage a spectacle such as might grace the offices of some future Secretary for War: some scene of indomitable strivings, with icy wastes stretching away.

'Naturally, the War Department will require a pictorial record of such discoveries as we shall make,' he said importantly. 'Could you rise to that?'

'I can try, sir,' replied the young man, whose soul had spaces that cried out to be filled.

After graduation he had roamed for a while among the wetlands of New England, living the life of the solitary artist. He painted silent, contemplative landscapes flooded with a suffused, incandescent light: numinous places where no humans were. *Pictures of nothing*, according to his uncle Ezra. At length the young man had begun to fear as much himself.

So, bowing at last to the urgent pressure of his family, he'd accepted the offer of a cousin to take him into his photographic studio. He still believed he was intended for transcendence.

'Very well,' said the Lieutenant, coming to a decision. 'I'll sign your papers. You can take the oath here and how.'

He still had a great deal to do. He'd completed requisitions for clothing, arms and ammunition, hospital stores, the usual field supply of medicines, camp equipage and subsistence stores. Arrangements were in hand for transportation and despatch from Baltimore to St John's. A stout Newfoundland sealer had been selected for charter under the direction of the Navy Secretary. Yet all these preparations and endeavours were stalled, could not go forward, not a single item actually procured, without an authority signed by the Secretary for War.

Days went by, and still the necessary papers failed to appear. General Sweetsir could do nothing. The good offices of Senator Clay were of no avail. With the Washington bureaucracies at a standstill pending the new president's removals and appointments, the whole matter of the expedition remained in abeyance.

At length, for he was not a man to do anything without reflection, Lt Parish took himself to the office of the Adjutant-General, who shot his cuffs, rested his elbows on the desk, and stared coldly over his glasses. At a mere lieutenant.

'That's a matter for the Secretary for War.'

Set-faced, the mere lieutenant rose to leave. Only the slightest tremor in the muscles of his face betrayed his anger.

For days afterwards he brooded on the matter.

'It's not as if I can just walk down the Avenue and buy these things,' he repeated to his wife.

She had not seen him so unsettled.

'I must have it out with him.' It was a question, for all his firmness. He was looking at her for support.

Silently she took his hand. William, she knew, would do his duty. Which, father used to say, rendered a man independent of powers and principalities. If need be, he would take it to the president himself.

A day or two after the confirmation of his appointment, the new Secretary for War slipped unnoticed into the vast *château* across the street from the White House. A gaunt, stooping figure, Secretary Crowell made his way by opulent corridors, past painted walls and ceilings, wrought iron mouldings, bronze balusters, a wealth of marble, porcelain and gilt. His appointment had not gone unopposed. The *New York Sentinel* poured scorn on the elevation of a penny-pinching Baltimore lawyer whose policies, it claimed, would so starve the Army of supplies as to leave them with neither the strength to fight, nor the speed to run away.

In one respect, at least, Elijah Crowell had shown himself the man for the job. He was taking charge of a department still under the cloud incurred by a previous incumbent, for whose downfall he was largely responsible. It was Crowell who had pursued and finally uncovered a long-standing conspiracy concerning the awarding of franchises to army contractors supplying the western posts.

In these early weeks of a new administration the business of government was taken up principally with appointments. Day after day the great temples of State were infested with a veritable plague of office-seekers. They thronged the halls and corridors, lounging against the columns, leafing through newspapers, or squatting on the steps of stairwells in covetous contemplation of the consulates, the foreign missions, the revenue offices, the postmasterships and Indian agencies, the contracts and the franchises that were the dues of faithful service. They had won the victory. Now they looked to enjoy the spoils. They saw nothing wrong in that. Inexhaustible in their expectation, they clung like the caterpillars of Egypt. Like locusts from the bottomless pit. And Elijah Crowell cursed them from the bottom of his soul. He cursed them with all the curses in Deuteronomy.

Groaning in spirit, he went through to his private office. He was deeply serious about his duties. In his pocket-book he still carried a tattered clipping, cut from *Harper's Weekly*, of the elephant which had become the emblem of the party of government. He regarded it as an image of the exaggeration and excess which had so disfigured the nation's life. Elijah Crowell would make war on the elephants.

Meanwhile he sat, a quixotic figure amid the Babylonian splendours of his office, and laboured on. There were tenders to be considered, allocations issued for every kind of Army procurement: horses, boots, beef, belts and webbing, blankets, uniforms, harness, saddlery, arms and ammunition; and every application to be looked into, every dollar accounted for.

He stuck at it hour after hour, day after day, checking tenders, scrutinizing contracts, writing instructions, confirming, denying: against the great corruption, the only armour was painstaking work.

One by one the petitioners were admitted, his clerk whispering in his ear.

Scarcely raising his head, Elijah Crowell worked on: listening in silence, missing nothing of what was said, his pen continuing to scratch.

They left their details with the clerk.

Lieutenant Parish waited the best part of three days to see the Secretary for War. Aloof, he kept apart from the office-seekers, drawing aside in spirit to avoid contamination. He took to pacing about the hallway, or simply stood with folded arms and spoke to no one. He would not bandy words with jackals vying for spoils.

Late in the afternoon of the third day he was finally admitted. He saw a stringy man, writing at a desk. A man of distinctly misanthropic appearance. He was clad entirely in black, with a wide, loosely tied cravat wound round his throat. A frowning mouth, turned down at the corners, soured a leathery face.

But the Lieutenant had gone down deep into his purpose. His will was set. He could not alter what he was fixed upon.

He crossed the room, his heels ringing on the boards.

Crowell looked up from his papers. The clerk whispered in his ear.

The Secretary for War stared long and hard at his visitor. Then, indicating a chair with his pen, he carried on writing. His pen scratched over the paper.

Minutes passed. The Lieutenant remained composed. He would not fidget in his chair. He sat, breathing evenly, his mind aligned to the ticking of the clock on the gilt overmantel.

Eventually there was a pause in the scratching. The leather face lifted like a trap.

'Well, Lieutenant. What matter of Congressional business do you have with me?' Secretary Crowell had a brusque growling manner of addressing folk that did not endear.

'Next year is set for the first ever International Polar Year,' began the Lieutenant carefully.

He had given considerable thought to choosing his words. He would be addressing a man with time for no more than the most succinct of briefings.

'From Siberia in the east, through Lapland and Spitsbergen, to Greenland in the west, the top of the known world will be ringed by a series of stations carrying out a simultaneous programme of scientific observations. Congress has decreed that the United States should take part in this international venture. It has assumed the entire project as a government undertaking to be carried out under the direction of the Chief Signal Officer.'

Crowell's black eyes were expressionless, his mouth shut tight.

'As its field commander, I am endeavouring at this moment to equip the expedition. To procure stores and supplies.'

'Well?'

'I cannot do it, sir. I cannot do it because, despite repeated application, I have not yet received the necessary authorization.'

Elijah Crowell laid his pen carefully on the stand in front of him, leant back in his chair, folded his hands and stared hard at the visitor.

'What is your name again?'

'Parish, sir. Lieutenant William Parish, United States Fifth Cavalry Regiment, presently assigned to the Signal Corps.'

'Have you any idea, Lieutenant Parish, what demands are made upon the Secretary for War?'

In New Mexico the Apache were murdering ranchers and miners. Congressmen, with the massacre at the White River Agency still fresh in mind, were demanding that the south-west be made safe for settlers pouring into Arizona. The papers on the Secretary's desk lay thick as leaves in autumn.

But the visitor had not come to make concessions.

'We are all busy men, sir. All my time is taken up with the

business of the expedition. It must be assembled at St John's, Newfoundland, no later than the beginning of July.' The Lieutenant paused, it might have been for a response.

None was forthcoming. Crowell's face gave nothing away.

'We are going to *Grinnell* Land, sir,' Parish added meaningfully. 'We must be in station before the onset of the Arctic winter.'

He looked intently at the man in front of him. He saw that the Secretary for War understood nothing, absolutely nothing, of what he was being told.

'I have to advise you, sir,' he went on, mildly enough, though with great earnestness, 'that unless I am given swift executive authority to carry out my duties, then the will of Congress will be frustrated.'

Crowell's gaze never flickered. He seemed to be registering every detail of his visitor's face.

'Very well, Lieutenant,' he said abruptly. 'The papers will be signed forthwith. Good day.'

Instantly he was immersed again in his work. Matters of no importance he set aside as if they never existed.

The dogged New Englander continued to go about his business, leafing through lists of medical equipment, household items, special articles of diet. He negotiated for supplies of coal; he enquired after dog food of the right kind and quality; he selected scientific instruments and many other items necessary for a polar expedition; he saw to it that chronometers were overhauled and calibrated, and that the specially built New Bedford whale boat was properly strengthened to withstand the pressures of the polar ice.

Now and then, though, he felt dwarfed by his own longing. There was nothing else in life except to conclude his preparations, and be gone.

The party was just about complete. The meteorological observers, non-coms from his own Signal Corps, were men he had trained himself: the enlisted men, all of them volunteers, inured to dangers and privations by long and hazardous duty on the Western frontier.

These hand-picked veterans seemed a world removed from the young fellow who took a seat one morning in the Lieutenant's office. Who hung his head and mumbled, and could scarcely look him in the eye.

The Lieutenant was thinking he'd never before seen a fair-haired Jew.

'Professor Sewell speaks very highly of you,' he tried, not unkindly. 'I understand you have been assisting him in his work on the moons of Jupiter.'

If the young man lowered his eyes again, it was because he found it easier to withdraw.

Jacob Asher, Dr Sewell had written, was outstanding at his job, but didn't mix much.

The Lieutenant, though, was recalling the tongue-tied farm boys with whom he'd gone into battle twenty years before.

'You understand you will be conducting your observations throughout the Arctic winter,' he said, almost gently. 'It is certain to entail some suffering. There will be long lonely hours in bitter cold.'

Parish surveyed the rather delicate face in which an elusive something hinted at a fugitive soul. What sort of place, he wondered, did this young man imagine lay out there. He seemed very young.

'You will be expected to undertake all the magnetic work, as well as the astronomical observations. Do you feel confident of doing that?'

Jacob Joseph Asher mumbled something that could be taken as affirmative.

The Secretary for War was still proving difficult. Though formal consent had now been received for the expedition to go forward, still the requisition for the appropriation approved by Congress failed to arrive. Elijah Crowell was seeing to it that a mere lieutenant should appreciate the full extent of his limitations. Meanwhile the Lieutenant's head was filled with innumerable items all clamouring for attention. Nothing seemed to come together. He was bogged down in detail, checking prices, poring over the many desirable items the limited sums at his disposal would not permit him to acquire, removing them, only to restore them to his list.

'A dollar twenty-five this fellow wants for his pemmican,' Martha Parish would hear her husband muttering. 'A dollar twenty-five!' The long face looking more severe than ever.

The whole burden of organization seemed to be devolving on to William's shoulders.

'Rainbird seems eager enough to brave the rigours of the Arctic,' he sighed one evening, 'yet he has but slight management capacity.'

She was sewing a silk flag for her husband to fly over points of land not yet visited by man.

'But I understood you thought so highly of Lieutenant Rainbird?'

Chronically uncertain, she was acutely conscious of her ignorance. She had no idea of what was needful to the life of an explorer: what things were true and important, and what were not.

One morning, changing the calendar to May, she was suddenly overcome with a longing for the settled certainties of home. She fell to wondering if the wood was piled, and the yard cleaned up. And the trees trimmed, and the garden made, and the manure got out, and the potatoes planted? But of course it was. Tom would have seen to all of that.

So, loyally, she busied herself packing away china for the officers' mess, seeking out gifts and tokens to make his Arctic sojourn more homely. She had begun embroidering the afghan with their joined initials, a conjunction that might diminish the sense of distance.

The margins of his world were all around her. Like a sea. Like a winter fog into which he disappeared. At night, as she sat quietly with her stitching, he was immersed in his work. He'd stepped into another world from hers, an enigmatic region,

43

baffling in its ability to confound whatever she tried to make of it. It was simply there: a mystery, far larger than her grasp. She was prepared to accord it the standing she accorded other mysteries of life. Only she did not want to lose him. Oh, she did not want that.

Though he refused to countenance any grounds for her fears.

'Doubt as to my fate cannot exist. We cannot be abandoned, nor cut off. Really, dear, could any such trial come to you as has come to Mrs De Long, I should never go.'

She clung to him, gathered up in his long arms, as he explained that he would be living in a sturdy comfortable house, equipped with ample supplies of fuel and provisions, while addressing a number of scientific problems. He would be as snug and warm as anyone living in New England. At the end of the first year, he went on, a ship would call with mail and fresh supplies. The following year another ship would come to carry them all home again.

He was smiling down at her. Holding his wife at arms' length, the better to hearten.

'Believe me, dearest, a brief parting is the worst we have to fear.'

He made it sound so simple and straightforward.

And so it undoubtedly stood, arranged in the Lieutenant's mind. He had read widely. He knew full well the desolate coasts he would soon be traversing were littered with the wrecks of ships, and frozen caches, never visited, and cairns with desperate messages, never read. He knew men had perished miserably there: dying of scurvy, gangrene, starved, frozen on the ice beside the hulks of ships burned for their last ounce of warmth. All this he carried in his head, or else it was stacked inside the books which, packed into boxes, were to accompany the expedition to the polar region. He had prepared himself as thoroughly as study and reflection can ever qualify a man for the unknown. But of the immeasurable loneliness of the Arctic, its fracturing cold, its vast indifference, all this was as remote from the Lieutenant as the Pole star itself.

FOUR

They slipped away all but unnoticed. Only the US consul in St John's, who'd come to wish God's speed, lingered to watch them clearing the Narrows.

'A strange fellow, that army lieutenant,' he remarked later that evening, spearing a potato. 'He seemed very put out folk hereabouts took such little notice of his expedition. "They seem to have no notion of what we are about." I don't know what he was expecting.'

His wife helped herself to cod. She was a homely woman with no great interest in her husband's duties, beyond smiling when it was required.

'"Well, Lieutenant," I told him, "I guess another sealer outward bound is no great shakes to them."'

Meanwhile, the *Petrel* was ploughing a passage through the North Atlantic. An oak-built barquentine, sheathed in iron-wood from above the water-line to below the turn of her bilges, she'd been built for work in the heavy polar pack. The small fore-hold had been converted to accommodate the enlisted men. Mostly infantrymen and horse soldiers from the plains, they lay on their bunks in a pungent reek of seal oil, which no amount of scrubbing had been able to remove. Nate Emmons, the dour top-sergeant, was darning a sock. A former barman, labourer, stevedore, he'd found in the army a manner of life with which he was in perfect accord. Sergeant Hewitt, the meteorologist, frowned over the chess board. He was having the worst of it with his friend and assistant, Sergeant Knowles. Private Schmidt was writing a letter to his father in Stettin of the great adventure that would make a famous man of him. His blue eyes were far away. Others, too, were struggling to bring themselves into correspondence with that mysterious place the Arctic, of which they had no conception, except as the fulfilment of some unrealized dream.

Up on deck the young astronomer stood clutching the rail, his cheeks buffeted by the salt wind. Life had sundered him at last from the bosom of his family, the most devoted members of which continued to clutch and moan. 'Ach, Jacob,' mourned Rachel Asher, 'Jacob Joseph.' 'What does he know,' cried her husband Yaakov, 'a young man with his head in the stars?' Strangers in the wilderness of the New World, they still harked back to their little town of narrow streets, and small frowsty rooms. Their grandson, though, was gripped by the strangeness of things: the creaking of sheets and timbers, the movement of the deck under his feet, above all the strangeness of a new identity ... *Sergeant ... Sergeant Asher* ...

It was a dark night. Few stars were out. Even the moon was no more than a fleeting presence, overborne by banks of cloud.

From an early age the night sky had soothed and pacified Jacob Joseph. Luminous nights especially seemed addressed to the soul. The solemn panoply of stars and constellations, so silent and far-off, would sink in and through his being, a tranquil presence. Folks passing the Jew house sometimes saw a pale face at a bedroom window looking up into the starry vastness, and guessed it was that queer kid, the motherless boy. The night sky was where he found his most searching questions. *Why is it so black, grandfather? Ach, nicht dray mein kopf*, the old man would moan, clapping his hands to his temples. Then one day Uncle Lou came over from Knoxville. *Hi there, Jake*, he called out cheerfully. *This is for you*. It was a telescope. Well wrapped up, at his grandmother's insistence, he would go out on winter nights, gazing up through vast and empty distances of space. He felt he stood on the threshold of a momentous darkness, and knew somehow he must go out and get lost in it.

The wind was rising. Holding on to the rail he made his way aft. A distant light shone faintly off the port beam, remote as any star. He was wondering where that might be when he heard voices in the darkness beyond the deckhouse. He couldn't make out what was being said. Only that one of the voices was raised, angry. Moments later a stocky figure brushed past him and clattered down the companion way. In the lamp's gleam, as the door opened, he recognized the yellow-haired lieutenant.

'Isn't that the Cynosure, sergeant? Above the mast there?'

The astronomer turned to see a tall figure outlined against the night.

'It is, sir. The Pole star.'

'It looks mighty cold and lonely.'

With that, Lt Parish stepped through a door in the deckhouse and was gone.

For a week the north-westerlies ran in without relenting. Thick weather held them back. The cramped quarters made for a certain amount of discomfort, especially for the two lieutenants Rainbird and Foxer, who were sharing a cabin with the ship's officers. The expedition leader's duties required that he be accommodated in the after cabin, the use of which he had insisted on as a requirement of the charter. Though he would, of course, eat with his fellow officers in the saloon.

One evening over dinner Lt Foxer, a conscientious and most personable young officer, confessed it had been his childhood ambition to journey to the North Pole.

'Of course,' he added diffidently, 'it was just a dream.'

'Do you know my dream?' offered Rainbird. 'To reach a point in life when you don't have to do anything you don't want to do, and can do everything that you do want to do.'

'I g-guess that's every guy's dream,' stammered young Foxer. He longed to accomplish some great thing himself.

The commander said nothing. Only the slightest tremor in the muscles of his face betrayed his disapproval.

He looked, thought the straw-haired man, more than ever the chapel elder.

The Lieutenant could have been entitled to a measure of irritation. Right up to and beyond the time for their departure, the expedition's tale had been one of continuing frustration. The Secretary for War had persisted in his obstruction. When the main party sailed from Baltimore, he had been forced to remain behind, relinquishing command to Lt Foxer, Rainbird having been sent on ahead to supervise the stowing of the cargo. Finally, when he could delay no longer and set out himself, still the appropriation had not been disbursed. Had it not been for the good offices of Mr Chance many special items of expenditure would not have been obtained.

Then, in St John's, he was faced with further delay, the circumstances of which he had communicated in a letter to his wife: *We are a whole week late in setting out. As you will recollect, I had hoped to sail on the first of the month. However, on my arrival, I found affairs in such a state as to render that impossible. Certain essential supplies had not yet arrived, while the stores on board the Petrel were in endless confusion, cases and boxes scattered about the deck, with scarcely a square inch of vacant space remaining.*

He did not add that he found them left in the charge of an enlisted man, who was evidently the worse for drink. Rainbird himself was nowhere to be found. Ensuing remonstration had resulted in an unpleasant atmosphere, his entirely reasonable rebuke having been received in tight-lipped silence, since when Rainbird had not spoken, beyond what was necessary for the execution of duties. Indeed, since leaving St John's, Rainbird had done little but clean and fondle his shiny new Remington rifle, and do his exercises. He'd rigged up a horizontal bar on the foredeck, where he would perform various feats of strength, to the embarrassment of the Lieutenant, though some of the men seemed impressed.

Punctually at noon each day he gave a talk on some aspect of expedition life. Trooping up the hatchway, the men would find the tall Lieutenant waiting on deck with a large chart pinned to the main mast. Black whiskers jutting, eyes looming behind their pebble lenses, his was an imposing presence.

His lectures were devoted to practical matters: the dangers of wet feet, and how to get out of a crevasse, and what to do if they fell into Arctic waters. He taught them how to navigate by

hand compass, and what to about frozen limbs, and the proce-
dure to be used for excretion when travelling in the field, and a
hundred other things a man must know simply to stay alive in a
cruel, unforgiving land. Again and again he stressed the need for
constant vigilance to avoid simple mistakes which, where they
were headed, could be fatal.

He was trying to convey to them the kind of place that lay
out there, a place utterly different from anything they'd ever
come across.

And the men were fascinated. The Lieutenant sure as hell
knew what he was talking about.

'He seems to have everything worked out,' quipped Private
Hanson, 'from taking a piss to having a shit on the ice.'

Seven days out, off Frederickshaab in the Davis Strait, the
travellers encountered their first intimation of wonders to
come. As the thermometer fell to zero, slender filaments of
frost-smoke began to wreathe, sun-shot eddyings like fiery
breath lifting off the surface of the sea. Then, as the mercury
sank further in the glass, the vapour condensed into a fog. A
bitter wind sprang out of the north-west. Ice, the captain
announced, was not far off. He could smell it.

Lieutenant Parish was most interested to observe the natural
phenomena. He noted that the swell on the water was subsid-
ing. Wasn't that another sign that ice was not far off?

Captain Quine grunted. He had not taken kindly to having
to share his cabin.

The fog grew denser. Sent aloft to the lookout, the mate
soon reported ice on the port bow. Then, ice to starboard.
Seamen, equipped with long poles, positioned themselves in the
stern, ready to fend off chunks of loose pack from the screw.
The members of the expedition lined the rails, gazing as they
might have gazed for the first time at the great plains or the
desert. The ice flowed past, mainly lumps from three to five feet
above the water. As the sea washed over it the ice changed
colour constantly, delicate blues shading imperceptibly to palest
turquoise, aquamarine to blueish white. Occasionally the level

49

pack gave way to isolated knuckles of ice, fifteen or twenty feet high, fantastically carved and pinnacled. Simple, monumental, they came and went in the fog, drifting past on the dark water.

Then, off Godthaab, the fog lifted sufficiently to afford them their first glimpse of the sun. For the first time since leaving St John's, Captain Quine was able to take a noon-day observation. Among the party excitement grew. At last they were within the Arctic circle. They passed the tidings on to one another with the cheerful zest of travellers arriving at their destination, though with no notion yet of where that was, since nothing had changed.

Gradually, as the fog dispersed, a soft primrose light began to filter through the void. Eastwards, opposite the dipping sun, a filmy radiance of pale blues, washed pinks and yellows lit a horizon of gleaming summits.

'Greenland's icy mountains,' murmured young Foxer, who was watching from the bridge. It was everything he'd ever dreamed.

The fog closed in again. After some hours of cautious progress Captain Quine stopped his engines and hove-to. Hour followed upon hour of tedious waiting before, as evening fell, the fog rolled aside like a curtain to reveal a forbidding fortress of rock rising sheer out of the sea.

The *Petrel*'s engines started up. Soon she was ploughing through a choppy sea, making for the cliff. Summoned by the thumping of pistons the enlisted men began to gather for'ard, gazing up in silence at the wall of rock louring over the masthead. They seemed to be making straight for it. Distinct, now, came the mewing of sea-birds wheeling out from the precipice, soaring up on currents of air, scraps of white against the enormous blackness of the cliff.

'Steady at that,' Quine muttered to the helmsman.

To the landsmen watching uneasily in the bow it seemed as if he were intent on driving the vessel in among the breakers, now plainly visible, crashing against the rocks.

The captain, though, had found his mark. 'Hard-a-port,' he said quietly.

Then, as the helmsman spun the wheel, the great black mass swung silently to port as the *Petrel*, curving in a graceful arc, turned in at the narrow bight that gave on to the hidden harbour of Godthavn.

As the sealer stopped her engines, a single cannon sounded a salute, its dull report echoing around the sullen crags hanging over the cove. A puff of smoke drifted upward. At the water's edge, where a handful of figures were waiting at a landing stage, the Danish flag broke out upon a flagstaff.

Washington was enduring another of its febrile summers. Days of intolerable heat were followed by sticky, stifling nights that settled on the city like a blanket

'It has always been a mystery to me,' observed Senator Clay, who'd invited friends to tea, 'that when Holy Scripture proclaims the virtues of a city set on a hill, our first president should have chosen to build the nation's capital in a fever swamp. I fear its effect upon the conduct of government has been incalculable. Mrs Parish, here, observed how very bilious some of our congressmen appear.'

Martha Parish, stirring her tea, reflected how very quickly every conversation turned to politics.

Since coming to the national capital she had tried to inform herself about the government of her country. She was utterly at a loss to make any sense of the conflict that had broken out between the new president and Senator Conkey. Were they not of the same party? Did they not subscribe to the same principles? The newspapers were no help. Written in a style quite unlike that of the *Hartfield Republican*, and allusive beyond her grasp, they could not enlighten. She was left in the dark.

'I do not understand,' she'd confessed, 'why Mr Conkey should be at loggerheads with the president.'

Senator Clay seemed to find nothing out of the ordinary in her enquiry.

'It is customary,' he explained, 'to allow senators to designate who should be appointed to fill certain offices in their respective states. Instead of consulting Senator Conkey, the president has nominated an enemy of his as Collector of the Port of New York. Now he's pushing hard to secure the Senate's confirmation for his man. Naturally, Senator Conkey is doing everything in his power to block the nomination.'

He was conscious of her gaze fixed on him. She was, he saw, one of those women of a characteristic New England type: earnest, high-minded, with a *conscience*.

'It is the most profitable and powerful patronage post in the country,' he went on brutally. There could be no wrapping up of the indelicate when explaining a fact of life. 'Two-thirds of the nation's tariff revenues pass through the Collector's hands. To have such a post within one's gift is, I'm afraid, very desirable to a politician.'

She guessed he was trying to outrage her.

'You mustn't be too hard on us, Mrs Parish,' he went on humorously. 'We're in politics to make a living, and if possible, to get rich. It's the American way.'

With the end of the Congressional session now in sight, Ithamor Conkey had been manoeuvring to have the Senate confirm the president's uncontested nominations, and then adjourn without acting in the matter of the Custom House. But then, in a manoeuvre of crushing simplicity, the president had counter-attacked. He had withdrawn all nominations except that one. Either the senators would have to confirm his man, or sacrifice the appointments of their friends. Outrage in the party was considerable. Many who had deserted Senator Conkey in the hope of securing office in the new administration, now returned to the fold. Meanwhile the president, confident that he had, as he put it, 'put the bag on that joker', prepared to join his wife in New Jersey.

Martha Parish, too, was going home. Though it discomfited her to admit that it still felt like home, the brick house on Willow Street. She might have stayed on in Washington and sweltered, as an act of penance, but for her promise to William, who'd been alarmed at the malarial vapours which had struck down the president's wife.

A porter took her bags. Hurrying after him, in her anxiety to board her train she let fall a glove, and might not have noticed her loss had it not been retrieved by a pallid fellow with slicked-back hair, whom she took for a railroad clerk or messenger.

The clerk had been trailing the president for several days. He'd packed a portmanteau with such personal effects as he thought he might require. A cab stood waiting to convey him safely to prison. Though he entertained no doubts as to the necessity of what he was about to do he was less certain of the bystanders.

Twenty minutes after leaving the White House with a small entourage, the president arrived at the depot. The clerk was watching as he passed by with the Secretary of State. Taking the pistol from inside his jacket, he stepped up behind his victim, and fired twice.

Martha Parish, settling in her seat, was aware of a distant murmur, a commotion, like a wind rushing through the carriage: 'The president ... the president's been shot.'

The news spread like wildfire through the city. In Saks' Emporium, on 7th Street, a white-faced man came bursting into the store. Congressman Potwine was buying a hat. Forever after he could never put on that hat without thinking of it. Within three hours most of the country had been apprised of the astounding news that the president had been shot by an assassin. Professor Cousins was in the office of the *Hartfield Republican,* delivering his weekly piece when the story clicked over the wire. Stunned, he sat down on a bench and thought of Lincoln.

A shroud of fog hung over the island, of which little could be seen other than a cable's length of dark water and a few wooden huts, scattered over a barren tongue of land. Lt Foxer gazed around with some misgiving. He was an amiable young man, ruddy of skin, with a smile that was particularly white. The idea of North had intrigued him since childhood. His father, thinking to improve the boy's mind, had given him the run of his library, which was filled with histories and biographies of great men. One day, bored with self-improvement, he went searching on his own account. In a tall old book, the cover of which was illuminated with a dragon ship, he came across a picture of weird women weaving at a loom. Underneath, some lines that made him shiver. *I see death in a dread place. Yours and mine. North-west over the waves, with ice and cold and countless wonders.* The boy was drawn as a moth to the flame. *Where does North begin?* he asked curiously, turning the globe, his fingers tracing the lines of longitude to their zenith at the Pole. His father stirred behind the pages of his paper. *Wherever you want it to, son.* Then, as the boy considered this enormous possibility, *In your head, if you like.* So there it grew, the idea of North, a magical land of countless wonders.

The commander was preparing to receive a short, broad-chested figure, at that moment mounting to the deck of the *Petrel*.

'I am Pederson. The Royal Inspector.' Thrusting out his arm he shook the Lieutenant's hand warmly. 'Welcome. Welcome to Disko.'

With purposeful stride the sturdy Dane led the visitors ashore.

The wooden huts that comprised the settlement of Godthavn turned out, at a closer inspection, to be sturdy dwellings, with walls of tarred, rough-hewn logs, painted window casings, and roofs of the same ochrous tinge as the dripping rocks. Further off loomed what could only have been a little church, with spire. Around one of the dwellings a small plot of land had been set out as a garden. At the door a smiling woman in a grey dress and apron stood waiting to greet her guests.

'I regret,' the Royal Inspector threw up sorrowful arms, 'Mrs Pederson speaks no English.'

Smilingly, the inspector's wife brought them to a long, low-ceilinged room. Several lamps, placed here and there, shed a mellow light on an interior which the Lieutenant guessed to be very much like that of any Danish home. Indeed, several of what might have been the latest books lay on a low table. Freshly laundered napkins and loaves of crusty bread were set out on a long board. A fire of logs burned in the grate. There was even a piano.

Then Mrs Pederson, who had slipped away to change her dress, suddenly reappeared as a strikingly handsome, fresh complexioned woman, with black braided hair – half squaw, Rainbird guessed – bringing with her tiny bouquets of flowers, which she set in each guest's place.

Young Foxer was suddenly reminded of home, and his mother. Though not by anything that looked the same.

By the fire, a little aloof, stood a thin balding man with a high brow, neat beard and moustache.

'Allow me,' began the inspector impressively, 'to introduce our good friend Dr Fabius, a noted Arctic scholar.'

He might have been older by several years than the rest of the party, yet it was difficult to estimate his age. His was a face lined by inward preoccupations rather than years. He was not old.

'The doctor has been staying with us, while making a collection of botanical specimens.'

Luther Rainbird put him down as a bookish fellow. Though sporty himself, he was prepared to be friendly.

Dinner being slightly delayed, Lieutenant Parish there and then administered the oath of service, which Dr Fabius, if slightly mystified, took smilingly enough.

He apologized for his English, which was impeccable.

'I have lived,' he added with the merest hint of a shrug, 'so many years abroad.'

To feel at ease with others the surgeon had to demonstrate his distinction. It was not enough to know it. Though American born, his soul was a complex dissonance of echoes. A French-speaker from birth, that language was the sea he swam in. The cast of his mind was sceptical, not visionary. Descartes, not Jefferson, was his instructor.

While they were waiting for the meal to be served he listened to questions regarding his experiences during the previous twelve months, which he answered very precisely, giving each enquiry its due weight.

Greenland, he explained, was very far from being the barren place most people supposed.

'On the cliffs across the lagoon here,' he said casually, 'I gathered over forty varieties of plants.'

Then the trim Eskimo maids were bringing in a peppery broth, speckled with herbs and barley: then fresh Greenland salmon, larded eider-ducks, and Arctic ptarmigan, accompanied by *akvavit*, and chasers of beer.

Mrs Pederson's gaze flitted smilingly from speaker to speaker as the conversation flowed humorously, with much laughter and good cheer. Mr Pederson, in between chaffing Rainbird whose yellow locks, he insisted, betokened Scandinavian descent, was proffering more *akvavit*. Indeed, urging, thought the Lieutenant, frowning, a most indiscriminate participation.

Inevitably, the conversation turned to talk of men and ships, and explorations past. Captain Quine had a store of doleful tales of Baffin Bay and its notorious 'middle pack'. To all this the surgeon contributed very little, though attending to everything that was said.

Eventually Parish sought to draw him into the discussion.

'You must be well versed in all this, Dr Fabius?'

It elicited a smiling acknowledgement.

'I have some slight knowledge of the Arctic.'

Each man was conscious of the other as, if not a kindred spirit, then a fellow addict, driven by the same compulsive hunger.

The Royal, though, was recalling some of the earlier expeditions that had put in at Godthavn.

Personally, explained the Lieutenant, he deplored this narrow preoccupation with the Farthest North. For a modern explorer there were far worthier objectives. Though there was no doubt that Fort Chance, as he intended to name the station in Grinnell Land, would make an excellent starting point for the Pole. Others might prefer to make their way via Spitsbergen or Franz Josef Land. But Smith Sound was pre-eminently the American route …

'I hardly think so,' murmured a soft, self-deprecating voice, as if embarrassed at the necessity of correcting a colleague. But would do so nonetheless.

'Correct me if I am wrong,' Doctor Fabius continued, in the faintest of accents, 'but I believe it was the Englishman Baffin who first sailed the waters of Smith Sound. Smith, too, was an Englishman.'

Head bent, Foxer busied himself with cutting up his duck. Rainbird scarcely bothered to conceal a smirk. The Lieutenant tightened his lips. He was not disposed to argue the point.

'This time it *will* be the American route,' averred Mr Pederson stoutly. 'All the way to the Pole.'

And called for more *akvavit*. There was no avoiding another toast.

'You know Franklin put in here?' remarked the Inspector. 'On that last voyage.' He looked round the table meaningfully. 'And we have the *Fox*,' he went on. 'You know the *Fox*? She went aground here.'

He sighed, out of respect for wrecks.

Lieutenant Parish was familiar with the history. Among the box of books set aside in his cabin for study on the journey was McClintock's *Voyage of the Fox in the Arctic Seas*.

The *Fox*, he began explaining to his officers, had been the first vessel to bring back some evidence of Franklin's fate.

'Ah, those poor fellows.' The governor sighed again, this time for the calumnies of men. 'Even here, alas, the ugly stories reached.'

Parish frowned. It was not a topic for a lady. Fortunately, Mrs Pederson was oblivious.

'The best authorities regard them as highly improbable,' he said firmly, helping himself to cheese. 'They were based entirely on hearsay. I cannot believe,' he concluded, with what should have been sufficient finality, 'there was any truth in them.'

'I believe it.'

The Lieutenant turned to gaze reprovingly at the speaker.

But the surgeon was addressing himself to Foxer.

'Lieutenant Foxer, would you say you have enjoyed your supper this evening?'

'I'll say.'

'You were hungry?'

'He's always hungry,' joshed Rainbird, who was beginning to enjoy himself.

'No, my friend. Real hunger is when you have eaten nothing for many days. You see yourself getting thinner and thinner. You become aware of your bones standing out, as the body begins to feed upon itself. Your sight begins to deteriorate. You cannot focus properly. Now you are driven to the last resort. You make the decision to live by whatever means possible ...'

He looked round in rational appeal. Was it not so?

Mrs Pederson's gaze remained fixed politely on her guest, who was addressing the company. Rainbird's eyes too were fixed on the doctor. His face wore a fixed gleam of amusement. Foxer, whose face was incapable of concealment, gazed open-mouthed.

'You can't mean ...' he stammered.

'I believe that under certain circumstances, you, I, all of us here, would come to the realization which faced the members of poor Franklin's party.

'Dr Fabius,' Parish interrupted firmly. 'This is not a fit subject.'

'Of course. I apologize. I was forgetting I am among laymen.' His smile hinted at realities beyond their comprehension.

But the Lieutenant had begun to enquire, with great earnestness, after the Inspector's garden, the sight of so green a spot having surprised him in what he took to be a barren isle.

The soil, the governor explained, had been brought from

Denmark. As for it being so green, the previous winter had been unusually mild. Then summer came earlier than usual. Not for fourteen years had it been so.

The *Petrel* remained a further day at Godthavn, during which time the Lieutenant negotiated the purchase of dogs, and the hiring of a pair of Inuit drivers. Having no acquaintance with either, he had been forced to rely on the expertise of Fabius. Parish had formed a most unfavourable impression of the surgeon. Cultivated, certainly. Well-versed, no doubt, in Arctic lore. He felt a dull stirring of anger at the memory of the man's persistence in dwelling on the fate of Franklin's companions, when he had plainly indicated he wished the subject dropped. Clearly, he'd done it in order to draw attention to himself.

The twelve dogs were chained in a line on the fo'c'sle deck, where the men had gathered to watch them being fed. Mitsoq, one of the drivers, was cutting up fresh seal meat with a hatchet. The other, Quisuuk, did the feeding. The dogs strained at their chains, following every movement with slanting, black-rimmed eyes. The meat, thrown from a distance, was caught in mid-air between snapping teeth, and swallowed in a gulp.

'They live for three things only,' remarked the surgeon conversationally, 'to mate, to fill their bellies, and to fight with other dogs.'

Parish studied his new acquisitions. They were Greenland dogs: supposedly the best, though of irredeemable viciousness, if appearance was anything to go by. He suspected he had paid too much for them.

It being the eve of their departure the explorers were invited to attend an Eskimo dance which was to be held in their honour.

'I believe you will find it an interesting spectacle,' remarked the Inspector. 'The natives here are naturally given to dancing. They take pride in executing the jig which was taught to them by the Scottish whalers.'

The Lieutenant felt at a loss at social gatherings of a frivolous nature. Shortly before midnight, having watched his men clumping around in clumsy merriment, he retired thankfully to finish his dispatches.

George Reade, too, had wandered away from the dance. He scrambled up the low elevation of land, a hundred feet or so above the settlement. Below lay Disko Bay. A distant glimmer across the water was the shimmering mother glacier of Sermeq Kujallew, forever calving its stream of ice. Westward, on the horizon, fabulous and golden, dwelt the midnight sun.

Reade sat on a rock, watching the bergs drifting south. Earlier that day he had tried to draw them, sketching the outlines rapidly in chalks, searching for the spirit in the mass, resolving it into light and shade: sunlit bergs on a matt-black sea. At length he sat back, dissatisfied with the line where it cut the surface of the water, remembering that what he saw was floating in the sea, not on it. He was conscious of the enormous volume, an unseen mystery, beneath each exposed form. So much was translucent: reflective, not defined. Yet he was stuck at the surface. He stared hard, as if sheer intensity could carry him beyond the curtain of appearance. Though the eye, he knew, was stupid. In the end he sat back, at a loss, simply watching the bergs, blinding white on the matt-black water. Baffling, they drifted past, beyond anything he could make of them.

Vaguely there came to him the shouts and whoops of his comrades exchanging partners in the reel. A glory of light enveloped the dancers, black twigs whirled in mellow flame, as they turned and promenaded in the dance. The lambent light coruscated on the surface of the sea. It fell, full and golden, on the western faces of the bergs; glazed with a sheen of rich egg yokes, or glowing richest cadmium orange, or buttery primrose, or rose-gold, or a far-off coppery wash, undershot with the glimmer of ice. Berg after berg, aloof, on a golden sea.

The prodigality overwhelmed him. Sitting there on his little hill, he was illuminated, and blinded too, by something inexpressible, a core of beauty he could never come at. He could never lay hold of the splendour that he saw.

Three hours after midnight the *Petrel* slipped her cable, inched out from her anchorage and turned her bow towards Baffin Bay.

In the fore hold the men lay on their bunks in reflective mood. Like all frontiersmen they were sometimes troubled by the fugitive nature of their lives, never quite knowing where they belonged, or what they were doing there. Private Diggs, born Dygalski, played softly on his harmonica. Others were adding to the entries in the personal logbooks issued to officers and men to record their own impressions. Now, at last, they were on their way. As to danger they scarcely thought about it, except to suppose that somehow or other they would manage to circumvent whatever perils came their way. But they had left behind the last sketchy outpost of security, and it made them thoughtful.

In his cabin Parish had completed the last of his dispatches, which would be put aboard the Danish brig sailing from the mainland two days hence. The writing of reports, usually so satisfying, seemed less sustaining than usual. It was with relief that he turned to adding some lines to the letter to his wife. She was ever present in his mind, a confidante for those anxieties and justifications which are the burden of command.

In those high latitudes the sun would not set for another month, yet the light in the little cabin was dim enough for the Lieutenant to require a lamp to write. The flame burned steadily in its glass, swaying now and then with the motion of the vessel.

Meanwhile the *Petrel* was gaining headway. Black smoke belched from her stack. All her timbers vibrated to the rhythmic stamping of her pistons as, under power alone, she nosed through the narrow channel.

The lamp swayed, sending a shadow lurching across the cabin, as the *Petrel*'s bow encountered the swell of open sea. Up on the fo'c'sle deck a solitary dog lifted its muzzle, scenting the cold salt wind. It broke into a long, high melancholy howl.

Instantly the pack gave tongue; wild, discordant, the crying of the blood.

Below deck, the harmonica fell silent. Private Fromm, flicking out cards on a blanket, held his hand. Mere men looked up from whatever they were doing, gripped by that ragged chorus drawn out on the air, a salutation to whatever lay out there; the jubilation of wild creatures returning to the wild.

The Lieutenant too had heard. As he raised his head to listen, he was seized by a sensation that could only have been excitement. He was sailing North: cutting the same water as the great names of old. Now, at last, he was of their company. At the thought of the illustrious compatriot whose stirring record had first awoken his own ambitions, Parish's mind turned to thoughts of the volume he would himself write on his return, a sober narrative unmarred by Kane's exaggerations. The letter to his wife forgotten, he dwelt on the additions to knowledge he would make, the agreeable prospect of undiscovered capes and bays in need of names.

In that genial house on the square, its windows shaded now against the sun, Senator Clay sat at his desk. He was writing his memoirs. If the task was proving a struggle, the fault lay less with the pitfalls of remembrance than with a more insidious discouragement. Sometimes he was painfully conscious that the country he was born in, and the country he'd been left to grow old in were not the same.

Now a second president had fallen victim to an assassin's bullet.

'What I want to know,' said Amos Potwine, sipping a brandy in the foyer of Willard's Hotel, 'is who put him up to it?'

On the Hill word had it that the fellow was well known as a supporter of Senator Conkey in the matter of the Custom House appointment. A statement from the White House reported that the president, now calm and composed, was greeting members of his Cabinet with words of cheer. The first bullet, ripping through a coat-sleeve, had done no more than graze his arm. The second, striking above the third rib, was lodged some four inches from the spine. The wound was discharging healthy pus: a promising sign of future recovery.

Meanwhile Dr Craigie, exploring the wound with an unwashed finger, was probing for the slug.

Since ancient times, as the first summer warmth opens leads to the north and west, ships have followed that same route along the Greenland coast. A warm current, sweeping around Cape Farewell, strikes the north-west bulge of the land. Pushed westward into Baffin Bay, where polar ice comes surging south from Smith Sound, it sets up a churning counter clockwise movement of the pack. This swirling of the current creates the ice-free polynya north of the pack long known to whalers as the North Water, the traditional killing ground of the Greenland whalers.

For several days the *Petrel* ran north-west along this northern coast. Fogs and sleety showers came and went under a low grey sky. The surface of the sea was inky black. The sergeant observers of the Signal Corps were kept busy, taking readings of the temperature at different depths. The commander was occupied with paper work. His instructions required him to send back by the returning steamer a full report, together with a transcript of all meteorological and other observations made during the voyage.

With the Berry Islands in sight, he was fast approaching his first operational decision: whether to take the notorious 'middle passage', or follow the coast and look for a shore lead. He inclined to the latter. He'd read about Melville Bay and its 'middle pack' as a crushing graveyard for ships. So he was somewhat put out to find the waters of the bay, stretching ahead to the north-west, serene and clear of ice.

'It's not what I expected,' muttered the Lieutenant, who believed experience in the field should corroborate, not contradict, what he'd come across in books. He was inclined to be unsettled by anything irregular.

As he steamed further north, he was increasingly troubled

by the non-appearance of the pack. He brooded over its likely whereabouts, its conditions and extent. He went so far as to solicit Captain Quine for an opinion. 'It's your decision, mister,' was all that cautious man would offer.

At length, with Holm Island showing to starboard, the Lieutenant decided to risk it. There was no indication of ice. The season was well advanced. And he had Inspector Pederson's assurance that the spring and summer had been unusually mild. He gave orders for a course to be laid direct for Cape York. At midnight when he went below, the ship was running at full speed through an open sea.

All the next day the sea continued clear of ice. The *Petrel* was running north-west through open water when the quartermaster, going aloft to start his watch, reported a whitening of the sky to the northward. Before long, a northerly breeze got up, and with the breeze, a thin, cold mist that closed around the ship. The mist thickened. By now the first fragments of stream ice were sliding past the vessel. Soon they were encountering larger pieces of close pack.

Rainbird, a moody presence, hung about the bridge clutching his rifle. He was put on edge, hearing for the first time the deep, exhausted groaning of the floes. 'A melancholy sound,' remarked a voice, it might have been to a friend. He turned to find the surgeon gazing into the mist.

'The Eskimo call it "the weeping of those who live under the earth".'

In the fore hold the men lay in their bunks listening to the noise, that was like nothing they'd ever heard before, and wondered what they were getting into. They had begun to suspect that their ignorance was extensive.

Shortly afterwards the *Petrel* shot forth from the mist into a glittering sea.

Later that day, Lt Rainbird shot a polar bear.

That night, having been photographed and skinned, the bear was cooked and eaten.

'Quite palatable,' opined the Lieutenant. 'It compares very favourably for flavour with our own cinnamon. If a trifle stringy.'

'The tongue is much coveted by the natives,' remarked the surgeon. 'Also the teeth and claws.' Made into a necklace, he went on, they ensured the faithfulness of a wife. The atmosphere in the little saloon was almost convivial.

Rainbird, having received the congratulations of all, and seemingly his easy-going self again, was contributing his own observations derived from his experiences as a hunter.

'Venison tastes best if you get in a clean head shot, and don't ruin it.'

'That pelt will sure look good upon a wall,' enthused young Foxer. Privately, he was resolving to secure one for himself.

The Lieutenant, though, had begun uttering that odd, throaty noise of demurral which his officers had come to recognize as the presager of Authority.

'I'm afraid the bear must be regarded as an expedition prize,' he corrected, not deterred by the pleasure it gave him. 'As such its pelt becomes the property of the Government.'

Still smiling, Rainbird turned to look at his commander. His face wore the expression of a man not quite understanding what he'd heard.

'The instructions are quite specific on that point,' added the Lieutenant mildly.

Rainbird seemed lost for words: the straw-pale head more startling than ever above a rising flush. He was struggling to suppress something.

'Isn't that a trifle officious?' he managed tightly. 'A trifle petty?'

The Lieutenant's lips cramped together. Only the slightest tremor in the muscles of his face betrayed any emotion. Suddenly he rose to his feet and left the saloon.

The three men, looking anywhere but at one another, heard him clumping about his cabin.

After some moments he returned bearing a document

which, having adjusted his spectacles, he began to read in the toneless voice befitting a General Order.

'*Careful attention will be given to the collection of specimens of the animal, mineral and vegetable kingdoms. Such collections,* etcetera, etcetera, *will be considered the property of the Government of the United States, and are to be at its disposal.*'

A glint of triumph, it could have been, reflected in the bottle lenses.

'I'm truly sorry, Rainbird.' He sounded almost apologetic. 'Your disappointment is understandable. It would have made a fine trophy.'

White-faced, Rainbird got up, and slammed out of the saloon.

Hot, unhappy, young Foxer sat with his eyes fixed on his plate.

The surgeon leant back, exploring his teeth for shreds of bear. It was no concern of his.

To westward now the coast of Grinnell Land was constantly in view. Four hours' steaming brought them within sight of the Carey Islands. By eight that evening they had cleared Hakluyt Island, and were entering the North Water.

Next morning, approaching the narrows of Smith Sound, the Lieutenant was wondering what to do. To the north-west, at Cape Sabine, where the bottleneck of the Sound debouched into the Kane Basin, was the first of the English depots. He was anxious to determine the exact location and condition of such stores, and perhaps add to them such supplies as might be a godsend to a boat party retreating southward from the Robeson Channel. The view to northward, for forty miles or more, showed a sea entirely free of ice. Yet he had read of the extreme rapidity with which ice conditions could change in these waters. He decided to risk no delay but press on directly for Cape Hawks.

The *Petrel*, her decks airy with light, steamed steadily northward into the glowing afternoon. Men standing at the rail could have been participants in some luminous work of Art. Or Nature. Even the dogs chained to the fo'c'sle might have forgotten they were savage in that healing light. They slid past umbrous cliffs, shingle beaches, the icy facets of far-off mountains, brilliant as if cut in crystal.

Distances were swallowed up in that magical air. Far capes and headlands gliding past, were, the Lieutenant pointed out, quite probably superimposed on one another. Such tricks of the light could give rise to topographical confusions. Opposite Bache Island, which an earlier explorer had copied on to his chart as a pair of islands separated by a strait, he stopped the ship for a few moments to enable Sergeant Reade to photograph the true facts.

'It is in the correcting of such errors,' he explained to Captain Quine, 'that the value of an expedition such as this consists.'

The tide was at the slack. The *Petrel* lay at anchor in a flat calm: sea and air utterly still: an entire coast, bays and headlands, faultlessly reflected, in a flawless ocean. The deep valley between the two high capes of the island was saturated with primordial light, slopes green with the freshness of the first dawn. Even stones had the sheen of something just emerged: the gloss on a fresh horse chestnut, the silky shimmer of a licked foal. It was a land devoid of memory: simply there; silent, untouched since the Creation.

'*Heilige Gott*,' breathed a voice, for once not blasphemous.

As they pushed further north, into the greater spaces of Kane Basin, the absence of sea ice continued to perplex the Lieutenant. In many of the bays, though, the harbour ice was still in place. From Dobbin Bay it reached out, solid and unbroken, to the north end of a forbidding island. Here, off Cape Hawks, at the only point at which a landfall looked possible, the *Petrel* dropped anchor.

The Lieutenant went ashore in the whaleboat to inspect another of the English caches.

In a small cove facing the cape they came across a cairn, and then the stores, cached on a rocky shoulder, some thirty feet above the sea: a few casks, and a quantity of cans arranged in rows on the bare rock. The strangeness of the spectacle, cans laid out just as a woman might stock a larder shelf, had a sobering effect upon the boat crew, who'd gone ashore in holiday mood. The lonesome sight, in such a place, far from all house or home.

The surgeon, testing one of the cans, pronounced the beef quite palatable. Some of the bread, though, proved to be mouldy.

As well as some samples of rum, the party came away with the English jolly-boat, which was found to be in an excellent state of preservation.

'I name this ship *Valorous*,' declared the Lieutenant humorously, in taking possession.

Now, for many miles to the north, the coast of Grinnell Land loomed as an encroaching vastness that might, the Lieutenant saw, be dispiriting. That emptiness. In winter especially. He prayed such endurance as was needed would grow out of contact with the wilderness. In this he was heartened by the re-emergence of Rainbird as an active member of the expedition. In addition to conversing again at meals, the deputy leader had presented himself on the bridge of the *Petrel* where he stood somewhat stiffly, a little apart from his commander, as if available for such duties as might be required. The Lieutenant, when he could think of anything to say, would hazard some observation, pointing out the dorsal fins of whales looping into the sea, to which Rainbird would respond with an appropriate rejoinder. Neither man made mention of the polar bear.

Cape Frazer came and went. Then Cape McClintock. Captain Quine, taking the noonday observation, reported them as having crossed the eightieth parallel. For the Lieutenant, little given to sentiment as a rule, it was a moment for reflection. In the whole of human history but three vessels had ever attained so high a latitude as this.

'It has been a most remarkable voyage,' he began gravely. 'I can't help but feel Providence has taken a hand in our behalf.'

'You struck lucky, mister,' grunted the captain, who sailed Arctic waters to earn his living, not to make a name for himself. 'Let's hope it holds.'

Further north, all the bays were choked with harbour-ice. Fringes of new ice, extending a mile or more from the shore, warned of the approach of winter. Soon, in fog and drizzle, they were running at half-speed, then steerage way. By morning, as they entered the long narrows of the Kennedy Channel, the fog had lifted sufficiently for both coasts to show up plainly.

Heavy floes pressing against the coast of Grinnell Land forced them steadily eastward. Captain Quine was hard put to thread a passage through the maze of ice choking the channel. South-east of Cape Baird, where sea-ice, driven down from the north, had impacted in mast-high ridges, they were stopped at last.

Then followed a weary and frustrating time. The phlegmatic captain, probing lead after lead, had managed to advance his ship a mile or two closer to her destination, when a rousing nor'easter, joining forces with the Polar current, began shouldering large quantities of heavy ice down the Kennedy Channel. The *Petrel*, giving ground continually, was driven south again. Continual snow showers blotted out all visibility. When the snow cleared at last the log showed forty miles of latitude lost to this southward drift.

At last the wind backed. Now, under a freshening south-westerly, they started northward at full speed. What little ice they saw was crowded well to eastward.

With the gale stiffening, the *Petrel* rounded the cliffs of a high rocky cape, and entered a wide bay.

The Lieutenant pointed where an arm of the sea ran between a rugged island and the high peninsula to the west.

'I take that to be the westward entrance,' he said. It was marked on the British charts.

Leaving a curving wake behind her, the *Petrel* steamed slowly through an arc of open water in the ice-bound channel. The men crowding her decks found themselves in a great land-locked harbour many miles in extent, with level ice stretching away to dark cliffs, silent, empty, under a brassy sky.

On the bridge the Lieutenant was scanning the shore, all the while reflecting what loss it was to the man who loved his own chimney corner, who never dared to venture beyond his own town end. Such a man could never marvel at the wonderful works of the Almighty.

Inwardly moved, he passed his field glasses to his deputy.

Rainbird studied the landing place, a pocket-handkerchief plateau within a semi-circle of blunt hills, on which he recognized the debris of an old encampment.

'I take it,' he said, 'the British left those cans.'

*

In the White House the president's condition was giving cause for concern. He'd had a bad night. By morning he appeared to be sinking rapidly. The team of physicians, gathered round the bed of the unconscious man, were at a loss

The Army Surgeon-General stuck a finger into the wound, burrowing along the tunnel dug out earlier by Dr Craigie. He shook his head.

'I fear the bullet has penetrated the liver,' he said. 'Surgery would be useless.'

All over the country folks were looking in the morning papers to see how the president was faring, pondering on what tortuous paths life might lead them, what calamities might lie in store. Amos Potwine, musing on the vagaries of political fortunes, didn't know but that bullet was as lucky a stroke as Ty Greig could ever have had. In the First Congregational Church, Hartfield, Reverend Dwight called for a day of prayer and supplication for the president's recovery. Martha Parish thought of her husband William. Remembering him, stubborn, dogged, suffering his endless frustrations with that curious look of patient endurance, she never doubted he would outlast all obstacles. He would wear them down. Cousin Thankful was reflecting that marriage seemed to have done nothing for poor Matty's sunken chest.

The thoughts and prayers of some, for whom no news could be expected, good or ill, were for loved ones far away. 'He has no idea,' muttered Yaakov Asher, 'he has no idea what sort of place he is going to,' beseeching the Holy One, un-nameable, answerable to no one, brooding over the chaos of creation. Only a man secure in his soul could be safe in the wilderness.

In the White House bedroom the Navy Surgeon-General, searching so deeply that his finger punctured the patient's liver, concurred with his distinguished colleague. The president could not live more than twenty-four hours.

The Lieutenant had pitched his dog tents in two neat rows on a lip of land overlooking the harbour. It was the only level place in a region of high hills and narrow, V-shaped valleys. Southward, rising directly from the shore ice, precipitous cliffs stretched for two miles to the headland overlooking the eastern entrance to the harbour. More hills rose to the north, divided by a V-shaped valley beyond which a snow-topped hogsback cut off any further view of the interior. East of the camp, between the sea cliffs and higher hills inland, another narrow valley ran to a low divide beyond which a frozen creek ran down to the sea.

Seated at the door of his tent, the Lieutenant was writing to his wife. He had begun a journal-letter which, in the long winter months, would bring her a little closer. At the same time he was striving for a certain resonance suited to a historic document which would, in years to come, no doubt be lodged in the Library of Congress: *So we made our landfall, not in the blinding snowstorm through which William Bradford found his way to Plymouth Harbour, but with every providential sign of God's good grace abounding. Here was a pool teeming with wild fowl; there, musk oxen grazing peacefully on a hillside; there, a pasture clothed with every kind of vegetation, with great drifts of Arctic poppy yellowing the slopes...*

It was indeed a lonely place, imbued with a desolation to

which numerous abandoned barrels, empty cans and other refuse added a forsaken air. If the lure of the fresh start will set men dreaming, desire is often perplexed by what it finds. Each morning they tore themselves from their buffalo sleeping bags for another fourteen hours' toil in a strange land devoid of memories, where there was neither dawn nor dusk, only an alien sun scarcely dipping beyond the horizontal: a land seemingly intended, as Private Hanson never tired of pointing out, for a man to be made to labour 'til he dropped.

'Hey, one thing for sure,' joshed Diggs, always the joker. 'No one gonna shoot at us at the North Pole.'

The Lieutenant looked up to where his men were carrying the timber sections, under the direction of Sergeant Emmons. They had set to work the moment he'd chosen a site for the long house. Within days uprights and rafters were in position. Now the carpenters were nailing tar-paper to the joists, preparing them to receive their covering of boards. The Lieutenant felt a sudden affection for these men he'd brought to this unknown shore, and for whom he was accountable. He was convinced that, as he came to know them better, he would be as a father to each man. In that tender light his perceptions were suddenly glowing:

I believe myself blessed, too, in my officers and men. Emmons, for instance – a good man, I should think, in a tight corner – always cool and collected, but when he tells a man to jump, that man jumps pretty quick. Rainbird, I'm happy to say, has returned to grace after a regrettable misunderstanding relating to the shooting of a polar bear, a prize which he insisted on claiming for himself, though an expedition capture for which I, as leader, am answerable to the War Department. General orders are quite clear upon that point. To tell the truth, I felt disappointed in him. Though twenty years of military service have caused me to observe that such gifts as these dashing fellows possess are rarely if ever bestowed on men with the character to put them to good use. Even so, properly harnessed, I believe they can be of immeasurable benefit to an expedition. Now leading

*hunting parties up into the hills, Lt Rainbird is himself again,
and merry as a boy.*

Generosity was tempered by a nip in the air, a reminder of
the freezing temperatures which were now a daily occurrence.
Mindful of many items of supply as should be got under cover,
the Lieutenant locked away his letter, and went forth to hurry
along completion of the work. Winter was on its way. Within
days the sun would begin to dip below the northern hills. Then
the temperature would plummet, the period of darkness would
grow rapidly. Already heavy ice, driven in by an easterly storm,
was piled up at the eastern entrance to the harbour. Though the
Petrel had been discharged, Captain Quine had got no further
than a small island off the point, where he was now anchored to
take on ballast. The Lieutenant would be glad to see her gone.
He was conscious of a certain wistfulness in the seaward glances
of his men.

Standing within the framework of uprights and roof
timbers, amid a furious hammering of floorboards, he felt well
satisfied with the start he'd made. Lt Foxer, having explored the
long watercourse beyond the divide, had just returned with
news of an excellent coal seam no more than four miles way.
Rainbird had come in from the Hogsback with a report of more
musk oxen killed. He was, at that moment, setting off with the
butchers to dress the carcasses. All in all, the prospects for their
first winter were most reassuring.

Astonishingly, the president had rallied. His pulse had fallen.
His stomach had resumed its normal functions.

'I am better,' he announced, if faintly. 'I believe I shall live.'

He was put on a diet of milk fortified with brandy. His
physicians, misled by the path excavated by Dr Craigie's finger,
continued to search for the bullet.

Meanwhile, a crisis had arisen over the vice-presidential
function. Certainly, no one could deny that in such cases the
vice president was authorized to assume the powers of the pres-
idential office. But now the matter had been thrown into

confusion, as some parties to the discussion discerned an ambiguity in the Constitution. Would Ty Greig serve merely as acting president, as the Speaker of the House was insisting or, as maintained by the Conkey faction, should he receive the office itself and thus displace his predecessor?

At the White House clinical investigation was continuing with the aid of a specially designed electrical device.

After several passes to and fro over the patient's body, its designer claimed to have pinpointed the position of the bullet. It was far, far deeper than anyone had suspected.

By now signs of septicaemia were unmistakeable. In the right lung an abscess had appeared. Faced with this steady deterioration in the president's condition, his doctors decided on surgery to remove the slug. They failed to find it.

Meanwhile, what had begun as a three-inch wound had been elongated into a twenty-inch canal, now heavily infected, oozing more and more pus with each passing day.

On that lip of land, by the edge of the frozen sea, the long house was taking shape. In outline it had the comfortable look of a country barn, a long sturdy building within which the reassuring properties of a rough home had begun to appear. The roof was on. The double walls, half-inch boards tongued and grooved, with a cladding of tar-paper, securely battened, had been fitted into position. Doors, windows and interior partitions were all in place. At one end, segregated from the officers' quarters by a central area comprising the cookhouse and bathroom, tiers of bunks for the enlisted men were already in position round the walls,

There were practical considerations for completing the work as soon as possible. For several days in succession the thermometers in their wooden shelter close to the house had recorded a minimum reading below freezing point. Each evening saw the sun dipping closer towards the northern hills. Soon the mercury would fall below the mark and not rise again before May.

Despite almost daily attempts to leave, the *Petrel* had so far failed to force a passage through the narrow strip of densely packed floes piled up at the eastern entrance of the harbour.

Its continuing presence had become an irritant to the Lieutenant. He got up at seven as usual, though, as he remarked to Rainbird, who joined him in the mess tent, he had not slept well. Fabius arrived shortly afterwards. Foxer was late *again*.

Private Wutz, coming in with the breakfast, thought the commander looked more sour than usual.

'Thank you, Wutz. Please to take the dishes back to the kitchen, and see that Lieutenant Foxer is called. When all the officers are assembled you may serve breakfast, and call me at the same time. I shall be in my tent.'

He had *repeatedly* requested that officers be up for breakfast at the same hour as the men. Seven a.m., Washington time, seemed to him a reasonable stipulation, particularly as Fort Chance being so far in advance gave them a generous margin of fifty minutes for lying in.

A full half hour had elapsed before he was able to return to the mess. Only that slight facial tremor betrayed his vigorous displeasure.

'I'm surprised I find it necessary to restate an order,' he said stiffly, helping himself to grits. 'Especially as I've already had cause to mention it on more than one occasion. Let me repeat it.' He looked up from his plate. '*All* officers must be up to breakfast with the men.'

Shamefaced, young Foxer mumbled an apology.

'I guess I'd rather stay in bed, and hang the breakfast,' said Rainbird with a doleful humour, it might have been in sympathy with a brother sluggard.

'Whether you eat or not, Rainbird, is, of course, your own affair. But the hour set for rising is a station regulation, and must be complied with.'

Rainbird exchanged a glance with the surgeon.

'Well, if you insist, Lieutenant,' he sighed, good-humouredly enough, 'I suppose I shall have to comply.'

The Lieutenant laid down his spoon.

'It astonishes me to hear an officer of the United States army declare that he will obey an order only if it is insisted on. What the army expects, Lieutenant Rainbird, is cheerful compliance. An officer who found that beyond his powers would cease to be a useful member of this expedition.'

'Are you suggesting,' enquired Rainbird, who had gone a dangerous colour, 'that I'm of no use to the expedition?'

'I have nothing to add,' concluded the Lieutenant firmly. 'Except to observe that the army seems a strange choice of career for a man with such a rooted objection to obeying orders.'

'You have no right to speak to me like that,' cried Rainbird hotly.

'I don't wish to discuss the matter further.'

On that note of disengagement the tall Lieutenant put his hat on his head, and went to inspect the works. In the officers' quarters, a curtained-off corner of which was to serve as his study, he was gratified to find his desk and rocker already in place. He'd already brushed aside the scene over the breakfast table. It was unfortunate, but he felt he'd handled it well enough. The matter was at an end. Rainbird really was an extraordinary fellow.

The Lieutenant made a mental note to add to his log a memorandum stressing the importance of selecting for Arctic service only officers and men of proven qualities.

In the White House bedroom the president had been sleeping quietly. Suddenly he woke, gasping at the pain constricting his chest.

Dr Craigie was summoned from an adjoining room.

'My God', he muttered. 'Call Mrs Swain.'

The sick man's eyes were wide open, and fixed upon his wife as she entered the room. Helpless, astonished, they followed her as she moved round the bed to take his hand.

In the long house the carpenters were putting in the kitchen range. Other men were lugging in the boiler. The Lieutenant went to lend a hand. He found release in practical tasks. Engrossed in the absorbing business of setting up a stove in the mens' quarters, he failed to notice that Fabius had entered the room and was requiring his attention. The stove was heavy. Diggs and Lawless were struggling to position it directly under the opening into the chimney, trying to lift while looking up, as the Lieutenant gave directions.

'No, no … a little more this way,' he was saying, when he became aware of the surgeon's presence.

'I have been asked to give you this.'

The surgeon made a stiff little bow, and withdrew, leaving a mystified Parish clutching an envelope, with the enlisted men struggling to cling on to their burden.

Dinner was a strained affair. When it was over the Lieutenant requested that the surgeon and Lieutenant Rainbird should step outside the tent for a moment.

Parish led the way, the two men following in silence. After a dozen yards he turned, addressing Rainbird abruptly with cold vehemence.

'You say in your letter that I as good as declared you had better go. That is quite untrue. I said no such thing. If I wanted a man to go I should tell him so very plainly. There would be no mistaking it, I assure you. What I *did* say was that an officer who felt unable to comply with orders was of little use to the expedition. Now, if you still feel my orders to be unreasonable, then I remain of the same mind.'

Rainbird flushed.

'I do think them unreasonable.'

'Very well. Then I shall put it to you stronger still. I will not say that any officer thinking and acting so had better go, I say he *must* go.'

The Lieutenant, altogether borne up by the warmth of his own indignation, was gratified by the impact of his words.

'I would sooner dispense with officers altogether and work with the enlisted men, rather than endure the company of officers disposed to question their orders. Now, you have heard the situation, Lieutenant. Do you wish to go?'

'I believe that would be best.' Rainbird had never backed down in his life.

An hour later, supplied with stores, bearing the order relieving him of his duties, the straw-haired man was picking his way over the rubble of the fore-shore towards the point where the *Petrel* lay at anchor. After all, a man had his standards. It was the only honourable thing to do. Lieutenant Parish was not the kind of commander he'd bargained for. He'd confessed as much to the surgeon, whose detachment seemed to invite confidences. 'Still, we're stuck with him for the next two years. We shall have to make the best of it.' He had to confide in someone. It would have been wrong to speak so to young Foxer. He'd meant what he said. He would have made the best of it. This coming to the Arctic was to have been a new beginning. A fresh start in a new land.

Rounding a curtain of rock he saw an ominous plume of black smoke. A mile offshore the *Petrel* was making another attempt to break through to the channel. He could hear the pounding of her engines as she nuzzled at the floes.

Burdened with baggage, his rifle slung from a shoulder, he hurried along the shore, eyes fixed on the vessel, shouting, stumbling, leaving in his wake a trail of useless encumbrances, first one bag, then the other, then his rifle.

Finally his hat went too as he ran and ran, his feet catching in the rubble of the shore, shouting, waving. Still she might be stopped. She'd been stopped before.

But the pack had shifted under a nor'westerly wind. The sealer was making headway. Already she was halfway down the ice-strewn channel. Gouts of black smoke hung in the air, falling in sooty flakes on the floes astern. Pistons stamping, her iron prow ripping through the loose pack, the *Petrel* was boring a passage through the floes that cut her off from open water.

Stripping off his jacket, waving it as he ran, stumbling, scrambling to his feet, the frantic man staggered on and on, out across the ice foot to Dutch Island, and up to the low summit of that tiny rock, last nugget of accessible land.

But Captain Quine had found the sea. A long beam of autumn sunlight, slanting down from the high plateau of Grinnell Land and out across the harbour ice, gleamed on her spars and masts as, skirting the pack, the *Petrel* put her bow to the south-east. She was homeward bound.

Rainbird knew it now. Exhausted, he fell to his knees. Throwing back his head, he uttered a long despairing cry.

All that morning Lucius Clay had been adrift again in the first fall of the war: for him, shut up alone in his house, months of black despair. He was remembering the jingle of accoutrements as the escort halted under the window, and the kindness of a sad-eyed man in dusty black; a man with a lined, leathery face under a stiff black hat, dropping by to pay his respects. Within weeks Lincoln too had lost a son.

Sunk in his reverie, the old man was brought back by the tolling of the bell across the square.

Then he knew at once that the president must be dead.

Startled, he turned his head towards the window.

'God help us,' he muttered. 'Ty Greig is President of the United States.'

FIVE

Secure as a great river in its bed, the government of the United States swept on its way unchecked. Within hours of the president's death Ty Greig took the oath of office at his home in New York City.

The next day, in his office in the Capitol, he took it again, administered by the Chief Justice.

'Listen,' said Lucius Clay, over dinner at Wormley's, 'I don't care how many times they make him take the oath, it'll make no difference. Ty must reckon this a gift from the gods.'

More generally throughout the country the new man enjoyed no lack of support.

Donning her spectacles, the widow Stevens took up the *Hartfield Republican* to read out loud a remarkable eulogium. '"*For character, ability, superb executive powers, absolute integrity ...*" No, it goes on, '"*... courage, temper, tact and good nature the new president challenges any man in Congress.*" My! Aren't we blessed?'

Matty took up her work basket and resumed her mending. She had a veritable siege of sewing to get through. Following William's departure she had returned to the house on Willow Street, where she found life lying like an old coat cast aside, waiting to be taken up again. She wound the clocks, and fed the chickens, and peeled apples for the pie, while consoling Lizzie Boot for injustices suffered in her absence. She dined at one, and supped at six, and was visited by her relations, who had come, it seemed, especially to bestow pitying looks, such as might be extended to an abandoned wife. William was never mentioned.

The sun, streaming across the meadow where a second crop of hay had been raked into heaps, brought with it all the colours of the wood where she used to walk with father: crimson, cherry, bright sulphur, fiery orange, against a backdrop of ever-green. Sighing, she laid down her work again. Sometimes, in Foggy Bottom, it was what she had longed for: the stability of a life regulated by New England constants; customs, crops, weather.

One day, when the cold east wind made it impossible to sit out on the back porch, she thought suddenly of Washington, of the balmy air filling the enormous streets, and recollected, with something of a shock, that she was a married woman.

There was a sense of release in announcing her intention to return.

She overrode objections with a firmness that dismayed mother. After all, as she pointed out, it was always intended she should return. Besides, all danger of malarial fever must be over by now. It couldn't be long before the *Petrel* docked at St John's. She must be on hand when William's letters were forwarded to Washington.

'I'm quite sure the War Department will send the mail to people's homes.'

'No doubt they will. But there may be duties William wishes me to carry out, things that cannot be attended to here in New England. Besides, my home now is in Georgetown.'

'That's as maybe,' said her mother tartly. 'But you have no family. No friends.'

Martha Parish might have contradicted her mother on that score, but had not entirely made up her mind about Senator Clay, whose teasing ironies she found somewhat unsettling.

'Won't you be lonely?'

No lonelier, she might have said, than here. At least in Washington she would be a lonely *wife*.

She went back with a set of New England scenes, with gold mounts, to brighten up the walls.

But in Georgetown she found nothing to return to: only the dreariness of rooms standing exactly as she'd left them. The ground floor suite was empty again. Her key grating in the lock, her footfall on the stair, were the only sounds echoing in a silent house. William's clothes, his uniform hanging in the closet, only brought home what was missing in the life she'd thought to take up again.

As the gloomy days drew in Martha Parish began to feel her isolation. Sometimes she would look at a photograph of the party which had appeared in *Harper's Weekly*. She had clipped it out, and mounted it in a silver frame. But the men's faces, remote, wary, told her nothing. Even William, sitting with folded arms, seemed changed from the man she'd married. Then she found herself sinking further into a half world. She would willingly have given up the intervening months if only she could curl up like a mouse, and sleep out the time until he came home. She felt as solitary as a cat.

Sometimes, at Lucius Clay's insistence, she went to sit by his fire of an afternoon. (*I shall send the cart*, he wrote, *at three o'clock. Do not fail me. I am low, very low.*)

As usual, what ailed him was politics. In his heart the old man hankered after a simpler, more home-spun republic.

'Do you know, I envy your husband, Matty?'

'So you have said before, Senator.' She looked at him askance, suspecting something not to her liking.

'It will be like sailing with the Pilgrims,' he went on musingly. 'He may rediscover things the rest have us have long forgotten.'

She sipped her tea, knowing he only said such things to shock.

He enquired about her life in Massachusetts. Loath to speak of mixing bread and feeding chickens, she told him of her membership of the translation society.

'We are attempting the Greek Testament,' she confessed shyly. 'Well, the book of Romans.'

The senator confessed to having read the Greek authors, when a young man at the University of Virginia.

'Though I fear my Greek,' he added gallantly, 'is hardly the equal of yours.'

Kindly as before, he sought to draw her into his circle. She was invited to attend a senatorial dinner which was to follow the president's address to Congress.

Martha Parish, though, had begun to pick up something of the bantering Washington arts.

'I fear I would be a most unsuitable guest, Senator. I have neither office, nor constituency. What would I talk about?'

The sea-grey eye surveyed her quizzically.

'I can see you are undecided. Let me advise you. Accept. On the principle that one should always say "yes" to life.'

She put up her hair in the severe old style, parted in the middle and drawn back in a Grecian knot, and wore the lavender dress William deemed suitable for social occasions, trying not to appear nervous, an endeavour in which she was hampered by the lumpy bodice. It was a burden of which the company seemed reassuringly oblivious, being occupied with their own uncertainties as to the president's intentions. His message to Congress, it seemed, had given little away.

'If Ty's holding the cards close to his chest,' she heard one grizzled congressman declare, 'it's because Ithamor Conkey don't want anyone seeing his hand.'

She went in to dinner on the senator's arm, a little hunched, and sat, the patient wife of Lt Parish, Arctic explorer. Who had, it seemed, done one of the most purely manly things a fellow could do. Several times, at intervals throughout the evening, Martha Parish was left in no doubt as to that.

Yet of the Arctic, she had no conception, except as lonely distances of ice.

One dismal, foggy afternoon she took her solitary tea at her window, gazing down the Potomac. The broad reach stretched before her, swallowed up in a brooding gloom. Once embarked, a man might journey to the uttermost ends of the earth. Only she could not understand why William should want to go there.

His letter told of a wild shore seemingly flowing with milk and honey, meadows radiant with wild flowers, and oxen grazing, and every kind of waterfowl. She had looked to find some reflection of her own loneliness. Only he was far too busy to be lonely, or feel sorry for himself. As she followed his account of the building of the fort, and the preparations for winter, above all as she read of the work of science that was going forward, she saw she had misjudged him. And felt ashamed, fearing she'd failed to offer him the support a husband was entitled to expect from a wife. She was made miserable at the thought of her own selfishness and feebleness of spirit. She was indeed a very weak woman.

Winter began with leaden skies, and flakes of snow travelling on a knifing wind. Then a sinister rustling, as of dry leaves, that left the slender branches outside her window clicking together under a freight of ice. She read, and re-read his letters, clinging especially to one particular paragraph in which she was assured that separation could be no barrier to an affinity of minds. Her replies were modelled on his staunch self-sufficiency. She would not burden him with her complaints. Loneliness was a sorrow best suffered in silence. She must simply hold out and win through.

Instead, she wrote of the tragi-comedy of frozen pipes; how glad she was to have thought to bring her 'Arctics' with her from New England, for the heavy snow had lain in the streets for weeks. Indeed, the poor horses could not be got out of their stables. She filled her letters with encouragement: the expedition would achieve great things, she was sure of that. He would return, she wrote, a famous man: *I've never had any hankering to leave my mark on the world. All I ever wanted was to love someone, and be loved in return ...* It might have been a confession of weakness. *Here in Washington my sun has just gone down. But he will be back tomorrow. I think of the long dark winter stretching ahead for you, wondering how many days and nights must pass – though it is all one night – before you see the sun again.*

At Fort Chance the polar night was well advanced. At first dusk had seemed endless, a dreary, level, steel-grey gloom that went on day after day. Men bringing back coal, hauling sledges through leathery autumn ice, or hacking out blocks of frozen snow to pile around the walls of the house, looked back almost in disbelief to nights when they'd lain under the stars, or climbed the rackety stair of some frontier bar with a woman.

Eventually the sledging petered out in deepening darkness.

It was never pitch black. Even when obscured by cloud there was always some light reflected from the snow, against which the black land loomed, impenetrable in its strangeness. The Lieutenant had anticipated, as chief threat to the party's well-being, not cold and darkness so much as monotony and stagnation. Accordingly, he devised a rota of daily chores: sweeping, cleaning, digging out supplies of snow, fetching food from the store, keeping the stoves going – tasks, as the men soon discovered, which were far more arduous when performed at fifty below. The cold was brutal. Men soon learnt to unfasten all the necessary buttons, belts and braces whilst still within the shelter of the hut before responding to a call of nature. Private Krug, feeding the dogs in their winter quarters round the back of the coal store, remarked how first they lifted one foot, then the other, as if the ground was burning them.

Curtained-off in his corner, the Lieutenant worked steadily for several hours each day, writing up his log, recording observations, or looking things up among the books in his Arctic library. Glancing at his rocker, his square of carpet, Matty's flag fastened to the wall, William Parish reflected with satisfaction that a man content with his own company was best suited to Arctic life. At the same time he was profoundly conscious of his responsibilities. His sense of duty was too austere for anything less.

Believing the human enterprise to thrive best when regulated in accordance with sound principles, he instituted a regime designed to minister to the whole man. Regular hours, daily classes in arithmetic and grammar, a weekly bath and medical inspection were buttressed by divine service on the Sabbath, the Lieutenant, taking cognisance of Sergeant Asher's presence, choosing his readings from the Old Testament.

Having read somewhere that within a month or two food

would matter more to his men than the absence of women, he gave the party's dietary needs his special attention. He declared the menus for each day a confidential matter, restricted to himself and Wutz in the cookhouse. Knowing with what eagerness men in camp looked forward to their meals, he saw to it that dishes greeted with particular enthusiasm were offered sparingly, whenever morale needed a boost.

Nothing that might contribute to the success of the expedition escaped his attention. On discovering it was Fromm's birthday, the Lieutenant promptly relieved him of all duties for the day. Henceforth, he announced, each man on his birthday should enjoy the privilege of choosing a dinner from the list of provisions. In addition, a quart of rum would be donated to enable him to celebrate with his comrades. Within hours of this announcement an unofficial flyer appeared on the wall of the men's quarters, with all the birthdays for the year plotted in sequence, a token of enthusiasm which led the commander to reflect with quiet satisfaction on the efficacy of his strategy. What harm in a celebration or two if it served to draw them through the winter?

If he had calculated rightly for his men, the icy atmosphere of the officer's quarters was very far from the comradely fellowship the Lieutenant had envisaged. Rainbird's return, in the wake of the departing steamer, had created an awkward situation. Nevertheless, as he noted in his log, Parish believed he had regularized the situation:

> Sept 30th: Having resigned from the expedition, Lt. Rainbird has, in effect, become a civilian and, as such, a guest of the expedition. I have explained as much to him. He, for his part, has agreed to abide by the police regulations of the station. For the time being, Lt. Foxer will continue as second-in-command.

After some reflection he'd made up his mind that should Rainbird ask for reinstatement he'd be prepared to consider the matter. Though such a possibility would not be raised by him.

In the meantime he was determined that any discomfort should be Rainbird's, and not his.

As winter drew on the Lieutenant found himself struggling against an increasing tendency to testiness. The habits of his companions seemed almost calculated to annoy. Every morning, at seven-thirty sharp, he would emerge from behind his curtain and sit down alone to breakfast, acutely irritated by the sight of his officers still sprawled in their bunks. Wutz would bring in the dish of musk-beef hash, or pork and beans. After some minutes the surgeon would appear, then Rainbird, just late enough to provoke. Hardly had the man sat down to his meal, before he was up again, still chewing, sauntering over to the shelf to change the date, and wind up the clock. Then, having finished his breakfast, the guest fell to a meticulous brushing of the ridiculous whiskers he had cultivated since the departure from St John's.

Always the first to rise, the Lieutenant was tempted to adjust the calendar himself, and wind the clock. Rainbird, though, would guess it had been done purposely. Seething with annoyance the Lieutenant bit his lip, and retreated behind his curtain.

Applying himself to mental work now required an effort of discipline which sometimes defeated even the best intention. At such times he would find consolation in his journal-letter: *I am called Parissuaq by our Eskimo drivers, 'suaq' meaning 'great one'. Though honesty compels me to add that, on occasion, it can carry the suggestion 'most ugly'. It is, apparently, all a matter of intonation.* He missed his wife. She had become a vivid presence, vulnerable in a raw way he'd scarcely noticed before: her hands, over-large for so slight a body, which he recalled with painful clarity, the red-rimmed eyes in the pale face, not crying now, yet inconsolable. He did not think he could ever bring himself to leave her again. *We are all sick for home, though not a man would acknowledge it, I least of all. It would be seriously damaging to morale for the commander to admit to any such thing. Yet I feel it, sometimes so acutely, I can scarcely bear to think of you too closely. It were easier, safer, not to think of you at all.*

All the party had begun to suffer the oppression of mid-winter darkness, its monotony, its numbing emptiness. They were discovering it was not the country they were up against but themselves. Every man tramping out to the latrines was conscious of his isolation. To be out alone in the silence of the polar night was to feel at once the weight of solitude. Only in the huddle of the hut could a man find homeliness, within the radius of a stove, or the kitchen range: or, feeding the puppies bits from the slop-bucket, seek solace in a snuffling and a whimpering, the lick of a warm tongue. Yet, since no one spoke of his feelings, each man suffered them in isolation, complaining instead of sleeplessness, and numbing migraines, for which the surgeon prescribed extract of ergot.

Over and above a reek of cooped-up lives, of cooking and of Lysol, an unmistakeable odour clung to the walls and ceiling of the bunkhouse: the smell of loneliness. At night, hearing the groans and mutterings of men reunited with old lives, Jacob Joseph lay listening to the loneliness. His indifference was a puzzle to the men. They thought him a queer fish. He never spoke about his family as others did, chatting over a mug after supper, telling of brothers and sisters making out fine in Idaho or Illinois, or else the old folks back home.

'How about you, Jake?' enquired the amiable Diggs. 'Ain't you got no folks?'

The astronomer shook his head. He had no father. And the word 'mother' now seemed but a projection into the infinite of childish longings, the ache of an old wound. For as far back as he could remember he'd known he was different, and that he'd brought great desolation on his family. Whatever his nature, that it was truly awful he concluded from the boundless pity he received. Small for his age, he'd found himself swung dizzyingly up into the air, or crushed against asphyxiating bosoms. Always they made much of him, the aunts and uncles. He'd always assumed it was because he had no mother. *Is she dead?* he once asked. He would have been very young, even then. *We don't know where she is. She couldn't cope with*

88

looking after a little baby, so she went away. You mustn't ever think badly of her. There were tears in Aunt Yetta's eyes. *She was very young.*

For Lt Foxer the long polar night was especially dispiriting. The troubled atmosphere of the officers' quarters upset him deeply. It threw him off balance; disturbed his sense of what was fitting. In resolving to keep well out of it the young man was thrown back upon his own resources. At night, unable to sleep, he lay on his bunk staring up into the darkness, wondering what he'd got himself into. Inactivity gnawed at him like a disease.

There were days when the darkness seemed to penetrate the walls. Meals passed with scarcely a word. Sometimes the brooding air seemed likely to crackle into a spontaneous discharge. But never did. The surgeon's politeness would become more studied. The Lieutenant's lips cramped together a twist tighter. That was all. In the stuffy, lamp-lit air the faces of his companions seemed to have acquired a sickly greenish-yellow tinge occasioning unwholesome fancies which crowded in upon the young man. He took his daily walk, lit sometimes by a feeble phosphorescence emanating from the snow. If the wind wasn't moving, nothing moved. He found the stillness unnerving. Not the stillness of winter woods at home. It was the profound stillness, the timelessness, of death. Harry Foxer shrank within the stiff animal hide of his buffalo coat. Sometimes, though, he was impelled to step into that stillness. He would stand motionless, listening to the silence roaring in his ears.

With the arrival of the solstice came a change of mood.

'If winter comes,' observed the Lieutenant, forcing a cheerful note, 'can spring be far behind?' It was a piece of poetry he had learned at school.

There was no visible difference. The sun was at its very furthest from the fort. Weeks were to pass before a faint, far-off glow appeared in the south. Holding his watch close to his eye, Harry Foxer was just able to make out the hands pointing to noon.

There were days when it was impossible to leave the house. The wind screamed. The barometer plunged alarmingly. The entire building creaked and trembled, groaning in travail. Young Foxer lay on his bunk and waited for the roof to be torn from the rafters, and the whole party whirled away to the frozen harbour. Yet the thought of the sun making its journey north was a rock to cling to. Day by day it was getting closer. Reveries of the Greenland coast and the sledging journey he would make in the spring began to figure in that inner sanctum of the soul where a young man's sense of himself is secretly forged. For whole days together he clung to his dream of life as an adventure of the spirit: travelling, always travelling; each day a plunge into the unknown.

Parish had already intimated privately the mission that was to be entrusted to the young lieutenant. He had brooded over it for weeks. It wasn't that he'd in any way departed from his conviction regarding the centrality of scientific work. Each day he sat at his desk entering the figures, a record of several hundred daily observations to do with tides, currents, winds, atmospheric pressure, air and sea temperatures, the movements of clouds, the strength of the magnetic field, and so forth. He took a quiet satisfaction in accumulating this mass of information. Even in the deep midwinter darkness the work of the International Polar Conference went forward.

At the same time, as he contemplated the despatches his orders required him to send back the following summer, he'd begun to fear that something more was needful, a more tangible image of arduous striving. How else was the drudgery of scientific labour to be translated into terms which people could appreciate?

At nights, twisting in his narrow bunk, listening to Rainbird's snores (he was sure it was Rainbird), the idea took increasing hold that some notable achievement was expected of him. The American people would expect it. He began to fear that if he failed in this, his own leadership would somehow be called into question. True, his orders were not specific on the point. The acts of Congress spoke of scientific observation and discovery in the Arctic seas. All the same, as the polar night wore on, the Lieutenant became increasingly convinced that among the despatches that would go back in the summer must be a message proclaiming a new record for the 'Farthest North'.

One evening, after Wutz had cleared away the supper dishes, he made the announcement.

'I can now reveal that I have finalized the programme for Spring sledging.' Unrolling a chart, he anchored it to the table with a pair of heavy rulers. 'As you can see, our present knowledge of the area is restricted largely to the coastal strip. I intend to embark upon a programme of mapping and surveying, the principal objective being an exploration of the North Greenland coast.'

Rainbird commenced to studying his nails. The surgeon, though, was following the briefing with every appearance of the keenest attention. Foxer, about to be honoured, sat with eyes modestly averted.

'The advance sledge will be led by Lt Foxer. It will be supported by four supply sledges, hauled by the fittest and strongest of the enlisted men. Lt Foxer will be authorized to announce, at such time as he deems appropriate, the payment of a bounty of one thousand dollars should the party succeed in making a northing further than that previously attained.'

Whether or not the Lieutenant's disclosure brought home to Rainbird a painful sense of his own exclusion, his face expressed the indifference of a man not affected by the matter under consideration. Rising from the table the house guest crossed to his bunk, and began a casual brushing of his whiskers.

The surgeon had been listening closely throughout. When Parish had finished his announcement, he proceeded to cap it with a startling revelation of his own.

'I, too, have formulated a plan. I intend to go round the coast to the east, here,' the surgeon indicated with a finger, 'then north to Cape Joseph and so out across the Frozen Sea.'

He spoke as if of a quite separate expedition, of which he himself was leader.

'I believe I shall be able to travel a great distance northward over the ice of the polar ocean. Certainly as far as the northing attained by Markham, who, you will remember, had neither dogs nor Eskimo driver.'

Suddenly Parish knew for certain truth what previously he'd taken to be the sour imaginings of a winter confinement. The surgeon believed that he, Maximilien Fabius, and not William Parish, should be leading the party.

At this disagreeable suggestion the long face grew more severe than ever. Not for the first time in his career the Lieutenant experienced the precarious nature of command. He felt particularly keenly the absence of a dependable second officer with whom he might discuss the surgeon's shortcomings. The man was a sluggard. He was not reliable. Even the monthly medical report was never handed in on time. He repeatedly irritated his commander by continuing to assert, through sly insinuation and despite the oath he had sworn, his status as a civilian, a professional man, a graduate of the University of Paris. Yet these were scarcely things he cared to broach with young Foxer. He rued the day he'd written that letter to Rainbird. He felt bitterly let down.

Bent over his desk behind his curtain, jabbing his pen in the slushy ink, he confided in his wife: *He is a clever fellow, certainly, with a good knowledge of the Arctic regions. But the fact is, whatever he may feel to the contrary, Fabius is simply not fitted for leadership. As a medical man I cannot fault him. But while medicine might exercise a man's intelligence, it contributes nothing to the formation of character. And it is in character that Fabius is sadly deficient. He and Rainbird are very thick.*

The Lieutenant watched them going off together, no doubt putting their heads together. In the polar night the two men were visible only as a thicker concentration of the general darkness.

Unless a storm was brewing, they never missed their daily walk.

Dawn began as an eerie twilight far to the south. The men couldn't see the sun, but they could see the glow of its coming, drawn out over many days, gradually ascending in a suffusion of bruised indigo, layers of deepest purple, now reflected in carmine bands of cirrus, then dense periwinkle blue on lavender above a long pale band of primrose yellow.

These early weeks were taken up with getting ready for spring sledging.

For the Lieutenant the long dawn took on more and more the promise of a New England summer's morning. He moved benevolently among his men in a space that suddenly seemed endless. He was estimating supplies, portioning them into daily rations sufficient for men hauling heavy sledges. In the officers' mess Foxer and the surgeon, when not tracing maps and sketches, were checking the records of previous expeditions. The men were kept busy sewing tents, soldering cooking lamps, stitching boots and mittens.

Chief among these preparations was the overhauling of the sledges. Dr Fabius, in a series of trial runs over the harbour ice, was experimenting with various modifications of the Greenland sledge. In reducing its length he seemed to have added to the difficulties of manoeuvrability.

The Lieutenant surveyed the latest spill. 'If anything,' he frowned, 'it needs to be longer. A longer sledge is less likely to be baulked by rubble ice.'

'That would make it heavier,' said the surgeon wearily, in a voice he would adopt for the inanities of others. 'My objective is to lessen the weight, not to increase it.'

Fabius was to set off first. After much deliberation the Lieutenant had decided to give his plan formal approval. It still rankled that the surgeon, in conceiving his expedition, had acted without consulting the leader. But Fabius insisted he'd seen land far to the northward of Cape Joseph. He was quite vehement about it. Parish remained sceptical. It was not uncommon for explorers to report sightings of coasts and islands which later were found not to exist. All the same, he did not wish to be thought of as obstructing legitimate exploration. However disagreeable the man, no chance of geographical success should be neglected.

'I have been giving some thought to your suggestion,' he remarked one morning, unrolling a chart and spreading it on the table. 'Your plan, I know, was to sledge northward round the coast to Cape Joseph. I venture to suggest that an alternative route westward, here,' the Lieutenant's finger crossed the peninsula, slid over the ice of James Ross Bay, and fetched up at Cape Hecla, 'would avoid the difficulties encountered by the English in journeying over the polar pack.'

The surgeon listened courteously, stroking his beard. He did not pay much attention to the suggestions of others.

He had conceived his plan in the course of a long reconnaissance the previous autumn. Parish had sent him as far north as he might make towards Cape Joseph, in the hope of finding some trace of Lt De Long. On a high headland above the Robeson Channel he had gazed across the level ice of the Frozen Sea. Somewhere out there, not so very much further north from where he stood, was as far as any man had ever ventured.

All winter long Maximilien Fabius had nourished that moment. That he had kept it to himself was entirely consistent with his dream of Arctic exploration. No man could aspire to the Pole without first casting off the world.

The Inuit were the first to spot the sun.

'*Seqiniliaq!*' they cried excitedly, running back to the hut. '*Sainang sunai seqineq!*'

And turning, bared their heads to the sun.

In the hut all work stopped. The men trooped out to stare at the sun, a cold, lifeless wafer looming over the rim of the southern uplands. For weeks they had yearned for the moment when they would stand in its light and bathe in its glory, and their disappointment was monumental.

The days went by. The sun was now a hand's-breadth above the horizon. A wispy vapour rose from cracks in the harbour ice. Hearing long attuned to the silence of winter was now sensitized to the slightest sounds, a sudden slither of snow, the dull

94

impact of a stone. The men drank in the freshness rising from the steaming earth, in the miracle of the visible world restored, that had been stolen from them in the long winter darkness.

Young Harry Foxer, breathless from his daily run, stood on a hill north of the camp, and gazed, heart-smitten, at the Greenland coast.

With the sun came light, though not yet warmth enough to melt winter ice. *Lt Rainbird*, the commander complained to his wife, *seems intent on making the most of his status as a guest. He eats, he sleeps, he does no work. Much of the time he spends playing cards with the enlisted men. A man might despair, having to spend his waking hours in such small-minded and uncultivated company, were it not for the work one had to do.*

Certainly, the Lieutenant had only to survey the line of depots, the snow-shelters and reconnoitred trails marked on his chart to feel well satisfied with his preparations. His estimate of the daily ration adequate for the heavy work of man-hauling had been thoroughly vindicated. He, and not Fabius, had proved the better judge in the matter of the Greenland sledges. He was especially gratified by the condition of his men who, a few minor cases of frost-bite excepted, had returned from arduous duties in excellent health. He had every reason to feel confident of their readiness for the tasks ahead.

Fabius set off towards the end of March. It was a perfect evening for Arctic travel, calm, clear, with the thermometer showing several points below freezing. To accompany him the surgeon had selected the photographer, who had proved durable on several autumn journeys. Emmons would follow for the first few marches with a sledge hauling extra supplies.

Those remaining at the station gathered outside the hut, registering their farewells with the gallows humour men reserve for comrades exchanging a place of shelter and attachment for hardship and uncertainty.

For the departing men, it might have been a relief to be doing something. Only the Inuit drivers were getting on with what they always did: looking over the sledge, tightening lashings, securing covers, checking the thongs which secured the load. These were tasks they did not care to entrust to any *qallunaaq*. If they seemed unaffected by the occasion it was because they were incapable, naturally, of appreciating the object of such journeys: so it struck the Lieutenant, in whom had begun to kindle the glow of a heart-warming story; an inspiring narrative encompassing burly haulers of sledges, patient observers at their instruments, younger men pushing forward the frontiers of the known world, even these simple fellows waiting with their dogs, oblivious of the tale in which they were destined to play a part.

He went with the teams himself for the first mile or two. Their departure, he felt, should not be soured by any past unpleasantness. Personal feelings were as nothing beside the responsibilities a commander owed to the men under his command. Such antipathy as existed between Fabius and himself had no place at such a moment. However objectionable the man, he went to do important work.

At the turn of the headland the party halted to exchange farewells.

Parish offered his hand.

The surgeon shook it gravely. It might have been an historic moment.

'Good luck,' cried the Lieutenant. His gaze embraced them all.

'Your safe return,' he added impulsively, 'is what matters most.'

'Please not to alarm yourself on our account.' Fabius was quite composed. 'Not for many weeks will there be any cause for anxiety. I do not expect to return much before the beginning of June.'

The dogs, restless from waiting, were sitting on their haunches, looking back and whining softly. The ice foot lay before them, a white strip snaking away between the dark cliffs of the coast and the rubble ice of the Robeson Channel.

Then, at a nod from Fabius, a sudden cry '… *aak* … *aak*'

from the Inuk, with yelps of joy the team plunged forward, runners crunching over the hard-packed snow.

In a speckless sky the Arctic sun hung clear and blinding. The Lieutenant shaded his eyes as he gazed after the departing teams. A northerly breeze was creeping up on him, congealing his breath in fragments of ice that clung to his beard. Though he held his arm raised in farewell, Fabius did not look back.

Despite the cold he remained watching until his men had dwindled to dots against an infinite horizon. Soon they would be swallowed up altogether. He turned away at last, conscious that other men had another version of the story. Fabius believed he should have been leader of the expedition. It was a situation no amount of tolerance and good will would change. It could only be borne.

He walked back between the tracks left by the runners. They were blurring already. By the time he reached the hut they had become no more than a dim impression in the snow.

In Washington too the trail had all but disappeared. Geography was against it. Situated between two great oceans, in a continent so vast and empty, it was all but impossible for the Lieutenant's fellow-citizens to be much interested in Grinnell Land, a region about which they knew next to nothing. There were, besides, intriguing matters far closer to home. The town was agog with the news that the new president had had more than twenty wagon-loads of junk removed from the White House, and was now busy with refurbishment. Meanwhile, his request that his predecessor's cabinet stay on temporarily was exciting much speculation as to who the new men would be.

Senator Clay was affecting indifference.

'Whoever they are,' he said dryly to Martha Parish, 'they're unlikely to be friends of mine.'

He had come with his cart to take her for an excursion across Rock Creek. It was a year to the day since she was married. They drove between mossy trunks, the young woman dreaming of the strangeness of a husband, taking up the life so briefly enjoyed, until they were both clothed in the same streams of cathedral light pouring between the bare forest branches.

That morning she had placed some stems of mignonette beside the photograph William had had taken just before he left. And wept a little.

That evening, when she returned, the room was filled with fragrance.

With the approach of summer preparations were already under way for the supply ship. It was due to sail in July.

One afternoon, arriving for tea with Lucius Clay, and finding General Sweetsir there before her, Martha Parish enquired about the collection of mail from the families. She was shocked to learn that no arrangements had as yet been made .

'You should become postmistress for the expedition,' suggested Lucius Clay.

She, with the diffidence of one not inclined to take anything upon herself, was far from convinced.

The senator, though, seemed dazzled by his inspiration.

'I nominate you,' he went on grandly. 'It is not an office requiring Congressional approval. It offers no remuneration. Only the satisfaction rumoured to reward a kindly act.'

'A capital idea,' boomed General Sweetsir, combing his moustaches. 'What more suitable postmistress than the wife of the commander?'

So, supplied with a list of names, she sat at her window watching the little steamer pounding the muddy waters of the Potomac. She shrank from the thought of addressing total strangers. In agonizing over what to say, she discovered her faculties had dried up completely.

At length, stirring herself, looking down the list, she came upon a Mrs Sedgewick, wife to one of the enlisted men. She felt she might perhaps approach another wife.

So, taking up her pen, she began: *My dear Mrs Sedgewick* ...

She found she was able to write quite simply, as she might have written to a neighbour, explaining that she was putting together a few comforts for her husband, promising to see that any items of mail were safely forwarded aboard the *Rattler*, sailing from St John's a few weeks hence.

She was startled by the vehemence of some replies. Writing from New Jersey, the father of Private Edge expressed his shock at finding himself put down for next-of-kin, believing his son to have married a wife out West. There was nothing he wanted to say to Chuck. But the mother of Lt Foxer sent back immediately a package of mail for Harry, with a most appreciative and neighbourly note. A number of families overseas were overjoyed to have news of sons with whom they had lost touch. Heinrich Krug, of Chemnitz, Germany, had not heard from Otto in seven years.

Jacob Joseph's Aunt Yetta read the letter to the old folks, to whom it came as a revelation that their grandson might be communicated with. They had given him up for dead.

Yaakov Asher was wont to talk aloud to God in his mother tongue. Lou, his humorous son, often joshed him for praying at times not prescribed by the *halakhah*.

'In Kalisk,' retorted his father, 'men were born with souls, not clocks.' Mystical, profound, the old man's Hassidic soul cleaved to the Eternal Now.

He still felt the pain of a daughter's defection. His youngest, she'd leaped early into the wilderness of the New World. She had given birth (since birth was unavoidable) at the country fair, on the wet trampled grass under the planking of one of the wooden stands, and came home with it wrapped in a piece of sacking.

'A *mamzer*,' the old woman wailed. 'She has brought home a *mamzer*.'

But the girl only hardened herself against them all.

And yet the infant yearning will survive even the least practising of mothers. At first he hallucinated her presence. She was still there, warmly reassuring, in the milky odours of his wrappings. He had no life other than the life he shared with her. Now and then a face loomed at the end of his cot. But no one soothed, or cuddled. Or rattled anything. Or offered more than the tip of a little finger for him to clutch at. Rachel Asher didn't want the *mamzer* taking her for his Momma, hoping the girl would take to him in the end. Who never did. Though nothing was left unsaid that might have worked toward that end. Meanwhile he was left alone in his cot. Though elsewhere there were dreadful scenes. Shouts, dramas, penetrating even his isolation. His shrieks eventually summoned someone, who settled him again, so that they could resume the struggle, fought out now in looks and bitter silences. *You want him. You look after him.* In the end it scarcely mattered. She left anyway.

Yaakov Asher never spoke of her, except in his prayers.

'Oh Perfect Rock,' he murmured, as he plied his needle, 'spare and have mercy on the parents and the children,' joining the boy's name with that of the mother.

She, too, might have been dead.

SIX

A mile or two along the frozen watercourse a fox was seeking a mate. It had stolen past the fort before sunrise, making a wide circuit of the sleeping dogs. Trotting busily on its short legs, turning aside to gnaw at the foot of a musk ox, resting, running up slight hummocks, quizzing the air exhaustively with its black nose, the dog fox had left a meandering track for the man to follow this way and that across the frozen creek.

Two days cooped up with Parish had left Rainbird edgy. He badly needed to kill something. He'd fired a shot a while back, seeing movement under the cover of a rock. All he found, though, were spots of blood in the snow.

He trudged on up the creek. Sometimes, looking back over his career, he couldn't figure out why he hadn't made more of his life. Fifteen years of service, much of it on the western plains, had not brought him the promotion he might have expected at his age. He liked to put it down to his lack of connections. At heart, though, he suspected it came closer, deeper.

The leaden sky contrasted drearily with freshly drifted snow of a deathly whiteness. He'd come to hate the snow, its no-colour blankness.

Rainbird regretted his resignation. Regretted it, just as he'd regretted storming out of the cabin over the business of the polar bear. Why was it he could not, would not learn? Yet a request to return to duty was out of the question. He couldn't serve under Parish. The crack shot still smarted at the memory of insufferable words. The Lieutenant had inflicted an injury which wouldn't heal. Rainbird's wounds never did. Though nursed with care.

Whatever it was he'd hit, he saw, was now leaking blood and entrails, yet still it struggled on.

Rainbird groaned in spirit. He felt utterly abandoned in his own mess. Sometimes, in the chilly silence of the mess, his mind went back to those evenings on the river just before sunset, gliding under the pillars of the old railroad bridge with the shell holding steady just inches off the water, the stroke flowing, continuous, at one with the river. Each swing of the body seemed a moment of sublimity; man and boat in perfect harmony.

Now, all he dreamed of was escaping home. Meanwhile he trudged on, one day at a time. As long as the days kept slipping by the ship would eventually arrive to take him home.

His glance arrested suddenly on a shiver of snow or white fur, it might have been, conspicuous against a dark rock wall. Another shot sent it tumbling. He had to scramble down the gully to recover it. When he bent to pick it up he saw the hare was not yet dead.

Rainbird marvelled that so small and pitiful a thing should cling so to its life.

However uncongenial daily life with a disagreeable companion, the Lieutenant was sustained by an unfailing aspiration. Foxer's expedition must now be well on its way. His orders were to proceed as far north-eastwards as endurance and weather conditions might permit.

Spreading the chart on his desk he fell to tracing the young man's route along a coast, the detail of which dwindled to no more than an outline, a notional continuation to the north-east, before petering out in thrilling blankness. It was a thought to savour: a party of men, obscure, unthought-of, pressing on to the utmost limits of the known world: following where the footsteps led, and then beyond ...

The Lieutenant never doubted the young man would return in triumph. His enthusiasm was wonderfully heartening: *You know the saying, sir. A Boston bulldog hangs on till death*.

William Parish's long anticipation of just such a moment had registered in a last-minute request.

'This flag,' he'd said awkwardly, producing, from under his

coat, a small strip of cloth, carefully folded. 'My wife sewed it herself. You may care to fly it on your sledge.'

Young Foxer had accepted it gravely.

'Who knows,' the commander added, in a sudden show of emotion, 'to what unknown shores you may yet carry it?'

As the days passed his thoughts turned to the fortunes of his other northern expedition. He wondered if Fabius had heeded his advice to take the overland route to Cape Hecla. It was, of course, a matter for judgement in the field. He had taken pains, nonetheless, to indicate the desirability of the peninsula route in his written orders.

As the Greenland support party prepared to leave, in advance of Foxer, he'd instructed them in the manifold practical considerations one was required to attend to, and how vitally necessary they were. Nodding solemnly, they undertook to apply the warm hand at regular intervals to the face to keep it from freezing, and to wear goggles at all times. 'Remember,' he'd impressed on the dependable Emmons, 'question them frequently as to their condition. Avoid overwork. Do not travel in high winds or stormy weather.' He was sending out men who, without him there to ensure their safety, would be left to shift for themselves. The thought of losing any of them filled him with horror.

These were anxieties he might have welcomed sharing with a second-in-command. Though such words as passed between them scarcely stretched to mutual support. Meals were taken at remote distances from one another. Sometimes in air so thin Parish could hear the drip of snow melting on the black roof of the hut.

'Bread?'

The commander, lips cramped together, handed down the bread.

'Thank you.' Rainbird was never less than icily polite.

'Butter?'

And this was the man who'd written: *I'm with you heart and soul. You shall find no truer friend and more devoted servant.*

We will not think of home, nor turning back, until the mission is accomplished. Only the flicker of the whiskery face betrayed the Lieutenant's scorn. He felt bitterly let down.

After supper Rainbird went to his card-playing. Parish heard the straw-haired man's high-pitched laugh coming from the other end of the hut. He couldn't imagine what he had ever found to admire in such a fellow.

In the strained circumstances of his domestic arrangements, the Lieutenant turned increasingly to his wife. He knew her to be kind and good, though of a sensitive nervous organization. Yet it was her gift of silent sympathy, as he now perceived, wherein lay her most precious quality. He wrote: *Rainbird continues to act the sulky schoolboy, though I have made a point of treating him with the utmost civility. We scarcely speak a dozen words a day. Even as I write he is making up to the enlisted men. It is hardly surprising he has not got on as he would have wished. Nor is he likely to do so. Thankfully, with the coming of the supply ship we shall be rid of him at last.*

One evening on the shore, while observing a small gull with pale blue mantle, the Lieutenant heard a distant yelping. It was a cool, clear evening. A light south-westerly was blowing. Out over the headland dark specks of what he took to be birds were in flight above the cliffs. He began to fear he must be experiencing that displacement of vision which sometimes affected men exposed to high latitudes. For the specks, now growing in size, appeared to be men. Soon, he could make out plumes of fine snow from sledge runners, streaming away like smoke to northward.

After a suitable interval for refreshment, Dr Fabius sat down with the commander.

The surgeon seemed greatly changed. The skin, stretched tight over the bones of his face, was blackened by frostbite, the flesh of his nose peeling, red-raw. He had discovered that the heaviest burden a man could carry on his sledge was the bitterness of defeat.

He made his report with the neutral voice of a man of science, taking refuge in the essential facts, using the chart to illustrate the incidents of his journey. The ice foot had made for arduous progress. Many of the northern bays were choked with rubble ice. Snow, waist-deep at times, had forced them into wearisome detours. It had not proved possible to reach Cape Hecla. Instead, he gone directly north on to the sea ice. It was ... *extrêmement formidable.*

At this point the speaker spread his hands in a gesture that suggested all too plainly the impossibility of conveying the reality to a man who had not experienced for himself the monstrous nature of the pack.

Here, some four miles north of Cape Joseph, they had made their first camp on the sea ice. For two days severe storms confined them to their tent. A memory of its frantic flapping, the gale snatching up dinner plates of snow, hurling them against the thrumming canvas, moved the surgeon to an uncharacteristic exercise of fancy. It was, he said, like being shut up in a kettle drum.

On the third day, when visibility returned, he'd climbed to the top of a floe berg. East and west, as far as he could see, the Frozen Sea presented an impassable barrier of upheaved floes.

Fabius shrugged. His manner expressed the weary resignation of a seasoned polar traveller rebuffed by a force of Nature. It was regrettable, but there was nothing to be done. No sledge, not even a lightly loaded sledge, could have made progress over that ice.

'I shall, of course, be writing a full account,' the surgeon concluded, 'of the many matters of scientific interest determined in the course of my journey.'

No, he had not seen land to the northward. Doubtless, he added somewhat stiffly, it was obscured by fog.

'No matter. With every failure, we learn a little more.' The Lieutenant felt he could afford to be magnanimous. 'You took what you judged to be the easier route. Now we know that even in such high latitudes the pack can be in motion.'

Later that day, talking to Reade, Parish leant how close his northern party had come to disaster.

The Inuk had given first warning of open water. Not believing him, Fabius had pressed on towards Cape Hecla with the intention of making land, then pushing west along the north coast of Grinnell Land. He had not quite given up hope of making his mark.

An hour later, from the top of a high berg, Reade reported a dark channel about a mile wide extending westward past the cape. There was no sensation of change, or movement. All was serene and still. Only Mitsoq's agitation betrayed the critical nature of their situation. Slowly, remorselessly, new lines of coast were gradually opening to the westward. First Cape Colan, then Cape Aldrich, and then Cape Columbia slid into view. The pack was moving north.

'Even then,' said Reade, 'the doctor would have it that the pack was touching C. Joseph. I fancy he thought he had a clearer grasp of the matter than an Eskimo.'

Meanwhile, to the north and east the sky had darkened considerably, an unmistakable sign of open water. The polar pack was breaking up. With water spaces to northward their plight would become fearful indeed should the wind blow up from the south-west. Fabius decided to return at once to Cape Joseph.

Arriving opposite the cape they found themselves, as the Inuk had predicted, cut off by a mile or more of water. Halted there on the ice, they heard a distant rumbling far to the south. 'A grinding, and a shuddering,' said Reade. 'As if the machinery was breaking down.' The pack was grounding against the lower coast. Now in the surgeon's mind possibilities were becoming certainties. Gripped suddenly by the fear that the channel itself was opening, he'd had visions of the ice around the southerly capes breaking up. The sledge was hastily unloaded. Abandoning his tent, his scientific instruments and the rest of his provisions, with Mitsoq whipping up the team, Fabius raced with all speed for the coast.

For hours they'd beaten back and forth along the foot of the cape, trying to get through to the ice foot, through a maze of pressure ice, compressed, packed together in blocks and splinters ten or twelve feet high, the Inuk, his face expressionless, chopping a passage for the sledge, with the dogs whimpering, flopping down, having to be kicked to their feet. The indefatigable Reade it was who had expedited matters by picking them up one by one and throwing them bodily, up and over the last vertical edge.

The Lieutenant was thinking it a great pity that the surgeon had elected to ignore his advice. It had been a rash decision, the more so since a thoughtful study of the map would have pointed to the likely condition of the sea ice funnelling into the Robeson Channel. No, even allowing for such natural hazards as had thwarted his journey over the Frozen Sea, Fabius did not come out of it well. It was not that he'd abandoned his instruments, though that would have to be accounted for to the Army quarter-master. He'd never used them. No observations had been made for longitude, latitude, nor any checks on compass variation, at any time during the journey. Even his most northerly position on the sea ice was no more than an estimate, arrived at by the sort of simple calculations a man might scratch out in a matter of seconds on a patch of wind-packed snow.

The doctor, he noted in his ongoing letter to Matty, *appears to be something of a Jonah*.

For George Reade, though, the whole thing had been a revelation.

'It was different, I don't mind telling you,' he confided to Jeremiah Knowles over a mug of tea.

Stretched out on a crust of windblown snow, with only a few feet of sea-ice between himself and three miles of Arctic Ocean, he had discovered how infinitely beyond what he thought himself to be a man's real being really was.

The days passed, and still there was no sign of Foxer. At Fort Chance anxiety was mounting. All speculations, even the unspoken ones, were directed at the Lieutenant. It was only a matter of time before he heard, floated casually across the breakfast table, the question which had troubled him for days.

'What do you intend to do?'

'I have every confidence in Lieutenant Foxer,' he replied stiffly. 'I expect him back within a few days at the most.'

Meanwhile, all his admonitions had come winging back to haunt him; not least, his warning not to continue the expedition when half the rations had been consumed. At the same time he knew what fever drove a young officer to attain the objective whatever the cost. If delayed by storms the young man, gambling on getting back to his line of depots, might very well be tempted to reduce rations in an attempt to go that bit further.

He had, of course, discussed with Foxer what kind of assistance he might expect. Yet the thought of actually committing himself to such a journey was thoroughly alarming. Like all polar travellers, he was forever fearful of misjudging the country he had to travel through. In a land where peace of mind depended on accurate intelligence, he was troubled by uncertainties which he found himself unable to resolve. His fear was of the ice in the channel breaking up. In confined polar waters, with the floes ceaselessly separating and reforming under the stress of wind and tide, conditions were never certain. The English had been forced back in early June, stopped by rotten ice and water pools. Forty miles further south, by means of boat and sledge, they had crossed as late as August. But that had been a desperate venture.

One thing at least was clear. He would have no option but to haul the whale-boat. That would require a large party. That, in turn, meant carrying a full complement of rations and supplies. The best solution would be to take Foxer off by launch. But to use the launch he would have to wait until the channel was open for navigation. If it ever was. And what if both parties, rescuers and rescued, were to find themselves marooned on the desolate

North Greenland shore? One thing was certain. He could not afford to delay much longer.

*

In Washington the annual purgatory had begun. Nights of sticky heat gave way to days when the mercury climbed into the nineties. And still Martha Parish delayed her departure for New England. She would go, of course. Eventually. There was Mother to consider. Meanwhile, she was conscious of the irksome shade of Matty Stevens, waiting to possess.

In Washington she felt closer to her husband, the echo of whose voice she would catch at odd moments. Or hear his step on the stair. He might spring up in a conversation at Senator Clay's. He came closest of all in the brooding, solitary woods.

So she lingered on into July. Lucius Clay declared she was falling into Southern ways.

As always, the senator's talk was of politics. *Quod in hoc mihi,* he said, should be the motto of the new administration. He expected it to be a forcing bed for every kind of corruption. The new president's nominations had, as expected, drawn heavily on the ranks of the Conkey faction. Of the cabinet it seemed only Mr Crowell had survived.

'Honest Elijah,' said the old man scathingly, 'is to be Ty's solitary fig leaf, while his old friends plunder the public treasury.'

Martha Parish's thoughts, though, were with William. In contemplating the perils and hardships likely to be encountered by the party, she prayed they be granted the fortitude and forbearance that would be required of them. She could not claim such virtues for herself, yet she felt drawn closer to her husband in a common travail. The months of longing, poured forth in her letters, had seemed all the more forlorn for being trapped beneath the lid of her writing desk. But now the *Rattler* had set forth at last. Sometimes, gazing at the map fixed to the wall, on which William had thoughtfully inked in places of interest, she wondered where it was, the little ship. William, she felt sure, would be bending all his thoughts towards it. Then, at some indeterminate point in the Davis Strait, their two long-separated souls were at their most joyful.

As courier for the cargo of supplies General Sweetsir had chosen his secretary, a nephew of his wife's.

The young man had been aghast when the full extent of the mission was made clear to him.

'You want me to go *where*, General?'

'Here.'

Sweetsir laid a finger on the top of the globe that stood beside his desk.

'Lady Franklin Bay.'

He had brushed aside his aide's misgivings.

'Nonsense, Bright. It'll be an experience for you. Think of it as a summer cruise.' It was the general's little joke. He did not doubt the voyage would prove routine.

At Fort Chance the Lieutenant's long anxiety was at an end. Blessed by firm ice and favourable winds, the dogs had come trotting out of a summer's afternoon with the Stars and Stripes streaming from the sledge. The commander's relief, as he pumped the hands of the returned men, even clapping the Inuk on the shoulder, was evident to all.

'He has been spared for the present,' observed the surgeon to his friend. 'Sooner or later, though, he will be put to the test. Then we shall see.'

Rainbird's rejoinder was lost in the cheers of men clustering round the heroes.

What could be seen of their faces was almost black from the sun's glare, and the smoke of stoves. Two months of bruising polar wind had left its mark. Young Foxer looked to have aged twenty years, the skin around his eyes stretched and cracked like old leather. Out on the trail he had dreamt of devouring mounds of Hansie Wutz's sweet fresh bread, then sleeping for a week. Or draining cans of peaches. Yet he did none of these things.

That night, though, he could be observed resting on his bunk, his hands behind his head, lost in another country. He was savouring those first few hours, unlike any others, when a man's achievement is still vivid as a dream.

That rapt focus evoked everything Rainbird felt lacking in himself.

To ease his pain he took a turn along the shore with the surgeon for companion.

And the Lieutenant watched them, consorting together, united in their wish to break him down. For the moment, though, his own deep satisfaction rendered him indifferent to their scheming.

Before supper he had written to his wife: *I write first to you so that you shall be the first to be told the wonderful news. Foxer returned this afternoon, having exceeded the highest latitude previously recorded, about ninety miles north of Cape May. He has brought you back a stone from that point, the most northerly ever trodden by man. He might have gone on, but the low state of his rations would not permit any further extension of his remarkable journey. So, your flag flies above all the rest, unfurled at a latitude surpassing that ever before attained by mortal man, a thought which must surely come as some recompense for the sacrifice you too have made in all this. The English lost three men in setting their record. Now we have bettered it, and all our men, thank God, are safe.*

Meanwhile, the two friends walked side by side, the midnight sun casting their shadows in slant companionship across the gravels of the shore.

'What was it? Two or three miles at most further than the Englishman.'

Hungry himself for fame, the surgeon was very much afraid he mightn't achieve it.

'No, my friend. There is land to northward. I know. I have seen it. The real task still remains.'

Action, as the ally of illusion, can be a powerful deadener. It will render a situation tolerable which might else seem insupportable.

Young Mr Bright, thrust on to a stage not of his choosing, would have done all that he could, and more. No spirit, though, however willing, can prevail over certain weaknesses of flesh. Or weather.

From the moment she cleared the Narrows, plunging into the troughs of the North Atlantic, the little ship had pitched and rolled unceasingly.

As well as fogs, Captain Spratt informed, high winds and blizzards were the norm for those waters.

Now, forty-eight hours out from St John's, the wind went round to the north-west. In two days it blew a gale. The roar rose to a shriek as the wind tore the tops from waves, flinging showers of spray against the rigging, drenching the topsail yards. Mountains of sea crashed on to her decks, sweeping over her hatches, streaming from her sides.

Eyes screwed tight, Secretary Bright clung sweating to his see-sawing bunk. To lift his lids on the wild flashing of the lamp, jerking frantically on its hook, only added to his misery.

The young man groaned again, and strove to fasten his mind on the men in the far north, men who were counting on him.

At Fort Chance the Arctic summer was getting under way. Everywhere the signs spoke of a land coming to life. The worn snow was spoiling. Gaping gutters under rocks betrayed the tunnels of small animals, now released from their long captivity. Here and there clumps of pallid grass emerged trembling in the unaccustomed breeze. The shoreline was imprinting with the tracks of birds and foxes. Already the ravines along the cliffs had begun to empty in spectacular cascades, falling into the sea. Out in the bay bobbed the first flocks of eider and long-tailed duck. Every day saw more and more birds returning; honking flights of dark-bellied geese winging inland, little parties of waders setting down along the gravels of the harbour.

Sledging was at an end. Around the fort there was nothing to be done but the routine work of observation and recording. The enlisted men, now that they'd accomplished what they'd come to do, were looking forward to mail, tobacco, the replenishment of stores, and that sense of reconnection that comes with parcels from home. All these good things, already at sea according to Lieutenant Parish, were no more than a few weeks away.

Nor did it occur to the Lieutenant to entertain any doubts concerning the advent of a vessel, the arrival of which was stipulated in General Orders. His mind was fixed on a long-cherished project. Leaving Foxer in command, and taking the astronomer as intellectual companion, he set out westward with a small party of enlisted men. Occupying his mind was a problem long a puzzle to geographers. He put it to Sergeant Asher.

'Why, do you suppose, are there no discharging glaciers on the coast? One would expect glaciers given the high latitude of the land mass.'

The Lieutenant liked to demonstrate a scholarly disposition.

'The answer,' he went on good humouredly, 'must lie in the interior of Grinnell Land.'

Their way lay up a long, steep-sided valley which formed a natural bed for the torrents pouring from the melting snows. The air was filled with the sound of rushing water. The men walked in a clear green light between hillsides on which hare and ptarmigan, still in winter white, stood out against willow green. Musk oxen, in threes or fours, were feeding on the willow leaves, snorting, stirring up clouds of insects, a prey for swooping birds.

In this rough country the party went in Indian file, the Lieutenant first, devouring the territory with his eyes. At last he could put on the character he'd chosen for himself. He was happy as a boy.

In Smith Sound, the heavy seas so discomfiting to Mr Bright were heaving again. Twelve hours of strong wind had set the big floes grinding and twisting. Captain Spratt, fearful of being driven in among the pack, sought refuge in a fjord south of Littleton Island.

Here, for nine days snug in her haven, the *Rattler* rode out a succession of south-westerlies. The secretary went ashore with the ship's officers. He shot a seal.

Meanwhile, along the western seaboard, gales were driving

the pack up into the vast waters of the Kane Basin, leaving a passage open to the north.

All this while the travellers had pressed forward, amid the conversations of many creeks, marvelling at the plentiful game, which they shot at whenever they could get within range.

On they went, twisting, turning with the stream. They came to its source in a small, reedy lake where shoals of minnows flashed in passages of light and shadow. Here, under cover of a rushy margin humming with flies and bumblebees, they stole upon a noisy party of long-tailed duck which, when plucked and dressed, would greatly improve the flavour of the pemmican stew. All around the flanks of hills were steeped in summer green. The men too were steeped in light. Walking up to their knees in grass, gathering armfuls of brittle willow for their fire, they might have been persuaded that supreme serenity had its dwelling place only in such a wilderness as this.

After several days they halted at a meeting of waters, where a fork ran back towards abrupt high hills. Here, in a grassy draw, rich with ferns and mosses, they stumbled on the site of an old encampment. Circles of stones, undisturbed for countless years, showed where tents had once been pitched. It was a matter for astonishment since Grinnell Land had been uninhabited for centuries, the Lieutenant was explaining, while his men, creatures of time and space, stood in wonderment at what was timeless, their kinship with other wanderers like themselves, and with the earth.

At length, her water casks filled, the *Rattler* had resumed her passage. Finding the main pack again solid to northward, Captain Spratt took his vessel across the Sound to the coast of Grinnell Land, looking for a change in the wind.

Squinting, in this country of endless light, the party of explorers continued their journey westward. Up on the high tableland the light shimmered, blue and hazy. It was most intense just before what would have been counted as dawn most other places. Stirring in their tents, the men rolled on to their backs, faces warmed by the light filtering through the canvas weave. Each evening, after the brief flaring of their fire, they were soon shivering in the cold, thin air.

To Sergeant Asher had been entrusted the important task of mapping their journey. He was content to be doing this work alone, in solitary concentration. One morning he set out to climb to a higher point on the ridge to take bearings on a lake, the western end of which lay out of sight. In doing so he all but trod on a bird sitting on its eggs among the sand and pebbles of the tundra. A small bird motionless as a stone.

Stock still, the man stared down at a thing no bigger than his fist: a small dun-coloured thing that might have been a rock, or a coagulation of the tundra dust, yet was alive. A living thing.

The bird cocked its head, the button-bright eye rock-steady in its out-gazing.

The *mamzer* felt a dim joy. It was nothing he could have spoken about. He couldn't have put it into words. Only he began to see, in the tundra stretching away, something infinite. Not emptiness, but a possibility of fullness.

He bowed. He bowed to the bird, at home in its world. He bowed to the wilderness that had seemed wholly negation, a rubble of shattered rock, yet a negation that did away with every distraction, so that what was obscure might at last be laid bare.

Off Bache Island, far to the south, the icefield heaved on the swell. With two of the crew stationed in the stern to fend off lumps of ice from the screw, Captain Spratt was working his vessel through floes. The *Rattler* had entered the pack.

For three days, set fast, her timbers grinding alarmingly, the sealer drifted with the pack. Carried north into Kane Basin, she had come within two hundred miles of her destination. Then, as the wind backed, she drifted south again.

Bright lay in his bunk listening to a muffled scratching at the ship's side, as of something trying to get in. It was all a nightmare.

From the edge of his high escarpment, looking westward, the Lieutenant gazed across a nameless land losing itself in a haze of sun and distance: immediately below, the gunmetal gleam of a small lake; beyond, a pearly tangle of braided streams; further off, the oyster sheen of what he took to be other lakes; further still, shimmering indistinctly, a *terra incognita* where the material world petered out in a country of the mind.

Summoning his men to follow, the explorer set off exultantly to take possession.

Breaking free at last, Captain Spratt commenced to zigzag back and forth, skirting the edges of the pack, searching for a lead. Further north a blackening in the sky betokened open water. But there was no way through. Progress, when it was possible to make progress, was never more than inching forward, the *Rattler,* nosing through heavy brash mixed with large loose floes, making headway only with great expenditure of power. Pack ice alternated with drifting bergs.

After three weeks turning back and forth across the Sound, Bright had begun to ask himself whether a reasonable man would be justified in concluding that further efforts to reach Parish were useless. In which case his instructions were clear. He was to cache a portion of his supplies, together with all letters and despatches, at Cape Sabine.

Torn between duty and desire, he pressed the captain repeatedly. *What were their chances? Was it now too late in the season?* He could not bring himself to utter certain words he longed to speak. Nor would the captain grasp the nettle for him.

'It's your charter, mister.'

Captain Spratt had his owners to consider. They would not thank him if a decision of his deprived them of their fee.

Meanwhile, the brief Arctic summer was drawing to its close. Most of the plants had ceased flowering. Quietly, unnoticed, birds were flying south. The party of explorers, packs laden with skins and specimens, were returning to the fort. For the Lieutenant it had been a deeply satisfying experience. He had explored something approaching five thousand square miles of hitherto uncharted territory. He had mapped lakes, mountains, glaciers, and rivers. Most gratifying of all, as he noted in his log, he had settled the question of the physical geography of the interior of Grinnell Land.

Aug 21st. There can be no doubt that the system of fjords and lakes, in draining the snowfall during the short Arctic summer, readily accounts for the absence of glaciers discharging into the polar sea.

So William Parish brought his party safely back to base. For all of them time had begun again. Any day now could be the day that brought the ship. The men waited eagerly for news from home. In the wind from the south, they felt the chill breath of the ice-cap, and the coming of snow. The commander, interned once more in the chill civility of the mess, *burned* to be rid of Rainbird.

He posted sentinels on the hills above the harbour to keep watch for the vessel. Sometimes the glass revealed open water for many miles to the south. More often, as the days slipped by, they came back with reports of pack ice driving down the channel and surging into the bay.

Meanwhile, the sun's ellipse had begun to tilt appreciably towards the northern hills.

Two hundred and fifty miles to the south a violent storm had broken over the Kane Basin, threatening to drive the *Rattler* south into Baffin Bay. In which case, even Cape Sabine might prove beyond reach. Captain Spratt was anxious lest the Sound should close behind him. With the pack bearing down he made for the nearest land.

On a small island, just off shore, Bright cached such stores as came quickly to hand, together with a whaleboat. The secretary scribbled a regretful note.

Then, with three quarters of her cargo lying in her holds, the *Rattler* turned for home.

SEVEN

The year was sinking fast. One evening, settling at his desk to write his log, the Lieutenant noted it would soon be necessary to light the lamps.

> Sept 1st. Tonight the sun dipped for the first time below the northern hills. The time is fast approaching when the launch will have to be put in winter quarters. It is a decision I intend to delay until the last possible moment, out of consideration for the men.

It struck him then that he had all but given up hope of the ship.

In the great land-locked harbour the first indication of approaching winter appeared as an oily film on the surface of the sea: then, as a grey sludge which, as it thickened, turned to a viscous, transparent layer undulating on the ocean swell. Pack ice, which for days had been driving down the channel, began to pile up at the eastern entrance.

At last the Lieutenant gave the order for the launch to be hauled to its winter quarters. For the men hauling on the ropes there could be no plainer indication that the ship they were longing for would not now come.

That night, for the first time the mercury registered below zero.

Those who had been hoping against hope now recollected that life's injustices were part of the general pattern of malevolence. They stared up at the last noisy parties of geese flying south with the eyes of men suffering the spite of arbitrary, capricious gods.

The failure of the mail was especially cruel: letters they would have hugged to themselves many times over in the coming months, comforts to console and sustain. It was as if arms reaching out had closed on emptiness. They suffered their separation and, though no one spoke of it, spirits were further depressed by the approaching darkness.

It came on with remorseless speed. Already the first stars were visible. Inside the hut the lamps were now in constant use. By the second week in October, the mid-day sun cut no more than a tiny arc in the southern sky.

On what the astronomer had computed as their last day of sunlight some of the men climbed the high ground north of the fort, and stood gazing south, watching, waiting for the sun. Just after midday a few rays broke through the clouds, gilding the snow on distant hills. Dense water vapour rising from the Kennedy Channel cut off all direct light from lower ground. They watched the bright clouds drifting slowly south, delicate shades of pearly grey giving way to mellow orange and fiery red. Once, for a few moments, rays of red refracted light illumined the inner harbour, rosy columns of fog curling in the dense cold air. Then red faded to yellow, pearly grey died to a dull leaden hue. The sun had passed, and the long polar night was now imminent.

Facing that frozen void men began to shrink into their clothing. Now, even the most private thoughts echoed more loudly. Some discovered their need of families they had not corresponded with in years, pouring themselves on to sheets of paper which would perforce remain at the fort for as long they remained themselves, a continual reminder of their own captivity. Their spectral existence gnawed at them remorselessly. Then the soul, a queer, burrowing thing running on soft-padded feet, was left with nowhere to hide.

One morning Sergeant Emmons reported a case of drunkenness. Sedgewick, the store room orderly, had been helping himself to spirit-lamp fuel.

Leaving the man to sober up, the Lieutenant entered the incident in the log. He was inclined to take a lenient view. He would administer a severe dressing down, and leave it at that. The man had left a wife at home.

In Hartfield, Mass. where all things were expected to fulfil the purposes for which they were created, life went on much as it had for two hundred years. Apples ripened in the orchards. Long skeins of wild geese crossed the sky on their journey south. Fall was running through its repertoire of shades, crimson to cherry, bright sulphur to orange yellow, clove to liver brown.

After three months Martha Parish had all but submitted to her other self. On her way to church, or in the store, it was *Hi, Miss Matty ... Morning, Miss Matty ...* Even at a distance, and from behind, she was unmistakably the figure known since childhood. She accepted it with resignation. Who else could she ever be for old Mr Snell, but the little girl who lost her new shoe in the mud?

So her life put on again the identity it was born to: that of a retiring but useful soul, executing with fidelity the duties of her station, banging spice for the cake, glazing pies, baking all the bread, Mother declaring she could eat no bread but Matty's. The hens clacked at the kitchen door to remind her of her chores. Pussy jumped back into a lap she might only just have vacated.

Her reticence, in the matter of her husband's absence, did not go unremarked.

'You'd think she'd be upset,' observed Aunt Babbitt. 'If I'd mislaid a husband so soon after marrying him I'd suspicion there was something wrong with my housekeeping.'

Lawyer Babbitt was carving the fowl.

'Well, she don't seem too put out,' he growled laconically. 'Perhaps she hasn't missed him yet.'

One evening, though hopelessly out of practice, she attended a meeting of the translation society, taking her place at the table littered with books, Webster's big dictionary, the Greek grammar and Testament.

They had, she discovered, all but agreed another chapter of Romans.

Afterwards, Professor Cousins chatted to her over supper.

'I believe the new president to be a remarkable man,' he told her gravely.

He seemed to have quite forgotten that remarkable man, her husband.

Then, rather like a part in a play, came the boy from the telegraph office. She was coming down the stairs when she heard his voice at the hall door.

'Wire for Mrs Parish.'

Lizzy Boot, who knew no good of telegrams, came bearing it with an anxious face.

General Sweetsir's message was short and to the point: *Vessel failed to reach LFB. Rattler returned safely.*

'Thank you Lizzy. It is nothing of any consequence.'

Martha Parish had always been able to exhibit a calm exterior, a gift which, if it led some to suppose her cold and uncaring, had the merit of not inflicting her troubles on others.

She stared into the stove. Mother, she knew, believed she had seen the last of William.

Suddenly, she crumpled up the wire, and dropped it in among the embers. It was no one's business but her own

She did, though, unburden herself to Reverend Dwight.

There was One, he said, whose watchfulness never slept or slumbered, who could do far more than ever they could for those they loved.

The kind old face overflowed with eagerness to reassure.

'Let us put our trust in Him.'

Together they knelt on the carpet while he offered up a prayer.

One morning, as she was knitting soles for the stockings she had knit the bodies for the previous week, Lizzie Boot came back from the post office with a letter. It had been forwarded from the Signal Office in Washington. Enclosed was a cutting of a brief intelligence, copied to the Knoxville *Argos,* reporting that the relief ship intended for the United States Arctic expedition had returned to St John's, Newfoundland, having failed to get through. The party, as a consequence, remained cut off in Lady Franklin Bay.

He and his wife, wrote Yaakov Asher, were in great agitation of soul, crying aloud and in tears, for their grandson, Jacob Joseph, who had been abandoned in the wilderness, where he would surely starve to death. So it went on, an anguished *cri de coeur*, scarcely coherent, in places fracturing into strange words and phrases quite beyond her comprehension, but which she took to be Yiddish. Yet if there was much in the letter she could not understand, there was no mistaking its assumption. She, the wife of their son's commander, had written to them in friendship. Where should they turn in their distress, but to her? They knew no one else.

Martha Parish was first shocked, then made anxious by this imputation of a responsibility she'd never imagined might attach to her. In her confusion, she remembered an axiom of father's. When in doubt as to a course of action, he used to say, call to mind the person you most admire, and ask yourself what that person would most likely do.

So it was she began to compose the letter William himself would undoubtedly have written. Indeed, it might have been his own voice enunciating the phrases in her head, they presented themselves with such conviction: *Of course, the news from St John's is indeed deeply disappointing, but really, there is no cause for alarm. The party is comfortably accommodated. They have ample supplies of food. Indeed, they are equipped for a stay of three years' duration. We may rest assured they will remain safely engaged in their scientific work until the ship arrives to take them off next summer.*

But would it? How could she be sure? She had given an assurance she was in no position to make. What if the difficulties encountered by the *Rattler* represented the normal conditions for those waters? What if William's remarkably successful voyage had been a lucky chance in a rare season? Then she was filled with foreboding for her husband, isolated at the very end of the earth, and no one able to do anything about it: not his friends, not his comrades. She, who loved him most, able to do least.

That anguished letter had awakened all her own anxieties. At nights she lay unable to sleep, harried by questions that pressed in upon her, conscious only of her own powerlessness in that realm of action which was the prerogative of men. Only the men had failed. And might fail again.

So, by degrees, she came to see that the difficulty lay in her own ignorance of all things Arctic, and that it must be mended.

As soon as Thanksgiving was over she would return to Washington to begin her education.

She began with such books as remained of her husband's library, setting about the chronicles of Arctic exploration as assiduously as, when a girl at Hartfield Academy, she'd studied the classics. Gradually, as she turned the pages, she was troubled by a notion of some other landscape co-existent with the polar region, some hinterland corresponding to the physical one but different, a shadowy realm where, freed from the confines of family and society, men explored their deepest desires. She had a sense of furred, hollow faces. Intent, preoccupied they looked past her, their eyes fixed on the far distance. There was something wolfish in that gaze. She saw it was a hunger for the thing that drew them on.

Then, in the Library of Congress, she came across McClintock's *Voyage of the Fox in the Arctic Seas*. There she read of the fate of Franklin and his companions: of ships fatally beset, signal cairns (never visited), messages left under rocks (never read), of snow strewn with a debris of civilized living, kid gloves, silk handkerchiefs, scented soap, china tea-cups, lying with the pickaxes, the shovels and the cooking stoves.

Martha Parish trembled at the spectacle of the destitute men marching on, not knowing where they were, or what they were about. She *saw*, and *heard* them, falling in their tracks.

That winter news finally reached Washington of the fate of Lt De Long. For two years drifting with the polar ice, his ship had eventually foundered in the Laptev Sea. De Long had got ashore, only to perish in the Siberian wastes.

Her first thoughts were for his wife. She thought of her loneliness and distress of mind, watching, waiting, with never any news. Hoping against hope. It struck her that hearing the worst finally confirmed might be preferable to knowing nothing. She made up her mind then and there that she must take a hand in the preparations to bring William safely out of that place. She was quite determined about that.

One morning she received a letter from General Sweetsir. Would she care to meet the leader of the mission which was to recover her husband's party from Lady Franklin Bay? This time, he assured her, he had picked the best of men.

John Leffingwell was indeed as likely a young fellow as had come out of West Point in those years after the war. Intelligent, good-hearted, he had been brought up in the light of ennobling ideals, and longed to make his mark. As a boy of fourteen he had been with his father the day a stubby man in a linen duster walked into the dining room of Willard's Hotel. The whole room had risen to applaud the new commander of all the Union armies. It was his first introduction to the world as a stage for the exposition of celebrity. Later, as a cavalry officer posted to Fort Missoula, he'd very soon discovered that the obscurity of the western plains was no place for a fellow seeking to get on. He secured an assignment in the War Department. Any one wishing to advance himself in the Army could not afford to be too far, or too long from Washington. And yet the young man was drawn by some ineffable element in his own nature, His spirit longed to be called beyond the confines of the Department where, he feared, a man might soon shrivel up like a pea in a pod.

No such withering anxieties were anywhere evident in the slim figure, sitting with a casual grace, an arm thrown carelessly across the back of Senator Clay's sofa.

So this, thought Martha Parish, was the young lieutenant she'd been summoned to meet. She saw a head finely set, soft golden hair, a dazzling fair skin.

He rose, smiling, as she approached. Like William, he was very tall.

Leffingwell, General Sweetsir was explaining, had a personal interest in the mission, since Lt Rainbird was a friend of his.

'Hardly a friend,' demurred the young man, who remembered Rainbird as a hot-headed fellow, quick with his fists. 'I knew him slightly. We served for a time in the same company.'

She was left to pour the tea as the two men, moving over to Senator Clay's globe, fell to talking of retreats and rendezvous, and caches left on various capes, and the movement of ice in the Kane Basin.

'Has a vessel been chartered?' she put in eventually.

'No, not yet.' General Sweetsir turned affably towards her.

'Might I suggest,' she offered hesitantly, 'we approach the owners of the *Petrel*? And Captain Quine?' Having proved himself already in getting through the ice, he seemed the obvious choice. He would have her confidence, she added, and that of the families.

'By all means,' said the general. 'An excellent suggestion.'

Though even Captain Quine, she went on tentatively, might not get through. That had to be faced. What would happen then?

The young man might have been about to reply, but deferred to a superior officer.

'I believe that to be most unlikely,' said the General firmly. 'But in such a case the vessel would remain in Smith Sound, to rendezvous with Lt Parish as he retreats south.'

What if the Sound were closed by ice? Presumably the vessel could not remain there indefinitely. Martha Parish gazed unhappily at the army men. In that comfortable room, by a warm fireside, her intervention in their discussions seemed all the more improbable.

Supposing William was delayed, she went on faintly, conscious of Senator Clay's sardonic eye. He would arrive to find the rendezvous deserted.

'I don't believe that will happen.'

General Sweetsir replaced his cup, before looking at her gravely over his half-glasses.

'But if it should,' he went on gently, 'in the very unlikely event of that happening, the intention is for the vessel to land a relief party, fully equipped with stores and a winter house, on Littleton island. They would wait there for the ice to harden, then Leffingwell here would lead a sledge party across Smith Sound and up the coast to meet the party and bring them all safely back.'

'I shall bring your husband home,' put in the young fellow impulsively. 'Even if the ship is not able to get through, I shall reach him myself with dogs and sledges. I shall bring him back to you.'

Several times, over the teacups, she was assured of that. No effort would be spared to effect the relief of the Parish expedition.

These enthusiastic pledges carried with them a disconcerting impression of a young fellow eager for an adventure in which he had already cast himself in the leading role. Even so, she told herself, that was no reason why he should not pull it off. And what if men needed to cast things in a certain light in order to do their duty? She had no means of knowing, being of a sex too gentle to venture in the dangerous places of the earth.

Martha Parish had a woman's tendency towards self-effacement.

Later that night, recalling the young man's smile of absolute assurance, she was suddenly put in mind of Lt Rainbird. William had written of his ill grace over the shooting of a bear. Unsoldierly, he called it. She remembered he'd complained before of Rainbird's shortcomings. And yet he'd spoken so highly of the man. *The real thing*, he called him.

For some moments she struggled with a notion of an excellence somehow closed to her, an understanding peculiar to men. Then, calling to mind her husband's tensed figure, and that of the dashing Indian fighter, she wondered whether it might not be identified more by virtue of something lacking in oneself, than truly present in another. They were utterly unlike.

She put out her candle, and stood a moment, gazing out of the bedroom window.

It was a cold clear night, the heavens stretched out like the psalmist's cloth. She picked out the Great Dipper, low in the winter sky. Up above, with blackness all around, was the North Star.

Suddenly she felt engulfed by the numbing emptiness of the Far North, a cavernous darkness that seemed to absorb and magnify whatever was carried into it. Now William and his men were enduring a second winter with no news from home, no cheer to lift their spirits. And the polar night, she somehow surmised, was never a healer. She prayed that he and Rainbird had settled their differences.

✳

No party, the Lieutenant reflected as he closed his log, had ever passed a second winter in such latitudes.

He was pushing into the unknown. Though his *terra incognita* were the men themselves.

His anxieties had been exacerbated by a blunder arising out of the surgeon's official report warning of the consequences of dietary deficiency. Fabius had so far forgotten himself as to forward the report via an enlisted man, with the result that its contents had become public knowledge before it reached the commander. Worse, he had apparently been willing to discuss the situation with anyone who cared to broach the subject with him.

Naturally, he took Fabius to task.

'Scurvy,' he said icily, 'is not a word which I expect to hear bandied about by enlisted men. Medical reports are a matter for my eyes alone. It is only your inexperience which leads me to take a lenient view of what, in any other circumstances, I should be compelled to regard as a gross neglect of duty.'

The reprimand, Parish concluded stiffly, would be entered on the surgeon's service record.

It was quite clear Fabius could not possibly have cared less.

Patiently, the Lieutenant set about retrieving the situation. His first objective was to create an atmosphere of purposeful preparation for the winter. The heating system was overhauled, and orders given for the external snow walls to be carried up to the roof. Sleep was now forbidden during the day. Instead, a programme of work and recreation was instituted, such as might keep the men from brooding. As well as supervising the preparation of food, the Lieutenant now extended his daily inspection to ascertaining the dryness of the beds, even enquiring into the regularity of the men's evacuations. Nothing was neglected that bore on the health and spirits of the party.

Thanksgiving presented an ideal opportunity to pull them all together. He turned his attention to the matter of devising some recreations for the day. Footraces, of course. Perhaps a race on snowshoes. A shooting competition. Finally a grand dinner, with the prize-giving to follow. Somewhere among his own personal effects there must be sufficient candies and cigars to serve for prizes.

Bundled up in buffalo coats against a temperature of minus forty, the men had little heart for sports and entertainments. In the snow-shoe race the handful of volunteers shuffled over the frozen ground to derisive cheers. Only the shooting, a contest in which no man cared to come second, kindled genuine rivalry. Private Hanson, shooting at a target lit by a candle flame, hit the bull a dozen times in succession.

That night the whole party gathered in the men's quarters. The tables had been pushed up, and the round dining table brought in from the officers' room. The Lieutenant was particularly anxious they should dine as one company, officers and men together.

'Let us remember at all times,' he impressed upon them as they sat down, 'however far from home, we are still a piece of our beloved country.'

'United we stand, divided we fall,' sang out Diggs cheerfully. The motto of his adopted state, it was his talisman, his touchstone of the New World.

Yet even Wutz's excellent dinner, and a double ration of rum, failed to lift the party's spirits. As he rose to deliver his address the Lieutenant feared he would not carry them with him.

'Our nation,' he began, 'originated with just such a small party as ours wintering on a wild and barren shore. How different their first winter. Not for them a dinner such as we have just enjoyed. They saw only a desolate wilderness, full of wild beasts and savages, and what multitudes there might be of them they had no way of knowing.'

Surveying the company ranged on either side of the long table, the Lieutenant perceived no answering spark: only faces deadened by the monotony of an adventure for which they had lost all enthusiasm: Fromm toying with his glass, Schmidt, Muller whispering in German: strangers still, in a strange land.

'But they stuck it out,' he went on. 'They came through that winter, to celebrate their first Thanksgiving.'

Rainbird was sitting back with folded arms, his bored gaze directed at his plate. He had positioned himself towards the end of the table, with his card-playing cronies, Lawless and Edge: all part of his campaign, thought Parish with sudden hatred, to curry favour with the men.

That night, as he lay in his bunk, the Lieutenant considered whether he should put a stop to Rainbird's little scheme. Break up the card game. Order it to cease forthwith. Then it struck him that to issue such an order would be to treat the man as if he were still under military discipline. As if, in fact, he were still on duty, a serving officer on station. If some mischance were to compel him to relinquish his post as leader of the expedition, wouldn't that give Rainbird a pretext for claiming the command?

Before falling asleep Parish made a mental note that he must speak to Foxer on the matter. He would speak privately to Emmons too.

The next morning, to his annoyance, the Lieutenant overslept. He emerged from behind his curtain to discover his officers already at table.

Wishing them a stiff good morning, he lifted a cover from a dish. Sauerkraut again. No one ever ate it except himself. He only did so because they had it, and it was served. He considered it his duty to set an example. Glumly, he helped himself to a portion, conscious of Rainbird's sardonic gleam of amusement.

The surgeon, though, was clearing his throat.

'I have been giving some thought to our position.'

As usual, he spoke as if he were leading the expedition.

The commander was reflecting that the sauerkraut was not improved by freezing. Chewing stolidly, he made no reply as Fabius began to outline his programme for the coming season. There should be no long spring exploration trips. They should concentrate their efforts on preparing a line of caches southwards.

Parish had no doubts as to what lay behind the suggestion. The man was eaten up with jealousy. He would stop at nothing to block Foxer's chances of improving his Farthest North.

He swallowed a few last fragments of sauerkraut.

'My orders are quite clear,' he said curtly. 'We still have work to do. We shall continue our exploration and scientific efforts until the relief vessel arrives to takes us off in the summer.'

'And if it doesn't? It's been turned back once. It can be turned back again. If so, you will have to retreat. A prudent leader would begin his preparations now.'

The reversion to that '*you*' was not lost on the Lieutenant, who had begun to suffer the singularity of command.

'I believe you may allow me to know my duty, Dr Fabius.'

There was a deal of ice in his reply.

The men grew more captious by the day. Time dragged by. Forbidden to sleep, they lay on their bunks, oppressed by the aimlessness of their existence. It was not cold and darkness that subdued, so much as a sense of life withdrawing, shrinking in upon itself. It was as if an iron band was tightening around the party. The dogs felt it. Sitting on their haunches, eyes half-closed, heads tilted skywards, they howled out their unhappiness, a long, wailing lamentation that went on for three or four minutes, before stopping abruptly. The men, though, retreated into themselves. Then the air grew thunderous.

Those with real work to do were the best served in this time of trial. Even on days of brutal cold and darkness the astronomer went willingly the quarter of a mile to his wooden hut. There were days when the weather grudged him every yard. Often he made his way, bent double, through the furious knife-slash of blown snow, into a wind screaming at him from another world. On such days his journey took him past certain snow-plastered shapes he knew to be musk oxen lasting out the storm. When the bad weather started they had gathered on the side of the hill, closed up like a fist, facing the blast. They would stand like that, motionless, for as long as it lasted; for days on end, if necessary.

Endurance, he saw, was everything.

One evening, just before supper, the officers were startled by a sudden, furious altercation flaring up beyond the partition: then a voice, high-pitched, trembling on the edge: 'Don't say anything. If you say anything, so help me, I'll kill you.'

Hastening to the cookhouse Parish discovered a wild-eyed Wutz, meat cleaver in his fist, standing over a cowering Fromm.

Supper was subdued. The normally good-natured Wutz seemed dazed by his aberration. The men talked uneasily in low voices. 'He's like the rest of us,' Lawless was heard to mutter morosely. 'He wants to go home.'

The strain was palpable. A vast distance separated them from all that they held dear, all that made life worth living. The weight of sea, of ice, pressed down upon them. Defeated, they were driven back to a core of sullen anger and resentment.

That night the Lieutenant, rummaging among his books, came across a reference to a strange winter hysteria among the Polar Eskimos, in which afflicted men went astray, lost in some tenebrous region of themselves.

The next morning he spoke privately to Emmons.

'I want you to keep a close watch on the men. At the first sign of any abnormality I want to be informed.'

Meanwhile, the surgeon continued to press his view as to their future course of action. He wouldn't let it drop. The Lieutenant would be at his desk in his corner, knowing Fabius was the other side of the curtain, with a chart laid out on the table, organizing the retreat. It was all retreat with him.

Increasingly, he found himself leaning on Emmons for support. Twenty years of soldiering had equipped Parish to recognize a rock when he saw one. And Emmons was a rock. Others, he feared, might prove distinctly shaky.

When wrestling with some predicament, the Lieutenant preferred to put his thoughts on paper. He began to draw up one of his lists. Brenner, Schmidt, Krug, who'd done such excellent work with the puppies, Nadel the engineer, were all reliable men. So too was Diggs. Wutz, he put down as unpredictable, remembering his aberration with the cleaver. But a man who was unpredictable must, by that very fact, be questionable. Sighing, he scratched Wutz from the list. The cheerful Hanson he thought on the whole a safe bet. Lazy, but strong as an ox. Top of the 'unreliables' he put the insubordinate Fromm, then Sedgewick, whom he'd reprimanded for drunkenness. After some hesitation he added the names of Rainbird's cronies, Edge and Lawless. It was better not to count on any man he couldn't be sure of.

He wondered whether he should enter his assessments in the official log. In the circumstances it might be prudent to place on record every significant event involving members of the party. In the end he decided against it, being unwilling to besmirch a man in the absence of any formal charge.

Engrossed in his deliberation, from time to time the Lieutenant was aware of low murmurings coming from the other side of his curtain. It conveyed the unpleasant suggestion of a command-in-waiting. As the idea took hold he became alarmed at the idea that Fabius might be communicating his obsession to the men. He was quite capable of it. In considering whether or not to have it out with him, he wondered if he'd been altogether too lenient with Rainbird and the surgeon. Or too aloof?

Knowing himself to be of an irritable disposition, the Lieutenant examined his conduct to discover when, if ever, he'd given way to immoderate anger, but could find no occasion. Indeed, he had been patient and restrained to a degree.

It was, he reflected, the best course of action. Restraint was of the essence.

The next morning he set off as usual on his run. In this, as in all things, seeking to lead by example, it was his practice to trot cautiously over the frozen snow for fifteen minutes or so, before returning to his desk. Each day he took the same route, jogging with short steps over the bluish ice. Out beyond the ice foot the hummocky rubble cast weird shadows in the moonlight. Wind had swept the tops clear of snow. All along the shore, and out into the bay, the burnished ice sparkled with a gemlike brilliance. The cold bit into the Lieutenant's nose. The hut loomed in the distance, standing up against the light reflected from the snow. He was looking forward to the warm stove and a cup of coffee.

He sensed, rather than saw, the figure. At first it struck him as a thicker, local concentration of the gloom, until it moved, emerging from the hillside as a silhouette darker than the twilight.

'Lieutenant …'

It was Rainbird.

'I'll give it to you straight, Lieutenant. Some of us have been discussing the situation. The feeling is, first chance we get, for sending a sledge party to Littleton Island. They could wait there for the relief ship and guide it the rest of the way back.'

'Absolutely not,' said Parish.

He was trying to breathe evenly, anxious that his lungs should not freeze in the icy air.

'You know you're alone in this, Lieutenant? Surely you'll allow one man's say-so oughtn't to carry when two dozen others think different?'

Rainbird paused, it might have been for an answer. Getting none, he pressed a little harder.

'The men are very depressed. You should know that. Even Foxer. Though he won't tell you so.'

'I don't believe you. Besides, this is not a town meeting, Mr Rainbird. This is a military expedition from which, may I remind you, you chose to remove yourself.'

With that, the Lieutenant resumed his slow trot. A sledge party! To include Rainbird, no doubt.

All the same, the encounter left him uneasy. There was something ominous, even a hint of threat, in Rainbird's specious invoking of a majority. Parish suspected Fabius' hand in it.

Then and there he decided he must give up his own plans for a spring sledging. With Foxer and Emmons absent in Greenland, he could not afford to leave the station in the hands of Rainbird and his friends.

With the start of the new year men began to look to the south. Each day at noon a little knot of shadowy figures could be found, gathered on the shore. They were watching, waiting for the first glow of twilight.

The Lieutenant saw in this an encouraging sign.

'With the coming of the sun,' he declared, 'we shall draw new life and strength.'

Among his command there was no such anticipation. Always at the back of their minds was a fear that perhaps the darkest day was yet to come.

Not even the commander went unscathed. Sometimes his whole being was crushed by the weight of this second winter. Sometimes it was difficult to believe that anything, even a seed could still be alive, alive and lying low, biding its time. Then his prayers blackened and died in a frost no promise of sun could ever thaw. Yet he knew that in wintery New England someone was praying, her prayers falling steadily through the iron darkness.

One day, trotting back cautiously over the frozen snow, he

rejoiced to hear the hoarse cry of a dog fox calling to its mate. Something had come through. Nature kept faith after all. And so would men. They would get through.

Winter was becoming spring. Now, with each passing day, the glow of noon stood higher in the sky. On the day calculated by Sergeant Asher for the first sunrise, the sun failed to show itself to the group of men gathered outside the hut. It was an omen suffered in silence by the watchers. Yet the Lieutenant's voice lacked nothing of fervour as he read a Sabbath psalm of thanksgiving. For all the surgeon's dire predictions, he had brought his party through.

William Parish was almost ashamed to think he should ever have doubted it, for the winter had been a great mental trial to him.

At the end of the month young Foxer set off north. All winter he'd talked of extending his journey in the direction of a lonely cape he'd seen glimmering distantly across a waste of ice.

Had he been carrying snow-shoes he believed he might have done so there and then.

This year, with a heavy sledge equipped with steel runners, he believed he could add a hundred miles to his own 'Farthest North'.

The Lieutenant viewed his departure with misgiving. Abnormally high temperatures over the past month were causing him concern. He feared there might be open water in the Robeson Channel.

'Take no chances,' he added, as they shook hands. 'Should the pack show signs of disintegration, you are to return immediately.'

Plunging temperatures came as a relief. Even so, Parish would not rest easy until the young lieutenant was safe again on Grinnell Land. Though perfect peace could only come with the ship. *And if it doesn't ...* The surgeon's question was never far from his mind. His orders were quite clear. He was to abandon his station not later than the first day of September, and retreat southward, following the coast, until the relieving vessel was met, or Littleton Island reached. In the event of it being unable to get through, the ship would remain in Smith Sound until the last possible moment before the ice closed off the Sound.

He studied the chart, on which were pinpointed the position of stores cached on the journey north. They should be able to make Cape Isabella. He gazed at the blunt headland projecting across the Sound in the direction of Littleton Island. If a ship came they could not well miss reaching it. If not …

'God help us,' he muttered.

The boats he had – the steam launch, and the New Bedford whaleboat – seemed scarcely adequate. There was also the English jolly-boat. Parish closed his eyes, and thanked Providence that had prompted him to pick it up at Cape Hawks.

Then he remembered that across the channel, at Thank God Harbour on the Greenland shore, was the large ice-boat cached there by the British. As a conciliatory gesture he decided to invite Fabius to bring it back. It would, besides, afford the man an opportunity to recover his self-esteem.

Gratified by his own magnanimity, the Lieutenant was quite unprepared for a cool response.

Fabius shrugged. 'But it is not what I am here for.'

Parish stared hard. A muscle quivered in his face.

'It is not my work,' explained the surgeon, who cherished his animosities with more solicitude than most. 'My contract is quite clear as to my duties. I am here as medical officer.'

'Very well.' The Lieutenant's lips cramped together. 'Then you will accompany the party as medical officer.'

'As you wish.'

Fabius bowed politely, that odd inclination of the head, assenting and ironic.

Parish watched him going about his business. It struck him as extraordinary indeed that men could not be counted on to act, even in their own best interests. It was a sobering thought.

Meanwhile, there was still the matter of the boat. In the end he entrusted the task to Reade. After Foxer and Emmons, Sergeant Reade was the best man he had.

One evening, weeks before he was expected, Foxer's team came trotting home.

The Lieutenant was at his desk engaged in an examination of the botanical specimens, some of which he found to be in a less than admirable condition, when he heard the welcoming shouts. He went out to find his deputy surrounded by excited men.

Foxer, though, was in despondent mood. Three days out from Cape Sumner, skirting the Greenland shore, he'd come across open water. No more than a hundred yards away was the solid polar pack. Cutting him off was a continuous belt of young ice.

'A stone would go through it anywhere. So that was that.'

Disappointment was alive and aching in his voice.

'You were right to return,' said Parish consolingly. 'Besides,' he added, for the benefit of the faces looking on, 'we still have a great deal of work to do before the ship arrives.'

This observation he uttered with every appearance of conviction. He did not wish it to be thought he entertained any doubts about the safe arrival of the vessel.

All summer the work of mapping and surveying went on as before. The entire collection of natural history items was classified and arranged, with a detailed description made of every object, in case of eventual abandonment. He was determined that nothing of their scientific labours should be lost. At the same time, he began his preparations for retreat. The expedition records, together with the photographic negatives, field journals, diaries and other official papers, he had soldered into water-tight tins for the journey. A third tin held a set of duplicate records made in case of any disaster. The scientific instruments, the thermometers and magnets, were stored in a strong wooden case. The heavy pendulum, packed in its box, and soldered inside a tin container, was secured with an outer layer of wooden boards.

The men threw themselves into the work with a will. The steady accumulation of boxes and barrels, neatly labelled, waiting to be loaded on to the steamer, proved an antidote to anxious thoughts. They were going home at last.

As he watched them hoisting the heavy cases, the Lieutenant felt a sudden surge of gratitude and affection for his men who had laboured so mightily throughout. He had selected them; now, at the end of their mission, he believed he had been vindicated in his choice. It was especially gratifying that he should have brought them through the dangers and privations of Arctic life without a single case of scurvy or frostbite, let alone serious injury.

As he looked back at the work completed, the territory explored, the wonderful achievement of a new 'Farthest North', William Parish felt he might be excused a degree of satisfaction.

EIGHT

Earlier that summer, on a bright day towards the end of June, young Leffingwell stood watching the *Petrel*'s prow cutting through the six-foot swells of blue-black water. From the first turn of the windlass, the rattle of the anchor chain as it was shortened in, he'd been in the grip of an excitement that filled the mind to the exclusion of all else.

He cut an exotic figure himself, the tall lieutenant, muffled up in furs, strolling about the decks with Rags, the huge Newfoundland dog he'd purchased in St John's, whistling and exclaiming at the wonders of the Greenland coast, that might have been the setting for some heroic drama, a skyline of raging, jagged peaks, with marbly glaciers racing down to long, fingery fjords, and, in the distance, Valhalla itself glittering above black bastions of rock.

At Godthavn he had taken on board the dogs and drivers, and the winter clothing that would be needful in the event of a sledging expedition. He did so hope there would be a sledging expedition.

His last despatch distilled the buoyant spirits engendered by a favourable voyage: *Good sailing. Excellent weather. Melville Bay reported clear of ice. So far the voyage has passed like a dream. Making all speed north.*

Speed was of the essence. General Sweetsir had been most insistent about that. 'Allow nothing to hold you up.' His written orders repeated the point in the plainest way: *It is essential you miss no opportunity to hasten the journey northward. Nothing should be permitted to impede your progress to Lady Franklin Bay.*

So far nothing had. The Carey Islands had come and gone. And still there was no ice to speak of. He could not have wished for an easier passage. Poor De Long had perished for the want of a rescue party. Lt Parish would not suffer the same fate. He would see to that.

Enlarged by these agreeable reflections, the young lieutenant's reverie flowed serenely to a homecoming, saluted by the yachts at Flushing, and the big Sound steamers, with flags dipping all the way up the East River, and thousands lining the shore, welcoming home the heroes. His enthusiasm engendered the most generous sentiments towards the needy object of his mission, reaching even to Martha Parish, to whom was allotted the role of grateful wife.

He had written her a bubbly letter, filled with optimism for the voyage: *You will rejoice to hear we are to enjoy the added security and protection of the US Navy. The* Yarborough *(Commander Young) is coming with us …*

It had been her own suggestion. For it seemed only sensible that two ships be sent, one to remain in Smith Sound, the other to push north along the coast of Grinnell Land.

That winter, pondering the plan prepared for the relief party, she had come to look upon General Sweetsir's strategy with increasing misgivings. The decision to leave a supply depot and winter house on Littleton Island would be of little use if, as seemed most likely, William retreated down the opposite coast, in accordance with his instructions. His party might be in no condition to cross Smith Sound. They would find no shelter at Cape Sabine, and the pitiful supply of rations left by Mr Bright would merely prolong their ordeal for a few more days. The fate of poor De Long was ever fresh and dreadful in her mind. What was needful was a full complement of supplies to be landed on the Sabine shore; tents, fuel, medical supplies and provisions sufficient to carry the party through another winter, though God forbid it should come to that.

Lt Leffingwell, though, seemed to entertain no thoughts of failure. His letter had reiterated his earlier assurances: *If the ship cannot not get through, rest assured I will myself with dogs and sledges. You shall have your husband home before the winter.*

The crux of the matter, though, was not what he planned on doing, but whether he could do it. What experience did he have of dogs and sledges? Or, for that matter, of seamanship? He did not say, and she had not liked to ask, not wishing to embarrass.

Suppressing her anxieties, she'd sent a wire of encouragement on the eve of his departure: *Having heard the golden opinions showered upon you I feel sure the safety of my husband's party could not be in better hands.*

The lieutenant had been gratified by this expression of confidence. Mrs Parish was just the kind of loyal wife he would wish eventually to marry. Though prettier, of course.

Meanwhile, he scanned the horizon with the powerful new telescope he'd purchased in St John's, sweeping the sea from east to west. The look-out confirmed his impression. The way was clear north to Smith Sound.

Such good fortune left the young man perplexed as to his course of action.

Stepping into his cabin, he opened the drawer of his writing desk and took out the packet of additional instructions he'd received shortly before departure. There was doubt about it. They required him *without fail* to leave a depot at Littleton Island on the journey north. Not having had an opportunity to discuss this instruction personally with the general, he was uncertain what to do. As if to complicate matters, the *Yarborough* had begun to lag. When he returned to the poop he was dismayed to see her prow falling farther astern.

Within the hour, rounding Cape Alexander, he received a signal to say her boilers were failing. Commander Young would put in to Pandora Harbour to effect repairs, then rendezvous at Littleton Island.

Weighing things up, Leffingwell came to a decision. *Allow nothing to hold you up.* The standing orders stated quite clearly that the Littleton Island plan was a measure of last resort, to be implemented only in the event of a failure to rendezvous with Parish, and the closing of the Sound. The barometer was set fair for the moment, but he'd had warning how swiftly, in these high latitudes, the weather could change for the worse.

He signalled back: *No ice anywhere in view. Conditions too good to be missed. Shall go directly north.*

Cape Ohlsen passed to starboard. Littleton Island fell away astern. The *Petrel* steamed slowly north, the mast-head man calling out his regular 'All-clear'.

An hour before noon, ten miles to the north-west, Leffingwell was tugging on his stick for Rags to chew at when he heard a cry from the mast-head.

'Ice dead ahead.'

At Fort Chance July was slipping past. Daily now, southerly gales were breaking up the floes in the Robeson Channel. The lookouts keeping vigil on the cliffs brought back the same report. The channel would be partly open for an hour or so, then fill again with ice.

The Lieutenant felt increasingly uneasy in the face of a situation which was becoming more ominous by the day. He remembered Pederson saying that particular summer had been exceptional, the aftermath of an unusually mild winter. In these high latitudes the reality was ice.

As the month ended he issued an order of the day: *In the case of the non-arrival of a vessel, this station will be abandoned this day week, and a retreat by boats begun southward to Littleton Island. Sixteen pounds of personal baggage will be allowed each officer and eight pounds to each man.*

The tone, unexcited, matter-of-fact, was something he'd laboured at. He wished to leave undisturbed the assumption that the steamer's arrival was still expected.

His preparations told another story. Over two tons of coal had been screened, bagged and stowed on the launch. Meanwhile, the boats were being thoroughly overhauled.

The men worked in an atmosphere of subdued apprehension, packing food, fuel, tents and clothing for the journey, moving the loads methodically down to the boats. When not occupied with duties, they would climb to the top of Prospect

Hill and look out across the bay, gazing south. Every heart still cherished the same unspoken question: *When would the ice melt, and the ship arrive?*

Faced with that wall of ice stretching away as far as the eye could reach Captain Quine had turned westward. For several hours he searched for an opening. Then, off Cape Sabine, he banked his fires and lay to. Asking to be informed of any change in the wind, the master went below.

It was Leffingwell, hanging restlessly about the poop, who first spotted a flaw-lead of dark water opening as the pack shifted with the turning tide. Frost smoke rose from the lead, tinged with flame by a dipping sun. The ice seemed to burn on the water.

The young lieutenant hurried aft and banged on the door of the master's cabin.

'Open water,' he shouted urgently. 'We must get under way.'

He burned himself to take the ship into that strait of golden fire.

Captain Quine had been asleep. Yawning, he emerged from his cabin, and crossed to the rail. Thirty miles to the north Cape Albert loomed dove grey in the thin Arctic air. The master stared at the surging waters of Buchanan Bay where, under an offshore wind, the moving pack had parted company with the shore-fast ice.

'The tide's turning,' he said shortly. 'That's all it is.'

And would, no doubt, have returned to his bunk. But the young man was insistent.

'No, no, we must get under way. My orders are quite clear. We are to take advantage of every lead.'

All that evening and on into the early hours, pistons thumping, her iron prow shoving aside loose floes, the *Petrel* followed the flaw lead.

In the morning, though, four miles off the cape, as the wind swung north, the ice closed in again.

Leffingwell was roused by shouts outside his cabin. He

became aware of a sullen, all-encompassing rumbling, as of heavy guns. He tumbled out of his bunk to find members of the crew, armed with boat hooks and long poles, digging away at the ship's stern. Heavy pack, surging into the strait on the incoming tide, had pinned her securely against the solid shore ice reaching out from the cape. She could move neither for'ard nor astern.

Leffingwell crossed to the starboard rail, then walked the whole length of the vessel, amazed at what was taking place. Around the ship chunks of ice, caught between moving floes, were jumping like squeezed cherry stones. Meanwhile, the deck he stood on vibrated to the thunder of the seaward floes grinding into the fast shore ice.

For a while he watched, fascinated, as the seaward ice, driven in upon itself, rode up in ridges ten or fifteen feet in height, before toppling forward on to the grounded floes. Then he began to feel somewhat apprehensive. There was something inexorable about those huge blocks, tumbling over one another in their slow advance upon the ship.

He went back aft and mounted the poop to seek out the master.

Captain Quine was staring thoughtfully at the ice, as if trying to gauge its intentions. Old whaling men told how it sometimes happened that a vessel, caught in an equilibrium of forces fore and aft, would be held fast until, with a change of wind or tide, the floes opened again. If so, she might survive.

'Can't something be done?'

Leffingwell had begun to feel rather nervous, and was striving to keep the strain out of his voice. He entertained a vague notion of something he'd read somewhere: whaling men sawing a kind of dock in the ice to contain a threatened vessel.

'You're in God's hands now, mister,' was all the master said as he crossed to the starboard rail.

Amid the continual roar of pressure Leffingwell was made aware of a low, guttural growling. Rags, crouching down, was backing away, the whites of his eyes like peeled eggs in the great black head. Leffingwell took him by the collar, and shut him in his cabin.

By midday the floes were crowding the vessel so closely great chunks of ice were piling up against her sides. Now the sullen grinding was accompanied by a keener, closer sound: a pleading, whining from within the ship itself, as the ice tightened its grip about her oaken ribs.

Captain Quine had placed the photograph of a loved one between the pages of his bible, which he was stowing in his bag. He was thinking either the keel must break, or the holds would fill with water.

'How much longer can this go on?' asked Leffingwell shakily

The master turned to glance at the strained face.

'Don't worry, mister,' he grunted. 'You should have time to step overboard and walk away.'

Leffingwell, though, had observed that some of the hands, who had gone below to get together bundles of warm clothing, were now appearing back on deck with their duffle. He tried hard to compose his mind. To judge things coolly. All this was rather more than he'd bargained for. All the same he was determined to do his duty.

Shouting, he dashed for'ard, summoning his own men.

'Get the stores on deck ... bring up the stores ...'

He had no idea what he would do when that was accomplished. He knew only that the stores must be secured, and that it was his responsibility to secure them.

In the desperate hour that followed Leffingwell led the work himself, seizing whatever came to hand, encouraging his men in a voice as calm as he could manage.

'Jump to, boys ... quick as you can ...'

Tins, boxes, cases of canned goods tumbled about as, straining, groaning, her beams beginning to buckle, the *Petrel* was shaken like a rat in a terrier's jaws. In the foreward hold the sound of running water rose above the tortured creaking of her timbers.

Coming up from the fore-'tween deck, a barrel of bread on

his shoulder, he heard a squeal and rattle of block and tackle. The ship's boats were being lowered.

Leffingwell, shouting frantically for his sergeant, found a bullet head at his shoulder.

'Ransome … thank God … Get our boats over the side.'

Then he was back in the hold with one of the enlisted men, salvaging the last of the barrels, with the roar of gushing water echoing beneath them, and the ship's beams cracking and exploding like pistol shots. They had each secured an armful of coats when they heard, from somewhere below their feet, an agonized interminable groan that ended in a terrible rending: then, as they stood transfixed, the sudden roar of a great sluice.

Leffingwell, dashing up the companion way, was swept into a mass of men rushing this way and that, clutching blankets, rugs, sleeping bags, struggling into heavy coats as they sought to salvage whatever came to hand. Most of the stores were still on deck, though the deck itself was already breaking up, folding along the seams like a concertina.

'The stores,' he shouted. 'The stores.'

He collared a seaman dashing past, but the man shrugged him off and began clambering over the starboard rail. With the ship done for, he had lost his pay, most of his belongings, and might very soon lose his life.

Then Leffingwell was profoundly glad to hear his sergeant's booming voice.

'Get these stores over the side.'

Scarcely heeding the shudders convulsing the stricken vessel, he threw himself into the task, working feverishly to salvage the stores: tins, cases, barrels, boxes, heaved over the side, some straight into the sea.

He was making ready to clamber over the side himself, when someone seized him by the arm. It was Ransome.

'The dog, sir … the dog …'

Only then did he hear a frantic barking.

Dashing back he threw open the door of his cabin. Rags bounded out, only to crouch, cowering. It took the strength of

147

both men to drag the terrrified animal to the port rail and heave him over the side.

No sooner had he landed on the floe himself than he noticed the two whaleboats, canted over on the ice. Thank God he'd got the boats. He stared at the boxes and barrels scattered at random. The stores: what was he to do with the stores?

He felt a pressure against his hand. It was Rags, eyes in the huge raised head fixed on him in mournful enquiry. Leffingwell groaned inwardly at the thought of Parish, waiting at Fort Chance.

Dazed, dismayed, his men stood in little groups of twos and threes, sensing the ocean under their feet as the floe rose on the swell. The Newfoundlanders, to a man, had all gone over the starboard rail, and were gathered with their possessions on the further side of the ship.

Slowly, surely, still on an even keel, the *Petrel* was settling lower in the water.

Soldiers and seaman, separated by a catastrophe not yet wholly grasped, gazed numbly as she went down, sinking with stately dignity; the ice, attentive to the last, holding her steady, upright, as the sea broke over her deck.

Her three tall masts, steadfast to the end, were the last they saw of her.

Then she was gone, leaving the silent men to stare at one another across a strip of black, bubbling water.

NINE

One evening, early in August, a frail flotilla of small boats sailed on the ebb tide towards the western entrance of the harbour. The steam launch, the *Martha Parish*, was towing a string of three small craft. A fresh southerly gale had been blowing all day. It had driven the greater part of the pack to northward. The Lieutenant judged the prospects excellent if they could but get ahead of the ice.

He had dressed for the occasion, though whether to invest the moment of departure with a solemn dignity, or else to affirm human identity and purpose in the face of the awesome prospect confronting the party, the Lieutenant himself might not have been able to say. Whatever the reason, William Parish had donned full uniform, with epaulettes, sabre and revolver.

He had taken up his station in the bow of the launch, with Foxer at the helm, and Rainbird in the cockpit under the canvas weather cover. Sergeant Emmons followed in the whaleboat, leading the English ice-boat Reade had brought back from Thank God Harbour. Bringing up the rear was the smaller jolly-boat they had picked up at Cape Hawks. In the bows of each a man stood ready to cast off the painter at the first signs of danger, as the Lieutenant had instructed.

The launch chugged steadily ahead, low in the water under its heavy load of coal and supplies. Foxer was keeping her well out in the channel as instructed, well away from the heavy ice fields separating them from the shore. Parish was under no illusion as to what lay ahead. The pack was constantly in motion. In the ripping of the current, in every varying of the wind, there would be danger.

The flotilla steamed slowly south-east, weaving among the floating ice-pans of the bay.

Parish glanced back at the small boats strung out astern. He felt a flush of anger at the sight of Fabius in the whaleboat.

The surgeon had elected to travel (since travel he must) in the whaleboat rather than the launch. It was essential to dissociate oneself from a course of action, the folly of which he had indicated in the course of a strained meeting with the Lieutenant, whom he'd come to regard as imprisoned by the military mind. The man was a slave to his orders. He was incapable of those acts of initiative which were supremely necessary in the Arctic. Fabius had pointed out, as civilly as a necessary measure of scorn permitted, that they were two hundred and fifty miles north of Cape Sabine. Yet the Lieutenant was proposing to retreat along a frozen, uninhabited coast, where his caches might be rendered inaccessible by ice or weather. The prudent course would have been to overwinter at the fort. Then, in the Spring, they could cross to the Greenland coast and sledge south, seeking out the Eskimo settlements which, in the past, had been known to have rendered assistance to explorers.

A slant light picked out the surgeon, a stiff figure buffeted by the wind, the image of reason outraged, intelligence defied. The Lieutenant gazed at him with loathing. He suspected Fabius had communicated his objections to the men. The fellow had no scruples.

His gaze took in the men in the boats, nervously fending off the floating ice with their oars. The Lieutenant reflected he had full rations for forty days, with supplies for another twenty cached to the southward. Enough to enable them to reach Cape Hawks with the same quantities as they'd taken from the fort. A nagging reproach was the abandoning of the dogs. It had given rise to a painful scene with Private Krug. *You might as well shoot them now, Lieutenant, and have done with it.* But he couldn't have shot them. If, by mischance, they were driven back to the fort, he would need the dogs for the hauling of game and fuel. Before leaving he'd ordered the breaking open of several barrels of beef and bread. The man had given him black looks ever since.

Angry-looking clouds were massing to the north, all but shutting out the midnight sun as they rounded the cape. The Lieutenant felt a stab of lonely longing as the launch turned her prow towards the Kennedy Channel. Far to the south lay home, and safety. What could sustain them now but the spirit of God and His grace?

The gale, freshening all the time, had backed north-east. Out in the channel the floes were surging rapidly southward, a turbulent mass of heavy ice charging down with the speed of a mill race.

'Stick close to the shore,' a voice shouted, above the wind. Rainbird was feeling the strain.

The Lieutenant, his nerve ground paper-thin, ran for shelter. He was profoundly thankful to find it, among the stranded floe bergs lining the shore south of Cape Baird.

Glad to stretch their legs after the cramped confinement of the boats, the men wandered about the narrow beach between the ice-foot and the cold black crags. Nobody said much. As the cooks prepared a meal, the rest fell to struggling with poles and canvas to construct a rudimentary shelter. Going among them with words of encouragement, the Lieutenant was conscious of their eyes searching his face with the gaze of unhappy children. At the thought of the countless perils that lay before them, he was assailed by a sense of his own unfittedness. He could only pray that such judgement as was needed would grow out of the journey south.

The small flotilla steamed slowly south. Foxer had yielded his place at the tiller of the launch to Reade. The better to see where he was going, the photographer elected to perch on a narrow transom raised above the stern, his Eskimo boots resting on the slippery spars. It was a position fraught with peril. Light snow set in, which soon wet everything unprotected by canvas. The Lieutenant directed operations from the bow, peering through his lenses at the streams of ice, that seemed forever to divide and close. Again and again he would follow a lead only to find it closing against him. Then the boats were hastily cast off, and drawn up on the floes. For the *Martha Parish* there was no such escape. Unwieldy, slow to respond, the launch became an increasing source of frustration to her pilot, whose urgent instructions to the helmsman seemed all too often to go unheeded.

After that, even in quite open ice, the Lieutenant thought it inadvisable to take chances. There was no telling what wind or current might get up to. The day would seem set fair for a fine run. Then the ice would come charging down on the frail boats threatening to grind them to atoms. Sometimes they barely escaped to the shelter of the shore. Sometimes, with the ice foot towering ten or fifteen feet above the launch, there was no escape. They were swirled along like twigs on the current.

The men were wholly out of their element, and their sense of helplessness was extreme. To some among them it seemed as if some capricious Spirit was playing a game of cat and mouse, stopping them, letting them go awhile, then frustrating them again as a prelude to stopping them altogether.

The Lieutenant blamed himself for every setback. Though he'd managed to bring off the first of his caches at Cape Craycroft, it was all taking far too long. In eight days, according to Sergeant Asher's calculations, they had steamed two hundred miles to make sixty miles of latitude. In his anxiety, fearful that they would miss their rendezvous with the ship, he harried the men continually. No chance of a lead could be ignored. Men at their breakfast would be forced to abandon a half-eaten meal to drag the boats into the water. If they couldn't make Cape Sabine before the middle of September, the vessel would have left. Their only hope then would rest with the relief party on Littleton Island.

Each journey's end found him ground down by the constant watchfulness.

'I don't know we wouldn't be better abandoning the launch,' he muttered one night to Emmons. 'Haul the boats on to the pack, and drift south on the current.'

The sergeant went to direct the work with troubled face. It seemed crazy to him.

The strain, the tension, returned with the morning and the prospect of another battle with the ice. As the men laboured to drag the whaleboat down over the ice-foot, the burly Hanson was backing off as usual.

Instantly, the Lieutenant flew at the man.

'Hanson, you goddam asshole … you piece of shit … Shift your ass *now*.'

The men gaped, open-mouthed.

Once in the boats, they sat avoiding one another's eye. No one joked about it. It was too troubling for that.

Then, off Cape DeFosse, they ran into fog. The launch crawled through sludge ice to the dismal honking of the horn. Nadel, posted in the engine compartment, sounded a long double blast every few seconds. The Lieutenant had now got it into his head that the relief ship might slip past them out in the channel.

Solitary floe bergs came and went, menacing shapes adrift in the gloom and uncertainty of fog. Parish perched in the bow, now and again wiping his spectacles, peering into the mirk. Somehow or other he managed to manoeuvre his squadron past every obstacle, creeping along by the ice-foot, several times all but grounding his vessel, until, his nerve pared to the quick, he found a refuge in the lee of an immense floe berg grounded a mile off-shore.

Light snow began to fall as the boats were hauled up on to a sloping shingle. Every man was chilled to the bone. Stiff and aching, Nate Emmons was stretching his legs along the shingle when he heard his name called. Looking back he saw Rainbird hastening towards him.

Step for step, they trod the beach together.

'What do you make of the Lieutenant?'

Warily, the sergeant waited for the other man to state his business.

'You've heard him these last few days. He's not right, is he? And this crazy notion to go floating off on the ice …'

Emmons knew without looking that the other man was studying him closely.

'He's not a well man, Sergeant. He's not normal.'

Emmons grunted non-committally. He had the impression Rainbird was looking for answers to a question as yet only hinted at.

'You're a professional soldier. So am I. Wouldn't we be failing in our duty if we allowed the whole outfit to be put in jeopardy by a crazy commander? By rights he should step down, but of course he won't.'

The sergeant stamped his feet. He was getting cold, listening to this.

'He has to be replaced,' Rainbird went on hurriedly. 'Legitimately, of course. It's a quite straightforward matter. The surgeon would make a formal medical examination. He'll report that in his judgement the Lieutenant is not fit to exercise command. As next in rank the command will fall on me. Lieutenant Foxer will have no option but to fall in line. Either that, or be placed under arrest. We would then turn back for the fort. There's enough supplies there to last the winter, and fresh game in plenty. Then, come the spring, we sledge down the coast. Now, doesn't that make better sense?'

The sergeant nodded consideringly. He was a big man, a good head taller than his companion.

'Isn't that a better idea than this crazy adventure?'

The devil of it was, Nate Emmons thought, it made good sense: winter at the fort, warm bunks, coal in plenty, then a spring retreat. It seemed infinitely preferable to what they were enduring now. What he knew best, though, were men; which men could be trusted. And he did not trust Lt Rainbird. He had no faith in an officer who played cards with the enlisted men. Besides, Rainbird had no standing. If the Lieutenant really was crazy, a possibility of which he had yet to be persuaded, then the command passed automatically to Lt Foxer. What Rainbird was proposing amounted to a breakdown of discipline. Go down that road, and who could say where it might lead.

Slowly Emmons shook his head.

'No,' he said, 'we must stick together.'

The gymnast smiled that strange, inconsequential smile. He shrugged.

'OK Sergeant. I guess we'll just have to soldier on as we are.'

Emmons watched him pacing back over the slushy shingle. He wondered whether he should speak to the Lieutenant. Though to do so would only add to his burdens. What if Rainbird and the doctor persisted with their plan? The sergeant considered the possibility, then dismissed it. Their only hope of success now was to go directly to the men. If they did that, he would certainly get to hear of it.

The sergeant shivered as the wind gusted suddenly, carrying the chill from the floes. Well, he'd done what was right. What his oath required of him. All the same, he was conscious he might yet live to regret it. What if the ship failed to get beyond Melville Bay? How would they fare at Littleton Island, assuming they got that far, with no supplies and winter coming on?

Still shivering, he set off back to see the men bedded down. It was a law of life with him that things generally turned out worse than anticipated.

Next morning, when the voyage resumed, it was George Reade who stepped on to the bow of the launch.

The Lieutenant had conceded defeat with unusual candour.

'I cannot claim any expertise in ice piloting,' he acknowledged, with a humility acquired by dint of repeated, mortifying lessons. 'My eyesight is not of the best. Sergeant Reade here has been steering the launch with great skill. I have every confidence he will pilot us safely.'

'A merciful release,' murmured the surgeon to his friend. 'He would have killed us all.'

The men greeted the decision with relief. That the Lieutenant knew nothing about ice navigation they had seen for themselves. Whereas they trusted George. That he was the right man for the job was evident in his handling of the launch.

What's more, they believed he was lucky. Several times he'd been knocked into the sea. He was hauled out, rubbed down with towels, his wet garments strung over the boiler. Then, kitted out in borrowed clothes, he'd resumed his post, perching like a bird on the stern of the launch. Rainbird thought him the best man they had. The sight of Reade side-stepping along the gunwale back to his post stirred a fierce admiration in the yellow-haired man. He would have given the shirt off his back to help George Reade.

Now, with the days that followed, came a general lightening of the mood of the party. The men drew on the comforting illusion that their fortunes lay in skilled human hands again, rather than at the whim of wind and tide. For his part, Reade had come to believe that perhaps a spirit of daring served best in a cruel, unforgiving region. Only after grievous trials and dangers could they hope to escape the Arctic wastes.

Now, blessed with good weather, and a favourable wind, they worked their way steadily south.

The pack, a vast snowfield fractured into a maze of shifting needles, spread out before them like a gigantic puzzle. Straddled across the bow, George Reade was immersed in the absorbing business of threading a passage from one black needle to another. They were opening and closing constantly, as the floes rolled off the wind.

Visibility was flawless. Ice pushed the light up under bluffs and headlands from whence it came streaming back, filling the sky with a presence which, to the pilot, communicated itself as a conviction of extraordinary lucidity. He might have broken through into a wholly different dimension, scanning as far as vision and the atmosphere permitted, staring with a gaze of such intensity his head felt airy with light. He seemed dispensed from the frailties of human personality, in favour of pure consciousness, filled with the brilliance and clarity of Arctic light.

Around midnight the basalt cliffs of Cape Lawrence came into view. The sea was black as scorched earth, the floes so blinding white it hurt to look at them. He couldn't see except in black and white.

'Are you all right, Reade?' The Lieutenant was peering at his pilot from the engine room. 'Never better,' he shouted back.

In that thin air the faceted cliffs slid past like polished gems.

North of Rawlings Bay came further proof that a change of pilot brought a change of luck. The pack, shifting under a freshening south-westerly, had begun to move against them. Then, drifting out of the bay came a berg the size of a small island.

Moving with the current, the huge berg ploughed down the channel through the oncoming ice, and they steamed southward in its wake.

After two weeks at sea Fortune turned against them. The sun, which had looked down benignly as George Reade took them through the ice, now refused to shine. At Cape Collinson they put in to take up another cache only to find the barrels smashed. What bread and beef were left had turned to a slimy mould.

A north-east wind commenced to blow, driving the pack rapidly to the south-west, crowding the boats against the shore. Soon they were cut off altogether from open water.

Flurries of sleet swept over them. For the men in the launch, under the weather awning or in the engine compartment, there was some degree of shelter. There was none for those in the boats. The wet penetrated everything. Cold, wet, miserable, they huddled in their bags with the helplessness of victims, waiting for the ice to open. There was nothing they could do.

Nor could the Lieutenant do anything to raise their spirits. He'd become increasingly agitated by the possibility of their being trapped north of Cape Sabine. The cold weather added to his anxieties. All around new ice was forming, cementing the floes together. Meanwhile, keeping the launch's fires banked was burning eighty pounds of coal a day.

As day followed day the wastes of sea and sky reflected the vanity of their hopes.

Rumours reached the men that the Lieutenant was again

considering abandoning the boats and riding south on one of the floes. They were thoroughly alarmed.

'Only a crazy man,' Fromm was telling, 'could think of such a thing.'

The men thirsted for a ship. Increasingly, as they journeyed further south, they could not understand why it hadn't been sighted. In mid-August it should have got through.

'We shall be in an unenviable position if we reach Cape Hawks and fail to find it,' the surgeon confided to his shipmates in the whaleboat. 'The season is late, our coal nearly gone, and food entirely uncertain.'

But no ship waited at Cape Hawks.

Parish went ashore with a party to see what could be salvaged of the English cache. Leaving the surgeon to examine the cans, he went to inspect his own record, left in the cairn. He found it untouched. Yet the ice to the southward, for as far as he could see, was largely sailing ice. A well-built steamer could run through it easily. He was at a loss to know what to make of it. The instructions were quite clear. For his part, he had kept to them implicitly. He no longer knew what to expect, or what, if anything, he could depend on.

One thing, though, stood supremely clear. If there was no vessel present in these waters it seemed highly unlikely there would be one at Littleton Island. If there was no party there, then their position was extremely serious. They had no more than a few weeks' rations. They would stand little chance of obtaining food during the long Arctic night.

The commander was recalled from his sombre reflections by a cheerful hail from Sergeant Reade. The pilot had climbed a spur south of the cape, from which vantage point, gazing across the mouth of Buchanan Bay, he had seen Cape Sabine glimmering in the sun.

'It can't be more than fifty miles away. If we make a straight run for it, we'd be there in no time. Two days at the most. There's bound to be food and supplies at Sabine. Last year's ship must have got that far.'

So they set off, with Reade piloting the launch through a brash that grew thicker, heavier, mixed with loose streams of heavy floes. Off Victoria Head they were met by a strong south-west wind, and much ice running north.

That evening, as the sun clipped the northern horizon, they were stopped in the pack. George Reade's luck had finally run out.

Morning found them frozen in, a mile short of open water. The Lieutenant ordered the boats to be hauled up on to the ice, and the launch tied to the floe.

The young ice grew steadily thicker in the continuing calm. In places it was more than equal to the weight of a man. The Lieutenant decided to let the fire go out under the boiler, to preserve their dwindling stock of coal.

He called the men together on the ice.

'I have extinguished the boiler fire so as to keep a reserve of fuel for when the ice breaks up.' It was a rule with him, when dealing with enlisted men, always to present the situation, however serious, in a positive light. 'Our chances of getting through remain fair. We still have coal for a day's steaming.'

As he surveyed their faces, he saw that the eyes fixed on him were ready to welcome any reassurance. He had brought them thus far. He was determined to get them back alive.

'Even if we remain fast,' he went on, 'we must eventually drift into Smith Sound.' The level voice made it sound a comforting prospect. 'Once there, we shall be within ten miles of the coast.'

His private assessment was far from encouraging. A few more windless days, and any chance they had of reaching Cape Sabine would have gone. They would have to abandon the launch, and at least one of the boats. Their only hope of breaking free lay in a storm.

That night the sun set for the first time. Under a clear sky the mercury plunged still further.

Day followed day. Some of the men slept in the boats, others in a makeshift tent put together with oars and canvas. Dispirited, their bones aching after three weeks in open boats, they spent whole days in their bags, getting out only for food or a call of nature.

The Lieutenant found an outlet in the twice-daily plotting of their position. He was forever angling for some improvement. Though they'd made little or no progress southward, they had moved appreciably westward. He pointed out that the coast was now quite close, with Victoria Head clearly visible, perhaps three miles away.

As the calm continued, he was confronted by a new dilemma. Should he stay with the floe, and wait for it to break up? Or should he abandon the launch, and try to drag smaller boats and supplies to open water? He had food for sixty days, taking into account the caches already picked up. Thinking to accustom the men by degrees to the privations he now feared were inevitable, he began to consider a modest cut in rations. There was no telling what might befall. In the end he rejected the idea. He did not believe they had reached that stage. Besides, he feared the effect upon the men. Idle, with nothing to occupy their minds but their own discomfort, they were a prey to every wayward thought. The indeterminate nature of their confinement gnawed at them constantly. The return of sunset had a lowering effect. For while it was never dark, each dusk they were reminded of what was rapidly approaching. The Lieutenant, it was rumoured, had been heard to remark that he did not believe there would be open water again that year. They were further disheartened to learn from Asher's calculations that the ice, and they with it, were moving further north. That night a fall of several inches of snow collapsed the makeshift tent, adding to the foot or so that covered the floe.

One morning, after a week in the ice, they woke to a dense fog. All day long it lay over them, a dank clinging curtain. An hour before high tide it parted sufficiently to reveal stretches of open water. Immediately, the excited men made ready for launching.

The Lieutenant had to go from boat to boat vainly trying to

hold in check the upsurge of euphoria. 'No, no, not in this fog. And with a full sea? It would be madness.'

The men, though, were clamorous to go on. Subdued at last, they continued to simmer. The Lieutenant was conscious of the whispered conversations that ceased as he approached. He received his vindication shortly afterwards when, on the heaviest tide of the month, the pack to northward set down upon them violently, piling up the young ice in ridges along the edges of the floes. Desperately the men struggled to remove supplies from the launch as she was lifted bodily from the water, groaning mightily, before shuddering down again.

That night, anxious in case of a further threat to the launch, Parish elected to take the first watch himself. He was passing by the tent when he heard a voice, low, yet clear enough in the still cold air.

'We should have moved when we had the chance. But we did nothing. Now we're stuck here, and who knows when the chance will come again.'

The commander was appalled. For a moment he considered bursting into the tent and having it out with Rainbird. But hung back, uncertain to what effect an angry scene might work upon the men.

Seething with anger, he returned to the launch. Huddled in his bag, he brooded on Rainbird's treachery. The man's disloyalty was beyond belief. He found it almost inconceivable that an experienced officer should behave so. Useless to remonstrate. The man was beyond shame.

Dusk, though, had stolen up unnoticed. The north was aflame with lambent fire, glowing through a screen of papery rose and salmon. The fire burnt upon the ice, an avenue of coals glowing red in the twilight. Meanwhile, a dense mass of heavy, impenetrable floes was moving steadily southward. Not far to the east was Rensselaer Bay where Kane had spent two terrible winters, living on rats, his party fragmenting, falling apart.

Suddenly the Lieutenant saw, with terrible clarity, the rocks which lay in wait for his command. *His* command. He felt another surge of anger. He couldn't have that. Mutiny? Desertion? Men splitting into separate parties, drifting off on some desperate venture with no proper leadership, no notion of where they were, or what they were about? He wouldn't stand for it.

A light snow was falling the following morning as Parish summoned his officers to a private council. Noticing that Emmons and Reade were also in attendance, Rainbird wondered uneasily what it might signify.

The six men huddled under the weather awning of the launch. It was bitterly cold.

'Before we begin,' the commander began, in a stiff voice intended to draw attention to past treacheries, 'I shall ask Lieutenant Foxer to take shorthand notes. In the past my understanding of what was said on these occasions has been called in question.' He resisted an impulse to glance meaningfully at the surgeon. He was determined to rise above petty recrimination. 'This time there will be a written record for those to whom it may fall to read it in due course.'

An uncomfortable silence followed this, an unmistakable hint that some posthumous significance might possibly attach to their deliberations.

Clearly, he went on, their position was very grave. It was for that reason he had called them together. He wished to hear their opinions. But before doing so he wished to point out the indispensable necessity for unity. Whatever course of action he decided upon must have their full support.

'I will start,' he said, 'with the most senior officer. Lieutenant Rainbird?'

'Make for the shore,' the athlete was in no doubt. 'Move from floe to floe.'

He might have had in mind a series of frog hops.

The surgeon, too, was for seeking the shore.

'If it were me,' he said, as clearly it should have been, 'I would send a boat over the ice to the water's edge and try to reach land.'

Parish turned to Foxer. But the young man's natural spirits

seemed clouded over. He had spoken little since their beset-
ment, and had nothing to say now. He would go along with
whatever the Lieutenant thought best.

'I'm against moving yet,' said Reade firmly, not waiting to be
asked.

The photographer had spoken out of turn, yet with a conviction the Lieutenant found reassuring.

'While there's a chance of a lead, I say wait for it. We have
supplies. The pack's still moving. We can get a darn sight further
day for day by boat, than ever we could on foot. I don't relish
hauling a sledge until I have to.'

The laconic Emmons took the same view. 'I think we should
stay put.'

Parish had not expected complete agreement. Moreover,
nothing had been said that changed the view he'd already
formed as to the course of action he must follow. But he was
reassured to know that the men he trusted most thought as he
did. Reade was right. The floes were still unstable, the pack constantly shifting. It would be foolish to exhaust the men in
fruitless endeavours. Slowly, surely, the current was carrying
them south-west. He still believed there was a party, if not a
ship, waiting with supplies at Littleton Island.

The thought of a welcoming band of fellow countrymen
only brought home his own isolation. He had called for unity.
He thought it unlikely he would get it. Rainbird would continue stirring up trouble. The surgeon too. Their chief wish was
to bring him down, whatever it cost. So far, they had not acted
openly. Sooner or later it must come to a head.

For the first time he noticed the moon riding up into the twilight, so faint as to be scarcely credible. Only the sullen grinding
of the floes conveyed an impression of absolute permanence.

*

Beset for fifteen days, they drifted hither and thither as wind or
tide decided.

Now, the daylight hours were increasingly overtaken by long washes of rose and salmon, of indigo and copper, staining the lonely immensity of the north above their heads. The sky above awoke a sky inside their minds. In their fixedness and yearning some of the men imagined they could see smoke far off to the south. Fromm swore he'd heard the barking of a dog.

Concerned to eke out the rations, the Lieutenant now sent his Eskimos to look for game.

From the outset the Inuit hunters had grown increasingly uneasy. They were baffled by practices which seemed incomprehensible: travelling while encumbered with quite useless belongings, articles that had nothing to do with food, or getting food, or shelter. They felt the reality of things eluding them. Now, rejoicing in their freedom, they became themselves again, hunting seals along the living edge of land and sea. Most days they went off over the ice, carrying their kayaks.

The other men, all too conscious of their own helplessness, were heartened to see the figures skimming freely over the black, oily water of a distant lead.

These daring forays amid the sharp-edged ice won the admiration of Lt Rainbird.

'He's a brave fellow,' murmured the ex-oarsman, with what could have been regret for former glories.

'Interestingly, there is no Inuit word for "brave",' observed the surgeon. 'They say *pissortut Inuit*. Doing what is needful. Doing what an Eskimo should do.'

On the third day a jubilant Qisuuk brought back a seal. At Fort Chance, when offered seal meat, most of the men had been revolted by the taste. Now, when Wutz served it in a fricassé with some bacon, they made no difficulty, but wolfed it down with relish.

Then, for three days, the pack was stationary. The winter floes seemed fixed. The men went walking on the new ice, now six inches thick, staring dolefully at the western shore where an isolated lead showed off Cape Camperdown, the only open water in a waste of close-packed ice. The mercury fell to minus eighteen: a sign, the Lieutenant confided to Foxer, fatal for any hopes they might have of continuing by boat. That morning he set the carpenters to work stripping the launch.

As the men began unloading the *Martha Parish*, the Lieutenant felt a clutch of apprehension. He was burning his boats, or all but one of them; and that one might carry, at most, a third of his party. Yet the decision made itself. He could only take one boat, and that the lightest.

Meanwhile, the tins containing the scientific records were being moved to the ice-boat. The pendulum too. The Lieutenant felt a qualm as he watched two of his strongest men straining to hoist the heavy case on to their shoulders. But there was nothing else for it. If the records were to count for anything, the instruments had to be checked for accuracy on their return. But everything else, the natural history specimens, the fossils, must be abandoned. He was faintly surprised it should still matter so to him. But it did.

For two days in succession the thermometer showed no rise. That night, having offered the customary words of praise, the Lieutenant addressed his men.

'We have waited long enough. Now the time has come for action. Tomorrow we must abandon the boats, and take to the sledges. So, let us have no repining over what is past. Let us put our trust in Divine Providence, and each one do his utmost, come what may.'

They pulled with a will, the officers taking their place in the drag-ropes. After so many days of inactivity, every man was taxed to the utmost.

'Remember, men,' gasped the Lieutenant, at the first halt, 'however laborious our progress, with every step we are closer to home.'

As encouragement it was somewhat vitiated by the fact that they had to travel twice over the same ground to shift all their load. Even so, the Lieutenant thought they might make three miles a day. Sergeant Asher had judged their position to be eighteen miles north-west of Cape Sabine. Bearing in mind the relieving steamer was expected to leave Smith Sound by the middle of the month, he still believed they had a chance of making the rendezvous.

Each day they hauled their loads over the hummocky, hateful ice, with nothing but the hard, enamelled pack for their horizon, and the sun, a pale chrome disc, dipping in a steel blue sky. A foot of snow added to their labours. They were hauling the weight of sea and sky, and approaching darkness.

Scouts went ahead with axes, chopping away the worst of the rubble ice, though they could do little to aid the progress of men whose steps were at best slow and uncertain. On sunless days no shadows formed to give definition to the surfaces they struggled over. Up and down, broken or level, were alike. Men stumbling, cursing, wrenched this way and that, would stagger on, their minds fixed on the hot stew Wutz would have prepared, or the measure of rum waiting at the end of each day's march. Each night they took what rest they could, some in a crude tepee fashioned from poles and the sails from the launch, some in the ice-boat, some sleeping out on the sledges.

The Lieutenant was as exhausted as the rest. In addition, he was ground down by his unceasing responsibilities. They had food for forty days. Time, though, was more crucial than rations. Each night the interval of darkness lengthened appreciably. He'd all but given up hope of reaching Cape Sabine before the deadline. With the ship gone he would find no shelter there. His hopes shifted now to Littleton Island. Failing that, they were left with winter, and the polar night. 'No, not that,' he muttered in his prayers. 'Let it not be that.'

Inevitably, the huge expenditure of effort began to take its toll. The surgeon reported several cases of frosted feet. The Lieutenant detailed those worst affected to sleep in the ice-boat, where they would at least have dry wood under them, and some measure of protection. At the day's end, huddled under the canvas cover, the exhausted men asked themselves how much worse it was going to get.

'I will tell you,' informed the surgeon. 'Much worse. Much, much worse. Only the Lieutenant won't admit it.'

One evening, having struggled all day in the teeth of a bitter wind, they made a crushing discovery. While they were toiling in their ropes, the pack had been drifting north. In a few hours they'd been driven further from Cape Sabine than they'd made towards it in as many days.

That night, since someone had to answer for their misery, some in the ice-boat fell to abusing the Lieutenant in the bitterest terms.

'He is not to be blamed,' a voice said, coming out of the night. 'The poor man does his best,' the astronomer thought to add, if diffidently. 'But what a situation he is faced with.'

Out of the darkness came a continuous rumbling, dull and harsh; the grinding of monstrous jaws.

That night a south-westerly sprang up. By dawn it was blowing hard. Within an hour or two the configurations of the western shore, glittering in the sun, showed very plainly the extent of their drift. Clear skies enabled Asher to take a noon observation. He placed them twenty miles north of Cape Sabine, at a point roughly equal to where they had abandoned the launch. They were back where they'd started.

'I think it best not to speak of this to the men,' said the Lieutenant. 'I shall acquaint them with our position when it confirms a more cheerful view.'

If he couldn't lift men's spirits, it was better not to depress them.

But the Spirit dogging their journey south had determined on discouragement. One morning, as they were preparing to set out, Diggs was dismayed by the sight of their own tracks coming back, as it seemed, towards them. It caused an outcry among the men, convinced that they were being led in the wrong direction.

'This is crazy,' cried Edge, who'd had almost enough. 'We're heading back the way we came.'

'No, no,' insisted Jacob Joseph, 'the floe has revolved. That is all.'

Even so, he had to demonstrate, with the aid of a compass and by diagrams drawn in the snow, that they were going the right way.

It was almost dark when they reached the edge of the last floe. Ahead lay open water. A headland loomed through the dusk.

Fabius was all for making for the shore.

'It can't be more than four miles away. Rainbird and I are prepared to take as many men as the boat will safely hold, and attempt a landing. If successful, we would then return for the rest of the party.'

The Lieutenant turned him down. In a loaded boat, across four miles of stormy water, with the pack constantly in motion? It was out of the question.

No poles or canvas were put up that night. They made their camp on the edge of the floe. The men were so cold and exhausted they lay in a stupor, the greater part of them on the bare ice.

At first light, as the cooks prepared breakfast, the men struggled to erect their shelter. A fresh north-westerly had got up in the night. It soon became clear they'd been carried out to sea again, and that the Sabine shore, no longer visible through the whirling snow, was now well to the west. The Lieutenant peered through the snow at a vague bastion looming to the south-west. He was at a loss to know what it could be. Then it dawned on him he was looking at Cape Isabella. It could only be Cape Isabella.

As the implications fell into place, he was seized with growing alarm. Beyond Cape Isabella, the Sound debouched into Baffin Bay. Once carried into those waters, everything they were counting on, food, shelter, the relieving party at Littleton Island, would be lost to them. Either they reached land, or they would be swept south into Baffin Bay.

While the men were eating, he embarked on a desperate calculation. Even now the falling tide was carrying them further south. Either they made a final effort to reach land, or be swept into the bay.

After breakfast, he summoned his council. He explained the situation with his usual brisk despatch.

'This is the position. We have been blown south into Smith Sound. The headland to the south west is almost certainly Cape Isabella. Beyond that, the Sound debouches into Baffin Bay. Should we be swept into those waters there is no hope for us. We must move quickly. I propose to take our records, plus twenty days' rations, and make for the Greenland shore.'

He could see from the stunned faces they were entirely oblivious of the danger.

'But we must be twenty miles at least from Greenland.' Rainbird was incredulous.

'We are drifting south,' repeated the Lieutenant. 'In three days, while making only four miles west, we have been carried twelve miles further south. Taking into account the topography of the coast, the further south we drift the closer we get to Greenland. A drift of a further thirty miles, along our present meridian, would place us two miles west of Littleton Island. Greenland, and not Cape Sabine, is our likeliest landfall. Now do you see?'

He might have been instructing a more than usually stupid class.

'I don't know,' began Foxer uncertainly. 'What about the other sledge?'

'We leave it.'

'But the load, all the supplies …'

'Abandon everything.'

The blackened, bearded faces were regarding him with unconcealed dismay. No amount of tortuous calculation could second-guess wind and tide. Another day might find them over again on the western shore.

'Emmons?' The Lieutenant turned to his senior non-com. 'Reade?'

He was appealing over the heads of his officers to the only men he trusted now.

'It is a great pity,' sighed the surgeon, 'that my suggestion was not acted on last night. We might now be safely on shore.'

Parish surveyed him coldly from behind his bottle lenses. Oh, yes. He, Rainbird, and their friends from the ice-boat. Lawless. Edge. That hulking malingerer Hanson. Meanwhile the wind would have set the rest of us further offshore.

The Lieutenant had begun to grasp the nature of the drama now unfolding around him, with its cast of characters over which he could exert, at best, a minimal control.

'I can see you are all against me on this,' he said stiffly. 'Nevertheless, I believe mine is the only feasible plan, for the reasons I have already given. Besides, we have seen no signs that there is anything for us at Cape Sabine. At Littleton Island there almost certainly is. We shall set out as soon as the blizzard has abated.'

The wind strengthened as the day wore on. It grew so violent it was impossible to light the stove. The Lieutenant ordered pemmican and water to be served to the men where they lay in their sleeping bags, listening to the roaring of the waves, and the furious shrieking of the wind. A number of them were now wretched in the extreme from sickness and cramping stomach pains. The whirling snow soon found its way into the bags, which were drenched with spray from the heavy seas crashing against the edges of the floe.

Some of the men were hating the Lieutenant worse than ever.

Drifting off from his command, William Parish would have given up all dreams of high endeavour in preference to lying quietly with his wife. They were riding the floe together. Their hands touched in the black night. He reached over intending to stroke her cheek, only to groan in spirit, encountering a void.

As darkness fell the gale increased in violence. The pack, a monstrous animal, shoving, jostling, was constantly on the move. The men were tense and frightened as never before, lying in the darkness, hearing the booming of the floes transmitted through the ice directly under their heads.

Morning found them east of Rosse Bay, with Cape Sabine falling behind to the north-west.

Westward, a pewter light fell on a foaming sea in which no

small boat could have lived for more than minutes. The falling tide had carried them south, and now the wind, which had shifted to the north-west, was driving the pack towards the centre of Smith Sound, and its notorious counter-currents. The Lieutenant, with Reade and Emmons, went over the floe to assess the situation. The noise was deafening. It seemed to be all around them, distant and close at hand, a ceaseless drumming coming from all directions.

The gale was driving heavy breakers over the seaward edge of the floe. The dark water frothed and foamed about the boots of the three men as they made their inspection. In places the ice had buckled, heaving up ridges of debris. Elsewhere the frozen snow was fissured with a network of narrow cracks.

All day long the pounding and the grinding went on. Fast in the pack, subject to conflicting pressures, the floe was being reduced to fragments. A crack would open a few yards, then the two parts come crashing together, one heaved up and up, almost to the vertical, then collapsing in huge chunks tumbling about the ice as the floe pitched and shuddered under the repeated blows. In the ice-boat the sick men lay in a stupor. The grinding of the pack was terrible to hear. Where edges met, the fractured ice had begun to accumulate as tons of rubble which, whenever the floes were carried momentarily apart, fell crashing into the sea in an explosion of spray. Then the floes clashed together again with a shock at which the sick men groaned in unison.

Shortly before dusk the Lieutenant conferred with Reade and Emmons as to their chances of evacuating to a larger floe across a narrow causeway of rubble, held in place by the enormous pressure.

As they were rolling up the tent a crack appeared under their feet. Now even the sick worked with a desperation born of terror. Boat, sledge, supplies, were shifted over the causeway by men who groaned, cursed, stumbled, uttered piteous little prayers as they shoved and heaved their loads over the rubble ice.

As dusk fell, the party finally gathered on the larger floe, a huddle of shivering flesh. Qisuuk was the last to cross. As he darted over the causeway with his kayak, the pressure eased momentarily. The Inuk uttered a single, wailing cry as he dropped through the ice and disappeared.

TEN

With General Sweetsir absent on a tour of installations, the Signal Office was ill-equipped for a crisis. His deputy, a modest officer in his middle years, was adjusted to the day-to-day routines of office business. His work had to do with supplies of wire and poles, and the provisioning of parties in the field. He was quite unprepared for the terse dispatch that came over the wire from St John's.

Petrel foundered. All taken off. Yarborough arrived safely St John's.

Greatly puzzled, Miles jotted down such questions as the wire left unanswered. *Who* had been taken off? Did that mean Parish and his men? Had Leffingwell pulled it off, despite the loss of the *Petrel*?

A second wire, three hours later, left him little the wiser. The *Petrel* had been crushed in the pack, but the crew and all Army personnel were safe. It seemed Leffingwell had somehow made his way across Melville Bay to Upernavik, where he'd joined up with the *Yarborough*.

Uncertain what to do, Miles had the presence of mind to wire back a crucial query.

What about Parish? What has been done for him?

Shortly after noon a further telegram conveyed the full extent of the fiasco. No stores had been landed, other than a few hundred rations cached at Cape Sabine. There was no news of Parish. Leffingwell believed it was now too late in the season to accomplish anything more.

Now badly rattled, Miles sought a meeting with the Secretary for War.

Summoning his departmental chiefs Elijah Crowell laid the telegram before them, and asked for their advice. By the end of the afternoon he had himself drafted a wire which went unerringly to the heart of the matter.

Why were no stores landed at Littleton Island? Did Yarborough leave supplies elsewhere? Is it feasible that sealer be chartered and provisioned for a year, dogs, sleds and drivers to be picked up en route, vessel to make northernmost attainable point on Greenland coast, from whence you lead small party with supplies to Littleton Island, or meet Parish?

Leffingwell's reply came in the following morning.

Sailing north now problematical. Dangers of ice navigation greatly enhanced with dark nights fast approaching. Chances slim, but am ready to make attempt if ship can be procured. However, officers and crew must be Navy personnel. Foreign civilians unreliable. Speedy decision crucial.

As the Secretaries for War and the Navy met to consider its implications, correspondents of the national newspapers had begun to gather in the lobbies of the State/War/Navy building. Somehow, a copy of the wire had found its way into the office of Associated Press. Though Congress was in recess, the news had begun to permeate the usual circles. There was talk of a tragedy in the making. The safety of the expeditionary party was giving rise to grave concern down at the War Department where, it was rumoured, hopes of a rescue had all but been abandoned.

The Navy Secretary, his back to the marble fireplace, was lighting one of the strong cheroots to which he was addicted. 'Read it again, Walt,' he grunted.

The chief clerk cleared his throat, and piped out in a reedy voice the telegram that had just come in from the commander of the *Yarborough.*

Second attempt so late in season would risk another disaster. Melville Bay impassable by end of month. Latitudes further north effectively closed to further efforts whether boat or sledge.

'That would seem to settle the matter,' declared the Secretary for War.

He wanted it settled. He had other things to see to. The Indian Bureau were pressing for action against Geronimo and the Chiricahua. He found the whole affair intensely irritating.

Secretary Hynes chewed on his cheroot. 'I guess so,' he muttered.

He would not himself have been averse to a stab at glory, having already elicited the intelligence that several whalers, fully coaled, were waiting at St John's. But without a genuine commitment from the officers on the ground, he could come out of it badly.

In Hartfield they were laying pipes all over the town. The moment the gang of teams and shovellers commenced digging up the road outside the house the widow Stevens had taken to her bed. Dr Bigsbee had diagnosed 'revenge of the nerves'.

Matty was doling out her drops into a tumbler of water.

'But Mr Harmer must get it done before the frosts set in,' she was explaining patiently to the invalid, when Lizzie Boot came up with the wire.

The next morning readers opening their Sunday papers were sucked into the most compelling drama since the shooting of the president. The US polar expedition had become grist to the mill of every editor who had some knowledge of the Arctic, or had none.

The sharpest speculation centred on the obscure Army lieutenant. What had become of Parish? Was he still at Fort Chance, or had he set off south? What would he do on reaching Cape Sabine, only to find neither ship nor shelter? Would he try to cross to Littleton Island, or would he seek the aid of the Etah Eskimos as Kane had done before him? The Lieutenant's character was the subject of relentless examination. Much was made of his defective vision, and a constitution which, while said to be allied to great energy and ambition, might not be sufficient for the strain now imposed upon it. Some believed he would try to make it back to Fort Chance. Some thought his best plan was to stay on at Cape Sabine, trying to subsist on whatever caches he could fetch in from the surrounding area, until a boat came to pick him up. Others had it he'd already crossed the Sound, and was moving south, following Leffingwell's line of retreat down the Greenland coast. It was imperative a sledging party be sent to meet him. It would need, they said, a good man. Others declared a further attempt that year was out of the question. The Secretary for War, they claimed, had already ordered Leffingwell's return.

'I'm asking you to think again, Elijah.' Senator Clay was closeted with the Secretary for War. 'Wait until the spring and I very much fear you'll find nothing but corpses.'

Elijah Crowell stared unblinking at his visitor.

'I don't accept your assessment of the situation, Senator.' He leant back in his chair, and clasped his hands across his chest.

'And I will tell you why. Parish's position is by no means as black as has been painted. Let us look at the full picture. Let us suppose he left Fort Chance before the beginning of September, in accordance with his instructions. He would have had plenty of daylight. He may have reached Cape Sabine already, perhaps as long ago as a fortnight. He will have learnt of that fool Leffingwell's fiasco, and formed a judgement as to his best course. Should he decide to continue south towards the Greenland settlements, he will have over seven hundred rations at Cape Sabine, and another two hundred on an island just off-shore. In short, sufficient food for approximately fifty days.'

His desk was littered with sheets of memoranda, yet the Secretary spoke with never a downward glance.

'Most probably, though, he will choose to return to Lady Franklin Bay, a distance of something less than two hundred and fifty miles. At Fort Chance, as well as fuel, clothing and medical supplies, he has canned meat, fruit, vegetables, bread, milk, chocolate, a range of beverages, and a variety of the best preserved foods. Enough for a full year.'

'You're very well informed, Elijah,' Lucius Clay said dryly.

'I believe I know my business, Senator.'

'You take a cool view, I must say, with men's lives at stake.'

'I don't believe they are at stake. It's those you'd have me send on a fruitless adventure who'd be at greater risk. I decline to gamble with their lives, Senator. I will not do it.'

In Hartfield the life of the spirit was undergoing its weekly starching. Martha Parish sat in her pew, eyes fixed on the pulpit where Reverend Dwight, turning this way and that, was toiling up the mountain of Truth. *The Army*, she remembered William saying, *looks after its own*. Surely they would not forsake him now? She'd recognized immediately that the chief purpose behind the Secretary's telegram was to dispel any suggestion that the party had been abandoned to its fate. Yet his whole line of reasoning was false from start to finish. He thought it most probable that Lt Parish had remained in station, though William's orders specifically instructed him to leave Fort Chance. Yet, in the unlikely event of him having set off southward, he assured her William would almost certainly retrace his steps to Fort Chance, where he had ample supplies to sustain the party until the summer of next year. He spoke of William *fortified* by supplies cached on route, of his being *comforted* in the knowledge that the most strenuous efforts would be made to reach him at the first practicable opportunity, though she *knew*, from the most powerful intimations while at prayer for her husband's safety, that he was in peril.

Reverend Dwight, though, had finally reached his summit. Even in the fires of affliction God was to be glorified. And who would presume to question the great Designer of events, whose wise purposes would one day be made clear.

If, Martha Parish was wavering, she could endure till then. Yet for that purpose, it was borne in upon her, were they given to one another.

*

Under a dismal crag, devoid of vegetation, the officers and men of the United States Arctic expedition were camped among the stones of a desolate boulder field.

They'd eaten a scanty meal of meat and potatoes, their first hot meal in days, and now they had dispersed to such shelter as was afforded them, some in the makeshift tent, others under the canvas cover of the ice-boat, some half-dozen, Parish among them, out on the naked rock. The Lieutenant deemed it his duty now to endure the worst with his men.

It had taken all the effort he could muster to rally them when, making land at last, they'd slumped exhausted among the boulders. The loss of Qisuuk had shaken them badly. The malignant Spirit, appeased, at least for the time being, had cast them forth upon the nearest shore, and they lay where flung down, with the passivity, the resistlessness of the defeated. Going among them in the cheerless half-light, he understood how that lone, light-footed dash across the ice, swallowed up in churning water, had plunged them all into the severing mystery in the midst of life. He was acutely conscious of the need to hold them together. Even the doctor, despicable fellow though he was, had to be drawn in.

His gaze shifted to the figure who lay beside him out on the stones. For a moment he thought of making a fresh approach to Rainbird. Breaking through to the sturdy figure who'd ridden out of the blizzard that time on the Powder River. If he and Rainbird were quite unlike, it had not mattered then.

But the drawn face had turned aside. There was no welcome there.

Sighing inwardly, Parish rejected the idea. He would not risk another rebuff.

He put their position at some twenty miles south-west of Cape Sabine. It was no more than an estimate. The sun was now so low, even at midday Sergeant Asher had not been able to take a reading. Parish badly needed to know what stores had been landed at the cape, and what intelligence, if any, might be gleaned as to their relief. That very morning George Reade had set off north with Mitsoq to find out what he could.

The Lieutenant uttered up a prayer of thanks for the continuing strength and cheerful fortitude of Sergeant Reade.

Rainbird had given up his place in the boat to the ailing Hewitt, where he would be sheltered from the worst of the weather. Huddled in his bag, face pinched with cold, the athlete's thoughts at that moment were also with George Reade. That they'd got this far was due largely to George. When the gale slackened, and their floe lodged against a grounded berg, it was George who'd piloted them ashore. Now he was off again, doing what he could.

There were certain moments, in the course of his death by a thousand cuts, when Lt Rainbird desired earnestly to be reborn.

The following day, the Lieutenant selected a site for his winter quarters. He settled on a low plateau on the south side of a glacier, a mile from where they had come ashore.

So the work began to build a hut. All day, labouring in temperatures made more bitter by the constant wind, the men dug into the snow and ice with bleeding hands to get at the heavy stones, then lugged them to the site. At the day's end, so stiff and aching they could scarcely stand erect, they crawled into bags rigid with ice, where they lay shivering until it was time to start work again. It was a wretched existence, scarcely preferable to death.

One morning the Lieutenant was compelled to reprimand Lawless publicly for remarks reflecting on Sergeant Emmons' fairness in issuing the ration.

The man declared sullenly he had only repeated what others were saying.

'He looks out for his friends,' he threw back defiantly, as he turned away. 'Everyone knows that.'

Parish chose not to hear. He judged it best.

The men stared at the rusty, boiling water that was served to them as tea, and muttered among themselves.

Later that day Rainbird shot at a walrus on the ice, but the creature sank before it could be recovered. The crack shot stared bitterly at the widening pool of blood.

The next morning Sergeant Emmons reported a small quantity of bread stolen from the store. A fox, he thought, to judge from the signs.

Ten days after they had set out, two figures were seen descending the glacier to the north.

The Lieutenant went out alone to meet George Reade. He was anxious to weigh up any news before it was imparted to the men.

For several minutes, watched tensely by the rest of the party, the two men spoke privately. Documents changed hands. Then all three joined their companions at the hut.

The commander gave the bad news first. The *Petrel* had gone down in the ice. However, no lives were lost. There were perhaps upwards of a thousand rations cached on an island, of which Cape Sabine formed the eastern tip.

A cheer went up from the men. Compared with their present miserable allowance, a thousand rations seemed the stuff of banquets.

Most remarkable of all, the Lieutenant went on, Sergeant Reade had found their abandoned whaleboat, still on its floe, which had come aground against a spit of land. He then read out in full the message left for them by Lt Leffingwell. It concluded with a postscript:

The USS Yarborough is, at this moment, on her way to Little-ton Island. A Swedish vessel too will shortly be cruising the North Water. I shall try to make contact as we go south. Rest assured I shall see to it that everything within the power of man be done to rescue the brave men at Cape Sabine.

The men could have swelled visibly, drinking in the lather of noble emotion. Lightheaded after sapping days on half ration, they flung their caps in the air, and gave three cheers for Lt Leffingwell. The relief was enormous. The marvel of the whaleboat abandoned on the ice, which the ice had now brought back to them, was taken as a sign. They felt certain now they would get through.

The ragged band hoisted George on to their shoulders, the astonished Inuk too, and bore them back in triumph to their miserable dwelling, cheering over and over again.

It was especially heartening to hear Lt Rainbird's confident remarking to the doctor:

'I know Leffingwell. Leffingwell's a good man. I'm damn

sure he's at Littleton Island at this very moment. I'd stake my life on it. He'll be over here the moment it's possible to cross.'

The Lieutenant, though, was doing his calculations. Leffingwell's note spoke of five hundred rations, plus a further two hundred and fifty left by the *Rattler*. Then there was the English cache left at Cape Sabine, the cache he'd failed to examine on the outward voyage. Reade put it at two hundred and fifty. A thousand rations would not go far, unless supplemented by game. And there was little daylight left for hunting. He foresaw a winter of starvation. The fuel supply alone would scarcely see them through.

Such considerations were weighing heavily later that day as he climbed the promontory, and stood on the headland overlooking the sea. The visibility was unusually clear. To the south-east, across the Sound, the blunt foreland of Cape Alexander stood up like a watch tower marking the Greenland coast. He picked out the rocky summit of Littleton Island, and the indentation of Lifeboat Cove a little to the north.

Had Leffingwell got through? Had he met up with the *Yarborough*?

Out of the Sound came the dull thunder of the pack, grinding on the falling tide. In the dark lanes between the floes, long streaks of grey slush ice were lining up with the wind.

He stood watching the ruffle of light over the young inshore ice, rippling like watered silk on the dark sea swell. Had the navy ship got though to Littleton Island? Was there a party waiting to come to their assistance? He had no way of knowing. All he knew was that he must abandon the huts that had cost his men so much effort to build, and move north to Sabine. If help was indeed on its way, that was where it would come.

✳

When Lt Leffingwell arrived back in Washington, friends were shocked by his changed appearance. Though the golden hair was well groomed as ever, the dazzling fair skin they remembered was now tanned as any hide, the consequence, they explained to one another, of weeks of exposure in an open boat.

The newspapers had more or less written off Lt Parish. Now they took up with relish the task of excoriating the scoundrel who had almost certainly sealed his fate, a blackguard who'd so far forgotten his responsibilities as to bring back from the wrecked ship a large dog, kept alive on food which should have been left to feed Parish and his stranded men. Leffingwell, it was confidently predicted, was sure to face a court martial.

The young lieutenant was expecting a roasting. Nonetheless, he refused to skulk in holes or corners, but went about the town, as if to demonstrate the composure of a man who had done no wrong, a man whose integrity would be vindicated when the facts were known. The great Newfoundland trotted at his side, pink tongue lolling, glossy coat aglitter. Rags had become something of a celebrity in the fashionable Washington salons to which the young man found ready admittance.

He sat, an elegant figure, picking off questions with such casual ease it was difficult for his admirers to credit that he'd brought his men five hundred miles through ice and fog, high winds and heaving seas. His worst moments? Being cold and hungry, mostly. His most vivid recollection? Oh, the grinding of the pack.

Yet of the circumstances that brought about the collapse of his mission, Lt Leffingwell would say nothing, not even when pressed directly by a young woman spunkier than the rest.

'And is it true what they say? Did you abandon Lt Parish to his fate?'

But the lieutenant only smiled. 'That's a matter for the Court of Inquiry. I can only say that I shall be vindicated when the facts are known.'

Though the facts continued a private anguish to Lt Leffingwell. Not least among his torments as he'd dashed to and fro, hauling out whatever could be salvaged, was the thought of the opprobrium he would suffer. The *Petrel* lost. Parish left without succour. Those were the worst hours of his life.

Acutely conscious of his obligations, yet scarcely knowing

what to do, he'd filled a whaleboat with such stores as came to hand and set off for the nearest land. Pure chance brought him ashore close to the cache left by Bright the year before.

Then followed a frantic time, regaining the floe, loading the boats with as many boxes as they could carry, then working his way to land on the ebbing tide, with the floes surging round. There, on the rocky tip of Cape Sabine, he'd stood in the rain and watched the ice littered with the rest of his supplies sweeping past into the Sound.

Times without number he'd asked himself, what else could he have done? To have waited at Sabine would have accomplished nothing, except to eat into such stores as he'd managed to salvage. If Parish stuck to his orders it might have been six or seven weeks before he arrived at the cape. To have set off north in the hope of meeting him? Out of the question. The likelihood of a chance meeting on that coast he still judged pretty slim. Besides, he had no dogs, no sledges. The sole, practicable course of action open to him had come as a moment of intense conviction, and he'd seized it with relief. The only hope of achieving anything lay with the *Yarborough*. He must cross to the Greenland coast, and travel south to intercept Young as he came up the coast to Littleton Island. He could leave a substantial depot for Parish at Littleton Island, then return to St John's for help.

Comforted by this resolve, Leffingwell had filled his boats with food for the journey, made a cache of the jumble of goods he'd salvaged from the wreck, and built a cairn on the headland.

There, on that bleak point of windswept rock, with the chill rain sweeping across, he left his message acquainting Parish with the news which, for very shame and mortification, he could scarce bring himself to relate.

The postscript was the addition of a moment. It had poured out unreflectingly, that impulse of the heart to offer whatever comfort an inspiring message might convey.

As it turned out, there was no Swedish steamer. And Commander Young in the *Yarborough* had steamed past Leffingwell, enveloped in a fog.

Ten days later, reunited at Upernavik, the two men agreed regretfully it was too late in the season to turn back north.

✳

General Sweetsir was reflecting that Elijah Crowell had been hostile from the start.

'I want you to know,' he assured Martha Parish, 'that every man at the Signal Office was for making another attempt.' He looked at her beseechingly. 'It could have been done. The ships were available. The precedent was there.' He believed William was already on the Greenland coast making his way south, and was desperately troubled that no stores were left at Littleton Island, a blunder for which he blamed himself.

'The government put them in this position,' she said consolingly. 'However slight the chances, they were duty bound to go to their aid.'

'I have every confidence in your husband.'

'Oh, so have I,' she said stoutly. 'If any man is able to endure a third winter in the Arctic, that man is Mr Parish.'

It was her own endurance that seemed in question. She had all but begun to buckle under the weight as the families, hanging on to one another for support, clung most of all to the wife of the commander; who was most emphatically *not* a Lady Franklin, and had no one to uphold and comfort *her*. Letters had poured in from next-of-kin, letters filled with a sense of numb desertion at loved ones abandoned. *I tried so hard to keep him from going*, wrote Sarah Sedgewick. *Not knowing*, wrote Mrs Foxer, *is the worst*. Though not knowing, thought Martha Parish, could come to never knowing in the end. And could not have replied to every letter, filling pages with hollow words of comfort and encouragement, only that William would have been so terribly disappointed in her.

One morning, on opening another envelope, she was greeted with the following:

Esteemed lady,

What troubles your heart most is that your dear William has left his station and is now suffering with cold, with hunger, perhaps sickness, in that dreadful place. Be comforted, dear lady. He is safe. He is with the Eskimos. My wife has seen him, and doubtless could show you more if you will allow us to call on you …

Her first shock of surprise, then anger, revulsion, soon crumpled into a pitiful longing to be told, indeed *shown*, what her heart yearned to be assured of.

Why the wife, she wondered. The poor wife who, *lightly clad*, had begun *to shiver dreadfully from the cold.* No doubt it struck as more convincing in a woman, the working of inexplicable powers in creatures who had such little strength themselves. Oh, that it were so, and that a woman's heart could be a vessel for revelations.

No second sight could fill the gap that separated her from William.

Yet emptiness, it seemed, tightened the bonds that held, even at the cost of pain. Whatever it was vouchsafed her *that*, it was closer than close. But oh, the longing: longing without promise of remission.

The loneliness was crushing. And the temptation to return to Hartfield was very great. Only it seemed too much like giving him up for dead. Constancy was all. Besides, nothing that happened in Hartfield could possibly have any bearing on William's fate.

Even so, she might have gone back where friends and family waited with a sort of life to offer, had it not been for Senator Clay. That fall, his quiet fireside became a haven where, for a while at least, she could escape the loneliness.

Often she would arrive to find him at his desk.

'Some day,' she smiled, noting the pile of manuscript, 'we shall all be in your debt.'

Her gaze lingered a moment on the photographs in their oval frames: one, a sweet-faced woman, dressed in a style of half-a-century ago; the other, a young man in the uniform of the Confederacy.

'He was killed at first Manassas.' The old man's voice was a quietly closing door.

Sometimes, though, over the tea things, he would hark back to kinder, more generous days when the lamentable events that had occupied his day were still undreamt of. *Before the Fall ...* as he put it. Almost, it might have been, before the war was *lost*.

'Did you never have regrets?' she dared to guess. 'You might have followed General Lee?'

The old man seemed taken aback, even as she recognized she had quite misunderstood.

'Lee went with his state,' he said abruptly. 'I went with my country.'

She saw then that he, too, had been thrust into a different, darker world: one that could never again be trusted.

✳

Days stretched to weeks, and weeks to months, as the Court of Inquiry laboured through interminable twists and turns. General Sweetsir haunted the hearings, sometimes accompanied by the faithful Miles, more often alone. He had become more and more an isolated figure.

As the evidence unfolded, those generally held responsible for the disaster seemed less and less inclined to accept their roles in the affair.

Commander Young, when challenged, invariably took to his quarter deck.

Yes, it was true he had come within an hour's sailing of Cape Sabine. Certainly, he could have landed stores.

'But look here,' he bristled. 'I had no orders to that effect. Besides, my first thought was for the shipwrecked men. They were my responsibility.'

He glared round, as if daring any man to challenge *that*.

'I may say,' he added, thrusting out his jaw, 'I had no fears then for Lieutenant Parish, nor do I have them now, knowing him to be well equipped, and stationed in an area abounding in game.'

'Be damned to his orders!' Sweetsir muttered fiercely. 'He turned back! He knew very well his fellow countrymen were counting on assistance, yet he turned back.'

Yet, as testimony emerged of arduous duties commendably performed, the tide of opprobrium began to ebb away from the principal witnesses. The disaster, it was becoming clear, had been brought about by feckless, rascally civilians. Captain Quine now stood unmasked as a half-educated incompetent, scarcely able to take a bearing.

He was, testified Lt Leffingwell, constantly bumping into rocks.

Stung by the criticism levelled at him by mere scribblers who had never set foot north of their own state line, let alone endured weeks in an open boat, bringing men to safety, the witness had begun to believe he had perhaps done rather well.

As he listened to Leffingwell's attorney steering his client clear of any culpability, General Sweetsir grew increasingly uneasy. Always now at the back of his mind, a blunder assuming ever more threatening proportions, was the grim fact that no supplies had been left at Littleton Island. Leffingwell insisted it was not in his Orders that he should have acted so. True, there was an inclosure instructing him to leave a depot there, but it was not signed. It was not dated. He had judged that memorandum subsidiary to his Orders, which required him to make all speed.

'Oh, the bastard,' groaned General Sweetsir. 'Oh, the son of a bitch.'

It was mid afternoon. Another dank November day was ending in a tide of darkness. Across the city Martha Parish was reading a letter from the mother of Lt Foxer: *Day follows day, and still not a finger lifted to help them. Worst of all is the agony of knowing that nothing is being done. We are told that because of winter cold and darkness everything must be held over until the spring. Only our dear ones cannot be 'held over'. They must go on enduring. I very much fear that when spring finally arrives there will be some, perhaps many, for whom endurance will have proved too much.*

Folding the letter, Martha Parish hoped it might be a comfort to the men to know they were held in the thoughts and prayers of others. Suddenly, she felt William very near. He had come so close she might have reached out to touch him. If they did not speak, it was only because there was no need for words.

The last of the light, spilling between ragged clouds, fell on the swollen waters of the Potomac. A livid glare lit up the dome of the Capitol. That whited sepulchre. Still the rain came drumming down. Then she began to suffer his abandonment afresh, suffering in her own spirit. A ghastliness came over her. In the midst of the populous town, its cruel indifference, she felt wholly alone.

ELEVEN

In the High North musk oxen had begun to gather in their winter quarters. Hares and ptarmigans too were moving uphill. Male polar bears were migrating to the edges of the floes, where seals had begun to form air-holes in the still-thin ice. Deep in the crevices of rocks foxes had laid in their store of eggs and carcasses. For weeks parties of geese and duck had been passing overhead in great numbers. The men were conscious now of the silence of the skies, and the emptiness of the land. Left alone amid the desolation, they felt the chill breath of winter, and the coming of snow.

They had been stunned, as the Lieutenant noted in his log, by the news they were moving on again.

> 5th. Oct. Eskimo Point. I have this morning given orders to strike camp. The men are devastated. It sickens me to abandon huts they laboured so to build, but I have no option. Even if we were able to ferry the caches here by boat, Leffingwell's note requires us to move north to Cape Sabine.

Sergeant Reade, with Brenner, had set off in the opposite direction. They were heading for Cape Isabella, fifteen miles to the south. It was, Reade argued, the most accessible point on that part of the coast, therefore the most likely site for the navy ship to land a cache.

Meanwhile, Parish had been studying his charts. With the shore ice not yet secure the easier route to Rosse Bay was not open to them. He estimated it would take several days to haul the sledge over the glacier, and then across to the island. By Reade's route it was a journey of more than twenty-five miles. Since it would require two journeys each leg of the way to haul their load, he had to think in terms of three times that distance.

For two days they struggled over the glacier. Setting off before first light, they hauled for as far as they could manage by midday, returning with the empty sledge for a second load. The wind sliced through the rents in their ragged clothing. In terms of distance covered, Parish estimated they were making about one mile an hour. At night they huddled together on the frozen ground, the blown snow drifting into their bags.

On the evening of the second day, they halted for the night beside a small lake on the far side of the moraine. Released at last from the ropes, the men stood about like exhausted beasts of burden. They could scarcely eat for weariness.

The Lieutenant was taking a reading from the thermometer, when he found himself confronted by the surgeon.

'Do you realize, Lieutenant, that you are killing these men?'

Taken aback, the tall commander stared down at his accuser.

'You will recall, of course,' Fabius went on smoothly, thrusting home a point he'd been sharpening for some time, 'that the English regarded forty-two ounces as a minimum requirement for sledge hauling. That is precisely twice … *twice* … the ration you are feeding to the men.'

The injury had the greater impact for being delivered discreetly, as from one colleague to another.

'I think you may allow me to do right by the men,' replied the Lieutenant stiffly.

That night, unable to sleep for the cold, he lay in an agony of uncertainty. Fabius, of course, had urged the matter in his usual antagonistic spirit. Yet the surgeon's charge continued to gnaw. *It is the truth I am telling you.* No doubt it was, in purely medical terms. At the same time, he had to be ruled by the need to conserve his supplies. At the last report they'd had enough food, in bread, meat and potatoes, for thirty-five days: about half the accepted Arctic ration, reckoning on thirty ounces per man, per day. Once in winter quarters, it would have to be reduced further still.

At four o'clock, roused by the stir of the cooks, he rose with them and spoke briefly to Emmons, who was weighing out the ration. They were the only ones up and about in the chill gloom. Sunrise was still some hours away. No man would stir from his bag until he had to.

The commander searched among the recumbent figures until he found the surgeon.

Squatting down, he muttered, 'I have decided to increase the ration. Henceforth, for as long as we are hauling, it will be set at twenty-seven ounces.'

'It won't be enough,' hissed the surgeon. 'But if that is what you intend to do, then my advice is that you reduce the hauling to a single load. The men are not capable of hauling everything. This heavy scientific equipment, in particular, should be abandoned.'

'That is also my opinion,' came a second voice, speaking from the gloom.

The Lieutenant might have guessed Rainbird was in it too.

He turned away, back to the glimmer of warmth where the cooks were squatting over the stove.

Rainbird, though, had struggled out of his bag, and was hastening after him.

'Lieutenant ... with respect ... I would ask you to reconsider. To halve the load might make all the difference. Surely things which are not essential to life could be cached now, and recovered later in the season?'

Why did I choose this man? thought Parish bitterly. As much for the question thrust so bluntly at him. It had been weighing with him since that first day toiling over the floe. Only he could not, *would* not, go back empty-handed.

Dawn rose at their backs. Below, a pearly glimmer in the gloom, lay the shore ice of Rosse Bay. Across the bay to the north, cut off from the mainland by a narrow strait, loomed the glaciated cliffs of a small island.

The Lieutenant could see no access there.

'Can you be sure of the trail?' he asked his guide.

Mitsoq, who had only to pass through a landscape once for it to be engraved in his memory, suffered this in silence.

He took a tortuous route, north-west through the strait, then round a headland to reach the northern shore of the island. Sharp flurries of snow drove at them as they crossed the bay, with the sun, a silver wafer, gleaming wanly through the swirl. Several times they met patches of young ice, whereupon the Lieutenant instructed the men on the drag ropes to fan out. Not daring to tread, they moved with a hobbled, shuffling gait over the black water clearly visible under the ice. Now and then a sudden gasp, an involuntary cry, told of a suddenly sagging surface. But no one stopped, or looked round, even.

It was dark when they finally came ashore. The cooks had been busy preparing the stew that now provided their daily sustenance. Supper took place in an exhausted silence, with the party huddled in their bags. Nate Emmons, contemplating one man or another, thought it very likely some of them would die. He made up his mind, as he'd done before in a tight corner, it would not be him.

Next morning the Lieutenant, with Sergeant Emmons, went ahead of the party to inspect Leffingwell's cache. They came upon the cairn just as Reade had described it, on top of a low cliff. Below, in a little cove, a dozen yards above the high water mark, they found the cache covered with a flysheet and weighted down with stones. A short distance away a snowbank, drifted over an all but covered whaleboat, marked the site of the depot left by the *Rattler*.

Together they removed the stones, and pulled back the flysheet from a pile of boxes and barrels. The cache had all too evidently been thrown together at random: hard bread, bacon, some canned goods, tea, raisins, a few sleeping bags, a box of lemons …

The Lieutenant, though, was totting up the tins of mutton.

'There's nothing like five hundred rations here.'

He took out Leffingwell's message from his pocket book.

'Five hundred rations of bread, sleeping bags, tea and a lot of canned goods.'

'He meant bread,' said Emmons dourly. 'Five hundred rations of bread.'

The famished men, though, greeted the sight of tins and barrels with simple joy, unclouded by arithmetic. Those deprived for weeks gazed longingly at a whole box of tobacco. The cheery Diggs even led them in hurrahs for the lemons.

The Lieutenant sent teams to ferry up the caches from the cove, and fetch in the whaleboat. Others he set to clearing a site for his winter quarters. He chose a level area on a neck of rock jutting out into the bluish ice of Buchanan Strait, not far from the caches, and close to a small lake of fresh water.

While the men were thus engaged, Reade returned with news of mixed fortune. He'd found no evidence of a landing. He had, though, uncovered a small cache of meat left by the English.

The Lieutenant climbed the glacier behind the camp in the fading light. He was thinking over the implications of Reade's news. He estimated the English cache at no more than a hundred and fifty pounds at the most. Six pounds of meat per man seemed a dubious reward when set against a winter journey of eighty miles to recover it. Asher had calculated they had eight days of sunlight left; eight days in which his frozen, half-starved men had a great deal of work to do. He decided they must make do with what they had.

From the top of the glacier he gazed across two miles or more of broken country to the bony digit of rock that was Cape Sabine pushing out into the Sound. South-east lay Littleton Island, an abrupt, rocky summit catching the last of the light. It would be spring before conditions would be right for a crossing. Was there a party there, capable of bringing them aid? He did not think it likely. Reade had found no sign of a landing at Cape Isabella. It was open to question whether the *Yarborough* had ever reached Littleton Island. In which case, even Leffingwell's fate remained uncertain. He might have reached Littleton Island, and be wintering there. Or, more likely, he would have been driven south. The most he could hope for at Littleton Island was the small depot left by the earlier expedition. If orders had been obeyed.

Down below the tiny figures of his men, strung out against

the biting wind, were hauling boxes and barrels up from the cove. He picked out the ever-willing Schmidt clearing rocks from the site. Over by the snow bank Diggs and little Wutz were building a shelter for their stove. The Lieutenant saw in their labour a touching pathos, struggling on because it was in the nature of men to do so. He cherished the possibility that out of this ragbag of imperfectly assembled human beings a sense of the common good might somehow crystallize. Though there was no guarantee. He could only pray that it would.

It took four days to build the hut, as the Lieutenant noted in his log.

> Oct. 15th. Work began in a temperature of twenty below. The remaining caches, together with the whaleboat, have been got in from the cove. As a sledging route to Cape Sabine is not yet passable I despatched a party comprised of the strongest men to fetch in as much of Leffingwell's cache of clothing as could be carried by pack: blankets, buffalo coats, bales of gloves, hats, footwear, even a couple of mattresses. I have distributed the clothing according to need. The mattress, by common consent, will be reserved for the sick. The men stick at it with commendable zeal.

Eyes swollen with cold, they laboured in the lengthening shadow of the glacier, cut off from what little warmth remained in the departing sun, lugging blocks cut from a drift of frozen snow, or bags of sand from the hill. They had acquired the stoical endurance of nomads for whom the first necessity is shelter.

Gradually there arose the low rock walls of what might have been a Stone Age hut, roughly rectangular, with a gap at one end for a doorway. The Lieutenant had given much thought to the construction of their winter lodging. Its proportions were governed by such materials as he had at his disposal. It could be no longer than the whaleboat, nor wider than the span of the oars, from which the blades had been sawn. The rough rock floor he had levelled with gravel, then carpeted with lumps of frozen sand, crushed underfoot. A framework of oars fixed to the walls served for rafters, on which was laid the upturned boat, its weight supported by a line of posts set down the middle. A covering of canvas, weighted down with snowblocks and secured to the oars, was laid over the boat to complete the roof.

That evening, before supper, the Lieutenant made a short announcement.

'You will, I'm sure, be heartened to know that this station has been designated in the expedition log as Camp Fortitude.'

It was what he looked for most in a soldier. Fortitude.

It was a hovel miserable enough by any standard. Yet, after eight nights in the open, any place seemed good to these men where the wind could not get at them, where they could lie in their bags free of the drifting snow. They were savouring an issue of chocolate and coffee, though in modest quantities, the Lieutenant considering stimulants aggravating to starving men. Sitting up, he ran his eye along the line of bags, toes to the centre, heads to the walls. It was cramped, certainly. His head was hard up against the roof. Only in the belly of the whale-boat, where Diggs was stacking dishes and provisions on the thwarts, could a kneeling man hold himself erect. But he was satisfied by what he saw. It struck him as disciplined and soldierly.

Even so, as the men ate their supper of stew, the Lieutenant reflected on the long night in which they would soon be swallowed up. He could not know what another winter might bring. No one had ever endured three winters in the Arctic. Nor could he be sure, as cold and hunger took its toll, whether he had what it took to bring them through this ordeal of starvation. Then it struck him that God gave nothing in advance, lest a man should come to rely on himself, and not on Him alone. Next to Divine Providence, he must put his trust in his own strength of will, which was considerable, and the disciplines of a military command. If they were all to perish here, then it would be done with decency.

Thus resolved, the Lieutenant put his mind to the business of surviving. His task now was to keep them together. It would be, he saw, a matter of painstaking planning: of scrupulous observance in minute particulars. Having made an inventory of all the food he set out about devising a subsistence diet, calculating the ration of meat, bread and potatoes to hundredths of an ounce. The Lieutenant weighed it out himself, on scales the ingenious Fromm had fashioned from a sheet of tin.

Twice a day, by the dim light of a blubber lamp fixed to a post, Wutz prepared a stew. Since the Lieutenant wished to conserve the lamp alcohol, he was forced to cook over a fire fuelled by wood cut from the staves of barrels, while the men coughed and hid their heads to escape the smoke. All heads, though, came out again for the dishing-up. Every eye was on the ladle. A man passing a plate down the line of bags would weigh it speculatively in the hand. Sergeant Emmons, slicing up the bread, was dourly aware of close inspection. The discrepancy of a single crumb was enough to nourish a grievance.

The Lieutenant, though, had embraced his new responsibilities almost with a measure of relief. He needed to have his teeth into something. For as long as the light held there was still a chance of pulling in some game. He deliberated with his officers the possibility of sending out a hunting party. It would be arduous in the extreme, camped at the Sound with little food, no warmth, no proper bedding.

He was reluctant to order any man to suffer additional hardship.

'I'll go,' offered Rainbird, who longed, sometimes, to cast off the burden of self.

He left with Mitsoq that afternoon.

At last the hardening of the ice allowed for a party, under the command of Lt Foxer, to fetch in the English cache from Payer Harbour.

Here, on the edge of the sea, Emmons found their whaleboat, still resting on its floe. He set about breaking it up for fuel, as the Lieutenant had instructed. Meanwhile, on the summit of a small island just off-shore, Foxer built a substantial cairn in which to cache the instruments and records. In among them he slipped a small package, wrapped in oilcloth: a journal of his 'Farthest North'. The long box containing the pendulum he set upright, a melancholy monument awaiting whatever posterity the Arctic storms or a passing ship might afford.

The English cache was pitifully small: three hundred sledging rations, and a couple of barrels of dog biscuits. When the first barrel was opened, at least half the contents were found to be covered with a green mould.

For once the surgeon was in agreement with his commander. 'Throw them out,' he sighed.

The men watched with avid faces as Emmons tipped them on to the snow. The Lieutenant was praying that a fox or a wolf would get to them first.

Thoughts ran constantly to food. They talked of nothing but food: of meals they'd eaten, or planned to eat when they got back. The famished men entertained one another in favourite restaurants, ordering raw clams and oysters by the dozen, bean soup, thick spicy sausages, served with apple and potato mash, roast goose and apple sauce with sweet potato pie, and bread pudding, with cups of chocolate to follow. When silence fell, they lay in their bags and dreamed of food. In his corner close to the door Sergeant Emmons stuffed down tripe and eggs. Jacob Joseph, in the candle light of Hannukah, lingered over dough-nuts and potato pancakes. Night after night young Foxer sent out for fancy cakes and pastries, only to wake before they arrived. Even the stoical commander, when no one was looking, slipped away to savour a *fromage de Brie* from Magruder's.

Meanwhile, work continued on the outer walls under skies of extraordinary beauty.

The sun had gone, and the firmament was stained with its leave-taking: level washes of indigo, shading to heliotrope and amethyst, above a bar of purest primrose yellow. The men were setting blocks of snow in place, filling the space between with snow and gravel. They'd added a passageway to an external entrance, with a small storeroom to one side.

The Lieutenant greeted the completion of outdoor work with relief. All they could do now was to sit it out and hope to win through.

That night, while the evening meal was in preparation, he lay in his bag and took stock of the situation. Now the heavy work of hauling and building was over, he knew he must impose a further cut in the ration.

Dimly lit by the glow of blubber lamps Wutz and Fromm were paring slivers of wood to heat the stew. Emmons was cutting up portions. He carved the hard bread with scrupulous exactitude. And the men watched him do it, eyes gleaming in the wasted faces.

The unpredictable element, the Lieutenant saw, lay with the men themselves. It was a disquieting illumination: men he'd rebuked for idleness, for drunkenness, men whose insubordinate comments he'd chosen not to hear. Now those same men had nothing to do but lie in their bags, wasting away from the starvation rations he was feeding them, and nourishing their grievances. And what of Fabius? Another conflict with the surgeon was now a looming certainty. And the thought of Fabius as spokesman for a party of discontented men was also deeply troubling to the Lieutenant. Even so, he was determined to eke out what food they had until March. Then, if the Sound was frozen over, rations for the last few days could be carried in a final attempt to reach Littleton Island.

He began counting the days. March 1st was a hundred and thirty-six days away.

That night, after supper, Parish revealed his plan. Quietly, he gave his reasons. It was possible rescue would come earlier. But, in the last resort, they must be prepared to fend for themselves. He would be failing in his duty not to make appropriate provision.

'So,' he concluded, 'from now on we must make do with less. As from tomorrow the ration will be reduced to fourteen ounces.'

He was bleakly conscious of the impact of his message.

'We cannot possibly live on that.'

Fabius was probably right. Though it was hard, it struck the Lieutenant, to have his medical officer speak so, when the responsibility was his and his alone.

He listened without interruption as the implacable voice set out, with clinical detachment, the diseases which would almost certainly seize hold. Recovery would be unlikely.

'I will not seek to minimize the dangers,' he said, at last. 'Nevertheless, I believe it to be our only chance.'

He waited, conscious of the eyes fixed on him in the darkness. He would not compel them. He did not believe he had the right to starve men without their agreement.

Yet military discipline will sometimes count for less than moral influence. Not for the first time the men were obscurely comforted by their commander's unflagging sense of purpose. He had interpreted their needs to them for so long now where else should they look?

'United we stand, divided we fall,' suggested Diggs. From the rest of the men came a half-rueful murmur of assent. They would go along with whatever the Lieutenant said.

With the extinguishing of the light a void of darkness descended on the hut. Though gratified, Parish was under no illusion as to their continuing confidence in him. As soldiers they expected to be asked to march till they dropped, or fight to the death. But he was asking a far harder thing: simply to lie in a bag and starve. Unable to sleep, he lay wondering which of his men were most likely to succumb. Hewitt and Sedgewick were both weakly. Nadel was complaining of chest pains, while Foxer, though he refrained from any utterance in the nature of complaint, was much reduced from his former vigour.

Before he fell asleep, the Lieutenant decided that whatever the dangers, the recovery of the cache of English meat was now a necessity. The next morning he would send four of his best men to Cape Isabella.

They whole party gathered to see them off. They stood awkwardly receiving handshakes and good wishes.

'Leave it to the Prussians,' said Muller heartily. 'Eh, Lothar? We shall bring home the meat.'

Lothar Schmidt grinned broadly. Never before singled out, he'd always known he was intended for some brave deed.

Far to the south, behind the glacier, a dim orange glow told of the sun tracking westward below the horizon. The sledge stood waiting. Muller and Schmidt were first in the drag-ropes. They waited as the Lieutenant cautioned George most solemnly that in the event of himself or any member of the party being incapacitated, he must return immediately.

'Remember,' he called after them, 'apply the warm hand to the face at regular intervals.'

They plodded into the darkness, and were soon swallowed up.

On a morning of bitter wind Rainbird arrived back at the hut.

The lieutenant's face showed plainly what he had endured. His cheeks were blackened by frost, his nose red raw against the leaden skin. Heavy breathing and a continuous dribble from his nose and mouth had built up a plaster cast of ice in which the bleached beard had frozen solid. But he had brought good news. They had made a kill. Though the credit, he was quick to add, must go to Mitsoq.

'We would have lost it, but for the harpoon. It would have sunk for sure.'

The Lieutenant had been hoping for walrus. Even so, he must be thankful for the seal. Now, for a day or two, they could look forward to fried steaks and liver, and rich soups thickened with the blood. He sent Emmons with a sledging party to bring it back.

When its stomach was cut open Wutz rejoiced to find a dozen fish, still more or less entire.

That night, after a fish stew thickened with mouldy bread and biscuit, there was the Sunday treat: a rice pudding with raisins. He was forever searching for ways to give them something to look forward to.

The wind had dropped earlier in the day. By early evening it had got up again, a faint, distant soughing as of wind through trees, slackening, then coming again a little stronger and with more direction. In its restless prowling about the hut the men sensed the presence of the animal that was the Arctic. They shivered together under their stiff buffalo hides, and drew forth oddments from a ragbag of recollections with which to comfort themselves.

They would have crept in any hole or corner that kept the wind away.

Around midnight they heard a noise outside the hut. Emmons reached for his rifle. Someone fumbled with a blubber lamp. There was a scratching and a scuffling in the passage way. Then something scarcely recognizable in furs, half-bear, half-man it might have been, crept into the dim light.

It was George. The bridge of his nose was bloody where the frozen face mask had sand-papered the skin. His eyes were mere slits between the swollen lids.

'Lothar ...' he gasped. 'Lothar dying ...'

What with stripping off the frozen clothing, wrapping him in blankets, feeding him brandy and hot water, it was some time before the exhausted man was able to tell them more.

It was a tale stuttered out haltingly between bouts of violent shivering, and the pains of returning sensation. The listeners, piecing together as best they could its fractured chunks, gathered that at first all had gone well: through the strait, across Rosse Bay, then over the glacier to Eskimo Point. The third night they'd camped on the ice of Baird Inlet. Next morning they'd pushed on with the sledge. Five hours saw them at the cape, climbing up to the headland.

'Could you see the Sound?' The Lieutenant had to know.

'O'en 'ater.' Words, squeezed sparingly from shrunken lips, came out numb at the edges. Some of the men were trying not to think of the ship that might have reached them even yet.

They'd found the cache of meat, and were dragging it back to their camp. Rough going over the ice foot held them up north of the cape. Schmidt had begun to falter.

'Eating sno',' whispered the voice. 'Hands and 'ace 'rozen.' It broke off to suck at the tea which Jacob Joseph held to the slobbery mouth.

The simple things, the Lieutenant was thinking bitterly.

Fourteen hours it took to travel the few miles back to their camp, that should have taken five or six. Bundled together in the four-man bag, they'd done what they could for Lothar, Muller and Stempel each taking a hand, putting it between their thighs to draw out the frost. The poor fellow howled all night.

The next morning, after a hot meal, they'd started back across Baird Inlet. Before long they were bogged down in deep, soft snow. Schmidt had begun to falter. His feet were freezing again. Leaving Stempel and Muller to haul the sledge, Reade had taken the stricken man under his arm.

'Had to 'e carried. Couldn't 'anage his legs.'

Before long they were double hauling; first Schmidt, then the meat. Again they were forced to camp on the ice. By morning Lothar was helpless. His legs were like logs of wood. It was now a question of saving his life. Reade took the decision to abandon the meat.

The speaker uttered a long, low groan. His frosted fingers were beginning to throb.

So it went on, the men were thinking. So it went on.

By the end of the third day they'd hauled the helpless man as far as the abandoned winter quarters at Eskimo Point.

'Had to 'reak u' 'art of the 'oat.' The swollen eyes were searching anxiously for the Lieutenant. 'Make a 'ire.'

It was the only way to thaw Schmidt out. He was howling all the time.

'No matter,' murmured the Lieutenant, who'd been reserving the English ice-boat against a possible journey south.

The next day Lothar's feet were frozen so solid he couldn't stand. Now too weak themselves to haul him over the glacier, they fought to pitch the fly in the teeth of the gale. First Reade, and then Muller had frozen fingers trying to light a fire. In the end George Reade saw he must go on alone.

An anguished figure, hunched into the wind, he'd plodded up the glacier in a mood of bitter self-recrimination. He blamed himself for what had happened. He should have prevented it. He'd been entrusted with the care of an inexperienced man, and he had failed him. And because of that he had failed his comrades who were counting on him to bring back the meat. Now the meat was gone, and Lothar was at death's door. But what was done was done. Shoving aside all other thoughts, he fixed his mind on getting back. It was, he told himself, straightfoward enough. You put one foot in front of the other.

So, chewing now and then on a chunk of frozen beef, he'd slogged the fifteen miles down from the glacier, across Rosse Bay and up through the strait to the hut.

At times it seemed unlikely he would get there. Once across the bay he met the full blast of the gale, funnelling through the strait. When it wasn't possible to stand, he crawled on all fours, lying flat in the fiercest gusts. Time and again he thought he was coming to the limit of his strength: but was resolved, if necessary, to cross that line.

So George Reade pressed on, and broke through at last into the solitary *there* of Nature he could never come at on a canvas.

The hoarse whispering ceased, that seemed to have been meandering interminably. The listeners, suspended in the lull that followed, were made aware that the high shrieking of the storm had given way to a low melancholy moaning.

The Lieutenant had been considering what to do. Emmons must set off at once with food and brandy. With him would go Mitsoq, whose night vision was profound.

Then, out of the darkness, came the voices of men reluctant to leave what had become a haven of warmth and security, but would do so if selected. Already the surgeon was preparing a pack. The Lieutenant, though, was juggling his resources. The doctor, of course, must go. The strongest men, if it made sense to think any strong after two months on half-rations, would be needed to haul the sledge. Here and there, among the figures half lost in shadow, a face suggested itself. Diggs. Brenner. He was reluctant to send Hanson. That left only Lawless, among the fittest men. The Irishman, too, was less than reliable. He would have to go, nonetheless. Who was to command? Foxer was too weak to make a forced march of nearly forty miles.

The Lieutenant's soul was churning at the thought of Fabius exercising any kind of authority over his men, when he became aware of a figure crawling across the sanded floor.

'Send me,' urged a low voice.

Somewhere, beyond sourness and acrimony, Lt Rainbird was imagining wholeness.

A day and a night dragged by. Those left in the half-empty hut were subdued by a sense of a surrounding vastness that swallowed up whatever was sent into it.

On the second night, as he closed the book after the reading, the Lieutenant concluded with a personal reflection. 'I believe we might find it strengthening if we spend some time before sleep thinking of those who are remembering us in their prayers. I believe we owe it to the prayers of others that we have been so often preserved in safety.'

His men, though, were too possessed by death for thoughts of fortifying arms held out to them.

Then, in the early hours, those dozing woke to a murmur of voices, and the crunch of boots in frozen snow. They were expecting the arrival of a corpse. Sure enough, what they saw, hauled in at the narrow door, was a dead man dragged to his tomb. For if Lothar was not yet quite dead, the stupor of death had already fastened about him.

They gathered round as the surgeon held a lamp close to the chiselled face. In that dim yellow glow the livid flesh, streaked with patches of white, suggested whatever hopes or dreams brought them to this place had been illusory.

Fabius slid his knife under the frozen boots, peeling them off, peeling away the fur inners.

Both legs, up to the knees, were waxy. A lifeless white.

'Frostbite is a condition of morbidity, not mortality,' remarked the surgeon, it might have been to his students.

Though death, he confided later to the Lieutenant, remained a possibility. Swathed in blankets, his marbly legs wrapped in fox fur, Schmidt was placed on a mattress, covered with the Lieutenant's sheepskin bag, which was cut open to receive him.

That night Fabius moved his bag to lie beside his patient. Though with the doctor often engaged in other duties it was mostly Jacob Joseph who tended the casualty, feeding him drinks, applying fresh cloths, wrung out in warm water, to the frozen limbs. A solitary whose only life lay up among the stars, he could not do much for flesh-and-blood, yet would not leave it to suffer. Hour after hour, with only the flap of the buffalo bag between him and the icy stones of the wall, he watched over the stricken man.

There was something steadfast about that patient presence which impressed itself upon the others. For the Lieutenant, it evoked a constancy that never failed. He turned, as he did increasingly, to his letter to his wife: *If I have learnt anything, over and above the great mass of valuable scientific data we have gathered, it is that the truths which matter most are wholly personal.*

As sensation slowly returned to his limbs Lothar Schmidt suffered acutely. His drawn-out, shuddering moans grated on the nerves of the other men.

For a week he lay in his bag begging noisily for death, while they listened, hating him, and hating themselves by turns.

Now, all along that empty, frozen coast the desolation of winter held full sway.

The first storms swept down from the north-east, ripping away the outside roof, filling the entrance, passage and storehouse with snow. It took three men several hours to dig it out. On the freshwater lake the ice thickened steadily. Foxes came down to the coast, searching along the shoreline for whatever they could scavenge. Over a period of days Rainbird shot several he found skulking close to the hut. They too were pitiful, wasted creatures, mere skin and bone. They all went into the stew. If the cooks were none too careful cleaning out the guts, no one cared.

Apart from exercising, when the weather permitted, the men lay more or less continuously in their bags. The monotony was such that any diversion served to pass the time. Some had begun to do deals over their ration.

'Who'll give me a bit of bacon,' cried Lawless, 'for this biscuit?'

Before long a regular market was in full swing as others took to trading in scraps of bread, corned-beef, mouldy biscuits, a cup of tea for a piece of seal blubber. Soon, portions not yet received were being pledged against a ration of rum, or a scrap of tobacco.

In the end the Lieutenant put a stop to it. It was not, he said, in the spirit of fraternity.

It was a constant struggle, this striving to hold them together, to keep them from slipping into the anarchy of each man for himself. He began to see a significance in establishing a framework for their lives: what happened one day would happen the next, and so on, until rescue came. He would have them hang on to each passing day as shipwrecked men clung to a floating spar. If days persisted, why not men?

He decided on a series of daily lectures on the geography of the United States, first in general, then with particular reference to each state. That afternoon, having spent the morning in preparation, he began with 'Mountain and River Systems'. The men dozed in their bags as he droned on. Always in their thoughts was the hope of rescue, and the succour all were certain awaited them thirty miles across the Sound. The wildest fancy was enough to set them agitating. What if a winter party was at that moment travelling along the coast? Something must be done. There must be a marker, high up on a nearby cliff.

In the end the Lieutenant let them have their way. He went himself with Sergeant Reade to fix a signal pole above the point.

One morning Emmons was in the store collecting rations for the day. Hearing a stealthy sound, he took his rifle, and crept softly to the entrance. Poking aside the canvas flap, he saw that what he'd taken for a fox was only Lt Foxer scraping in the snow where the rotten biscuits had been thrown away.

The young man was constantly famished. At meals times he would stretch out the act of eating for as long as possible, lingering over every mouthful, teasing it to a paste, cherishing its presence in the mouth. The question of when to eat his bread had become a daily anxiety.

'If I eat it before I get my tea, I wish I'd kept it,' he said plaintively to Parish. 'But if I wait until the tea arrives, I drink it too quickly, and get no satisfaction.'

If Foxer seemed to be failing, the Lieutenant drew some consolation from the fact that Schmidt, at least, was making progress. He'd ordered that a small fraction be cut from the daily ration so the injured man could have a few extra ounces. It was a very much smaller increase than the surgeon had been urging. All the same, it was asking a great deal. No one objected. The Lieutenant had taken silence for consent. If any were reflecting that a hundred and fifty pounds of English beef had been left on the ice of Baird Inlet, and the useless Prussian hauled back instead, they weren't going to say so.

He was still helpless. At meal times the doctor spooned food between his lips, while Sergeant Asher held the mug for him to drink. Though suffering much, he kept his spirits up. He often spoke about his folks in Germany.

'How 'bout your folks, Jake? What they think, you join the army?'

The astronomer shook his head

'They don't know.' A faint smile lit the rather wasted face. 'There is no Yiddish word for *army*.'

Lothar Schmidt stared, then threw back his head and roared with laughter.

'Such cheerfulness in adversity,' declared the surgeon dryly, 'is much to be admired.'

That night he cut off another of Schmidt's fingers. One by one they had blackened and dried up. As the stock of vaseline ran out, the Lieutenant, at the surgeon's prompting, had turned over all the lard to the medical supplies. Jacob Joseph dressed the wound with lard, mixed with a little salicylic acid. He wound on a fresh linen strip cut from clothing thawed out against his own body. In these small acts of self-forgetfulness the *mamzer* found a way of emptying himself. Sometimes, holding the pan for Schmidt to piss in, he tried to recall what had brought him to this place. *There's real work to be done in the Arctic. For a young man like yourself.* No. That was not why he'd come up here.

Some journeys, he began to see, had destinations of which the traveller was unaware.

With the approach of mid-winter came days of unceasing wind when the temperature in the hut fell sharply. The mercury registered thirty below. Schmidt's comrades on the ice suffered it most. The cold left their flesh as sore as if it had been cruelly beaten.

Elsewhere, the first cracks were appearing. Hewitt was now very demoralized, he believed he would never reach Littleton Island, while Fromm's constant whingeing had become a source of irritation. He whinged endlessly: about the cold, the food, the insufficient bedding, about the neglect of his health.

'He believes he is dying,' said the surgeon dryly. 'It is my fault, *naturellement*. I have a down on him.'

The Lieutenant trudged doggedly along his lecture trail. He had reached the State of Maine: his voice plodded through the darkness and the wind's lament.

His own health had begun to suffer. His feet were sorely cracked, and he was sleeping badly. That night he was roused from a light doze by a furtive scratching. It seemed to come from directly opposite, where Schmidt lay on his mattress between Asher and the surgeon. So distinctly was it etched upon the silence, there was no mistaking. It was the scrape of fingers in a bread can.

Instantly the thought flashed through the Lieutenant's mind: *someone is stealing Schmidt's bread.* Since the can, he knew, stood between Fabius and his patient, it could only be the surgeon.

He sat up, peering in the direction of the sound, but the darkness conveyed only the slurry exhalations of sleeping men. He began to wonder if his senses had misled him. Though the sound had been unmistakable. And he was quite clear in his own mind of the can's position.

The Lieutenant lay agonizing over what to do. He could not keep his discovery to himself. His second-in-command, as possible successor, should certainly not be left in ignorance as to the surgeon's character. But Foxer, in his present weakened state was no fit recipient for such news. Indeed, he might not survive. And Rainbird and the surgeon were thick as thieves.

Not knowing what to do for the best, William Parish reached out for his wife. Increasingly she had become the confidante for disclosures too perplexing to be entrusted to any but her. He had become aware that she was smiling at him. He saw that her smile was unexpectedly tender and forgiving. In his weariness he allowed himself to sink into that solicitude, and would have reached out a hand to touch her cheek, but for the frozen hide imprisoning his arm.

Next morning, though, the revelation was vivid as a waking dream. It seemed to him, though he knew it couldn't have been so, that he'd actually *seen* Fabius stealing bread from Schmidt's cup.

Under the belly of the whaleboat, the cooks were preparing breakfast. The feeble light of a solitary rag dipped in seal blubber illuminated a scene, it struck the Lieutenant with painful irony, such as a painter might have recorded for posterity – Sergeant Hewitt passing a dish along the line of bags, Wutz on his knees beside the stove blowing up a flame, Schmidt sitting up, mouth gaping to receive his portion from the surgeon's hand – an inspiring spectacle of comradeship in adversity

William Parish fell to wondering if he might have been mistaken. Night thoughts were never trustworthy. The more he pondered it, the more shameful it became: an emanation born of layers of mistrust that gathered in a man's head when he was too much on his own. Was that it? An ugly imagining, bred of the repugnance he felt for the surgeon. Had he dreamt it, even? It shocked him to the core to think that his aversion should so work upon him as to creep into his dreams. Besides, what could he possibly say to the man? A direct charge would only meet with denial. And he could not afford an open breach with the expedition's *surgeon*.

Later that day Fabius was due to make his medical report, a confidential matter which generally took place under cover of the polar night. It was bitterly cold, with a low wind, as the two men stepped out towards the point. A full moon, slipping from behind a cloud, shed a glacial light over the chaotic rubble heaped up along the ice foot.

For a few moments they trod the brilliant snow in silence.

Casting around for something to say, Parish remarked on Schmidt's powers of recovery which were remarkable in the circumstances.

'Since he seems to enjoy smoking,' he went on, 'the frostbite to his face cannot be troubling him now.'

The surgeon heaved a sigh. 'The poor fellow will lose his feet, and most of his hands.'

'Are you sure?' This was a blow not looked for.

'Most assuredly. He has suffered major tissue damage. The blood supply is destroyed. The lines of demarcation are quite clear, running through the fingers and just below the ankles.'

That night, holding a lamp while Sgt Asher changed the dressings, Parish saw for himself. Poor Schmidt's feet had mummified. As Asher unwound the linen strips chunks of blackened flesh sloughed away, leaving the bones exposed.

Later, preparing to write his daily entry in the log, the Lieutenant agonized over the situation in which he now found himself. His duty as commander was quite clear. He was obliged to care equally for every member of the party. Indeed, if any favour was to be shown it should be to the sick and wounded.

Suddenly, he saw his dream of a swift dash across the Sound, a light sledge, a minimum of food and equipment, for the foolishness it was. He couldn't understand how he'd been so blind not to have anticipated the inevitability of this outcome. Yet it was something he'd never considered. It simply hadn't struck him that some men might have to be hauled.

As he contemplated the enormity of hauling a helpless man across thirty miles of chaotic ice, it struck him that if, and when, the Sound was frozen over, the likelihood was that none of those still left alive would be strong enough to make the crossing.

That night, writing up his log, Lt Parish duly recorded the fact that he was not prepared to abandon any of his men.

Filthy, sluggish, the men lay in the cold and darkness. They had to grope about for anything laid down. Mug, can, whatever a hand encountered, had its patina of ice. And the ice was black with soot. Every surface was coated with soot; stones, timbers, sleeping bags; the urine frozen in the common tub by the door, was coated with soot. Bags, too, were firmly frozen to the ground, the buffalo hair stiff with frost which, by morning, had saturated their clothing. As soon as they got up the bags froze again.

Mostly, though, the men lay in the bags in their cold blubbery clothes, and waited for whatever was awaiting them.

On all sides now it was a waiting game. The Lieutenant was conscious of it, and it made him uneasy. He had become watchful, without knowing what it was he was watching for.

Meals had become a time for simmering suspicion. One evening, as the first mess were preparing to receive their supper, Diggs, serving up the stew, was accused of favouring some men over others.

'I'm sure,' said the Lieutenant firmly, 'Diggs does nothing of the kind.'

'We know he *does*,' shrieked Fromm. 'The officers get more.'

Later that day the obscure object of the Lieutenant's fears finally declared its hand. It was Emmons, intercepting him outside the hut, who broke the news.

'I've found a slit in the store-house roof.' The sergeant had been expecting something of the sort. 'Someone's fetched out a piece of bacon.'

That night, after the meal, the Lieutenant broke the news to the men.

'I regret to have to tell you,' he said soberly, 'there is a thief among us.'

His announcement loosed a flurry of allegation. Some had missed scraps of bread from private hoards. Others told of hearing, after the lamp was doused, a faint, furtive scraping, that could only have been someone scooping out the oil from the can. Wutz revealed he had warned the sergeant, only a day or two before, that a cut of meat issued to him for cooking had been taken from one of his pots. Outrage, though, soon crumbled into entreaty, as the men grew more and more fervent in their pleas.

'Whoever it is,' cried Lt Foxer excitedly, 'I'll give an ounce of bread a day to keep him from temptation.'

'So will I,' shouted Hanson. Though reduced from what he was, he still seemed well able to afford it.

Then broke out a regular babel of voices offering their scraps if only the thief would confess and repent. Amid the continuing pleas and supplications came a reminder of a Higher Authority before whom the guilty soul would one day be called to account.

'I urge that man,' croaked Sergeant Hewitt with terrible earnestness, 'whoever that man may be, to throw himself at the Mercy Seat.'

His very salvation might have depended on it. But the thief refused to be drawn.

The last word lay with Sgt Emmons, less concerned for the redemption of a sinner, than with stopping the bastard in his tracks.

'I'll just say this. I'm rigging up a spring-gun in the store-house. Anyone goes in there without my say-so gets a charge of shot.'

That night darkness was tense with a straining after any sound that might betray the thief at work.

It was now the very dead of winter, the island shrouded in snow. With storms setting in from the north and north-east no one ventured out for long.

Doggedly the shipwrecked men clung to the raft the Lieutenant had constructed to float them through the days. The cooks roused at six. Breakfast, eaten in the bags at seven was followed by the surgeon's medical inspection. Weather permitting, Mitsoq and Rainbird might set out to look for signs of fox. Someone would chop ice from the lake. Someone else would empty the tub. A period was set aside for exercise. The Lieutenant was punctilious in giving a lead. On bad days he used the belly of the boat were there was some headroom to do his bends and stretches. His good example, though, was lost on his men, and the effort to nag them into it wore him out. Two hours were occupied with the Lieutenant's lecture, after which Emmons issued the cooks with rations for the following day. A dogged, persevering man, able to apply himself to any job that needed doing, he had completed work on a door and lock for the store, though in no doubt that the thief would strike again. At three the knot of rags was removed from the hole in the roof, and the fire lit for supper. As the cooks prepared the meal the hut filled with choking smoke from the damp, burning wood. The men crawled down into their bags. The meal, served at five, was followed by readings. Little remained of the library of books and magazines. The men had opted for a gaudy historical romance of lords and ladies. It was scarcely a subject the Lieutenant would have chosen. Yet better that, he reasoned, than to leave each man a prey to crushing thoughts. He and Fabius took it in turns to read a page or two, the wretched lamp held close to the page, while those able to follow it drifted off into a resplendent world of gowns and decorations. Then Hewitt read a passage from his bible. At eight the lamp was doused.

After lights-out each man sank into an impenetrable darkness. Only on favourable occasions could he see the face of his neighbour touching him. Stuck down in their own stink, in their frozen bags, they might have been atoms falling endlessly through coal-black space.

The coming of the solstice brought a glimmer of deliverance. The sun had reached the end of its journey south. Now, with every day that passed, it would be coming closer. All they had to do was to stick it out, be patient, and let the sun pull them through.

That night the surgeon severed the flap of skin that held Schmidt's right foot to his ankle. The Prussian was quite oblivious of his loss. He was conscious only of the doctor attending to him in the gloom, while his good friend Jake held the lamp.

The new moon brought another surge of spirits. The men trooped out to stare where it hung, the thinnest of crescents, lit by the returning sun.

'Not much longer now,' Rainbird was telling those around him. 'You'll see. Leffingwell will soon be here.'

No one doubted it. Leffingwell's noble message had established him in every heart. Such was the rush of fellow-feeling that when Foxer's tea spilled from his hand every man tipped in a little of his own to fill up the lieutenant's can.

The young man was showing signs of increasing weakness. He was often sunk in dejection. In the course of listening to his troubles, Parish discovered he'd been keeping back a small amount of each day's ration, hoarding it in his bag.

'As long as you haven't eaten it, you've still got it,' he whispered plaintively. 'But if you eat it, it's gone.'

One morning Lawless, whose turn it was at the water hole, came back exhausted. He had been unable to break through. It took the efforts of half a dozen men, chipping in turn at the ice, to reach fresh water. Returning to the relative warmth of the hut after their exposure, they were close to collapse.

This gradual enfeeblement of his men was deeply troubling to the Lieutenant. The surgeon's latest medical report reflected an increase in cases of rheumatic cramps and painful, swollen joints.

Several of the mouths he'd examined were showing signs of bleeding gums. Both the cooks were chronically affected by the constant inhalation of smoke and fumes. In addition, Fabius concluded, Lt Foxer's condition was giving cause for concern.

The Lieutenant scarcely needed to be told what was only too apparent. The surgeon, though, rarely failed to take advantage of an opening.

'Some of these men,' he murmured, 'will never cross the Sound. Not in their present condition.'

Parish remained silent. It was a silence of pure hatred. He couldn't bring himself to speak. It didn't help that Fabius' words were so obviously true. Poor Foxer was now so weak he could scarcely move. He had to be turned in his bag.

That night the Lieutenant suggested gently that the young man write to his family.

'It is the prudent thing to do,' he said quietly. 'Indeed, I shall be doing so myself.'

Foxer appeared quite resigned. Though now very weak, he seemed clear and tranquil in his mind. He revealed that when the time came to attempt the crossing, he wanted to be left behind with his ration.

'You could conceivably haul one man, Lieutenant,' he whispered. 'Never two.'

The sick man had reached the place they both had to get to way ahead of his commander, who still lagged some distance behind.

No, he couldn't think of it. Sometimes it is preferable to suffer desertion than to do the deserting. But his protestations carried no conviction. Not in his own soul. What if it were not a single man, but three or four … or half a dozen?

Lt Parish was learning that the unthinkable happens: that the thing which is almost beyond contemplation has to be contemplated, because it may have to be endured.

TWELVE

In Washington the Court of Inquiry dragged on, churning out its thousands of words of testimony, and never a word to spare for those in peril.

'Every day that passes may be costing lives,' General Sweetsir complained to Senator Clay. 'We must have ships at Upernavik by the middle of May if we're to push through Melville Bay as soon as the pack opens. Yet nothing is being done. Nothing.'

The Senator, too, was troubled. He well knew what difficulties lay ahead, obstructions that had nothing to do with the middle pack. It would require a great deal of money to equip a rescue expedition. Yet the president's message to Congress, delivered earlier that same day, had made no mention of any appropriation for that purpose.

Next morning Lucius Clay, as chairman of the Senate Committee on Navy affairs, took himself to see the Navy Secretary.

'We both know this Leffingwell business was a fiasco,' he remarked, when settled.

'If so, it was the Army's fiasco,' quipped Hynes cheerfully. 'Not mine.'

A lean, hungry man, he was said to be in too great a hurry to eat much.

'Still, you've come out of it pretty well,' Clay pointed out. Commander Young, the navy man, had won glowing headlines for an arduous duty, commendably performed.

'And might do better yet.'

'It's an Army matter.'

'It's an Army expedition, certainly. But it will take the Navy to bring them back.' The old man cocked his head enquiringly. 'It could play well in New Hampshire.'

It was well known the Navy Secretary was nursing a Senate nomination in his home state.

'Elijah never wanted this particular chestnut in the first place,' continued the senator, swirling the bourbon in his glass. 'He'll be more than glad for someone else to pluck it out of the fire.'

As he drove off down the Avenue, Lucius Clay reflected that he'd cast his bread upon the waters. He did not doubt it would come back to him. The whole art of governing others – it was a truth he'd remarked times without number – lay in knowing one's man.

It took the Navy Secretary a little over three weeks to formulate a plan. Within a day or two, he had submitted his proposals to the Secretary for War. By the New Year they had secured the president's approval.

Over the tea cups Lucius Clay was explaining to the wife of Lt Parish what steps were in preparation to assist her husband.

'The president will send a message to Congress, asking for money to outfit a rescue bid. It will be read, first in the House, then during morning business in the Senate. Our friends will see the resolution through the House. I shall myself then bring it to the floor of the Senate.'

He fastened on her one of his cautionary looks.

'You must expect a battle,' he thought it best to warn.

'A battle?'

'Senators don't like spending money.' He was trying to make a joke of it.

'The bill will be opposed? Opposed by whom?'

'By the president's enemies. Since his elevation Ty's become possessed of an outlandish notion that the office of Chief Magistrate should embody the moral authority of the nation. He's jumped out of the pocket and into the frying pan, so to speak.' He sipped at his tea. 'Ithamor Conkey will be a formidable opponent, Matty.'

Lucius Clay knew the issue might go either way.

'I want you to come to dinner at Willard's,' he went on.

'There are some gentlemen I would like you to meet.'

For all his Southern blood, the old man had been seduced by her New England soul. In her devotion to her gangling Lieutenant, he recognized that image of wifely duty he knew would impress itself upon his fellow senators. Worn down in the service of Mammon, they yet retained a queer respect for virtues they might not practise but could never quite abandon.

'Politicians like to cherish American womanhood,' he told her lightly. 'It makes them feel good. Also, it makes them look good. And there are votes in looking good.'

He could see it irked, this dependence on others more powerful than herself.

'You are the strongest card we have,' he flattered.

'Couldn't you arrange it here?' She felt more at ease among the tea cups.

'They'll expect a dinner, Matty,' he said drily.

She wore the lavender dress William had declared suitable for social occasions. She wished she had something that fitted better. But sooner that than face the ordeal of a store. So, submitting to the embarrassment of the lumpy bodice, she set off once more to ride to the assistance of her husband. She was dreading the evening. But what other option did she have except to trust to Senator Clay's judgement in these matters?

As the carriage swept them through winter streets and up the Avenue towards Willard's, he described the men she would meet, and the strategy to be served by dining with them that evening. For the House, it seemed, was Democrat, the Senate Republican, a discrepancy Lucius Clay hoped to turn to their advantage. There would be Congressman Potwine whom she knew, a power in the House, and Senator Peachey, whose good offices would be required if the Senate appropriations committee was to be circumvented. There would also be the Honourable Pliny Cutpurse, from South Carolina.

It would be worth it, he promised her, for that alone. Senator Cutpurse was one of the wonders of the Senate.

'You will be dining among the Olympians, Matty,' he said drily as he ushered her through the lobby.

Zeus himself, it could have been, came forward to greet them, an old man with magnificent white whiskers and big curled moustache.

As the senior member of the party, Senator Cutpurse insisted on taking her in to dinner.

'This is the real heart of Washington, Mrs Parish,' he said, as they settled themselves at table. 'More so even than the Capitol. This is where the nation's leaders gather. Here you may hear our most illustrious men. Orators, statesmen, presidents in the making.'

As the old man continued to trot out his tour for a constituent of the gentle sex, Matty's glance strayed to a neighbouring table where a ponderous man with a huge, granite face under a thicket of iron grey hair was holding forth to his dinner companions. Not wishing to stare, she lowered her eyes to the fish. Yet throughout the meal the grating voice, audible in snatches, continued to exert a baleful fascination. He seemed to her a most extraordinary specimen.

But Senator Peachey, on her left, was asking if she found Washington as cultivated as Boston.

'I am not well acquainted with Boston, sir. But I believe Washington to be a cultured town.'

'Cultured or not,' averred Senator Cutpurse, 'we have something here you'll find in no other city in these United States. The machinery of government, ma'am. The hub of a whole continent.'

'Even so,' remarked Senator Peachey, a sad-eyed man, 'I regret to say there is much here that is dishonest and corrupt.'

'Never,' roared Senator Cutpurse loyally. 'Never say so.'

But Martha Parish's attention had been caught by cries of approbation, and a sudden ripple of applause from the table opposite. The stone-faced man was sitting back in his chair as a flaming pudding was set before him.

'Perish the thought,' the jovial Cutpurse went on, 'that our

US Congress should harbour dishonesty and corruption. Isn't that so, Mrs Parish?'

'Some of its members, it seems, may partake of hellfire with impunity,' she ventured drily, eyeing the flames wreathing the pudding.

It was an observation which greatly entertained her fellow guests. Martha Parish, though, was covered in confusion, for the remark had just slipped out.

'I do hope he is not a friend,' she stammered.

'I hardly think so,' murmured Lucius Clay. 'Though I did once have the satisfaction of escorting him from my house at the business end of a shot-gun.'

'Mrs Parish, ma'am,' Peachey cleared his throat, then added in a low voice, 'that is Ithamor Conkey.'

It was towards the end of the following week when Lucius Clay rose to call up the bill on the floor of the Senate. Forgoing his usual ironies, he addressed his colleagues with a gravity that reflected the seriousness of the situation. There was, he said, a common ground beyond the arena of party advantage, or personal vendetta. He appealed to his fellow senators to meet him there to discuss this measure, for that was where it belonged. It was, he freely acknowledged, an appropriations matter but, given the extreme urgency of the situation, he had by-passed the appropriations committee in order to save time.

Senator Peachey, he went on, would indicate his willingness to let the action stand.

From his front-row desk Lucius Clay was unable to see, somewhere behind, and to his left, the senator from New York, but he was conscious of his presence: was fully expecting a grating interruption: *Mr President, will the senator yield?* Ithamor Conkey had a sharp eye for irregularities of any kind. But no intervention came, and the speaker passed on to the urgency of the matter, as evinced only that morning by the Secretaries for War and for the Navy, in testimony to the standing committee. He spoke plainly of the extreme peril – not his words but their words – in which Lt Parish and his party now stood, and of the need for a speedy passage of the bill, if a rescue was to stand any chance of success.

He yielded courteously to questions from the floor which, for once, he was able to answer with a candour born of truth.

No, the money would be for the saving of lives, not for further exploration.

No, he did not believe there should be a limit placed on the appropriation. Neither the president nor the Secretary of the Navy should have their hands tied when it came to saving life.

Then, all questions answered, Lucius Clay yielded up the floor to the opposition. It took the form of a succession of amendments seeking to impose the very penny-pinching limitation he had counselled against. Each one, as it was defeated, gave place to another, set at a lower figure than its predecessor.

The clock over the president's dais was touching four. The attendants were turning on the gas lights. Lucius Clay turned in his seat, and raised a hand to the ladies' gallery, where Martha Parish had been joined by Amos Potwine. He was about to ask for the question to be put, when a stir round ran the gallery. A little way back, across the gangway, a man in a black coat and hat had risen to his feet, an old man with blazing eyes and a knife slash for a mouth.

'Mr President,' he began, in a sonorous voice, 'not for nothing did the pagan Northmen of old set their abyss in that fearful region of eternal ice and darkness.'

The venerable senator from Massachusetts was of that generation of implacable old deacons who yielded never an inch. Nor would he now. Netherwards and northwards lay the way to Hell. Yet expedition had followed expedition into that desperate domain, and always with the same result. The senator adverted to the voyages of Franklin, of De Long and Hall. They too had sailed away. Where were they now? In their lonely graves, if graves they had – or else their poor bones long since scattered to the winds.

'Mr President, whatever secrets may lie hidden in that mysterious zone, Providence has decreed there is only one thing waiting there for men.'

Lucius Clay groaned inwardly, and closed his eyes.

'If men there be, foolhardy enough to venture their lives in such a place, then let them do so at their peril. But I will not ... no, I cannot ...' – at this the grim old man, his white locks shaking, hammered the floor with his stick – 'I cannot grant the president power to assign whomsoever he chooses to this dreadful service.'

A murmur of approval ran round the chamber.

'I move,' the senator continued, 'that any expedition for the relief of these hapless men must be composed solely of volunteers.'

The gallery, which had hung on every word of this dramatic peroration, rewarded the speaker with tumultuous applause.

There was never any doubt, Lucius Clay reflected afterwards, that Eli would win his motion. No one was going to oppose it. He had been outmanoeuvred. And all afternoon Ithamor Conkey had not said a word.

Up in the ladies' gallery, Martha Parish turned with shining eyes to Amos Potwine.

'It's been passed. The bill's been passed.'

'No, Mrs Parish, ma'am,' the congressman was trying to explain.

For it was, it seemed, only a delaying tactic. Congress had approved different versions of the bill, and now it was up to some committee to resolve the difference.

'It will then have to be reported back to the House,' Mr Potwine continued, 'and approved there before it comes back to the Senate.'

His tone of cheerful assurance belied the congressman's true feelings. The prospects for a speedy outcome were not favourable. A measure could be stalled indefinitely if Congress had a mind to do it. Ithamor Conkey had a mastery of procedural niceties, when they could be used to obstruct any business not to his taste.

'We will get it through, Mrs Parish. Never fear.'

Over the next few days Lucius Clay had several lengthy meetings with the Secretary of the Navy. Together they took the first delicate steps towards negotiations with certain ship owners in Dundee and St John's.

The senator secured from Secretary Hynes a written undertaking that none but volunteers would be sought for the rescue mission. Armed with this assurance, and acting as the Senate's senior representative on the conference committee, where normally he would have been expected to uphold the Senate's position, he declared he would not insist on its amendment. He did so to avoid delay. Certainly, it helped to speed the conference report through the House. Yet, a week to the day following Eli Stearns' amendment, as he rose to his feet to submit the conference report, with the amendment stricken, Lucius Clay feared he'd succeeded only in presenting his opponents with further opportunities for obstruction.

Again he stressed the urgency of the situation, the need for swift action directed towards the saving of lives, lives for whom time was running out. He drew attention to the Navy Secretary's assurance, an undertaking which, he said, should reassure the anxieties of the senior senator for Massachusetts.

Yet the strong, clear-running current of his argument spent itself, as the afternoon wore on, amid a morass of pettifogging procedural points as speaker after speaker complained that once again the regular transactions of the Senate had been by-passed. One protested that the resolution had been sent to the wrong committee. As a money matter it should have gone to the appropriations committee, not the navy committee. Another declared that the Senate had deferred to the House yet again over the matter of an amended resolution.

'This chamber,' he went on, 'is well on its way to becoming a sub-committee of the House.'

Martha Parish, on the top tier of the gallery, was sitting too far back to see the bulky figure holding the floor, but there was no mistaking that grating voice.

'Now, Mr President,' continued Senator Conkey, with ponderous scorn, 'as to the message from the Secretary of the Navy, and the confidence placed in it by the esteemed Senator from Virginia. I have read that message. I have studied that message carefully, and I say this: if, and when, all is prepared for departure, and insufficient volunteers have presented themselves, what then? Are we to believe the ships won't move? Is that it?'

Martha Parish quivered at the harsh voice grinding out its jeering questions. She could not endure it, the prevarication, the refusal to see what mattered most.

Yet worse was to come as, one after another, the anti-spending lobby took the floor, trundling round and round the same worn rut, for all the world like good Aunt Buffem's mule. A gaunt, dyspeptic man with a twitching cheek had begun recalling how, when first he went about speaking at meetings, people would toss bills and coins on to a blanket spread on the ground. He produced one of the coins from his pocket. He held it up. He carried it, he said, to remind him who was 'paying his way'. So it went on, a general leave-taking of senses.

She was scarcely able to believe her ears as the senator from her own state, *her own state*, spoke of the bill to rescue William and his men as the most dangerous piece of legislation he had ever had to consider, a measure which, in conferring unlimited powers upon a Cabinet officer, could scarcely be exceeded for folly.

Down below in the chamber senators were coming and going, attending, or not, as they pleased, as if this managing of the nation's affairs was the most casual matter imaginable.

Meanwhile Senator Stearns was picturing the awful spectacle of the Navy Secretary entering the vaults of the Treasury, taking away whatever sum he chose – then selecting some officer, towards whom he bore a grudge, and serving him as King David had served Uriah the Hittite.

It seemed the purest lunacy to her.

Even so, when the request came for the *yeas and nays*, Martha Parish could not but believe men of good conscience must do the proper thing.

So she was stunned, as the clerk called the roll, to hear so many, voice after voice it seemed, cry:

'No.'

'No.'

'No.'

After the vote she sat, unable to move, her fingers twisting together in her lap, twisting her wedding ring. Oh, the hypocrisy, the hollowness of hearts.

Below her the chamber was emptying. The clerks had begun clearing papers from the desks. Senators were filing through the doors, or lingering in small groups. Prominent amid the rubi-cund cheeks and well-filled coats, the distinguished whiskers of Senator Cutpurse could be seen enjoying a joke with the presiding officer. Suddenly she saw that the plight of William and his party had no meaning for these men. It was beyond them. The truth was as simple, and as terrible as that.

Slumped dejectedly under the gas light, raw amid the marble busts, Martha Parish sat until found.

'Come, Matty,' a voice said. 'I will take you home.'

The hansom hurried them through the dark, winter town, and out towards G Street.

They sat in silence, the old man reflecting bitterly on a setback for which he felt responsible. He knew he'd blundered in striking out the Stearns' amendment. Fourteen days had passed since the President sent his message down to the House. Now he would have to start all over again.

'It is unjust,' she burst out at last. 'It is unjust and cruel.'

She was close to tears.

'We undoubtedly have the best form of government the world has known,' sighed Senator Clay. 'Unfortunately,' he added, 'it requires the best men to make it work.'

He wanted to explain that it was only the conference report which had been rejected. The measure itself had still to be resolved. But now was not the time.

'"*Government of the people, by the people, for the people …*" I was required to learn those words by heart,' she went on, somewhat unsteadily. Unbitten, her lip could have quivered then.

Lucius Clay sighed. She was a New Englander. Naturally, she put her trust in the big idea.

So the anguished wife juddered on in fits and spasms.

'I did not hear a single senator,' she flared up suddenly, 'speak of those men as fellow-Americans … fellow …'

But words had broken down again.

He took her hand in silent commiseration. He was thinking that everything came down to politics in the end. And politics was mostly about men. Managing men.

Suddenly he felt the bony fingers tighten convulsively.

'My father used to say there should be someone in every family prepared to say "Damn". I say it now, Mr Clay. Damn them ! Damn them all.'

Now, with the resolution at a standstill, Senator Clay set to work to pick up votes.

If he considered Congress a pitiable spectacle, the old man did not despair of his fellow senators. He had faith, if only in their frailty. He believed he must deal with men as he found them: and he found them to be venal, vain, unscrupulous and ambitious, often most ignorant when most convinced. In the corridors and committee rooms of the Capitol the revelations of the Court of Inquiry had fired up the zeal of the 'spend-nothings'. It would, he knew, take all his twists and sleights to procure a majority. If there was only one way of doing business with them, why, he would do it.

Several times, at the end of a frustrating day, Lucius Clay returned to find Martha Parish a visitant at his fireside. The wife of Lieutenant Parish was seeking sanctuary from the clamour of voices, a lamentation going up from the families that those they loved had been abandoned in their hour of need: Mrs Sedgewick, Mrs Foxer, the Stempel sisters in Pennsylvania, the Knowles family in Illinois. And what of those who had no folks: Private Lawless … Private Fromm … Private Muller … Their faces stared at her from the *Harper's* photograph. Now it seemed they had no country, either.

One afternoon she arrived to find a stranger in the drawing room. The senator introduced him as a Mr Chance, from Pennsylvania.

She took the hand of a youngish man, clean-shaven, with a shadow lurking beneath sallow skin. He was, he said gravely, turning his dark eyes upon her, honoured to meet the wife of Lt Parish, a man he greatly admired.

'I believe, Mrs Parish, that all nations are driven to seek out new horizons, but we Americans above all others. It is our national character.'

Shortly afterwards he took his leave. Evidently he'd completed whatever business had brought him. She could see he was not interested in her.

'There goes one of our great men,' Lucius Clay remarked, as she refilled his cup.

'But who *is* Mr Chance?'

He came away from the window.

'He is from Pittsburgh,' he went on, 'a satanic place if ever there was one. I went there once. It took days to get the brimstone out my clothes.'

'Then I wonder at your association with Mr Chance.'

Lucius Clay smiled his slow, self-deprecating smile.

'I'm a Virginian, Matty. I was born with a long spoon.'

It had been a dull day of routine legislation in the Senate. All afternoon Lucius Clay had remained resting in his room. His arthritis had its good days, and its bad days.

As four o'clock approached the old man hoisted himself from his chair, and was picking his way gingerly along the corridors when a bulky figure with a lumbering gait fell in beside him.

'You know, Lucius, if you were to allow a ceiling of say, half a million dollars on this appropriation, we could see the measure through in fifteen minutes.'

The old man cocked his head on one side, a gesture that had the effect of bringing the black eye patch into play.

'Why, Ithamor, I take that as a kindness. I surely do.'

Then the two senators, the ponderous Yankee and the old Virginian, exchanged smiles of improbable sweetness before Lucius Clay passed on his way into the Senate chamber.

No sooner had he settled himself in his seat than the Clerk of the House pushed through the swing doors. He ducked his head to the presiding officer, and declared it to be the insistence of the House of Representatives that an appropriation be made for the relief of Lt Parish and his party.

Senator Clay heaved himself to his feet to ask that the bill be considered at once. The time had come, he said, to look at the issue. They were facing a crisis. The question was, would the Senate take steps to rescue Lt Parish's party? Or did it prefer to abandon them to their fate? He wished senators to be in no doubt as to their responsibilities. Failure to act now would render any future action unnecessary. It would be too late. He had secured from the Secretary for the Navy a further undertaking that none other than volunteers would be selected for the rescue party. Nothing now stood in the way of approving the resolution.

The old man's speech offered no concession of the kind Ithamor Conkey had been seeking. To go down that road, Lucius Clay well knew, would send the whole matter back again to the House.

'Will the senator yield?'

Lucius Clay subsided, while raising an accommodating hand.

'I have heard,' the grating voice continued, 'that the Navy Secretary, unknown to Congress, is at this very moment negotiating to buy British ships. Is it true? If so, the esteemed senator from Virginia is indeed faced with a crisis, and Congress had better look into it.'

Ithamor, reflected Lucius Clay wearily, was never more disagreeably in character than when smelling a rat. Though it was a nasty moment, for the deal was done and the ships in question already at sea.

'Certainly, the Navy Secretary is looking into the possibility of obtaining suitable ships. He would be failing in his duty not to do so.'

There was a murmur of approval from some desks at the senator's nimble negotiation of the rocks.

'There are in the world very few ships suitable for such a task as we are contemplating. Most of them are presently to be found in Scottish or Newfoundland harbours. If Senator Conkey would prefer the Navy Secretary to wait until those ships have left port for the season, he had better say so.'

Having yielded up the floor, Lucius Clay sat indifferently at his desk as his opponents forked over their old ground. There was nothing more to be said. It was no longer a matter of argument. It was now a matter of votes.

Across the chamber a senator began a pitch for his own state. Weren't American ships as good as any in the world? Why, three suitable vessels could be built in sixty days in the state of Maine.

If his own votes stood firm, the old man reflected, just a little instability on the other side would swing it his way.

He'd spent much of the previous week on the telephone, having but recently had an instrument installed in his house, though an innovation which, he prophesied gloomily, enabling you to lie to a man without having him look you in the eye, could only bring about the death of political skills. He had called in favours from Atlanta to Chicago. He drew a line at Boston. He had, he said, no influence among the saints.

(Americans, the senator from Maine went on, should be rescued in American ships.)

Lucius Clay, though, waited to see who would answer the

quorum call. More importantly, who wouldn't. With the clerk about to call the roll, came the reassuring announcement that two senators, one from Pennsylvania, another from Ohio, had been taken ill in their rooms.

It was just as well, Lucius Clay reflected afterwards. For all his efforts at persuasion, only two of Ithamor's votes had switched to him. No matter, it was enough.

Though Martha Parish thought it scandalous, with the urgency of the situation made crystal clear, that only two from the other side should see fit to vote for the bill.

'Still,' she said, not wishing to belittle Mr Clay's efforts, 'at least you won over those two.'

'They're honest men, Matty.' Lucius Clay poured himself a glass of wine.

'And an honest politician,' he couldn't resist reminding, 'when bought, stays bought.'

She saw he was teasing her again.

THIRTEEN

At Camp Fortitude there was now an increase in those reporting themselves to the surgeon. Men complained of breathlessness, of dizziness, of chest pains and feebleness in the legs. All were subjected to an examination of the mouth. Fabius, with Asher to hold the lamp, would go his rounds, probing teeth, alert for swollen or discoloured gums. Then, by the dim light of the lamp he would write up his notes, and make his report to the Lieutenant. Hewitt, Edge, Nadel and Muller were all bleeding from the gums. In addition, Muller had suffered several minor haemorrhages. He had never recovered from the night he'd spent succouring Schmidt at Eskimo Point. The surgeon expected to see a progressive weakening in his condition. He thought it unlikely any of them would be able to cross the Sound unaided.

'Foxer's mouth,' he went on, 'is very bad. Quite raw in places. He puts it down to drinking his tea too hot. Of course it isn't so.'

The Lieutenant was now seriously alarmed by Foxer's condition. There were days when he would seem to rally, only to relapse again into moody silence. He seemed to have difficulty grasping what he was told. He complained of sleeplessness, and the long lonely hours when everyone else was sleeping, as a consequence of which the Lieutenant let him have a lamp fixed to the timbers above his head.

Waking one night Emmons found him crawling down the passage in his sleeping socks.

After that, Parish took him into the two-man bag, putting Hewitt in his place. It was a move not undertaken without some anxiety, for the meteorologist, resisting all the restorative efforts of his friend Knowles, had fallen into a very depressed condition.

As reports of thefts continued, now a potato, now a portion of butter taken from the shelf in the thwart, the Lieutenant began to wonder whether he might not have been mistaken about Fabius. He no longer knew what to believe, whether it was the surgeon or another, or whether there were two of them preying on the rest. Whatever the truth of it, he blamed himself for the damage the thief was doing to the rest of the party. Sullen, surly, they had become an unknown quantity. The knowledge that any one of them might be the thief had engendered a sense of estrangement, spilling over into quarrels, often springing from the most trivial disagreements. It was as if some hostile thing had got inside the hut, some malevolence in the natural order of things. The slightest thing could flare up in a squabble. A man turning over in his sleep would provoke his bag-companion to a string of oaths and threats. The Lieutenant agonized over these ugly flashes of hostility. Yet the only sure way of retaining his influence over them, he told himself, was to refrain from interference. Except to keep the peace, he did not intervene.

So the men continued to grind at one another. Fromm's whinings and complaints were now perpetual. He bewailed his craving for tobacco. He was driven almost mad by the gnawing pangs which, he seemed convinced, were the spasms of his stomach shrivelling up. The men would have to endure rambling accounts, over and over again, of his hungering for elaborate meals: smoked sprats followed by eel soup, calf's sweetbreads served with cream and butter, Mettwurst with apple and potato mash seasoned with black sausage, served with a thick slice of black Rhenish bread ...

It was the first time, complained the laconic Emmons, that he'd been made to suffer another man's bellyache. Others, made conscious of demons they were themselves struggling to keep in check, were less tolerant. They abused Fromm fearfully. Yet no one was more tormented by his paranoid imaginings than the sufferer himself. He cursed the cooks for cheating him of his proper ration. He berated the top-sergeant for picking on him unfairly. He especially reviled the surgeon, whom he seemed to hold responsible for his own state of mind.

One morning, having been sick in the night, he rounded on Fabius, who happened to be feeding Schmidt his breakfast.

'I saw him. He keeps back bread for himself.'

'You are mistaken, Fromm,' said the surgeon with commendable control. Coolly, he raised another spoonful to the lips parted to receive it.

'Liar!' The whites of the accuser's eyes gleamed furiously in the dim glow of the lamp. 'He is a thief.'

Self-righteousness swept the handyman to desperate heights.

'All Frenchmen,' he shrieked for good measure, 'are thieves and liars.'

Disdaining to speak further to his accuser, the surgeon addressed himself to the commander in the language they reserved for confidential matters.

'Je ne soignerai pas cet homme,' he said levelly: 'il faut qu'il s'excuse son cela, je ne lui donnerai aucun médicament.'

The Lieutenant saw he could not let the matter to pass.

'You will apologize to the surgeon, Fromm,' he instructed sternly.

But the man only glared wildly, his tongue flickering over his lips.

'Nein!' The word shot out eventually.

'Ich hab's gesehen,' screeched the frustrated teller of truth. 'Er ist der Dieb! Alle Franzosen sind doch Diebe und Lügner!'

The soft yellow glow shone upward on the ring of bearded, soot-blackened faces. They looked on with gleaming eyes, hungry for any diversion that might deflect them from the wretchedness of their condition.

'Then you will leave the hut. When you are ready to apologize you may to return.'

Instantly Fromm scrambled from his bag. With such

affronted dignity as a man on all fours could muster, the little tinsmith crawled out through the canvas flap.

A whole hour passed before he was reduced to the right temperature.

Later that day the Lieutenant took back the supply of lard he'd handed over for medical supplies.

'I intend to issue two ounces a week to every man,' he said loftily, against the surgeon's protests.

He felt entirely justified. Whatever the surgeon was using it for, judging by the quantity remaining, it certainly wasn't for dressing wounds. Over the days and weeks, as the ration was steadily reduced, the doctor had continually urged increases in Schmidt's rations. Parish had known he was being mocked by these cynical requests. Yet how could he refuse without a public explanation? Seething, he'd yielded up another ounce or two of bread.

Supper that night was rich in seal blubber and extra fat, though the contentment it engendered was soon spoiled when Emmons came in with a half-empty tin of frozen milk. He'd found it hidden in a cavity chipped from a block of snow.

The rest of what he had to say was lost, drowned in a torrent of angry voices.

Lawless, though, was examining marks on the tin, that had been made by a knife with a serrated edge.

'Hanson's got a knife like that.' The Irishmen shot a hard, sideways stare across the hut.

'Sure, I had a knife like that,' said the big man casually. 'I lent it Krug weeks ago.'

This production of a *name*, after so much uncertainty, created intense feeling among the men. Krug's protests that he'd returned the knife were unavailing.

As the pressure mounted the wretch began to crumble.

'Sometimes I take bread,' he faltered. 'Others take bread. Not milk. About milk I know nothing.'

The clamour grew more ugly by the moment. Hanson, scrambling over to where the accused was lying, drew back his

234

fist, threatening to take his face off, with other expressions of such gross obscenity as outraged the Lieutenant.

He restored the peace at last, though the strain of it left him trembling and exhausted.

Breakfast next morning was a bacon stew, garnished with rancid tallow, a dish much savoured by the men on account of its strong, rank flavour. As the cooks set about their preparations, the Lieutenant announced that the bread ration would be increased with immediate effect. It was an option he'd been keeping back since Sgt Emmons discovered the bags of bread were over-running his earlier estimate. He was taken aback by the satisfaction brought about by his announcement, for the increase amounted to no more than half an ounce per man per day. It struck him that these were indeed men and not brutes.

After breakfast Parish played his second card.

'One week from today,' he began, his solemn emphasis masking an uneasy conscience, 'Sergeant Reade, with Eskimo Mitsoq, will attempt to cross the Sound and reach Littleton Island.'

The ragged cheer which greeted his announcement tore at his heart.

'United we stand, eh, Lieutenant?' sang out Diggs.

Parish knew it to be at best a forlorn hope. If most of the men still clung to the belief that Leffingwell was in winter quarters on Littleton Island, it was not a faith he shared. Though reluctant to dishearten, neither would he hold out false hopes.

'It might be best,' he warned, 'to count on no more than a small cache.'

The men, though, would entertain no discouragement. At last things were beginning to move.

Later that afternoon, when Sgt Emmons came back with a blue fox he'd shot, all agreed it was an excellent omen.

Hopes were high as the party set about outfitting the travellers. Edge and Lawless were stitching up the best sleeping bag. Fromm, a different fellow when exercising his skills, began work on a lantern. Others were making candles and cooking utensils, sewing blanket socks and mittens. In these endeavours the men once again drew strength from the figure of their leader bent over his labours, pebble lenses glinting in the blubbery glow. The Lieutenant had thrown himself into the illusion, completing letters to Leffingwell and General Sweetsir, copying out records to be carried to Littleton Island and there deposited, though the effort of writing revealed to what extent his own powers were failing. A page at a time was as much as he could manage.

The day set for departure was a calm, clear day. The cooks had roused an hour earlier than usual to prepare a special breakfast for the travellers. For a week they had been built up with extra rations.

Sick at heart, the Lieutenant watched as they set about their ounces of beef. He believed he was sending men to their deaths.

Far away in the south a faint reddish glow transformed the polar night to a dead half light. The gloom, it might have been, of an underworld. The Lieutenant led George Reade a little way apart, in order to speak privately. Shivering in the still, cold air, the men felt buoyed up with a readiness to count present troubles as all but passed. They were in a mood to clutch at anything. Though the sun's reappearance was still more than two weeks away, the months of darkness were behind them. Already to northward the long dark loom of Bache Island stood out distinctly against the grey half light. In contemplating the preparations for departure they were enjoying the illusion that their destiny once again rested in dependable human hands. If anyone could get through, it was George.

Seemingly at peace with himself, the object of their confidence stood listening, nodding, as the Lieutenant issued some final instructions. To Luther Rainbird he seemed a man who had found his work.

'Should you find a party on Littleton Island, I have included a list of articles that are badly needed here. My fear is that you will find no one. In which case your orders are to proceed to Etah, and hire natives to cross with dogs and sledges. I have put together a small package of gifts, needles and so forth.'

Emmons and Rainbird had volunteered to carry the packs as far as the shore. Strung out in single file, the four men trudged over the tundra. No one had much to say. The uncertainty of the undertaking hung too heavy for words.

As they came down the final fan of scree into the cove the travellers were made aware of the nature of their task.

A hundred yards from where they stood, beyond the fast shore ice, what might have been a wild sea of billowing breakers was frozen in the act of motion. It was a place of chaos, an abomination of desolation over which the moon, just then emerging from a bank of cloud, shed a deathly pallor.

Rainbird shivered. He felt sucked back into his own dark undertow.

The carriers set down their packs on the pebbly shore. Reade handed over a sealed letter.

'I dare say,' he said, shouldering his pack, 'we'll laugh about this. In a week or two we'll be sitting in the sun on Littleton Island, having a good laugh.'

At the crest of the first pressure ridge he turned, a shadowy figure in the moonlight, and raised a hand.

The two men on the shore remained watching until their comrades were lost to view in the chaos of ice. Distantly, like gun fire, came the booming of the floes.

On his return Rainbird sought to inform his commander that the pack was in motion.

'I hope I can rely on you not to speak of it to the men,' said Parish stiffly. 'It is better their minds should remain in a hopeful state.'

The straw-haired man might have flushed under his grime. He took it as another snub.

Later that day the surgeon, with scissors and a scalpel, severed the flap of skin that held in place Schmidt's remaining foot.

Strong winds, sweeping down from the north, continued for several days and nights. Violent gusts tore at the hut. At night

237

the mercury froze in the glass. Unable to sleep, with Foxer shifting, muttering, in the bag beside him, the Lieutenant's thoughts were with his men out on the ice. At least the moon would be shining down on them in their crossing. He hoped against hope that the Sound was frozen over. He prayed that it might be. Even if Leffingwell failed them at Littleton Island, Reade would get through to the Eskimo village at Etah. They had helped Kane, and Hayes. He believed they would help them, too.

On the fourth night Parish awoke to find Foxer partly out of the bag. He was barely conscious. The Lieutenant supported him as Fabius spooned in brandy. Foxer offered no resistance, submitting to the soup which they insisted on administering, after which he sighed, and sank back into whatever arms were holding him. How long he sat in the flickering candle light, shoulders pressed against the stones, the Lieutenant couldn't have said: only that he remained, clinging on. He was thinking of their first meeting, and the young man's restless desire to accomplish something. The icy stones struck through to the bone.

He continued to clutch the body from which, he'd all but concluded, the last vestiges had indeed departed, when the sunken eyes, as if at a great distance, opened wide, the dying man turning his head slightly to fasten on the Lieutenant's face in a long, steady look.

'Not yet …' the faint voice whispered '… a Boston bulldog …'

Later that day Fabius certified life was finally extinct. With Asher holding the lamp, the surgeon peered into the dead man's mouth.

'C'est le scorbut,' he muttered. 'Sans doute.'

The Lieutenant thought it best to pass over the dread word. He gave out the cause of death as a dropsical effusion of the heart, caused by insufficient nutrition.

The dim light cast the dead face into dreadful relief. It fell across the sharp ridge of the nose, spilling shadow into the socket of an eye. It gleamed on teeth which the shrunken lips were no longer adequate to cover. *I can't sleep, Jake, for thinking of the folks back home*, the dead man had whispered, only the day before. *I guess they think we're all goners.* In contemplating a remoteness beyond all connection, the Jew suffered a sharp pain. It was not an echo of Foxer's loneliness. It was his alone, and it left him no less solitary than before.

Then, with a knowing deeper than his own knowing, he saw that what one is lacking, another must make up for.

So it was that the *mamzer* came to carry out the last service tender hands could render the dead lieutenant, a poor corpse far from the care of those who'd loved him, straightening his limbs, sewing up his body in a covering of sacking and canvas.

The Lieutenant read the burial service from Hewitt's prayer book. He uttered the words a commander must utter in such circumstances, urging the party to take courage, not to let the lieutenant's death depress their spirits, with the men sitting with bent heads, clutching their fur caps, the wind driving into their thoughts like awful certainty: *this* was the moment that waited for them as they'd journeyed towards it, the moment they'd carried with them from the start.

Six men dragged the body on its sledge to the low summit east of the lake. Rainbird trudged at their head, lighting the way. A solitary mourner, hunched against the wind, the Lieutenant followed the cortege. It was too cold to risk exposing more of the party than was necessary. They dug as decently as they could manage. It wasn't deep. Parish scattered the earth.

That night, in the loneliness of the hours before sleep, the silence of the grave descended on the hut.

After a hundred and fifteen days of darkness, the sun returned. The men had to be chivvied out to let its reviving energies soak into their bodies. For the commander, seeing them crawling uncertainly from the hut, they might have been the dazed survivors of some disaster. Stooping after months of confinement, matted hair hanging about their shoulders, they gathered to gaze silently at the huge, swollen disc, purple in the dense vapour hanging over the Sound. Filthy, stinking as they were, the veiled Presence would not look on them.

As the mist continued to wreathe and eddy, several of the men exclaimed at a figure that might have been stepping from a dream. Their first thought, since longing told them it must be so, was of Leffingwell. Leffingwell had arrived at last.

But it was only Reade, with Mitsoq following, and they were alone.

Grey with fatigue, George was too done in to say much. They had gone perhaps ten miles out into the Sound before being stopped. There was open water as far north as the eye could reach. They'd turned south, travelling as far as Eskimo Point, ten miles across from Littleton Island. In all, he reckoned they'd gone fifty miles.

Had they seen anything, a voice asked that might have been praying for a signal of some sort, a flag, a column of smoke.

'Only the pack.' Bruised, battered by repeated falls, at that moment he craved sleep more than anything on earth. 'The fast ice was covered by water clouds. We never saw the shore.'

Then followed a doleful time. Huddled in their bags, the men were subdued by lonely, crushing thoughts. One or two of the worst afflicted gave vent to bitter murmurings directed at the land that had abandoned them to their fate.

'Don't give up on your country, men,' said the Lieutenant sharply. He was determined not to let fear rule over him, nor yet that ordeal of the spirit which Providence would no doubt lay upon him. Yet flesh is sometimes less susceptible than spirit. There were those among the party who, in their wretchedness, would gladly have died then and there.

Meanwhile, the surgeon brooded on the safety that would have been theirs if only his own wiser counsel had prevailed. Better than most, he understood the reasons for the calamity that had overtaken them. Having abandoned the fort, their best hope of survival lay in making contact with the natives of North Greenland. Instead, they had been betrayed by a bungling fool who, under the impression that the workings of Nature must somehow or other fall in with his orders, had led them down a frozen, lifeless coast in the hope of stumbling across a ship that never came.

At length the leader-in-waiting, for that was the part he had chosen, directed his bitterness where it was most deserved.

'The time to cross was in December. In December we could have crossed by sledge.'

The Lieutenant had been brooding on the breaking-up of the boat that might have carried them all across the Sound. He should never have put his trust in Leffingwell. That promise of assistance had effectively pinned him to this spot as fatally as any act of God. He began to wonder if there might not be, woven into this pattern of misfortune, some design, a dark message that was meant for him alone.

'You have brought this upon us,' screeched the surgeon. 'You are responsible.'

It was a charge William Parish would not deny.

They were hating one another worse than ever.

Day followed day in a lethargy of helplessness. Some of the men had begun to pass the whole time almost entirely covered up. As he brooded on the figures stretched out in their bags with the flaps pulled down, Parish was conscious of heads close together, of murmurings, of lips put close to ears.

With Foxer dead, the Lieutenant had begun to suffer his isolation. In his anxiety he considered restoring Rainbird as his deputy. He began piecing together phrases for the draft of a letter which might convey a magnanimous offer, setting differences aside, pulling the party together after Foxer's death, only to reject the idea as too risky. It would be playing into the surgeon's hands. He regarded the surgeon as foremost among the whisperers.

With one mouth less to feed it had become possible to announce a slight increase in the ration. In addition, there would be an increase in the weekly allocation of lard and blubber. In reality it was all a pitiful game of brag. He knew very well the bread ration would have to be cut again before very long. He dreaded having to announce it. For several days he racked his brains, considering how it might be managed without risking what was now his constant dread.

At last he saw that if he was forced to take, then he must give something too.

That evening after supper the Lieutenant announced that preparations would begin for another attempt to cross the Sound. He spoke with all he could muster of that self-assurance which in the past had been both shield and weapon. And since a commander must justify to himself whatever he asked of his men, he was clinging to the possibility, less likelihood than hope, that the Sound would freeze over by the beginning of March. He had observed from records taken at Ft Chance that February seemed to be the coldest month.

'I believe we can afford to deny ourselves a little,' he went on, 'and so I intend to cut the bread ration by a couple of ounces. We may then stay on here until the 6th, and therefore have fifteen days' ration with which to cross the Sound.'

Once again, the Lieutenant was at his most persuasive with those who wished to be convinced.

They set to work strengthening the sledges, stitching canvas, repairing ropes and runners.

They were blessed with a succession of bright days. Though it was still too cold for signs of life returning, the Greenland coast stood clear thirty miles across the Sound. The sun, lighting up a horizon of gleaming summits, told more and more of the far country they all longed for. It was George Reade, now rested, who brought the best tidings. He had climbed to the top of the glacier, from where he'd gazed upon much open water, with many large floes which, further east, appeared to afford a continuous passage across the Sound. To the north, beyond Cape Louis Napoleon, a horseshoe curve indicated fast ice in that direction. All they needed was cold weather.

That night the mercury froze solid. A week of such low temperatures, men promised one another, must surely bind the floes together. There were still those who supposed themselves due a recompense for all they'd suffered.

Later that day Nate Emmons walked over the tundra looking for signs of fox.

He'd completed an inventory of the remaining stores and equipment that would have to be hauled across the Sound. He calculated it as not far short of a ton. He was remembering the long haul from Eskimo Point, and the huge expenditure of effort. Then, they had been relatively strong. And were they now to go through it again?

A dense vapour drifted up from the Sound, through which could be heard a dismal thunder.

Emmons reflected it was perhaps a mercy they would be spared that trouble.

FOURTEEN

All through the dark months, as the pipes froze and snow solidified in the streets, Martha Parish had been writing letters of encouragement; heartfelt, yet painstakingly composed to keep back all traces of the bitterness she felt. She had no doubts, she told the families, of Lt Parish's ability to safeguard the party through the winter. They were not deceived. The fears she'd sought to suppress came back as a clamour of voices, a lamentation going up from anguished kindred, that those they loved had been abandoned in their hour of need.

Other mail of an unsolicited nature continued to arrive: communications in which her husband was reported, sometimes living, sometimes dead, his features clearly visible, though cased in ice. Spiritualized fingers, moving over charts and maps, had located him in a dozen different places. He had appeared in dreams, visions, mesmeric trances, or else projected on to walls and ceilings, an indomitable figure tramping at the head of his men, or leading them in prayer, or received with open arms by grateful natives, whose humble huts he seemed to grace, a Doctor Livingstone in furs. He had been glimpsed fishing through a hole in the ice, grappling with a bear, even raising the flag over an icy mound presumably intended for the Pole: or else, a cat's paw in the schemes of others, her William had conveyed, through spirit voices, messages of hope and love. Not one of the clairvoyants seemed to have any sense of that iron darkness, of the cold that shattered rocks. So she continued to hold him close, even at the cost of pain. Meanwhile, Martha Parish struggled to keep her mind fixed on the likeliest reading of the case.

She believed he had set out for Cape Sabine. But there was no telling where he would be now. He could be wintering at the cape. Or, with the failure of a ship to come to his assistance, he might have set off south by boat, and gone ashore at any point along a thousand miles of coast.

She did draw some comfort from reports of the naval officer appointed to command the squadron. Commander Stannery seemed to have made a powerful impression on the press. A high forehead, an unwavering gaze set deep in the bushy face, gave him, they said, a look of Stonewall Jackson.

Yet it would need, she sighed, not three ships but a whole flotilla.

As she pointed out to Lucius Clay, what with the heavy bay ice and the constant fogs a party on the shore might easily be missed. Hadn't Commander Young in the *Yarborough* steamed past Leffingwell in a fog? Could not the whaling fleet be induced to keep a watch? After all, the British had offered a bounty during the search for Franklin. Only it must be done quickly. Time was pressing.

Now, at Camp Fortitude, days were possessed of a monotony of cold and hunger. Listless, apathetic, the men rarely stirred from their bags. If they did not communicate their thoughts to one another, it was because they needed no telling. Even those rare incidents which might have distinguished one day from another seemed cast under the same fateful aspect. There was the day Sergeant Emmons spotted a fox, the first in a month, but the gun failed. One morning they were visited by their first bird, a raven. That too flew off before it could be shot.

One evening the Lieutenant saw that the surgeon's report contained a memorandum.

It is now beyond dispute that we cannot hope to cross the Sound as a party. That being the case, I propose, with your agreement, that I, together with the strongest men, cross over to Littleton Island to make contact with the Etah Esquimaux.

The possibility of a crossing was, in his view, little more than a dream. Even so, there was only one construction to be put upon the surgeon's note. It represented an attempt to abandon the weakest to their fate.

The more he thought about it, the more uneasy he became. What if the surgeon communicated his proposal to the men? It would very likely attract the malcontents. It might even bring about what he dreaded most, the division of the party.

The Lieutenant lay sweating in his bag, watching his command draining away. Suddenly, they were no longer men he'd known and commanded for three years. They had become an unknown quantity, dangerous, unpredictable. Only by getting in first , he thought, could the surgeon be forestalled. Though it would be a desperate tactic.

After a meagre supper of rancid tallow and bacon with a few ounces of bread, Parish made an announcement.

'I have received a proposal from the surgeon.'

His heart was in his mouth at the thought of what he was about to say. All his instincts were against it.

'A proposal,' he went on, 'which, if it were acted on, would affect every member of the party. Dr Fabius suggests that I should send him, with a party consisting of the strongest men, to Littleton Island, there to make contact with the natives.'

He paused, it might have been for the enormity of the suggestion to sink in.

'As you all know,' he went on, striving for that note of calm assurance which, in the past, had always reassured, 'our preparations for the crossing are almost complete. When the time comes we shall set off together, as a party. No one will be left behind. The surgeon claims we cannot hope to cross as a party. Well, that has still to be put to the test. But as long as I am in command, no one will be abandoned. Not until all efforts have been exhausted.'

He was conscious of a blankness in the air.

'United we stand, eh, Lieutenant?' piped up the faithful Diggs.

If the rest were silent it might have been because they were reflecting that the very opposite was closer to the truth. They had not forgotten their struggle over the hateful ice five months before. This time, Schmidt would have to be hauled. Muller, too, for sure. Most likely others. The thought that some were fitter, stronger, and could therefore be called upon to devote their strength to supporting the weak, struggled with the recognition that these would die anyway, and might perhaps be better left to get on with it.

Not long afterwards the lamp was put out. A darkness fell in which thoughts were thrumming.

The commander was contemplating territories, as yet unexplored, which he had still to traverse.

Brooding over his reverse, the surgeon was considering his next move.

The following morning after breakfast, a few ounces of canned tomato thickened with some crumbs of dog biscuit, Fabius spent some time perfecting the riposte his dignity demanded.

He toyed with several versions, before settling on a final draft:

I wish to notify you that I no longer consider myself a member of the United States Arctic Expedition. Only my duty as a physician compels me to render aid where it is needed. For that reason, Lieutenant, and for that reason alone, I shall continue ministering to the men as if nothing had happened.

The surgeon enjoyed some moments savouring the magnanimity of this satisfying document before dispatching it to the recipient.

Within minutes it had been thrown back in his face. The Lieutenant had pencilled in a couple of lines. *I would remind you that you are contracted up to 1st July. Until that date you remain perforce acting-surgeon.*

The commander was outside the hut doing his stretching exercises when he was confronted by a furious figure.

'I refuse,' shouted the surgeon, waving the note in Parish's face. 'Je refuse reconnaître aucun de chose.'

'Then you may consider yourself under arrest.'

'Nonsense.'

'I repeat, I place you under arrest.'

The two men stood glaring either side of a jagged fracture of the air.

247

'It will be noted on your Army record,' the Lieutenant added for good measure.

He spent the rest of the morning working out a specification of the charges. The surgeon was entitled to have them served in writing.

At the same time, he went ahead with preparations for the crossing. He had the small sledge brought into the hut, and the lashings renewed. *We try to delude ourselves*, he wrote in his log, *that we shall have some opportunity of using it. But no one is deceived.*

They had entered the territory of last things: the last of the seal-meat, the last of the onion-powder, the last of the peas, the beans, the carrots, the corned beef.

That night they ate the last of the English beef.

Then a westerly wind sprang up that raised the temperature above zero. It brought about a continual drip, drip, of water inside the hut which added to their wretchedness. The wind freshened to a gale. All day the storm continued, piling snow against the hut. There was no venturing out, except to bring in water.

The men lay listening to the howling of the wind breaking up the new ice in the channel. The commander was trying to settle on his best course of action, should they be forced to remain where they were. He concluded he had about two weeks in which to come to a decision.

Yet as the storm raged unabated the Lieutenant felt his grip on things dissolving in a flux of shifting calculations:

March 3rd. At the present rate of consumption we have enough food to keep us alive until the first week of April.

March 4th. If unable to cross Sound before the 16th, all hope of leaving Sabine must be abandoned.

March 5th. Without game, I can't see us living much beyond 15th April.

The only constant was the relentless fury of the gale. After three days snow had covered the hut completely. Inside, between the stones of the wall, and in the timbers of the upturned boat, it formed a frost which, when dislodged, rained down continually, chilling them to the marrow.

Faced with the futility of any hope that the straits would freeze over while the storms continued, William Parish wrote in his log:

March 9th. I think our chances of crossing are about gone.

That night Emmons issued the last of the corn, the soup, the tomatoes, the evaporated milk.

Next morning saw the gale abating. Dense water clouds suggested it was still raging in the Sound. After breakfast Reade came to the Lieutenant. He wanted to bring back the meat he'd been forced to abandon in Baird Inlet.

'I'm sure I can find it. I'm still strong enough. I've been there twice, so I know the route.'

He spoke, now, as acknowledged leader of all forlorn hopes.

'Nothing venture …' he suggested, for the commander's face had clouded over.

Parish shook his head. 'I cannot allow it.'

He could not see, thought the Lieutenant, that for some situations there was no help.

'Why not, for God's sake?' protested Reade to Emmons. 'There's a hundred pounds of beef there for the taking.' Privately, he wondered if the commander was losing his nerve.

Supper that night saw the last of the onions, the coffee, the dog biscuit.

Unless they found game soon, they were done for. In two months they had obtained two foxes. The commander had been poring over charts and maps. A few miles along the coast west of the island, over the bay ice of Buchanan Strait, was Alexandra Fjord. The English had recorded many signs of game in the vicinity. If there was winter pasturage there for reindeer and musk oxen then they were safe. He resolved to send Rainbird and Mitsoq to Alexandra Fjord to look for game. He was persuaded he had seen a change of heart in Rainbird. As a preliminary to entrusting him with this vital mission, he informed his former second-in-command that, if he wished it, he would be restored to duty.

'I shall, of course, write out the order in due course.'

Gravely, the straw-haired man took the proffered hand. He couldn't resist a sour reflection that in the end it was Parish who had come to him.

'Your mission is to search for game,' the Lieutenant added. 'But new lands too, wherever possible. Do your best,' he said, clasping Mitsoq by the hand. 'If there is winter pasturage there for deer and musk oxen, then we are safe.'

The sun was touching the top of the hut when, an hour later, the hunters took their leave. To the men, this, the first initiative in many weeks, reawakened optimism. They were specially heartened by the Lieutenant's letting it be known that the British had recorded many signs of game in the area. They would have embraced any deception.

The two men now hauling on the ropes were used to one another's company. They had hunted together since the autumn. It was a partnership of nods and gestures, for they rarely spoke. A hunter by instinct, the Inuk habitually kept silent to keep the edges of his senses sharp. Thrust in the thick of life, he was spared the superfluities of words. Which were, in any case, of less moment than the vibrations of air blowing from far away, the sounds and colours of ice, the dampness or dryness of snow, the smell of earth steaming in the summer. He was not quite separated from the animal world.

With the bay ice much broken up, the two men kept to the ice foot. In places it was little more than six feet wide. Rainbird, hauling on the seaward side, was acutely conscious of the black water below his boots. He could hear the waves booming under the ice. He was fearful of the ledge collapsing.

It was almost dusk when they reached the fjord. Leaving the sledge the two men climbed the crest of a moraine. Cobbles clattered in the wet cold. Patches of wind-slabbed snow squeaked beneath their boots. The solitude pressed down with a weight of desolation. Rainbird was profoundly glad to have his companion close at hand.

Mitsoq narrowed his eyes. He was scanning the ice for the black dots of sleeping seals. At a zigzag fissure, where the pack was breaking up, he bent down and scooped up water, sniffing its salt sea freshness, smelling the flesh of the blubber animals that brought life and strength.

✳

In the office of the Secretary for War a private meeting was taking place. The Navy Secretary was facing a dilemma. A slick operator, he prided himself on staying ahead of the game. Buying those whalers while Congress was still making up its mind had given him particular satisfaction. His chief clerk was thunderstruck when news that the deal was done came over the wire. *What'll we do*, he wailed, *what'll we do if Congress turns us down?* Hynes had clapped him cheerfully on the shoulder. *Don't worry, Walt. We'll start up in the whaling business.* He enjoyed sailing close to the wind.

Now, though, the wind had backed unexpectedly.

'The worst of it was, I wasn't even consulted.'

Elijah Crowell took up the *Congressional Record,* and looked again at an item marked in red ink.

Senate Resolution 224: That the Government of the United States will pay to such ship or ships, person or persons, not in the military or naval service of the United States, as shall discover and rescue or satisfactorily ascertain the fate of the expedition led by Lieut. William Parish, a bounty of $25,000.

A thin smile glimmered an instant on the glacial features of the Secretary for War. Sam had been outflanked. Now he'd come to do a little manoeuvring on his own account.

'Now the Bill's already with the Committee on Appropriations.' It still angered the Navy Secretary to think he'd known nothing about it. However, it wasn't anger he needed to register, but a note of caution.

'I am advised,' he said, with all the reluctance of a man wishing he wasn't, 'that it would be extremely unwise of us to induce civilian captains to make risky detours into inshore waters.'

He glanced sharply at the Secretary for War.

'What worries me,' he went on, 'is that should any of them get into trouble then we would be morally obliged to go to their aid.'

'So diverting the Navy from their mission of looking for Parish.' Elijah Crowell could extemporize an argument whenever needful.

'On the other hand,' Sam Hynes indicated the difficulty with a fresh cheroot, 'I'm reluctant to pass by any chance of finding your man.'

'I appreciate that,' Elijah Crowell said drily.

There was a pause as the Navy Secretary leant forward to accept a light. Gazing thoughtfully, Crowell allowed the spill to burn down to his fingers before tossing it into the fire.

'Perhaps,' he suggested, 'this is a matter for the president.'

That same afternoon they sent in a joint report.

They kept going now on pemmican and rancid bacon. Wutz served them up in a ragout of so pungent a flavour, George declared it a cause of wonderment so toothsome a dish had never found favour with the folks back home. Reade's unflagging spirit was a rock to cling to.

Even so, the Lieutenant prayed that his hunters would return with fresh meat before long. Camped on the ice of Alexandra Fjord they had spent four days in fruitless exploration, scanning cliffs and headlands, scouring the slopes of deep, steep-sided valleys. All were filled with snow. There was no pasturage for animals. No seals were anywhere hauled out on the smooth, empty ice.

The fourth evening found them once again traversing the mouth of the fjord. They had reached a place where a gravel spit slipped under the sea ice. Twilight was almost on them. The sun, a cold red orb, had begun to sink below the western hills.

Leaving Rainbird at the sledge, Mitsuk went out to the end of the spit. The Inuk recognized in his companion's inner darkness, an emanation of the blackness which, in evil times, afflicted all his people. He had himself been struggling against it now for many days. He cursed himself for coming on this trip. He cursed the folly of entrusting himself to *qallunaaq* who'd brought about this dearth of animals. Some evil was at work. He didn't know what it was. He didn't know whether *Parissuaq* was responsible, or some other man. Only that the evil was sticking to them like shit in a man's hair, in consequence of which the sea Spirit was withholding the means of life. He'd made what shifts he could. He'd used the sacred word. But he had no illusions. For the sea Spirit answered only the prayers of the great shamans. Only they knew how to speak to her.

Rainbird shivered in a cold, congealing wind. His gaze had wandered to the distant leads of dark water, and the wind's passage, scudding over the surface of the sea, when the Inuk came racing back to the sledge.

'*Taku … taku … Aaveq!*' He had spotted walrus. In the shore lead a female was playing with her calf beside a floe.

Rainbird saw only the black water, littered with chunks of ice. He reached for his rifle. A walrus, for sure, would see them through.

Already Mitsoq had unstrapped his kayak, was sliding it into the water, breathing his thanks, '*Soo, Nerrivik … soo …*' to the sea Spirit. His gear lay ready to hand: the harpoon, slotted in the groove of the throwing board, his line coiled in front of the cockpit, the sealskin float behind the small of his back.

He paddled in a wide arc, well to windward, keeping the setting sun at his back.

If he feared anything in the sea, he feared an angry walrus. Yet in his bones, his flesh, in the strings of his nerves and sinews, the Inuk carried centuries of experience. He would not let fear rule over him.

He was whining softly to the mother.

'Aiee ... ee ... Aiee ... ee ...'

Curious, she raised her head, weak eyes widening in wonderment.

'Aiee ... ee ... Aiee ... ee ...' sang the hunter, mingling all his faculties with the mystery that was the animal he was intent on killing. At the same time he was praying to his guardian spirit that she let herself be killed, since his need was very great.

He was watching her intently. He had to strike at her neck, where the layer of fat was thinnest.

'Aiee ... ee ... Aiee ... ee ...'

Across the water came a throaty, answering whine.

At the edge of the ice Rainbird could just make out the small round head raised above the water. Instinctively he raised his rifle, only to lower it again. To shoot before the harpoon hit might be to lose the prey. He waited, watching in the fading light, as man and kayak, no more now than a black outline against the satiny surface of the sea, gliding with scarcely a ripple, closed on the quarry.

Ten yards ... eight ... six ...

Staying his craft, the hunter took up the throwing board in his right hand, first finger passing through the hole by the side of the groove, his thumb closing on the notch on the left side, holding the shaft of the harpoon with the tips of his fingers. Then, rising in the cockpit, he hurled it with all his force, and was back-paddling with short, urgent strokes, when suddenly he disappeared from sight in an explosion of water.

Rainbird caught an ivory gleam of tusks as a thing the size and shape of a huge boulder rose up and came crashing down.

For the man, rifle raised, watching his comrade struggling to free himself from the wreckage, a lifetime seemed to pass, though it could have been no more than seconds before the huge beast rose again, and crashed down in a column of spray

When the boiling sea finally subsided all that remained were a few shreds of the kayak bobbing on the blue-black water.

One morning Wutz, who kept a record of such things, solemnly announced the arrival of the Lieutenant's fortieth birthday. In acknowledging the congratulations of his men, Parish declared that the last of the lemons would go into a rum punch that evening. He was glad to grant them a celebration.

Brenner had gone out with his rifle, vowing not to come back without a gift. Within an hour or two he had returned in triumph, flinging down a string of small black bodies at the commander's feet. They were dovekies, shot on the foreshore.

Great was the joy that then enlivened the wretched dwelling. Diggs blew a bar or two of *Dixie* on his harmonica. The hut rang to cheer after cheer.

Everything went into the stew: heads, claws, intestines, everything. Only the feathers were left out. It was pronounced very fine, very satisfying. 'Brenner,' Schmidt declared in the after-dinner glow, 'has the evil spell *gebrochen.*'

Over the next few days, as more birds were added to the pot, the men began to feel that perhaps Fate was coming down at last on the side of flesh and blood. Already sea and mountain were showing promise of reviving life. Little flocks of ptarmigan had been spotted, returning to their feeding grounds. George Reade, pondering the chances of catching shrimps and mussels, had devised a trap from a hessian bag attached to a hoop, which he baited with the feet of birds and fox skin sewn around stones. Going along the ice foot at low tide he found a place, a mile east of the point, where a grounded berg overhung the tidal crack. Lowering his trap into the sea, after several minutes he raised it again to discover the bait crawling with tiny crustaceans. He brushed them off into a bucket, and sank his lure again.

So he continued every day, setting and drawing his trap repeatedly until he was too cold to stay longer, or the floe, lifting on the rising tide, closed against the face of the berg. It was cold, lonely work, but George kept coming back with his ten or twenty pounds a day. It afforded each man a few more ounces in his stew.

The Lieutenant was buoyed up by this change in the spirits of his men. For some days past, in an attempt to rally the party, he'd talked of the mapping expedition he hoped to send across the mountains west of Alexandra Fjord. Now he began to expand on his plans for the trip later in the spring, when they'd regained their strength.

'I shall need you then, Hewitt,' he warned cheerfully.

'A few more stews, and he'll be right as rain,' Knowles promised stoutly for his friend.

'I trust so,' said the surveyor feebly. 'God grant I may be sufficiently recovered to be included in the party.' He had not flesh enough to grin.

Such were the changes wrought by a few days of content, men began to claim for themselves a future in which they would attempt all manner of things. April had assumed the promise of a land of milk and honey.

'It was April that brought the seals,' murmured Charly Hanson, whose eyes shone at the memory. He longed for a rich stew thickened with the blood and blubber of a seal.

Others who'd done nothing for weeks now vied with one another in their eagerness to haul back the game from Alexandra Fjord. Laughter, not heard in a long time, was rolling round the hut, when all merriment died suddenly at a crunching of snow, followed by the gasping of an exhausted man crawling down the passageway.

For a long time Rainbird had waited, not knowing what to do.

The appalling moment played over and over in his head: the sudden, uprushing violence, the ivory gleam of tusks, the threshing water. Now there was nothing. No trace of Mitsoq. Nothing. Only the fragments of the kayak, scarcely visible in the dying light.

A pale moon was rising behind Bache Island, slipping in and

out of cloud. The lone man, who had subsided on to the sledge, remained staring dully at the bay ice, bluish in the moonlight, and the water, inky black. Still he did not know what to do.

Absently he raised a hand to his face: discovered, with dull surprise, there was nothing there where his nose, his cheeks, should be. The cold had been stealing up on him. Clumsily, the lieutenant began tramping about the ice, stamping and grimacing, creasing his face repeatedly, thrashing his arms about. Then, joining the ropes and looping them about his shoulders, he set off along the coast, dragging the sledge.

Only when he felt the warmth returning did he stop to brew some tea. He took it with a swallow of rum.

If it was too dark to travel further, it was far too cold for sleep. Huddled in the double bag the lieutenant sought to sustain himself with thoughts of his comrades. Then, as he felt the weight of the hopes that were hanging on him, he was rocked by wave upon wave of anguish.

Relief came at last in the thought of action. Only in action could he shake off the malignant Fate that seemed to dog him at every turn. The straw-haired man set himself the task of getting back with the sledge and equipment. Restoration lay there: in fulfilling the task.

Stiff and numb, he set off at first light, stopping for food when he'd warmed up.

Dawn, grey and cheerless, broke over the desolate floes of Buchanan Bay. The lone man took his warm rum with spirits of ammonia, and four ounces of bacon. As he ate he looked around for some sign of life. The tracks of a fox, or a bird even, would have been companionable. He saw only the dreariness of sea and sky, and blank no-colour ice. The only sound was the motion of his jaw. If he stopped chewing, the whole world fell silent.

Setting off again, he found the sledge had acquired a will of its own. It kept slipping sideways. Somehow, in re-packing, he must have upset the balance. He knew nothing of packing sledges.

Several times he was forced to stop. He loosened the thongs, re-distributed the load, and tightened them again. It made no difference.

'It kept veering to one side,' he said later, with baffled helplessness. 'It just wouldn't run straight.'

This, and more, Rainbird recounted with the anguish of a soul desperate to be rid of a burden: the passage of the ice foot, the endless stops to clear stones and chunks of ice, the water lapping under his feet as he leant on the rope to compensate for the sideways drift, the sledge veering one last time, the runner tipping over the edge, his despairing efforts to hold on, to haul it back, until he was forced to throw off the ropes, and watch it go.

No one said anything. The men felt dwarfed by the relentless nature of their own misfortune which, it was now evident, could not have been otherwise.

'I had to let it go', said the speaker wretchedly. He was looking round, pleading to be understood. 'I'd have gone with it, otherwise.'

And might have wished he had.

That night, as others slept, the Lieutenant lay reviewing his command. He had twenty-one starving men. Two of them couldn't walk. Half a dozen more couldn't haul a pound between them. There was, in any case, no ice to cross. Nor could they look for help from Littleton Island. Nothing had gone according to plan. Now they had lost their best hunter, they had lost one of their two remaining sledges, and the kayak, their only means of retrieving game from the sea.

In this remorseless stripping away the indwelling spirit, from whose dark illumination William Parish's Puritan soul was never wholly free, had begun to discern a chastening hand. God's purposes were nourished, even by man's disasters. And what if his pride had brought them all to destruction? In that instant the Lieutenant achieved a moment of bleak lucidity. Returning home, not having lost a man, had been an integral part of his story, the story he'd told himself about his expedition. And what if that too was only another aspect of his pride?

Now, unless Brenner could kill a seal or a bear, death was inevitable.

He was surprised how calmly he viewed the matter. At Antietam he'd expected to die. In those days death appeared the likeliest outcome. It seemed to him now that one supreme effort, going forward at the head of his men, would have been infinitely kinder than this long drawn out agony.

Then, as he reflected that they must all perish, some sooner than others but all none the less, he saw there was a kind of comforting solidarity to be found in this fellowship of the dying. It occurred to him that he might perhaps say something to the men on the subject. What was expected of them, and so forth. Just as he would instruct them in any other duty they had to perform. He must see to it they died with decency.

None of them, the Lieutenant made up his mind, should die in loneliness.

And yet, it struck him uneasily, it wasn't the end that dismayed.

It might have been another illumination. Or else a reading of the famished air. That night morbid whisperings passed between the occupants of certain bags, unsavoury speculations as to the nature of their latter days. Little Wutz, wedged in with Edge and Lawless, couldn't sleep for thinking of things too horrible to contemplate.

Next morning he spoke to George about it.

'It's just talk, Hansie. That's all it is. Just talk.' All that day, though, he couldn't get it out of his head. Tramping up and down in the bitter cold, waiting for his trap to fill, the cook's fears stirred up in him a grim conjecture as to their final days: the Lieutenant enfeebled, men demoralized, reduced to there was no telling what.

It so happened, as he returned with his catch, that Edge, with the burly Hanson in attendance, was clearing snow from the top of the hut. Glittering eyes, in a blackened face all but swallowed up by a mass of fur and matted hair, turned towards him.

'Hi there, George,' the big man grinned, with a show of greenish-yellow teeth.

Reade's soul shuddered at a memory of those teeth tearing at the raw seal intestines.

As he stooped along the passage with his catch he heard the sound of a handsaw. Emmons was cutting up the bacon. Suddenly, the need to speak to that dependable man was overwhelming.

Pushing open the storehouse door, George Reade voiced the fear that had been troubling him all day.

'Have you thought what might happen if no help comes? It could get very ugly, if we come to extremes.'

Breathing heavily, Emmons sat back on his haunches. It was exhausting work, this daily struggle with the frozen meat.

'It has to be faced, Nate.'

The two men gazed searchingly at one another. Each might have broken through to the same anarchic space.

Sighing, the sergeant put his hand to the saw.

'I have my own gun, George. If I have to, I shan't hesitate to use it.'

*

In Congress, the Bounty bill had stalled. The committee on appropriations had fragmented into a series of informal conferences and private meetings, as senators pursued their various objectives.

Meanwhile, a modest tide had begun to flow in favour of the bill. Among the letters published by the Washington *Inquirer* was one from Lieutenant Leffingwell. *No possibility*, he wrote, *should be ignored, no avenue left unexplored, no stone unturned, in our efforts to rescue the gallant men of Cape Sabine*. They were sentiments widely shared by the writers of editorials. The American people, it was pointed out, expected vigorous action. They would know what to think, especially in an election year, of a Congress which failed to live up to their expectations.

Lucius Clay was by no means confident of the outcome. He feared that when the measure was reported back to the Senate there might follow another lengthy wrangle over the amount of the reward, with further amendments, and more references back to conference committees.

His suspicions horrified Martha Parish. She was especially shocked to hear of the opposition of the Navy Secretary, whose homely welcome had contrasted so agreeably with the Babylonian splendours of his apartments. He had been so enthusiastic for the rescue. She couldn't make sense of it.

'But Mr Hynes has been so helpful.'

'Mr Hynes is a politician. Generally speaking, politicians are pleased to do good, but they expect to take the credit for it. It will do him no good at all for your husband to be rescued by some Newfoundland whaler. On the other hand, rather than make the wrong decision, it is better to make no decision at all. Especially when time is on your side. Sam hopes that while the president dithers the fishing fleet will sail.'

'What worries me,' he added, 'is that he knows his man.'

She saw that he was troubled.

'That is why,' he went on, 'I believe the time has come for you to appeal yourself to the president.'

Martha Parish looked sharply at her friend.

'If I remember rightly, you described him to me as "a great booby".'

'He is still the president,' said Lucius Clay reprovingly. 'He has control over any amount of money.'

She supposed he was intending a private meeting, which he would arrange on her behalf.

'Oh, no,' he said. 'It must be at the public audience. You must be as visible as possible.'

'I have no intention,' she declared firmly, 'of making a public spectacle of myself.'

'But that is precisely what you must become – a tragic spectacle.' He was addressing her with the utmost seriousness. 'You must arouse the president's sympathies. Awaken him to the plight of the wives and mothers. Put all your heart into it. Appeal to him as a woman to his manhood.'

'I would prefer to appeal to him as a fellow citizen.' Martha Parish felt faintly sick.

'Believe me, it is the way to go about it,' he replied, observing her look of disgust. 'Unless, of course,' he added slyly, 'it is beneath the dignity of a lady from New England?'

'I am proud of my origins, Senator,' she told him tartly. 'But I believe I have the courage to creep out from under them when needful.'

*

Now, with the coming in of March, the Arctic day began to lengthen. The men were gladdened by the returning sun. Every day Brenner was out with Rainbird looking for seals. The lieutenant was much reduced since his return from Alexandra Fjord, yet he seemed incapable of rest.

One afternoon they came back early. The straw-haired man was soaking wet. He had fallen through thin ice. The Lieutenant offered to dry some of his clothing. Stiffly, he declined the offer, and crawled down into his bag. He would endure his misery alone.

With both the cooks now suffering alarming fits of coughing, the Lieutenant was forced to look elsewhere for fuel. One night, Wutz was kneeling under the thwarts as usual, heating supper over an alcohol lamp, when suddenly he swayed, and toppled sideways. Seconds later Diggs, who was kneeling beside him, also collapsed. In the ensuing confusion, with bewildered men peering out from bags, demanding to know what was happening, the astronomer's voice rang out suddenly above the hubbub.

'The lamp ... the lamp ...'

Crawling across the bags he snatched out the rags which Diggs had forgotten to remove from the chimney.

Meanwhile, those that could were scrambling for the exit, scurrying to get out, gasping for air which, at twenty below, hit the lungs with a shock that sent them tumbling like ninepins.

When the Lieutenant got outside he found Rainbird sprawled on the snow. Then Emmons, too, collapsed at his side. As he went to help him the Lieutenant's knees buckled beneath him.

He came round to find Asher trying to force a pair of mittens on his hands. Then he too collapsed. As Parish pulled the astronomer to his feet, all around him he saw figures rising, staggering, falling again, as they tried to get back to the warmth of the hut.

Revived with an issue of rum, the shaken men chewed at the restoring bread distributed by the Lieutenant. All were still stunned by the realization they could have died in minutes.

Wutz knelt again over the stove, preparatory to continuing the supper, only to discover a piece of the bacon, set out to thaw, was missing from the thwart.

Then every voice was raised in a collective howl of fury and despair at their own helplessness.

That night they had to make do with what remained of the ration. The men waited with their pans as the meat was divided.

Charly Hanson was still feeling dicky, as he confessed to the man next in line. He took his portion all the same.

'I'll put this away for later,' he was heard to say.

He had been burrowing in his bag for no more than a moment when, heaving suddenly, he was copiously sick into his pan.

Knowles was closest. Snatching the pan, stirring the vomit with a finger, he picked out what could have been a chunk of bacon, scarcely-chewed.

'That's my ration,' the big man was protesting.

As they stared.

'It's what I've just been given.'

No one was listening. The pan, lit by candle light, was going the round of peering faces. No one doubted they had found the missing meat.

The discovery let loose a flood of accusation volunteered by men who, it turned out, had never trusted Hanson. They'd always known it was him.

'Didn't I say it was his knife,' shrieked Krug. 'It was Hanson stole that milk.'

Fromm, to howls of disgust, remembered him taking his place in the line twice for the issue of rum.

George Reade was recoiling from a memory of those greenish-yellow teeth ripping at the seal intestines, gulping 'em down like any ravening beast. Revolted, he thrust it away.

'I say cut out the evil now.' He greatly feared what would become of them if they didn't. 'I say he should be shot.'

George's verdict was greeted with shouts of approval. All those who had ever pilfered a can themselves, as well as those who had not, would have competed there and then for the pleasure of letting some daylight into the bastard.

'I vote we put a bullet through him now,' the frightened man heard a voice declare, that could have been a friend's.

'There will be no vote,' said the Lieutenant sharply. 'There will be no shooting. This is a military command. I alone have authority over such matters. I will reflect on the case, and give my decision in the morning.'

For much of the night the commander agonized over what to do. He felt complicit in what had happened. *He'd* long known of the thief in their midst. Yet he'd done nothing. Worse, he had colluded in the crime. And it was no defence to plead that the surgeon's services were indispensable to the party. Should he, on that account, be given a free hand to rob his patient? Was not this a corruption in their midst which he, the commander, should have confronted? If ever a man had a right to demand a life, it was George Reade, who had so often laid his own life on the line. Yet was he to take the life of a private soldier, when for months he'd allowed the corrupt officer to go unchallenged?

Next morning, the mood of vengeful anger had all but evaporated. The men were too far gone to sustain anything for long. They gathered in a semi-circle around candles arranged at intervals around the hut. Hanson, his arms gripped by two of his comrades, was shuffled from the confinement of his bag, and left squatting before the commanding officer.

A soft, yellow glow shone on the ring of faces as the Lieutenant invoked the claims of solidarity and comradeship. He spoke of the gravity of such a crime at a time when all their lives were at stake, and the damage it did to all of them, to their morale, to their chances of survival. A man, the Lieutenant said, who would steal from his comrades in such circumstances would almost certainly desert them in their hour of need. As he spoke his eyes, it might have been of their own accord, were seeking out the surgeon. Fabius' face wore an expression of solemn concern. At one point, the man even nodded gravely. *Hypocrite*, he could have snarled, under his breath.

Instead, the Lieutenant addressed himself to the prisoner.

'Private Hanson, I believe it to be proved beyond doubt that you are guilty of this crime.'

He spoke with that measured note of authority his men expected of him, and that had always reassured them. They glowed at this vindication of the right, as against what Hanson stood for, the law of the frontier, the anarchy of each man for himself.

The commander, though, was mocked by his own hollowness as he came to pronounce sentence.

'You will be placed under close arrest, and confined to your sleeping bag. You are not to leave it without permission, nor to go outside the hut unless escorted.'

One day the Lieutenant sent Emmons up to the top of the boat to cut openings in the roof.

As the first holes appeared, shafts of sunlight pierced the darkness of the hut. No rescuers, breaking through with their picks to men trapped underground, ever shone a more affecting beam. The sweet yellow light cut through the coal black air. It brought home, as nothing else could, the wretchedness of their condition. Strewn among the filth and squalor of five months were tins, pans, mugs, each with its coating of soot. Floor, walls, sleeping bags, the timbers of the boat, everything was black. Even the melting ice was black, and the sooty droplets clinging to the timbers. In that illumination the ragged figures crouching on all fours identified, as if for the first time, the blackened faces of other men, though scarcely recognizable as such, that could have been beasts in a cave. Then all they had suffered of squalor and deprivation, and despair at their own helplessness, rose up, and overflowed. Many were moved to tears to see one another so.

All were showing signs of some deterioration or dysfunction. Muller's condition was the most serious. He lay in his bag without speaking or stirring, except for meals. He had a wheyish look about him, only yellow, and transparent. After Muller, Hewitt and Nadel, who was fetching up blood, were now among the weakest. Even the fittest had begun to suffer bleedings, ulcerations, swollen hands and faces. Costive for weeks, Sedgewick could not manage any movement of the bowel. The surgeon had prescribed doses of calomel, and prepared suppositories, but without effect.

There was scarcely a man who was not experiencing difficulty in evacuation. The Lieutenant came back one morning very much exhausted. He was shaking all over. It troubled the astronomer enough to mention it to Fabius.

'I hardly think,' the surgeon murmured, 'he realizes how weak he is.'

Others were all but crushed by bitter thoughts. One night, out of an oppressive silence, a solitary voice was heard to mutter: 'I vote we share out the rest of the food right now. Better all die together, than dragging on like this.'

Inside, they were dead already; dead to all hope, all faith. Meanwhile, they continued their slow progress through the circles of Hell. They had food enough for a leisurely descent. Brenner would bring back a ptarmigan or a dovekie, the feet of which would furnish bait for Reade's shrimping expeditions. Twice a day, at low tide, he went out to set and draw his nets. It was a cold and lonely vigil by the stranded berg, drawing up the bait with frozen fingers, combing off the tiny crustaceans, no bigger than grains of wheat. Sometimes it seemed a pointless labour too, for the shrimps were mostly shell, and of questionable value. The men had to force them down. Fromm complained they made him sick.

George, though, had to be pegging away at something every day, if only in his head. It was what kept him going. Often now, nursing his frosted fingers, he lay in the bag he shared with Brenner, contemplating the hundred pounds of English beef lying at Baird Inlet, and what it would mean to try to bring it back. Weakened as he was, he would be taking his life in his hands. And yet self-recovery sometimes lay in attempting the only thing possible, the thing that had to be done.

One night, just before lights-out, he visited the Lieutenant's bag.

'This summer a ship will arrive for sure. If we're to stand any chance of being here to meet it, we're going to need that meat.'

Earlier that day Emmons had come to the Lieutenant with the same offer. The arguments against were very strong. The cache might no longer be there. Even if it was, the chances of finding it, after five months of winter storms, struck him as highly unlikely. 'No, Sergeant, request refused.' Seeing the look on Emmons' face, he'd added, 'I can't afford to lose you.'

Somewhere in the hut a feeble voice had begun a rambling monologue. Muller couldn't last much longer. Suddenly Parish knew that to give his men a chance he must grasp at any straw.

Next morning the sledge was loaded for the journey: stove, axe, rifle, rations for six days. A two-man bag for shelter. No tent. They hadn't strength to pull a tent.

To avoid the long detour by the strait, Reade elected to go straight over the glacier. Rainbird insisted on giving him a downhill start to Rosse Bay. He set off with a party of four to drag the sledge to the summit.

Later that afternoon, bruised, battered from repeated falls, he was the last to return.

All day Muller had been slipping in and out of consciousness. After supper he began to call feebly for water, entreaties that upset his comrades who had none to give him. It was a relief when finally he slipped away again.

That night George Reade spent the time before departure writing letters, that cost him much in silent reflection. At last, as his own bag was packed and loaded on the sledge, he crept in with the dying man for an hour or two of sleep before departing. From the icy chill which closed around him he realized Muller must have died some time before.

Just before midnight the two men got ready to depart. Ahead of them lay a round trip of seventy miles. Their comrades gathered round them with the helplessness of men who could do no more than offer their good wishes. Raising himself on his elbows Lothar Schmidt, with tears in his eyes, gripped Brenner's hand between his stumps. Even the prisoner under punishment was hating his baseness. 'Good luck,' he called, from the confinement of his bag. And would have given anything for a reply.

Subdued, the rest of the party went out with lanterns to speed the travellers on their way. Muller's death seemed the worst possible omen. As they gazed at the torn clothing, pitifully inadequate for the rigours of their journey, above all, at the emaciated faces, in which huge eyes had the beseeching look of victims, they recognized the enormity of the undertaking that was being attempted on their behalf.

Amid the final handshakes the commander, who had begun to yield to the conviction that his own particular judgement would be to lose, one by one, the men for whom he was responsible, embraced the two men with a fervour that might have been reluctant to let them go.

Rainbird, who had taken a sealed envelope into his safe keeping, looked on with bitter foreboding. Remembering George's words spoken privately to him – *I'm pretty well used up, Luther …* – he felt suddenly outsized by his own swelling breast.

To a faltering cheer, the two men set off. They went with slow, containing steps, breathing evenly, leaning into the slope. Above their heads the night was filled with luminosity but they, eyes fixed, saw nothing but blue ice and snow as they plodded upward, the only sound the crunch of boots, the steady rasp of breath.

At the top of the glacier they found the sledge where Rainbird had left it, chocked with stones.

As Brenner worked to loosen the stiffened ropes, his companion gazed out across the Sound. The night was silent with a wonder that was inexhaustible, that could never be wasted. It was so still he could hear a remote sighing of breakers washing against the cape. Below, the bay ice seemed shivered into a crazy paving, the ice blue with a fiery phosphorescence, at the horizon a haze shining with starlight, above which hung the starry firmament. The vastness of the sky, the solitude of ice and stars, brought back the old life and its days of failure among the rocky shores of New England, striving for something that always seemed to elude him, that haunted him because he never could possess it. It struck him that the transcendence he sought was not, as he'd imagined, something infinitely remote, but close at hand. All the time it was close at hand.

Suddenly George Reade was filled with a gladness wholly unlooked for. If there'd been times when he'd asked himself why he'd come on this adventure, with all its toils and perils, it struck him now that perhaps only through sufferings and strivings could a man come at the mystery of his life. Another surge of joy swept over him. He hadn't done much. Only what was necessary. What had to be done. And most of what he'd tried had come to nothing. All the same, he was glad he'd come here, glad to have had the chance. Only this way could he have learnt what he'd learnt.

Turning to the sledge, he looped the harness across his shoulders.

'Time to go, Rudi.'

He went on his way without regret.

FIFTEEN

One Saturday afternoon, the regular open day, Martha Parish stood with Lucius Clay waiting to enter the Executive Mansion.

Not without great misgiving had she been persuaded to this. Yet the need could scarcely have been greater. She greatly feared that unless the reward were proclaimed within the next few days, the fishing fleet would have already put to sea. She had repeated to herself times over that it was an old and honourable custom for the people to call upon the Chief Magistrate with their petitions. *Our president*, Professor Coussins used to say, *is the first citizen of the Republic, nothing more.*

At length the shuffling queue conveyed them through the east entrance, and so to the threshold of the public audience chamber.

'You must have been here many times,' she remarked, made nervous by a racket of male voices from within.

'Not since the refurbishment. I shall be greatly interested to observe the effect. I have heard it said,' he went on airily, 'that if our current president is to be remembered, it will be chiefly for the number of potted plants he has added to the White House.'

Her first impression, though, was of sweeping drapery, and towering windows. Indeed, a person of coarser breeding might very well have gaped at an interior the very opposite of homely, a room in which embellishment ran riot. All was richness and display on a scale beyond her comprehension. Never had she seen such a wealth of fluting and gilding, of moulded plaster-work and panelling, of glass and vegetation. It might have been a riverboat saloon, the haunt of thieves and gamblers. Vast mirrors, in which reflections strove together with bewildering effect, ran from floor to ceiling: a *silver* ceiling studded with gilded bosses and pendants, supporting the weight of two great chandeliers. Below, across a carpet of gold and magenta medallions, a press of frock-coated bodies swarmed like bees round some invisible core of sweetness.

She had cherished Professor Coussins' words about the people calling on their Chief Magistrate. But these weren't the people. These were the men she'd seen at Willard's Hotel. She recognized Mr Potwine, and that old senator with the curled moustaches.

'Go forward,' Lucius Clay was urging her.

Dismayed, Martha Parish froze. She shrank from any contact with that crush of bodies, of smoke, and whiskers.

'Go *forward*.'

Up on the wall a full-length portrait of General Washington gazed down reproachfully, radiated Father's distaste for all huckstering, fist-slamming politicians.

'Where virtue won't serve,' she sighed, 'I suppose one must make do with vice.'

The old man leant on his cane, the better to fix on her a gaze of ironic admiration.

'My dear Mrs Parish, we will make a politician of you yet.'

She had been spotted, though, and was instantly hailed by Senator Cutpurse.

'Come forward, Mrs Parish, ma'am,' he called out in his deep voice. 'Come forward.'

Offering his arm the old man led her, floating like a bride over a dozen plush medallions, his deep rumbling bass announcing, 'Make way, there … make way for Mrs Parish …' with the press of congressmen parting like corn in Kansas, to reveal a stout person in lavender trousers. It was, she thought faintly, all quite ridiculous.

The president advanced to greet her with a welcoming smile. He had moist, brown eyes, and hefty whiskers bordering a florid face. 'Let us sit over here,' he suggested. Leading her from the throng, he drew her to a circular settee, surmounted by a potted palm .

He seemed a kindly man, evidently desirous of putting her at her ease. But Martha Parish was trying to remember her words, that succinct statement of the situation she had rehearsed with such deliberation, for she feared she could expect no more than a few moments with the Head of State.

The president, though, was asking if she found Washington as cultured as Boston.

'I am not well acquainted with Boston, sir,' she was able to answer, being well rehearsed in that particular line of questioning. 'Though I believe Washington to be a cultivated town.'

But he had passed on to his great admiration for her husband. 'Lieutenant Parish is embarked upon one of the most manly things to which any of us could aspire.'

The Arctic had no meaning for Ty Greig, except as a great white blank. He could not imagine why any man should want to go to such a place. Yet he loved to roll the great phrases under his tongue, and was doing so now, savouring grit and backbone and the pioneering spirit. Martha Parish, inclining her head politely, caught a glimpse in an enormous mirror of a small plain woman sitting beside the President of the United States. Who was clearly in full flow. And might, she feared, continue so indefinitely.

'Mr President,' she began, seeking to bend the conversation to some purpose, 'this coming summer offers the last chance of bringing my husband's party back alive. The relief squadron will do everything in its power, I know, but there are thousands of miles of coast to search, hundreds of bays and inlets.' In such surroundings, amid the potted plants, the thought was desolating. 'And there is the fog ...' she faltered.

The spaniel eyes gazed consolingly.

'My fear,' she could not help confiding, 'is that their sufferings will already have proved fatal to many of the men.'

She looked most earnestly at the rather puffy face, which had arranged itself in an expression of kindly concern.

'That is why,' she said, recovering her composure, 'I consider it crucial to enlist the aid of the fishing fleet by proclaiming a reward.'

Martha Parish fixed the president with a gaze some folk would have considered uncomfortably direct.

The Chief Executive looked grave.

'Well, you know, the matter lies with the Secretaries for War and the Navy.'

'But they are opposed to it,' she said, surprised, for he must know that very well.

Then, in the same instant, she saw he was embarrassed, and that she was being trifled with.

The president smoothed a finger over his whiskers. He stood up. Not knowing what to do, Martha Parish rose uncertainly to her feet. Meanwhile her host had begun easing into his closing formula; was suggesting they rejoin the company, had already taken her arm, and was steering her back towards the throng. It was all too much. Alarmed that she had lost her opportunity, Martha Parish forgot whom she was addressing, forgot where she was. Most of all, she forgot herself.

She swung round to confront her escort, digging her heels fiercely into the Wilton. She was trembling with indignation.

'Is it not grotesque, Mr President,' she demanded, '*grotesque*, that American wives and mothers should have to come begging money from the government to go to the aid of loved ones in peril of their lives?'

A sudden hush had fallen on the buzz of conversation. She was conscious of the startled expression in the wet, brown eyes.

He would, he said, almost galloping her back to where Senator Clay was waiting, be sure to communicate her anxieties to the Secretaries for War and the Navy. He did not doubt they had the matter in hand. Everything that could be done would be done.

Martha Parish, exposed to that smile of absolute assurance, was made aware of numbing emptiness. She had had her few minutes with the president. She had come away with nothing.

*

At Camp Fortitude anxiety was mounting for Reade and Brenner.

Seven days had passed since they set out. Within hours of their departure a boisterous wind sprang up, battering about the hut, the racket swelling relentlessly to the high roar of an Arctic blizzard. Three days the storm had raged, before abating. Clear weather followed. Rainbird had climbed to the top of the glacier, scanning the ice of Rosse Bay through the glass. There was no sign of them. Then the weather worsened. It was too bad to leave the hut. Only Emmons, who'd taken over the shrimping duties, still ventured to the fishery.

One morning, as he was setting out, he saw a solitary figure coming over Cemetery Ridge.

As the sergeant got up to him, the exhausted man sat down heavily on a rock. It was Brenner.

He looked up mutely. Tears welling in his eyes told Nate Emmons all he needed to know.

Right from the start they were up against the old malevolence. First it was deep snow swamping the sledge, pitching them into drifts as they floundered down to the bay. Then, on the bay ice, it met them face to face. Screeching insanely, it became recognizable as a demented voice, whose worst ravings they could not withstand, but had to scramble on all fours, or else flatten themselves on their bellies. They struggled on for as long as they could, until forced to crawl into their bag. For the rest of that day, and all the night that followed, the storm howled over them, covering them with snow.

At daybreak they set off again, traversing the bay ice under dark, blustering clouds. They slogged on hour after hour, past the grey remains of decaying bergs, below the snouts of glaciers, until nightfall, when they came at last to their old camp at Eskimo Point. That night they bedded down in the abandoned hut. Reade put them six miles from the point where the meat had been cached.

The next morning was calm and clear. Leaving the bag and

part of their rations, they hurried on with a lightened sledge, hoping to find the cache and return to their camp in a single march. But pressure ridges in the ice foot forced them to make long detours out into the bay.

By mid-morning a gale came down from the north-west, whipping the snow into a frenzy. They were unable to see any distance. All they could do was to follow the loom of the shore, to the sound of grinding, as the ice field heaved on the swell. It was mid-afternoon before they'd reached what Reade took to be the site of the cache.

'We searched,' said the big Saxon simply. 'We found nothing. No rifle. No meat.'

The Lieutenant was reflecting it was just as he'd feared. He should never have let them go.

'We should have turned back then.' An inconsolable anguish coloured the speaker's voice. 'We should have turned back.'

But Reade wouldn't hear of it. He'd come to find the meat.

For another hour they roamed over the snow, blankness behind them, blankness in front of them, until George began to stagger.

'All the strength went out of him. Only the wind was holding him up. If it slackened, he fell over. When it blew hard, it pitched him on his side.'

Somehow, Brenner got them both to the lee of a grounded berg where he fed George tea and rum, with spirits of ammonia.

'I tried to get him going. But he couldn't stand without me holding him. He said his feet were cold. He wanted me to tell his mother what he wanted doing with his things. There was a ring he wanted to go to a young lady in Pittsburgh.' Fumbling in his clothing, the speaker might have been intending to produce the item in question.

The listening men saw how it was. George had given and given, until there was nothing left.

Meanwhile, Brenner was recalling merely how he'd laid his comrade full stretch on the sledge. Of other small acts of kindness – taking George's head and shoulders into his lap, easing out of his own seal-skin *temiak*, wrapping it round the frozen feet – he said nothing, confessing only that somehow or other he must have fallen asleep, for he'd heard, or maybe *dreamt* a voice, and the voice was saying *Wake up, Rudi … wake up …* He'd started suddenly, and there was George smiling up at him.

How long he sat there on the edge of the sledge, eyes screwed up against the driving snow, cradling George's head in his arms to protect his face, he was unable to report. His whole body, even his mind, had seemed suspended. He couldn't move, he couldn't think. He only knew he must remain, clinging on to George until he died.

When that was accomplished, and finding himself still alive, Brenner had struggled back to the camp at Eskimo Point.

Next morning, taking the axe, he'd walked back the six miles to bury George. He wouldn't leave him there, exposed to the wild beasts.

Then, still dragging the sledge with the axe, rifle, and double bag, he'd started back. It had taken him four days, trudging, resting during the dizzy spells, the frequent blackness before the eyes, then trudging again. He had to get back. If he failed, he knew another party would set out to search.

'I had to leave the sledge,' he added apologetically. 'It was too much for me.'

Fumbling again in his breast, the speaker produced the package he could have been searching for before, and handed it to the Lieutenant.

'George's rations.'

One man, Krug it was, broke into loud sobs and groans which were most dismal to the ears of the men, who berated him soundly, being glad to have someone to take it out of. Their fear now was that the best they'd had of indomitable courage, of strength and purpose, had been taken from them, and they did not know what would become of them.

*

A week had passed, a week in which Martha Parish had relived, over and over again, her visit to the White House. She couldn't believe she had spoken so to the President. It was not in her character to raise her voice to anyone. Though Senator Clay had made light of it.

'Congressmen are none the worse for the loosing of a little fateful lightning now and then. As for the president, believe me, Matty, your sword could not have fallen on a worthier neck.'

Afterwards, whisked away in the carriage, she sat shrinking with mortification as she recalled the stunned silence that had greeted her outburst. How the congressmen had stared. Even so, it was nothing less than the truth. Had they no wives, no families?

Then she thought of William, and the struggle for life going on far away at the very top of the world. She hoped he would not think badly of her. How heartened he would be to know of the enormous public enthusiasm for the rescue mission.

She took up the copy of the newspaper Mrs Stacey, who had lately taken the ground floor apartment, had kindly brought back from New York for her to see.

The *New York Sentinel* told of crowds of onlookers visiting the Brooklyn Navy Yard to inspect the progress of the work. It was reassuring, after so much incompetence and prevarication, to know that the preparations were going ahead by day and night. There was no doubting, the *Sentinel* assured its readers, the Navy Secretary's zeal for the expedition. Secretary Hynes was determined that nothing should be left undone that might contribute to a successful outcome of the mission.

Yet he would not enlist the aid of the fishing fleet. Oh, the hypocrisy ... the *hypocrisy* ...

It was with growing disbelief and anger that she read the rest of the article as it ran on, secure in its foolish assurance, ignorant of the difficulties of the search, ignorant of the likely condition of the men awaiting rescue, though concluding with a caution addressed to the squadron commander, should he be tempted to an early passage of Melville Bay:

The fate of earlier parties should be sufficient to persuade him of its unwisdom. If Lt Parish and his party have survived the winter and are alive in June, they are likely to be alive in July and August. A delay of a few weeks will be of little consequence.

Suddenly, she saw the whole enterprise for what it was – a sham, a swindle.

She was furiously, helplessly angry. Passion and frustration strove together, and she broke down in tears. Still shaking a little, she was setting pots of hyacinths in her window when the Western Telegraph boy brought a wire to her door. It was from Senator Clay. *Report forwarded to Congress. No recommendation either way.*

So the President had indeed done what Lucius Clay feared. Now it was up to Congress.

Her eye fell on the *Harper's* photograph in its silver frame. Always, now, the faces of the men evoked thoughts of wives and families undergoing their own ordeal of abandonment: Mrs Sedgewick, who had tried so to keep her husband from going, now left with a baby; the estranging bitterness of Mr Edge of Ohio, who had nothing to say to his son Chuck; of fathers to whom she had brought news of long-lost sons, Herr Krug in Chemnitz, Herr Stempel in Potsdam, who might have been kindlier served left in ignorance. She thought of that buzz of congressmen milling about the president that day. Whatever was happening at Cape Sabine had no meaning for those men. And General Sweetsir disgraced. General Sweetsir, for whom William would have pledged his life. It was beyond belief.

Martha Parish had lost all confidence in the masculine command of affairs.

*

Decreasing intervals of twilight now separated the lengthening Arctic days.

Twice a day, at low tide, Emmons went off to his fishery,

setting his net in the tidal crack, dredging for kelp, while waiting for the shellfish to collect. Sometimes, toiling back over the ridge, his eye was caught by the glint of sun on a brass button where Lt Foxer lay under his thin covering of soil and gravel.

The hunters, too, went out turn and turn about. Brenner was now joined on these expeditions by Klaus Stempel, replacing Rainbird, who had become much abstracted from what was happening around him. They spotted seals quite frequently, but never in accessible places. Weary, after long hours roaming the length and breadth of the island, they came back with little to show other than the occasional dovekie or ptarmigan, mere scraps of nourishment which, on the Lieutenant's orders, they consumed themselves.

'Our only chance is to keep them going. If their strength fails, we are all finished.'

Daily he noted in his log the steady deterioration of the party. His own strength, the Lieutenant might have added, was not of the best. His bowels seemed to have lost their function. Despite dosing himself, the ordeal of evacuation could be managed, if at all, at the cost of considerable pain and tearing of tissues.

One morning, after a terrible passage, he came back exhausted, having lost much blood. It brought about an icy exchange with the surgeon.

'I am bound to tell you,' Fabius informed, 'that these exertions must place a strain upon the heart.' He was thinking that were the Yankee officer to suffer a myocardial infarction while in the act of defecation, it would be *une drôlerie*, to say the least.

'If, and when, you form the professional opinion that I am not likely to survive, I wish you to inform me.'

'Of course.'

'Do I have your word of honour on that?'

'*Naturellement.*' Such a request could, of course, be taken for granted. Who else could any of them look to but himself? Only a medical man was now qualified to direct the affairs of the party.

His daily examinations were uncovering a wealth of observations relating to the progress of gradual starvation. His clinical notes, written up in painstaking detail, recorded fluttering heart actions and diminished pulse, marbly limbs from which the veins had all but disappeared, the torpidity of bowels, the painful passing of motions hard as musk-ox beef. This valuable testimony to the frailty of flesh and blood stirred up in the surgeon an increased determination to survive. It was imperative that he deliver in person these contributions to the scientific literature.

He was unsparing in his attentions to the sick, and the men were comforted by his devotion to duty: that in this desolate place something of the human spirit yet persisted. Some, though, had become so loathsome to themselves as to sink beyond all consolation. Hewitt, in particular, was much distressed by grotesque swellings to the lower half of his body.

With Asher holding a candle over the affected parts, the surgeon made slits in scrotum, legs and abdomen. A large quantity of water flowed out with the blood.

So, as the party's strength diminished, the surgeon began to figure ever larger in the Lieutenant's reckoning. Almost daily now he loomed, a disturbing presence, as Parish struggled to hold on to his command. His insistence that extra rations be issued to those whom he declared sick was a persistent irritant.

'Nadel is really very weak. He complains that he can't collect his thoughts, a sure sign of a poor blood supply to the brain.'

Reluctantly, the commander agreed to an increased ration. Yet this constant juggling of rations was a continual anxiety. Should ailing men be given the nourishment they needed, or should the meagre ration be eked out even further so that the strongest might survive? So, while giving way, he resolved to make up the loss, at least in part, by taking less himself. They simply had to last out until the spring. This determination led him into yet another calculation, weighing days in ounces, setting them against the likely activity of the middle pack in

Melville Bay. Yet if they were to stand the faintest chance of surviving until a ship might reach them, it would mean hanging on until the end of May.

There is an obscure comfort to be found in lists and workings-out. It will foster an illusion of control where events might otherwise seem insupportable. Even so, the strategy the Lieutenant now pieced together, a blend of supposition and self-denial, was flimsy enough whichever way one looked at it.

That night, after their meagre supper, he revealed the details of a plan involving the alternating of the meat ration with shrimp and sea-weed stews.

'This way,' he concluded, 'we can expect to make a daily saving of four man-ounces. Then, with the better weather, it should soon be possible to gather plants and lichens, and so stretch out the ration further.'

He looked round the ring of faces, impassive in the candle light.

'I believe it can be done,' he added encouragingly.

They might have been too far gone to care.

The surgeon's opposition, though, was wholly predictable. 'I cannot permit it.'

The Lieutenant stiffened.

'I speak, of course,' Fabius added smoothly, 'as a medical man. As such my first consideration must be the welfare of my patients.'

Parish was conscious of the muscle ticking in his cheek.

'We have to stretch out the ration,' he contented himself with saying. 'It is our only hope.'

'It is madness. For the weaker men it is certain death. They are in need of more food, not less. Already the shell-fish you feed them are making them sick.'

'You appear not to have grasped a simple fact. Our situation is desperate.' It did not help that the surgeon's observations were entirely correct.

'Then let Emmons' ration be cut. Or Brenner's. They are the strongest.'

'We must keep the hunters on their feet ...'

'And let the rest of us go hang,' cut in a truculent Irish voice. 'There'll soon be a lot more graves on the hill for sure.' A tense silence greeted this, the voicing of a truth, it could have been, too long suppressed. 'And someone,' Lawless added menacingly, 'will have to answer for it. Before God, they will.'

A murmur began that might have swelled to vociferous agreement, had it not been swiftly overtaken.

'Any more talk like that will be dealt with severely. It is incitement to mutiny, and is punishable by death.' Painfully, the Lieutenant hoisted himself up in his sleeping bag, well aware he'd been dragged into a public dispute that could only damage his authority.

'Let me repeat,' he went on, his voice shaking slightly, 'in such extremity as we are placed, the punishment for mutiny can be nothing less than death.'

The men were silent: silent, and subdued. It was as if something fearful had got inside the hut, some unknown quantity, and they were at a loss as to what might happen next. Huddled together in twos and threes, they burrowed into their bags as the frost tightened its grip.

Next morning, as the cooks were serving breakfast, a note was passed to the Lieutenant.

My professional duty compels me to inform you as follows: It is my belief that your general debility, coupled with insufficient nutrition, is now impairing your mental powers. Your judgements, while made for the best, are likely to be impaired. I beg you to consider the implication of this deterioration for your conduct of affairs. My sole desire is to help you all I can in this trying ordeal. You are, I know, doing everything for the best.

Parish folded the note. His first thought, as he stored it carefully among his papers, was that Rainbird was behind it. A moment's glance at the former athlete, feebly spooning up his stew, told him it wasn't so. Though Fabius would still need Rainbird. The surgeon had no military standing. Yet what could they do? They had no alternative plan to put to the men. The party would be no less helpless whoever was in command. Indeed, they would be in greater peril. Yet the more he thought about it, the clearer it became that Fabius' attempt at resignation had been a calculation. In distancing himself, making public his withdrawal, he evidently wished to be seen as raising his own standard. Well, he'd scotched that.

Even so, the Lieutenant was assailed by a fear that the surgeon's note might represent no more than the truth. In which case, he must regard his own judgement as questionable.

Later that day he wrote a memorandum naming Emmons as his successor. This, too, he stored in his log. He decided not to make it public yet. At the same time he resolved to restore the ration by a couple of ounces.

That week a third grave was dug up on the ridge. The Lieutenant gave out the cause of Hewitt's death as resulting from the action of water on the heart, induced by insufficient nutrition. If he avoided the dread word *starvation,* none of the men were fooled. They had given up talking of the meals they would eat when they got back to New York or Philadelphia. Their thoughts now were of the past, never of the future, for they had no future.

Yet for one man among them even the years gone by seemed to count for nothing. A frontiersman most of his adult life, for years he had roamed the far side of a desert that separated Luther Rainbird from himself. Now, all but swallowed up, he had become a tiny speck in his own wilderness, waiting for the end to come, waiting without hope. He was vaguely conscious that he needed help. But George was dead, and he didn't know where to turn. The Lieutenant had urged them to seek the consolation of prayer. Only he didn't know what prayer was. He didn't know how it happened.

What he needed, he told himself, was some exercise, something to divert his mind from this infernal brooding.

Dragging a piece of planking from the last of the timber

scattered outside the hut, he steadied it against the sledge. Then he took up the bowsaw and started work. Gasping for breath after two or three passes, he was suddenly startled to feel the life draining out of him. It was gushing from his nose.

Astonished, he sat down heavily on the sledge, where Emmons found him, a few moments later, his beard a mess of blood.

'No use ...' he groaned. 'No use.'

＊

A light drizzle was falling as the *Louisa Soames*, her paintwork glistening, was towed out into the East River.

That morning hundreds of well-wishers had boarded her to smother her foredeck with floral decorations as she lay at her pier in the Brooklyn Navy Yard. The Navy Secretary made his usual buoyant speech. 'Earlier attempts failed,' he told the press, 'because they were too cautious. Success in a task like this calls for two things: thorough planning, and boldness in execution.'

Brooklyn Bridge was lined with thousands waving down as the little ship slid out into the upper harbour. Thousands more waved from the Battery, and the Brooklyn side.

Whoops and whistles rent the air repeatedly, as every ship and tug in sight gave three blasts for the *Louisa Soames,* steaming on past Governor's Island, down through the Narrows to Sandy Hook, where Lieutenant Bostock stopped to swing ship for compass deviation, then turned her head to the Atlantic.

＊

Now, towards the end of April, the men of Camp Fortitude enjoyed a spell of good weather.

The temperature was not always above freezing. Even in a light breeze the weaker men suffered intensely from the cold. But when the air was calm, and the sun high in the sky, the sensation of heat was a blessing indeed. The entire party went out to soak up the sun. Those too feeble to crawl were hauled out by their friends.

Even Hanson had been paroled, and allowed outside the hut. The Lieutenant could not bring himself to withhold God's light and warmth from any man. Besides, with the steady drip from the roof now saturating everything, removing ice had now become a priority.

That day, watched sourly by the invalids, Hanson carried out six tubs of ice from inside the hut. When that was done he set about tearing out the insides of the boat, dragging out the timber, laying it to dry in the sun.

For the enfeebled men stretched out on bags this flaunting of a vigour nourished at their expense seemed to mock their infirmity.

'It's the first time I've seen the bastard do any real work,' muttered Sedgewick to Edge.

The burly man began to sing as he hauled the timber. He sang in a cheery bass:

> 'Over the garden wall,
> The sweetest girl of all,
> There never were yet such eyes of jet ...'

They all knew he was doing it on purpose. Some would have killed him if they could.

Then, in the south, the sky grew low and leaden. A south-easterly swept down from the glacier. It began as a faint, distant soughing, the stirring of a forest. Emmons, returning to the hut with a bucket of sea-weed, felt a prickle of spindrift against his face. Already dust devils of dry snow were scuffling across the ridge ahead of him. Within minutes the gusts had turned to gale, and the gale to a storm. The cold was intense. The sergeant could feel the skin over his cheekbones tightening. Every few yards he had to stop, turning his back to catch his breath.

All that day the storm prevailed. Cooped up again, the men lay silent, spiritless. Nor could the Lieutenant do anything to rouse them. Feverish, aching in every joint he rested now, at Emmons' insistence, in the single bag, laid on a mattress.

The astronomer, feeding the sick man with beef extract, feared he could not last much longer.

'He's at a standstill,' he confided in the sergeant. 'It's cutting his own ration has done this.'

Meanwhile, it was becoming clear to the surgeon that he must himself assume supervision of the party.

Later that day, having busied himself with pencil and paper, he approached the bag where the Lieutenant lay to communicate the results of his deliberations.

'I have drawn up a roster of hunting duties. It is designed to share out the task, and so conserve our strength.' Confident of his standing, the doctor believed the time had come to convey his thoughts in English.

'That won't be necessary,' said the Lieutenant shortly. 'We have our hunters.'

The surgeon shrugged. 'But they must be rested.'

He might have been soothing a sick child.

'I do not consider either of our present hunters unfit for duty.'

'Surely I alone am judge of that?'

Flat on his back, the Lieutenant was in no shape for a debate.

'I repeat, we have our hunters,' he said wearily, and closed his eyes.

'I repeat, they must be rested.'

Throbbing in every joint, the Lieutenant raised himself painfully on one elbow. 'Then let me make myself clear. As surgeon you may nominate the fittest men. As commander I shall stipulate the best hunters.'

For a moment Fabius seemed struggling to check, hold in the flood: then it broke, the phrases leaping, tumbling to an exchange of furious French that could have been a flurry of blows, or clash of weapons, until the Lieutenant – by now real mad, as every man could see – barked out the language of Command.

'I have given you an order.'

'I do not consider you in a fit state to issue orders.' Borne up by his own singular authority, the surgeon could tolerate no contradiction.

'What's that you say …'

'I repeat, you are not in a fit state.'

'Why don't you listen to the doctor,' cried Fromm, beside himself with excitement. 'He's only telling you what we all know.'

'What's this? Mutiny? There'll be no mutiny. I'll not stand for it.' Leaning across his bag the Lieutenant snatched up Brenner's rifle and was levelling it, when Emmons knocked up the barrel.

A single round crashed into the roof, showering the men with ice.

Long after the shock of the detonation faded on the air the stunned company, now with dread in their hearts, lay wondering what it might portend. The wind resumed its battering as the blizzard surged with renewed passion about the hut. At length, under cover of the wind, the murmurings began. Some men took the doctor's side, seeing he was doing everything a man could do to keep them alive, and declared themselves sorry not to have discovered his true worth sooner. Others argued it was none of the doctor's business; it was right to select the best men to be hunters, and favour them too. Brenner and Stempel were bringing in a steady trickle of birds. What other hope did they have?

The Lieutenant was all but drained, yet the reverberations of this latest challenge to his authority would not let him rest. The thought that the surgeon would almost certainly survive him brought with it the outrageous possibility that the truth about the man might lie for ever undisclosed. Weak as he was, he saw that he must leave some record of the facts. Then it struck him: Fabius was a thief and a liar. Such a man, with most of the party dead or dying, would not scruple to tamper with the log.

As he lay racked by the duplicity of men, and the iniquity of righteousness denied, the rest of the party subsided into the lethargy that now followed any excitement. Wutz lit the stove, and busied himself preparing the midday drink. Asher brought the commander his watery extract of beef. He was somewhat taken aback to be asked for his logbook.

He returned to find the commander trimming a pencil.

'I'm afraid I've not written much.' The astronomer might have been ashamed to have so little to show.

Selecting a blank page towards the end of the book, for several minutes the Lieutenant wrote with great concentration, pausing now and then to consider his words. Then he closed the book, and returned it to its owner.

'What I have written here,' he muttered, 'is highly confidential. I ask for your solemn word that you will speak about it to no one.'

A short while afterwards Parish summoned Emmons to his side. He handed the sergeant a folded slip of paper. 'I entrust this to your safe keeping. See that it reaches the Chief Signal Officer in Washington.'

Then, on a strip of paper torn from his journal, Lt William Parish pencilled a final message:

Believing myself close to death, and believing also the surgeon, Dr Fabius, as one of the strongest of the party, most likely to survive, I leave this record as a corrective against whatever account he may, in due course, seek to give of himself. It is a matter of plain truth, now clearly discerned by all, that Dr Fabius considers himself the fittest person to lead this expedition. Unsuited by character to the constraints of military discipline, he has continually resisted the authority of the commanding officer. He has at every opportunity fomented unrest among the men. In addition, while attending to Private Schmidt, he has for many weeks now systematically helped himself to his patient's food. I testify to this as a dying man, far beyond all rancour or personal spite.

Signing it with his full military style, the Lieutenant stowed this last testament among the packet of letters intended for his wife. Duty done, he sank back into his bag.

The high wind continued all that night. By morning the

storm was still too violent for hunting. Now much weakened, the men might have withdrawn completely into their bags had it not been for the interest aroused by further evidence of the commander's eccentricity. Ranged round him he had assembled various small items, to which he was observed to be attaching small slips of paper.

'I am putting my effects in order,' he remarked, as if conscious of their scrutiny. 'Every man,' he went on, 'should consider making some similar provision. As legal instruments they may have little value. But in such circumstances as ours, I feel sure no man's wishes would be disregarded.'

With a resignation none of them found surprising, they turned to settling the disposition of a motley assortment of rings, knives, watches, letters, pocket books and other mementoes, assigning them to brothers, sisters, old army friends, comforted by the thought that they were doing the right thing.

So, bunched up for safety's sake, they rode on together towards the unknown region.

Here and there though, where the territory was infiltrated by marauding fears, the frontier had moved inward.

'Are you a believer, Jake?' Edge enquired, in what was no more than a fumbling in the dark.

'In Hebrew,' said the Jew obscurely, "*to believe* is *to support oneself*".'

'I believe we may in some manner be cherished by our Maker,' averred the Lieutenant gravely. He considered it his duty to shore up faith where it might be sagging.

He collected in the testamentary dispositions, all of which he labelled carefully and placed with the official papers of the expedition. Even Hanson, he was gratified to note, had needed his advice. The black sheep so far lent himself to the occasion as to address a note to his old commander: *Well, this looks like the end. We done our best, hanging on as long as poss. Six are already dead and the rest of us now very weak indeed.* The brawny man enjoyed a pleasurable frisson at the tragic spectacle his words evoked. He licked his pencil, and added a phrase or two, by way of entering into the spirit of the thing. *We have food for six more days. Tell them all back home we met our end like soldiers.*

So far, he felt little in the way of ill effects himself. He was, as he reflected with some satisfaction, by far the strongest of the party. In any case, he had supplies stashed away in various nooks and crannies, under boulders, buried in the snow. He intended to last out until the boat arrived. Meanwhile, he entertained agreeable reveries of a hero's welcome back in Uncle Sam.

Next morning the last of the bread was handed out. In announcing the news, the Lieutenant revealed they had nine days' meat remaining.

He surveyed the faces, which were more or less abstracted from events. They had grown used to these deprivations, with each of which a little more of life was stripped away. No one said anything. Some had all but renounced speaking altogether, for the bitter flavour of such words as they had left. Others were less particular, chewing them over, relishing the sourness, before spitting out the husks.

The one consoling moment in their lives was the warming drink issued each day at noon.

One day, as Wutz lit the stove to mix the moonshine, he discovered that the ration of alcohol, issued to him that morning, was not where he'd put it. Missing too was Hanson.

In the outcry that followed, several men spilled out of the hut, only to stand gazing about, uncertain in which direction to set off after the thief who, doubtless, had put some distance between himself and any pursuit, before settling down behind some rock to get drunk.

Rainbird, too, had emerged from the hut. Mumbling something no one, it turned out later, seemed to have caught, he set off, clutching his rifle, though in no particular direction. If his general trend took him downhill, it might have been because descent demanded the least effort.

In five days he'd scarcely slept two hours together. Wakefulness seemed to have transfigured his perceptions with a clarity not known before. Distantly, as through a dream, came the shouts of his comrades searching for Hanson. As he went down the neck of land he fell to wondering if he might not be sleeping after all, asleep and floating through a dream.

Though the worn snow was spoiling, nothing green broke the monotony around him, nothing recognizable as life. In the barren stones of the tundra, the dreary bare relief, the man saw only a dead land sunk in stillness. So he went on, his boots crunching over beds of frozen snow, clattering down a fan of loose scree until he saw he had reached the limit of the land.

Here the sea floe came right in to the shore, a chaos of pressed-up rubble: jagged shards piled in ruinous heaps, huge blocks heaved up on the heavy tides and toppled, one on top of another. Rainbird was aware of a continuous groaning, low and dismal. The tide was at the full.

His life seemed wholly without meaning, a succession of incomprehensible illusions reflected in a mirror: oarsman, athlete, performer on the bar, impostures the more tormenting for the continued labouring within him of a figure that might have been struggling to get out.

Somewhere he heard a muffled echo of collapsing snow. Rainbird shivered. If all places were alike it was because none of them had any use for him.

In that moment of complete conviction, Luther Rainbird saw that things were as they were. Without value. Wherever he went wilderness went with him. Everywhere was wilderness.

A faint clamour, as of angry voices, came floating from the direction of the camp. Hanson had been found. The big man lay in a stupor, slumped against a boulder, eyes half closed, regarding his pursuers with a dreamy smile. Some were for settling with him there and then.

Fromm snatched up a rock, and might have used it too, but for a sudden *crack*, its reverberations rolling over the island.

Eventually, they found Rainbird lying where he'd fallen. Emmons got a rope under his arms and pulled him out of the ice crack, though not without some difficulty, for the body was wedged between the icy walls.

Ever practical, the sergeant went further down to look for the Remington, but without success. He reckoned it must have dropped into the sea.

Meanwhile, the rest of the searchers were gathering to stare at the body where it lay on the scree. The dead lieutenant's face still bore the blank look it last wore in life. A glaze of ice had sealed the black blood clotting the wound.

For hours afterwards the men were uneasy and withdrawn. They were suffering that loss of spirit men feel when gathered into the impersonality of death. They couldn't see it. They didn't know where it was. But it had them in its sights, and was picking them off one by one. And the manner of it made no difference, whether in the course of nature, or by misadventure, as in the case of the lieutenant falling into the ice foot and his gun going off.

It was a verdict confirmed at the reading of the burial service by the commander.

'No doubt Lieutenant Rainbird was pursuing a bear or a seal. We can only conclude that he must have stumbled into the ice foot, dropping his rifle, with the tragic consequence that followed.' The Lieutenant preferred to speak well of a fallen comrade. 'The lieutenant died,' he concluded, 'in the performance of his duty.'

He set it down as such in the log. Indeed, he would have had no reason to think otherwise, had it not been for a scrap of paper passed to him by Sergeant Asher who'd come across it while preparing the body for burial. It was torn from a government-issue log book, the personal record Rainbird would never use. Turning it over, he read a scrawled inscription: *A useless soldier, a faithless friend, he went gladly to his grave.* His thoughts went back to that first meeting at the Powder River. Rainbird's cheerful greeting, materializing out of a whirling void, was a warming recollection still. He felt drawn again to the dead man, closer than ever was possible in life. Even those feats of strength on the bar seemed poignant now. Then William Parish was all but overcome by distress at his own neglect. The truth was that in Rainbird he'd picked, for second-in-command, a man he scarcely knew, a man he'd not allowed himself to know, nor could he ever have done so, given his own want of feeling.

He looked round at the closed faces of his men: at Fromm, fiddling with a piece of wire; at Lawless, staring sullenly. They had suffered another blow in this war of attrition, and had put up the shutters.

What had he known of any of them? What did they know of themselves? They were all, all ignorant of what lay waiting, of what they were taking on. Only here, in the field, in the Arctic wilderness, was a man weighed in the balance; weighed, and found wanting.

*

On the first day of May the *Louisa Soames* tied up at the Queen's wharf in the harbour of St John's where she was to take on coal and dogs. The town alive with talk of a bounty. A few days earlier the bill had been reported to the House. After an hour's rambling discussion it was passed without dissent. No congressman felt it worth his while to voice a 'Nay'. Not in an election year. At least ten vessels of the whaling fleet, it was rumoured, intended to skirt the Greenland coast as far north as Littleton Island, before crossing the North Water above the pack to fish the west of Baffin Bay.

Bostock lost no time in telegraphing the news to the Navy Secretary in New York.

'I don't have to tell you,' said Sam Hynes to Commander Stannery, 'what it would mean if we're bested by a fishing boat.'

That afternoon, on the ebb tide, the *Samphire* slid out of her dock in the Brooklyn Navy Yard, past the spires and towers of Manhattan, past wharves and piers, and tall masts, under the echoing hulls of iron-black lighters, under that newest wonder of the world, the great Brooklyn Bridge, to a tumult of acclamations, of waving handkerchiefs and wild hurrahs.

The broad water-way, everywhere rolling with packets, ferries, freighters, coastal steamers, bustling little tugs, resounded to ear-splitting whistles and the whoops of sirens.

Off Governor's Island Stannery dipped his colours in salute to the guns. He was reflecting on that last, private meeting with his chief. *Bring them back if you can. At the very least, find out what happened to them.* The commander had ventured a grim smile. Neither man confessed what he believed: that there was only the remotest possibility any of the Lieutenant's party would be found alive.

a tumult of acclamations, of waving handkerchiefs and wild hurrahs

SIXTEEN

As the land warmed up, melting snow rained down upon them constantly. Everything was wet from the constant drip. At night the temperature dropped below freezing as the hut fell under the shadow of the glacier. Flesh, already pared to the bone, gave no protection. The men huddled miserably in their saturated bags and brooded on their own disintegration, the teeth loosening in skulls, nails flaking away from toes. Wounds long-healed were throbbing again. In those worst affected, as the surgeon recorded in his notes, the classic symptoms of starvation were now unmistakable. Feeble, emaciated, they were unable to walk unaided. Nadel, a wasted figure, now rarely left his bag. Krug, too, had grown very frail. Edge had broken out in ulcers. Schmidt, though he fared better than most, was also suffering from sores.

Some of the sick were heartened by the surgeon's determination not to despair of life. Knowles put it down to firmness of mind. 'The doctor's made up his mind he's going to survive.'

If survival still seemed a possibility, it might have been because life had begun to surge so insistently around them. They heard it in the cry and cackle of birds setting down along the edges of the floes, in the strutting gulls, and the high-pitched honking of geese. Out on the ice of Buchanan Bay seals were undergoing their annual moult. They sprawled indolently on the ice, waiting for their pelts to dry. They were big bearded seals, five times the weight of the little ringed seals they'd eaten in a past life. And the men dreamed of tasty fried seal liver and seal-meat steaks, of seal stomachs full of fish, and soups rich with the blood of seals.

But the hunters had no means of retrieving game from the sea. One day Brenner came back with a scrawny raven. He was awarded the liver, with the rest set aside as bait for shrimp, until Fromm, snivelling, begged for his share. In the end, over the protests of the other men, he got his way. 'Oh, give him his share,' said Brenner wearily, 'and shut him up.'

That evening Emmons came in from the store, and spoke privately to the Lieutenant.

'We have food,' he murmured, 'for three days at the most.'

The Lieutenant had been struggling with his journal-letter to his wife. He had become distressed at the thought of the straitened circumstances in which she would be left. He found it a great effort to collect his thoughts, and it upset him that he could form no sense of her at all. Wearily, he tried to fix his mind on this latest anxiety. A moment of weakness, it might have been, caused him to consider ordering what remained of the rations to be divided among the party. Then it struck him that one or two of the worst elements might seek to exploit the situation.

'Very well,' he sighed. 'Give out the rations in the usual way, until the last has gone.'

Sighing again, he returned to his letter. He had written: *I'm afraid very little of my personal property will come back to you. Much of it was of necessity abandoned at Fort Chance. I would like to believe that Congress would agree to reimburse you, but am not hopeful. A set of photographs has been set aside for you. They are packed and labelled with your name. They are quite unique, as depicting subjects never before seen. It would be worth your while to have negatives made of the more striking examples. Enlarged, and finished on canvas, they might sell for anything up to a hundred dollars apiece. Do not take less ...*

He was mulling over what might constitute a realistic sum, when deflected by a feeble voice.

'Lieutenant,' whispered Edge unexpectedly. 'What d'you think we'll find when we get back?'

The Lieutenant, accused by duties neglected, looked vague.

'Well,' he hazarded, 'I guess things will have gone on pretty much the same as always. Folks will be bringing in the sheaves, and putting in the winter rye. Some folks will have died. Babies will have gotten born. The bobolinks will still be singing in the hay meadow. Nothing much changes.'

A monstrous indifference, it might have seemed, to the suffering of starving men; and still the dearest hope a man could have. Chuck Edge had become a four years' boy again, carried through the woods to school on his father's shoulders. Others, who had started life in another country, were reminded of their epic quest to find a home.

Out of the shadows came the strains of Digg's harmonica, a plaintive tune unknown to the Lieutenant. One by one, though, the Germans took up the melody, singing softly in the wistful voices of men whose thoughts were far away. In the Lieutenant's hay meadow the bobolinks were silenced. He'd talked of home, but he had no home. He'd joined the Union army that first April of the war, and never since been out of quarters. Quarters, or rented rooms ...

The plaintive tune ran through its handful of notes again, the melancholy German voices swelling softly, filling the wretched hut with dreams. The Lieutenant was fixing on a house, with an acre or two of land, enough to put down roots. Apple trees. A vegetable garden. A barn. There would be a calf in the barn. Yes, a brick house, with an iron gate. Then he was walking up the hill, past the church, rounding the bend between the willows ...

Into his reverie the wife of William Parish slipped as readily as if entering a room. She seemed altogether too slight to bear the burden he had placed upon her. An uncompromising light fell full on her face, searching out the hollows of her eyes. She had the raw look of a woman who had just stopped crying, a woman whom there was no one to console.

He saw that in marrying him Matty had endangered her interests very much.

Go home, he wrote. *That is my advice. Leave Washington. Go back to Hartfield.*

The thought of her restored to the verities of her little town was easier to bear. At least on her mother's death she would have the security of the property.

Remember, he thought to add, *in Massachusetts a widow's house incurs no tax.*

Meanwhile the *Brave* had set out to a twenty-one gun salute. At last the whole squadron was at sea. Already entering the Davis Strait was the *Louisa Soames,* with the *Samphire* several days behind, escorting the collier *Aberdare.* The little ships met with heavy seas and snowstorms driven on strong north-easterlies. Drift ice, heavier than expected, was moving south along the Labrador coast.

In strange waters, with unreliable charts, the Navy skippers made slow progress.

✳

Eight days had passed since they'd eaten regular food. They were now a party split in two, the surgeon having warned that unless the weaker men were moved to warmer, drier accommodation they would die within days. Sgt Emmons had found a sunny, level spot, a few hundred yards from the hut, where he'd pitched the tent. It would take, he reckoned, eight or nine at a pinch. Though he'd agreed to it, Parish was troubled by this severing of his command. It left the strongest, most quarrelsome men under the same roof as the surgeon. The fact that there was no food left to squabble over brought little comfort. He felt instinctively that men like Hanson, Lawless and the unpredictable Fromm should be where he could keep an eye on them. Fromm especially. Since Rainbird's death the fear of another breakdown was never far from his mind.

'I want you to stay at the hut,' he told Emmons. 'Keep an eye on things. Wear your revolver. Keep it on your person at all times.'

Later that afternoon the invalids removed to their new quarters. Those able to do so walked the three hundred yards up the hill. The Lieutenant, giving an arm to Asher, brought up the rear. Though still weak, he was able to walk short distances unassisted. One morning, by dint of frequent rests, he succeeded in getting himself as far as the nearest rocks where he set to, scraping off the lichen which grew there in considerable profusion. It had occurred to him that the men of Franklin's first expedition had made daily marches on little more. What if, at this eleventh hour, the means of survival lay spread out like manna all around them?

Relations with Fabius had deteriorated since the Lieutenant offered to shoot him. On the commander's instructions, the medicine chest had been removed to the tent, a snub which might have been calculated further to affront the surgeon. Only some extrusion of their professional selves maintained a tenuous connection.

As the stronger men gathered at the tent to a breakfast of saxifrage, boiled with spoonfuls of shrimp, Parish had accosted his medical adviser, holding out a hand in the palm of which lay some grubby slivers of grey-green scrapings.

'I have collected these *tripe-de-roche* from the rocks,' he said stiffly. 'I take the view that they may contain some nutriment. What is your opinion?'

'*Informed* opinion is against it.' The surgeon was equally starchy. 'Hayes and Franklin considered it extremely dangerous. Richardson records that it caused his party considerable suffering.'

'That may be so. But it kept them going, when they had nothing else.'

'Those that survived.'

The Lieutenant was chewing a mouthful, which tasted of nothing.

'If, in our present condition, any of us were to be taken with diarrhoea,' the surgeon went on ominously, 'it would certainly be fatal.'

'I take note of your warning, of course,' said Parish indistinctly, his tongue impeded by a gummy paste. 'All the same, I intend to make a trial.'

That evening Wutz presented Lt Parish with the first fruits of his labour. Cooked in a kettle, they boiled down to a thick, syrupy tar which, upon tasting, the commander pronounced not unpalatable.

As his own recovery progressed, the Lieutenant drew strength from the continuing persistence of the human venture. The dogged endurance of his men, going about their duties, touched him deeply. Wutz, with never a word of complaint, cooked what was given him in the way of food. Emmons worked at his nets. The hunters brought in the occasional bird. He was especially moved by Asher who, though barely able to rise from his bag for the painful swellings of his joints, continued to nurse the sick.

In addition to his medical duties, Fabius had taken on the role of water boy. Every day, sometimes going out at two and three in the morning, he went on hacking at the ice.

Men lying in their bags would listen to the comforting sound of blows struck on their behalf.

'The doctor's at his daily dozen,' joked Lawless to Knowles.

The Lieutenant noted it sourly in the log:

> May 15th. The surgeon's strength and energy lately are quite remarkable. He seems to have remembered his avocation is the care of the sick.

Unable to ward off death, he could at least minister to suffering, doling out chloride of mercury for the costive, quinine for the heart arrhythmias, ergot for the blinding headaches, alcohol compound for the painful bowels. Sedgewick, now groaning fearfully, he quietened with opium. Nadel, of course, was not expected to live. He seemed quite reconciled to his fate. 'You know, Lieutenant,' he whispered, 'ever since I get my papers, I wonder what it means to be an American. Now I shall never know.'

Death when it came was kindly. It led the quiet man by a wandering, but never agitated route.

Fabius expressed surprise he'd lingered as long, being so reduced.

'The hold some men have on life,' he observed, 'is truly remarkable.'

Parish sniffed. He was thinking that, though stringier than when he joined the expedition, the surgeon certainly appeared relatively hale and hearty.

To the enfeebled men the doctor had become somehow absolved of the general frailties of mankind. It seemed almost intended that he should continue fit and strong so as to tend the sick. He watched over their ailing bodies, writing in his book, the agent of a dispassionate Fate that governed them inexorably. Alone among the party Fabius was acquainted with details of what lay in store for starving men. Such foreknowledge was, of course, entirely consistent with a superior being.

Lothar Schmidt, in particular, was living testimony to the doctor's skill and care. Their crippled comrade, in his undiminished will to live, had become their touchstone for survival.

Meanwhile, Schmidt seemed to go from strength to strength. Jacob Joseph had fixed a spoon to his stump. Had him practising spooning up the stew.

'Hey, Lieutenant,' crowed the invalid, 'look at me.'

'The man is a phenomenon,' remarked the surgeon drily. 'He will outlive us all.'

He was taken aback, though, when Sedgewick went so suddenly. It came as a complete surprise.

'Very likely he incurred an inflammation of the bowel,' Fabius advised the Lieutenant. Unable to make his stool, the poor man had been working with his fingers in his rectum. 'Certainly, it will have hastened his end.'

Parish entered it as such in the log. He'd become almost matter-of-fact in registering this tally of the dead. Somehow or other they'd come through the winter with the greater body of the party still intact. Of nine deaths so far, leaving aside the special case of Reade, only five could be said to have succumbed as a consequence of starvation. As he closed his ledger the Lieutenant still dared to trust some might hold out after all.

It was a hope soon to be dashed by a sudden flurry of mortality.

Its swiftness astonished even the surgeon. Certainly he'd never expected Knowles to be the next to go, nor that the effort of eating would bring about a collapse.

Those who'd come up from the hut clustered round the tent to peer in at the stricken man.

'He only came up here to get his supper,' murmured Hanson, for once shocked out of unfeeling.

Coming round, Knowles asked faintly for water. Raising him up, Jacob Joseph held him in his arms, spooning him mouthfuls of tea as he lapsed in and out of consciousness, until he slipped away altogether.

Later that morning Emmons, with three of the stronger men, took turns to drag the remains up to the ridge. Scarcely had they covered Knowles with earth, when it became evident that Edge was sinking fast. He died that same evening.

Parish read the service over him, then the dead man was lugged out and left in the open for the time being. They had not the strength to drag another body to the ridge.

The whole party was shaken to the core. The expectancy of death, so long a vague and deadening feeling, had suddenly sharpened to an acute apprehension that they were perhaps all locked together in what could be the last days. Not one of them but shivered at his own mortality.

Even the surgeon was reduced to clutching at the tatters of life.

On the morning following the burial of Edge, and with Emmons at his shrimping, he entered the tent and removed the remaining iron pills from the medicine chest.

It was a manoeuvre of which the Lieutenant soon got wind. 'What, I know not,' declared the watchful Schmidt, who did not trust the doctor. 'But something he has taken.'

Brenner had just returned with a brace of birds he had shot. Summoning the hunter for support, the Lieutenant went totteringly to confront the thief.

'You have taken medicines,' he accused, 'without permission.'

'Permission?' The surgeon wetted his lips.

'You will replace them immediately.'

'It is a medical matter ...' he began, reaching for his customary loftiness.

'You will replace those medicines, Dr Fabius, and you will do so immediately. If necessary, at gunpoint.'

Brenner, though not instructed to do so, levelled his rifle.

Smiling uneasily, the surgeon shrugged, and raised a soothing hand. It might have been to humour a lunatic.

Spring sunshine now gave way to showery days of sleet and snow. For the men still quartered in the hut conditions had become increasingly intolerable. Emmons and Stempel, stitching laboriously at blankets and old canvas, managed to patch together an extension large enough to accommodate them all inside the tent. Though for failing men, it took some gritting of teeth to get there, plodding so many yards, stopping, gasping for breath. The sergeant, watching Diggs and Fromm holding on to one another as they toiled up the rise, marvelled how they managed to put one foot in front of the other. He did not give either of them more than a day or two.

Even the surgeon had begun to sicken, swaying like a drunken man as he came up the hill. His behaviour had become decidedly odd. He had given up chopping ice, and become obsessed with the matter of diet, repeatedly urging the desirability of wholesome nourishment.

'Yes ... fresh vegetables,' he insisted, licking his lips. He might have been slavering for the good greens.

Yet at mealtimes he refused all food, taking only tea. He seemed to have an aversion to eating anything.

'I do not understand it,' said the Lieutenant. 'Up till now he has been one of the strongest. You have heard him chopping ice.'

'He's been dosing himself,' said the astronomer. 'Dover's powder, for sure.' The surgeon had taken a lot of that. 'I'm not sure,' he added charitably, 'he knows what he's handling.'

Attentive as ever, Fabius continued to care for the sick, though his pills and potions, now seemingly prescribed at random, bewildered his patients.

'What for,' asked Diggs, perplexed, 'this syrup of French lettuce?' Others were more candid. 'The doctor has gone mad,' declared Emmons, who'd turned an ankle, breaking through a crust of ice. 'He's given me bismuth. Bismuth for a twisted foot.'

Only in the case of the commander did an earlier condition seem to have stuck.

'For a costive bowel, I advise chloride of mercury. A half grain is usually efficacious.'

The Lieutenant stared in astonishment. 'I'm quite recovered I assure you,' he said, with dignity.

Fabius, though, grew worse. His dreams were fearful. After a night in which his crying out against nameless terrors alarmed them all, it was plain the surgeon was in a bad way.

'I am quite well now,' he gasped.

To the men watching from afar, he seemed locked into some impenetrable fever ward.

'Yes,' he insisted, with great eagerness. 'Ah, yes.' He stared at them with bulging rabbit eyes. The yellow face glistening.

All day he went about declaring to anyone who would listen that he was in the best of health.

'I am much stronger than I was.' He swayed, and might have fallen had not Brenner stuck out an arm. 'Yes,' he said firmly. 'I am as well as ever.'

During the night he grew worse. He could smell burning. He complained of thirst, of nausea, retching repeatedly, groaning with the pain that was racking his body.

The Lieutenant offered an opium pill.

'Non ... non ...' moaned the surgeon, who had begun to bubble up a greenish slime. 'Rien ... je ne veux rien.'

By morning his limbs were seized by involuntary twitchings, spasms that soon spread to the rest of his body.

'He's having a fit,' shouted Emmons. Thinking to do something for him, he seized the bag, and with Brenner's help, began dragging it out of the tent, to the great terror of the sufferer.

'Non ... ah, non.'

The surgeon's face was milky white under its grime. He could have been pleading for his life.

They hauled him out, and laid him gently on a mattress covered with a blanket, where he continued to thrash about. To the bewildered men, looking on in horror at the jerking limbs, it seemed as if something had gotten hold of the doctor and was shaking him to death.

Not wishing to see them further demoralized, the Lieutenant sent the men away to search for vegetation. Meanwhile, he thought it proper he should remain with the sick man. He felt completely at a loss. He did not know what was wrong with the surgeon. He had seen nothing like it before. Suspecting some sort of poison, he wondered whether in the collecting of vegetation some noxious substance might not have found its way into the stew. The surgeon had been utterly opposed to the eating of *tripe de roche*. Yet no one else had been affected. Not yet.

He bent down, his lips up close to the surgeon's ear.

'What's wrong, Fabius? What is it? Can you tell us?'

The surgeon, clenching himself to meet each spasm, was cut off from all but the pain convulsing his body.

Between times he would gabble incoherently.

'What's he saying? I can't make it out.' It was nothing any man could have made sense of.

'Yesterday he took away extract of ergot,' Asher told the commander. He spoke in a low voice, it might have been out of respect. 'He must have believed it was the iron he was taking. He has since drunk it all.'

By mid-afternoon the grey face wore a bluish tinge. Fabius had begun to gasp, sucking air in queer, hiccuping spasms, as the iron band about his chest tightened inexorably.

The Lieutenant was thinking that men choose the manner of their death. Day by day it took root in the gut of their obsessions. Didn't he know in his *own* soul the corruption of that hunger which would make a man break through all the laws of the Almighty? It had drawn him from his desk at the Signal Office, from the arms of his dear wife, to this dreadful place.

In ones and twos the men were returning. They gathered round to watch as the life was squeezed out of the surgeon. Staring up, he seemed no longer conscious, the gasping punctuated by intervals that grew longer, the breath shorter and shorter, until it ceased altogether.

Later that evening Lt Parish entered a brief record in his log.

> June 3rd. Fabius died at 6 p.m. Whether by design or accident, he had consumed a number of conflicting medicines, to the evident unsettling of his mind. Until a few days ago he was among the strongest of our party. It now appears, for reasons best known to himself, that he dosed himself repeatedly. It is to this that I ascribe his unexpected collapse.

He broke off at a ponderous sound, as of some heavy object dragged along the ground. Men were lugging the body away from the tent.

He wrote:

> Dr Fabius has been a first class surgeon. In addition, he went out voluntarily on a dangerous mission to bring back a stricken comrade …

… whose food, he almost continued, *he later systematically purloined.*

Lt Parish was suffering afresh that raised eyebrow, the mocking smile.

Conscientiously, he strove not to think ill of the dead. After all, Fabius had cared for his patients with commendable zeal. And yet a man might do good, and still choose that in his own nature which was defect and error.

So the Puritan Lieutenant finally understood how it was that Maximilien Fabius, graduate of the University of Paris, for whom it was not enough to be a good physician, fell into the limitless abyss carved out for him by his pride.

Too weak to dig another grave, it took the men two days, hauling in fits and starts, to drag the surgeon's body the three hundred yards to the ice foot. Then, pushing, heaving, they tumbled it into the tidal crack.

＊

Hollow eyed under his fur cap Commander Stannery was once again making the long climb to the crow's-nest. He'd spent many hours on watch, gazing over an endless white expanse, littered with blocks and boulders. The more he saw of it, the less believable it seemed. A cable's length off his port bow the *Louisa Soames* lay hove-to with the fishing fleet. Eight miles to the south the *Brave*, with the *Aberdare*, waited at Upernavik where they would remain until assured of a safe passage.

The commander was greatly irked by this waiting game. A newcomer to the Arctic, whose career had been languishing in the doldrums, he'd made up his mind to act on some advice given him by a Navy engineer who'd sailed with De Long, and come back alive. *The great thing is not to allow yourself to be shackled by the experience of others. The Arctic is a place where initiative pays off. Sounds crazy, I know. But there it is.* Though he had on board a Newfoundland ice pilot, he'd come to the conclusion there was little point in taking instruction from a fellow who would follow the same tactics as the rest of the fishing fleet, when what was needed was to get ahead of them. They were waiting for the ice to open. He would fight his way through it.

Reaching the cask at the masthead, he swung up and into his vantage point, only to see the same dreary band of white light sealing the horizon.

Then, on June 1st, with a storm blowing down from the north, a strong tide carried the pack to westward, opening a shore lead.

Later that day the lead closed, and the ships were stopped again.

For two weeks, sometimes strung out in a line, sometimes stationary for hours, the flotilla advanced by fits and starts. A wind from the north or east would separate the pack; a southerly, or a westerly wind would close it up again, as dense as ever. Then a crew-man would clamber up the top-gallant mast with more hot coffee, and a fresh cigar for the commander.

In fourteen days, they made fifty miles.

As he sipped his coffee Stannery studied the whalers hove-to line abreast. He watched the skippers far below walking over the floes to take counsel with their brothers. So far, they'd left him to make the running. Well, he fancied he'd shown them a thing or two.

The dull thump of another explosion juddered through the ice, causing the barrel to shudder, slopping the commander's coffee over his glove. Up ahead, his men had been boring a line of holes, sinking charges in the floe. Backing off, the *Samphire* ran at full speed, ramming into the ice, with the crew lining one rail, rolling the ship so as to lever the floes apart. As she hit, she stopped dead in her track, shivering from truck to keelson. Hanging on, a hundred feet and thirty feet above the deck, Stannery stared at the crack starting under the bowsprit, and the bows driving forward, cleaving a passage, splitting open the ice.

And where the *Samphire* led, the whalers followed.

Then the pack shifted under a stiff nor'westerly wind. A big lead opened northward. Racing ahead of all but two of the whalers, the *Samphire* and her sister ship closed on Cape York.

There they were stopped again. Perched aloft, Stannery gazed across another vast snowfield, broken to the south-west by channels and lagoons. The two whalers, he saw, were already turning, as if for Baffin Bay and the fishing grounds. Fearing a feint, he signalled Bostock in the *Louisa Soames* to follow them.

Meanwhile, as the midnight sun broke through the clouds, the *Samphire* edged further north.

SEVENTEEN

For forty miles the good weather ran as far north as Smith Sound. Every cape and headland, from Grinnell Land to the Greenland shore, rejoiced in warm sunshine.

A spring light lay over Camp Fortitude. Set free at last, clutching its shift of sparse grey-green, the land stepped into the light. The glacier gleamed wetly. The bleached grass was greening again where clumps of muddy turf had been exposed. Already the first flowers were resurrecting through a film of softened snow. Some of the weaker men, feeling themselves slipping away, were mocked by this renewal of life, its promise of a summer they would never see. Private Hanson, though, sniffing the air, surveyed the reawakening earth with the relish of a man who felt assured of survival. True, he'd suffered a mild diarrhoea from eating *tripe de roche*. But he'd recovered. It seemed to have left him none the worse. It was a restoration from which the big man drew much encouragement. He was by far the strongest of them now.

He had thrown off most of the constraints of military discipline. Even his thefts had become more blatant.

'I guess it's each man for himself,' he said, reaching a hand into the general pot, winking at Schmidt, who saw him do it.

The weaker men were alarmed. If he took their food, what could they do to stop him? They were quite helpless. 'Hanson says he's going to look out for himself,' complained Fromm querulously to the sergeant, 'and let the rest of us of go hang.'

The Lieutenant, too, had been a witness to the theft. He'd already spoken privately to Hanson, hauling himself painfully to his feet to do so.

'If you have no conscience, man, at least have a little common sense. If any of us are to survive, it can only be by

309

sticking together as a party, not by preying on one another. Don't you see?'

No more than skin and bone, still his bottle lenses loomed over the more powerful man.

'All for one, and one for all,' he thought to add, having read it somewhere.

The enlisted man took this as an invitation to a blunt exchange.

'That's bullshit, Lieutenant. It's the strongest who'll survive. Those who take what they can get.'

Sighing, the Lieutenant reverted to rank.

'Very well. But I give you fair warning. Continue on this road and you will come to grief.' The bottle ends focused a *look*. 'Now, do I have your word on this?'

Grudgingly, the big man had mumbled something of the sort.

Parish didn't believe him. He didn't even believe his own cautionary warning. The man was right. It was the fittest who survived. It was Nature's way.

All the same, the Lieutenant was repelled at the thought of Nature's triumph in the shape of such a thing as Hanson. If man's chief good was survival then the tyranny of the strong over the weak, and all that it implied of ruthlessness, became his virtues. No, men were worth more than that. He'd fought a war on that account.

As he watched the burly lord of creation slouching off, the Lieutenant was comforted by the thought that his reflections were largely notional. He thought it unlikely any of them would survive.

Meanwhile, days continued fine and warm. The members of the American Arctic Expedition were enduring that rarity, a spell of settled weather. In that unpredictable land where nothing can be taken for granted only the decay of men was never in doubt.

Of those still living, barely half of them had strength enough to search for the necessities of life. Unable to gather vegetation, the Lieutenant had crawled to the entrance of the tent, and was lying in the sun. Too restless for sleep, he had begun to explore the process of his own disintegration. He had read somewhere that the body of a starving man begins to feed upon itself. For sure, most of the fat and muscle was long gone. The skin hung from his limbs in flaps. His abdomen was so sunken it must have dropped right back to his spine. He couldn't smell his own body odour, but guessed it to be foul. He could still hear well enough. The *chip*, *chip* of Wutz's axe carried quite plainly from the lake. His vision, though, was beginning to blur. Even so, he thought he saw a figure emerging from behind the abandoned hut. Only when it drew level with the big rock below the tent did he see that it was Hanson.

Raising himself on an elbow, Parish called him over.

The fellow appeared to hesitate, then came on up the hill. It seemed to cost him little effort. Under one arm he was clutching a bundle wrapped in a cloth.

'What have you got there?'

The big man stood over the frail commander. He could have put a boot on the Lieutenant, snapped him like a twig.

'Sure, I got some seal skins, Lieutenant. I'm gonna keep 'em too. And there ain't a thing you can do about it.'

Parish's first thought, as he watched the fellow sauntering off, was that he must have the guns put out of that man's reach.

Only as an afterthought was it borne in upon him that his command had finally collapsed. It all sprang from his failure to take action against the surgeon. That omission, he saw now, had bred a kind of vanity on his part. Unable to act against an officer, he, the scrupulous, the high-minded, would not discriminate against an enlisted man. Yet his first responsibility at all times was the safety of the whole party. The greater good. What good had been served by dealing leniently with Hanson? George Reade, he remembered, was all for shooting the fellow.

Suddenly, he saw what he should have done – saw it beyond all question. He should have dealt with Hanson, meanwhile biding his time with the surgeon until such time as he might be charged and tried. Even now, it was not too late. Even if only the slightest chance remained of a few men surviving, he might, by acting now, tip the balance in their favour.

Reaching for his despatch book, he wrote out an order. Usually so laboured and painstaking, for once words fell into place with a fateful gravity.

Camp Fortitude, June 6th. 188-

To Sergeant Emmons:

Despite a most solemn undertaking given yesterday, Private Charles Hanson has today freely admitted to having again, earlier this morning, stolen seal-thongs from the store. Such obduracy and effrontery, if not terminated immediately, will be fatal to us all. Private Hanson is to be shot.

He stared at the words. Two hundred yards away, the condemned man was unconcernedly picking saxifrage for the pot. There was no other way. Leniency, in colluding with his crimes for so long, had only nourished a man whose physical strength was now a danger to them all. He wrote:

Stempel and Brenner will assist you. Take whatever steps may be necessary to ensure your own safety. Remember, the man's strength is greater than any two of us.

William Parish.
First Lieutenant, 5th Cavalry, U.S.A.

As an afterthought he added,

This order is *irrevocable*. Any hope of survival hangs upon it.

Then, with the order clutched in his hand, he watched anxiously for Emmons.

An hour dragged by. Wutz came back from the lake with his bucket of ice. Still there was no sign of the sergeant. At last, seeing the sergeant coming over the ridge with his bucket, he sent Wutz to intercept him.

Anxiously, Parish strained to follow the events now beginning to unfold a couple of hundred yards from where he lay. He could make out Emmons reading the order, then the sergeant handed his bucket to Wutz, and moved off in the direction of a figure – was it Stempel, by the flat rocks? Then both men moved off to meet a third figure coming up from the shore.

For several minutes the Lieutenant continued to peer uncertainly at what seemed, from a blurry waving of arms, to be sharp disagreements animating his firing squad. Alarmed, he feared lest his order was deficient in some particular. Suddenly it struck him that he'd forgotten the protocol of military execution. He should have written: *Determine manner of death by two ball and one blank cartridge.* Then he remembered Brenner's was the only serviceable rifle they had left.

At last, to his enormous relief, he saw two of the figures making their way towards the hut, and the third, evidently Emmons, setting off for the rocks where Hanson now appeared to be sunning himself.

The condemned man had found a caterpillar amid the saxifrage, when Emmon's shout summoned his attention. He popped it in his mouth – it was too good waste – then set off in a leisurely fashion after the sergeant, who had turned and was heading for the hut.

As he turned the wall of the hut, he came face to face with his executioners. Though it was more the look on their faces than the rifle Brenner was cradling that betrayed them. Hanson stopped dead, knowing, yet not believing. It could have been a voice heard in a dream telling him he was to be shot. That he might, if he wished, have a minute to say a prayer.

There was a brief moment of uncertainty. None of them knew quite what to expect.

Then the doomed man hurled himself at Brenner. As he did so, Emmons and Stempel each made a grab, clinging grimly to an arm or a shoulder, as Hanson, now with the strength of desperation, swung them about.

So began a deadly *quadrille*, as the three men, locked together, lurched this way and that, with the rifleman backing off, circling, looking for a shot.

To Emmons, hanging on like death, an age passed before it came. A shrewd stopper, as it turned out, which knocked all the fight from the big man. His partners, as if taken aback to find themselves suddenly holding him up, let him drop to his knees.

A second shot toppled him sideways.

That afternoon a filmy vapour began to spread across the sky, forming a halo round the sun. Within half an hour of the first light wind a yellow pall lay over the island. Soon the air was heavy with thick wet flakes.

For another day and night the storm howled over the island. Drifting snow crept into the tent. Without food or water, the men lay in their bags, snow-plastered shapes that might have been a part of the landscape, rocks that would lie until shattered by cold, eroded by the wind.

Then, abruptly, the weather turned round. Stiff with cold, those who could crawled out into glaring light, and the diamond sparkle of fresh snow.

Two days of fasting had taken their toll. That morning Jacob Joseph found himself unable to rise. He complained of the cold. Several layers of extra blankets could not keep him warm. Lawless, relatively strong a few days back, was now alarmingly weak. Diggs could be got to sit up only with great difficulty, and then only when his food came to him. The previous day, his term of service having expired, the Lieutenant had written out his certificate of discharge. Diggs then re-enlisted. He died, as he wished, a soldier.

For those still living there was nothing left but to wait for the end. None of them knew when death would come for him. Though they always recognized it when it came for others. The dying man wandered first into a twilight state, with no suspicion that his time had come. All craving for food had ceased.

Only he would call repeatedly for water, before slipping back into unconsciousness. So it was with Fromm. That same night Krug too began to unravel. Roused by his ramblings, Emmons watched over him till he died. Then, not having the strength to remove the remains, nor any will to do so, he went back to sleep.

Next morning he and Brenner managed to drag the dead a discreet distance from the living.

Meanwhile, they continued with the meagre business of staying alive. With the Lieutenant not able to walk, only four were left now to go scavenging for lichen, reindeer moss and the blossoms of the little purple saxifrage with which bumblebees had also begun to fumble.

So they struggled on, living off the land in much the same way as hares and ptarmigan, though these fellow creatures took pains to keep well clear of the men. Emmons continued fishing for shrimps, until a Spring tide washed away his net. Brenner went out with the rifle, coming back with reports of walrus bellowing out in the bay. One evening he failed to return. Those still alive were too far gone to search for him.

So they continued to observe the practices that comprised a simulacrum of existence. Denied shrimps, they started on their bedding. The Lieutenant cut off the filthy, oil-tanned covering of his sleeping bag for Wutz to boil up with the lichen. Though all desire for food had perished. They ate out of a sense of duty, as it were. Sergeant Emmons even erected a flag of distress on a rocky point overlooking the sea, the season now approaching, to the best of the Lieutenant's recollecting, the average date for whalers reaching the North Water. He was tormented now by that great absence in his life, the ship that hadn't come. He felt at an infinite distance from the world which had sent him, and had now abandoned his party to its fate. That world, he knew, was not recoverable. Never. He was afflicted, too, by thoughts of what he might have done, possibilities that beckoned the more accusingly for having been discarded. He could have taken the whaleboat, so providentially restored, and crossed to the Greenland shore. Or sailed south – anything, rather than allow himself to be pinned down here by Leffingwell's empty promises. And yet he strove with himself not to be bitter. He shrank at the thought of a sour, rancorous death.

The *mamzer* was spared that anguish. He had, in any case, grown very confused. Laid in the sun to soak up some of its goodness, he was absorbed in a mystery, the approach of which had been so gradual, so unobtrusive as to be scarcely noticeable. Silence had given way to the trickle of water. It was flowing all around him. It welled up from under ice. It bubbled over stones. It fell, a distant roar, from cliffs. In the wilderness, he remembered, shall waters break out, and streams in the desert. Quiet in himself, he drifted on the living waters. A streamer of light, he might have been, floating with the stream. He was profoundly grateful for this gift of water. It struck him that perhaps the ability to receive was also something given, and that it called for a thanksgiving. He thought of the words of prayer. *O our Father, merciful Father, ever compassionate ...* But the God of his fathers was not here. Not in this place. In this place there were only starving men. Suddenly he was brimming with tenderness for his comrades. An overflowing, it might have been, of something all-pervasive, for it was nowhere and everywhere at once. It was present in the ceaseless rushing waters; it was present in the stars in which, as a child, he read the unintelligibility of his fate; it clung, a bluish mist, to the stones of the tundra, it was present in the stones themselves, which were also one with the stars. It left him shaking, trembling, this welling-up that saturated everything. In the midst of his own disintegrating existence he felt himself opening like a flower to this mystery over which he had no control.

Suddenly Jacob Joseph, a miserable, starving creature, began to speak, though wordlessly, into the infinite distance that was God: *When at last we come to you this yearning, which goes on and on and never comes to you, will cease.*

For the rest of the day he drifted in and out of consciousness.

Towards the end he asked for water. The Lieutenant managed to raise him sufficiently so that he could suck at the spoon. Of all the lives demanded of him, this one he was least willing to let go. So he continued holding him, clinging on, thought the effort was considerable. But the young man showed no great desire to stay, especially now he found he could float about unhindered. He had this sense that someone who loved him was very close. An urgent feeling of closeness all the time. Though there was nothing but light all around. He was wholly in the presence of light. He seemed himself to have turned into light. Light within light.

The dying man had begun to whisper, though so feebly his commander, an ear bent close, could make out only a faint sibilance that might have been a sigh of wonder.

＊

Enormous bergs, with flocks of sea-birds swooping, screaming, now drifted south as the *Samphire* steamed through the thinning pack, past capes and islands, past floes with families of walrus, and craggy rocks, the colonies of wheeling gulls. The sailors, deprived of the rhythm of days and nights, still bemused by a sun that went round in circles, gazed in wonder at the great bergs gliding past. Eastwards, under a fiery cloud-scratched sky, snowy domes flushed coppery-rose.

'Greenland's icy mountains,' murmured someone, *sotto voce*.

It was the young ensign, Bitzer. The allusion struck him as worth remembering. He made a note of it in the journal he was keeping.

Beyond Hakluyt Island, the *Samphire* broke through into the North Water. Now the open sea stretched beyond Cape Alexander to Smith Sound. The sou'westerly had stiffened to a steady gale, bringing with it flurries of snow.

Commander Stannery took his ship on to the weather-shore, north of Littleton Island.

He went himself to supervise the shore party. They came across much driftwood, an oar, a piece of ornamental scroll-work, and a portion of a ship's deck, as well as a wet wad of paper, too far gone to be distinguishable. There were, too, many cairns, mute testimony of earlier landings, circumstances unknown. Only as the line of searchers was returning over the island did a seaman, probing a snow gully, uncover the barrels left two years before by young Mr Bright, still labelled for dispatch: *Lt. W. Parish, Fort Chance, Lady Franklin Bay, Grinnell Land.*

Back on the bridge of the *Samphire*, the commander gazed at the shore, now barely visible through the blizzard. He thought it very unlikely Parish had remained at Fort Chance. His orders had instructed him to retreat south, and from what he'd learnt of the man, Stannery was convinced he would have followed his instructions to the letter. Yet he found it hard to credit that Parish could have reached Cape Sabine and not sent a party over for the supplies. The most likely explanation was that he'd been stopped somewhere along the coast of Grinnell Land. In which case he might very well have turned back north to try to regain his old quarters.

Stannery considered his options. Should he wait for Bostock? Should he cross the Sound to Cape Sabine, and search there?

He was spared further agonizing by the tall masts of the *Louisa Soames,* just then nosing round the point.

*

Now that they had learnt it was defeat and death, and not imperishable glory, that awaited men, the terrible land stood forth in all the joy and splendour of creation. Clad in airy light, it had the clarity of a polished gem. Rocks glittered in that spangled light. Giddy with warmth and light, delirious hares flashed to and fro. Everything that lived praised life. Out in the bay, where the sea ice had begun to melt, a lagoon of shimmering light rang with the cries of waterfowl and squabbling geese.

Floes laden with harrumphing walrus floated in and out on the tide. Squadrons of duck flashed on urgent errands, past colonies of seals scattered over the blueish ice. And the seals barked their praise. With every day more and more birds came winging in to the promise stored all winter long, and were not disappointed. Waders, scuttling up and down, took as their due whatever the dragging wave uncovered. Tiny flies buzzed among the tussocks. Bumblebees nuzzled the tundra blossoms. The land was keeping its word.

In the flux and clarity of Arctic light every thing came into its own. Rocks glowed, or glittered with starry points. A dull bank flared suddenly with the colours of wild flowers. The burnished face of a king eider, see-sawing on the swell, was charged with its own particularity. Emergent light, streaming from gunmetal beach to jade hills, lit suddenly on folds of crumpled silk, kindled the illumination of another world around, within. Not emptiness but fullness. And the land lay content under the blessed light.

To the Puritan Lieutenant it seemed an emanation of divine joy. Though it had killed him, William Parish could find no fault with it.

Searching in his pockets, he found his wedding ring. He'd taken it off some weeks before, when his fingers began to swell. Now he managed to work it down over the top joint of his finger. He wanted to die wearing his wedding ring.

That done, he lay back on his mattress. He found himself walking down the hill from the inn where he'd put up, walking under a grudging sky, with flakes of snow travelling on a blustery wind. A cold welcome too: the mother mute, the guests keeping their distance. Then, sitting again behind the sorrel, he felt his wife's presence, or was it absence, her hand slipping into his. He knew then, present or absent, whichever it was, she had never been far from his side. She had always been there, waiting somewhere on the fringes of his need, waiting to be noticed. He too was content now to wait, comforted by her faint smell of cinnamon.

A gull flew past the tent. Out in the bay the bellowing of walrus reminded that God was to be glorified, even in the fires of affliction.

Meanwhile he held on to her hand, springing from the bones of a wrist he might have encircled with a finger and thumb. And room to spare. All that agitated wrestling with ships and promises of help, he was free of that at last. It was an enormous relief to have let it go. It seemed to him that true deliverance was to be looked for only in love, through love. He had, besides, his wife, whose loving presence was now a constant reassurance. He only prayed she would be taken first, so he would not have to leave her behind a second time.

It was the eve of the solstice. A strong southerly wind got up, carrying squalls of snow, battering at the tent. Inch by inch it gave way before the gale. Too weak to straighten it, the men lay in their bags and endured. So, hour by hour, the wind continued pushing at the tent, rattling the heavy canvas, snatching at the guys, tugging the flaps from under the rocks weighting them down, until it had all but collapsed, shrouding the men, pinning them to the ground.

EIGHTEEN

Six miles to the south-east, the relief squadron lay at anchor in the lee of a small island at the mouth of Payer Harbour. On the bridge of the *Samphire*, the flaps of his fur cap tied up despite squally blasts of snow, Ensign Bitzer stood a little to the rear of the commander, ready to make such signals to the shore party as might be required. Meanwhile, he peered through his glass at the island, on the summit of which, barely visible though the snow-swirl, he could just about make out a tall cairn topped by some sort of post.

A young man whose high cheekbones and dark, darting glance excited much admiration among the wives and daughters of Annapolis, he had entered the Naval Academy as a matter of course. There was never any question of him doing other than follow in his father's footsteps. He could scarcely have known, nor did his superiors inform him, that he was joining a service all but moribund from neglect. Since graduating from the academy, he had spent a number of years devoted largely to drilling, polishing, coaling, drawing up rosters, and other operations necessary to the general management of ships. It was not long before he began to ask himself what the navy was really for. An eager young fellow, he was tormented by those questions which time alone could answer. Where would he be in ten, twenty years' time? Twenty-one, and what had he done? *Nothing*. What was he doing? *Nothing*. The thought that he might live and die without achieving anything, unknown outside a narrow circle of family and friends, was more than he could bear.

As soon as the call came he had offered himself for the expedition, though not expecting to be chosen, such was the response from officers, many of them old Arctic hands. Though experience counts for nothing that cannot sail through the medical examination.

Nor, as it turned out, were health and strength all the young man had to offer.

Commander Stannery stroked his beard as he studied the report.

'What else can you do? Can you operate a photographic machine?'

'I can, sir.' No doubt he could learn.

A sharp young fellow, he would snap up whatever fell his way. When approached by the *New York Sentinel* to serve as its correspondent for the expedition Gene Bitzer jumped at the chance.

As the squadron battled north through Baffin Bay, through fogs and blizzards, he dreamed of an historic encounter with a haggard figure, emaciated no doubt but still of military bearing, and Commander Stannery approaching, hand outstretched. *Lieutenant Parish, I presume ...*

Ah, he did believe he was on the threshold of great things.

Meanwhile, enlarged, excited, he stared through his glass, waiting for the story to unfold.

As, sure enough, it did, in the shape of a seaman espied stumbling back from the island. He was shouting, waving as he came on, splashing through pools of water, his voice, whatever he was yelling, drowned in a sudden burst of cheering from the men lining the bow. Out of which emerged the fragments of a message, snatched out of the air by Bitzer, and flung aloft.

'All well ... Parish at Cape Sabine ... all well ...'

The young man was ablaze with excitement at the photographs he would take.

Not long afterwards, a box was brought aboard the *Samphire,* and carried to the ward room. Commander Stannery unpacked it, laying each item, notebooks, sets of photographic negatives, on the wardroom table. His officers, turning pages, gazed wonderingly at tables of figures, field notes on the *cetacea,* the *ungulata,* the *rodentia* and *carnivora,* the mosses and lichens, the *medusae,* accounts of fossils, auroral displays, petrified forests: the painstaking work, it might have been, of several Harvard professors.

Lt Austen, the exec officer, was opening a small package wrapped in oilcloth. He uncovered a small stained notebook. Turning the cover, he read out loud what he found written there.

'"A journey to the Farthest North, being the journal of Harry J. Foxer, 2nd Lieut. 19th Infantry".'

Meanwhile, the commander had discovered what he needed to know.

'We've found them,' he said quietly.

He read from a sheet torn from an army despatch book. '"My party now encamped immediately south of a small point of land midway between Cocked Hat Island and C. Sabine. All well."' Gravely he set the paper on the table.

'It is dated Sunday, October 21st. Eight months ago.' He forbore to add what everyone was thinking.

Even with the caches, reflected Bitzer, they could have had little more than a month's supply of food. Meanwhile, the commander was giving orders for the manning of the cutter. The young ensign heard, above the shouts of the coxswain, a whirr and screech of block and tackle. Yes, they must be dead. He took it as a personal disappointment. But brightened, imagining what scenes of horror might greet the landing party.

Meanwhile Lt Austen was supervising a hasty assembling of supplies. A couple of seamen began lowering boxes into the cutter. The young correspondent looked on enviously. He wanted desperately to go along. Suddenly, as the inspiration possessed him, he dashed below to the steward's store, and was back on deck in moments, his arms filled with blankets.

Stannery seemed mildly surprised so essential an item should have been overlooked.

'Oh aye, blankets. Aye, take 'em along.'

The tall commander watched the cutter pitching, rolling in the choppy sea. Midsummer day, and a coast still sheathed in snow and ice.

They must be dead.

NINETEEN

It was a sparkling morning for a homecoming. The electric air vibrated with excitement, from the green bluffs of New Hampshire, with its dancing spires and pinnacles, to the shimmering Isles of Shoals, see-sawing on a dazzling, light-soaked sea.

On the bridge of the *Samphire,* well muffled up in greatcoat and fur hat, Lieutenant Parish stood clutching the rail as Commander Stannery pointed out familiar landmarks known since boyhood. The salt wind pricked at the Lieutenant's eyes as he gazed at a filmy cluster of white houses that was sliding past. Meanwhile, the lacquered coast of Maine was closing fast.

The Sound stretched smooth as a mill-pond to the New Hampshire shore as the *Samphire* swung her head towards the narrows. Dead ahead, the Whale Back Light was coming into view.

As she cleared Fort Point she fell in with hundreds of pleasure craft waiting to escort her home. Air trembled at the thunder-crack of guns as she steamed towards the ship-hemmed haven of old Portsmouth. Clustered together in the bow the survivors stared at the fluttering handkerchiefs, the waving parasols. What they had so long despaired of ever seeing lay all before them, in the gables of Kittery and New Castle, in the old green town itself, nestling in its foliage. And yet desire is often perplexed by what it finds.

Up river, where the Navy Secretary had assembled the entire North Atlantic fleet, dozens of ships were riding at anchor, their rigging filled with cheering crewmen. As the *Samphire* came abeam of the flagship, the bluejackets mustered on the fo'c'sle head broke into cheers. Thousands more, packing wharves and jetties, waved from the shore.

Aboard the *Pensacola,* the wife of Lt Parish, fluttering her handkerchief along with other wives, was straining her eyes for a sight of William, though the figures aboard the little ship were too far off for her to make him out. She had been polishing the door knocker when the Western Union boy came bounding over the patch of grass. 'He's safe and well, Mrs Parish, ma'am,' the youth sang out as he handed her the wire. Glad tidings had given him the buoyancy of angels. Only when she was alone again, did she sit down weakly on the stair to read the news for herself: *Safe and well, but weak. Shall request long sick leave. Did what we came to do. Foxer carried your flag to Farthest North.* Meanwhile, the official party of admirals, generals and congressmen, among whom were mingled dignitaries of the town, was growing quite convivial. Then the navy band struck up *Home Again*, and choirs of thousands, seemingly, were welcoming her husband home.

'I have arranged for you to greet Lieutenant Parish in the privacy of Stannery's cabin,' the Navy Secretary was murmuring in her ear. 'No one is to board the *Samphire* until after you have been reunited.'

Thus cut off from the scene, members of the press were forced to rely on other sources to secure for readers the tenderness ('*Oh, William*' ... '*Oh, Matty*' ...) of that reunion. Engravings depicted the good commander, while tiptoeing discreetly from the cabin, directing a backward glance at the explorer, who had knocked over a chair in his eagerness to embrace his wife.

Intense activity had followed the arrival of the first despatch from St John's. Next morning column after column was devoted to the news. The story shut out all other items from the front page of the *New York Sentinel*.

LIEUT. PARISH SNATCHED FROM THE BRINK
Sad Death of Brave Survivor
Commander Stannery's Intrepid Feat
'*D**n the Icebergs. Full Speed Ahead!*'
Grim Task for Rescuers

Their correspondent, a junior naval officer sailing with the squadron, the first to leap ashore, had been met by one of the survivors, a ghastly sight, tattered, filthy, emitting a sickly odour. Wordlessly, with skinny hand, the scarecrow figure, had motioned rescuers in the direction of a wind-battered tent. With beating hearts they approached, through a litter of broken cans and scattered worn-out clothing, and raised the canvas flap. On one side, eyes fixed, glassy, with hanging jaw, lay a man to all appearance dead. Across from him, a pitiable sight, a poor fellow with no feet, a spoon attached to the stump of an arm. On hands and knees, red skull cap surmounting a black thatch of matted hair, a man in a filthy ragged robe squinted up at the newcomer. His beard was long and tangled, the dirt thick on his hands and face. On being asked, *Who are you?*, he'd groped for a pair of spectacles, fixing them with trembling fingers, peering vacantly at the enquirer. *That's the Lieutenant*, whispered the limbless fellow, *Lieutenant Parish*. But for a pan of evil-looking jelly, there was no food of any kind.

Thus, and much more, young Bitzer. He stuck to truth wherever possible, but would not spurn its gaudier imitation where the real thing proved elusive.

There was huge speculation as to the contents of Lt Foxer's journal, of the existence of which the *Sentinel* had been apprised by its correspondent. A leading article posed the question exciting the hearts of millions:

> Who knows but that these will indeed prove to be the dauntless men who have reached the goal of two millennia, and planted the Stars and Stripe upon the axis of the world?

That weekend a multitude of visitors flocked into Portsmouth from surrounding towns and villages. The Navy Secretary had ordered that the ships of the relief squadron be opened for the inspection of the public. The decks of the *Samphire* were crowded with hundreds of visitors, chatting with the crew, hearing at first hand the story of the rescue. Many were moved to tears by the tale of poor Schmidt whose wounds, corrupting in the unaccustomed warmth of the ship's sick bay, had proved beyond the surgeons' skill.

Rufus Chance, who had emerged as principal patron of the expedition, held a reception in his suite at the Rockingham Hotel.

'I like to think,' he mused, amid a cluster of reporters, 'this land was placed here between the two oceans to be found by a special kind of people.' The magnate paused to make room for his words. 'We are an exceptional nation. Naturally, we expect great deeds of our best men.'

Meanwhile, the men in question had been assembled on a balcony, a focus for the grand parade organized by the mayor and a committee of citizens. Huddled together on their cramped perch, they seemed bewildered amid the huge enthusiasm of the crowd below. The Lieutenant, a tall, whiskery figure in a white linen suit, was instantly recognizable. He wore a white Panama as if to shield his face from the glare of so many staring up at him. The others might have been trying out disguises. Nate Emmons, now crop-headed, had shaved off beard and moustache. Klaus Stempel's hair, gleaming like patent leather, was licked back over his scalp. Paddy Lawless's upper lip wore a big droopy moustache. Hansie Wutz sported a short square beard and burnsides.

In the street below, cramming the hotel steps, spilling onto the grassy banks, or lodged in trees, a crowd wild with excitement was cheering the men who had endured for them, striven for them, the men who had gone the Farthest North.

A banner, *Hail to the Heroes*, jiggled up and down in front of the balcony, appeared to distress the white-suited Lieutenant, who was seen to shake his head, and made as if to leave, but was taken by the arm.

'You must accept the part,' shouted Senator Clay above the din. 'It's expected of you.'

Meanwhile, the flags waved, the bands played, and the public continued to applaud its finer feelings as the sailors, the

fire companies, the marines, the midshipmen marched round
the town, those too dignified to march being conveyed in car-
riages, the blue-uniformed volunteers of Stannery's squadron
throwing a smart salute to the survivors on their balcony, who
could have been wishing themselves anywhere but there.

On the following morning, the admirals, the generals and the
congressmen departed.

Commander Stannery sailed south with the bodies of the
dead, to be restored, where possible, to their families. The survivors were returned to the Navy hospital to continue their
recovery.

The Lieutenant and his wife had been settled in quarters on
the Navy reservation. Secretary Hynes was proving a most
genial host.

'What you need,' he said, 'is some time to yourselves. You'll
not be disturbed there.'

So Martha Parish started out a second time on married life,
now in a clapboard cottage framed by apple trees, facing the
harbour mouth. And found herself confronted, if not altogether
by a stranger, then the strangeness of a husband restored. *You're
bound to find some change in him*, cautioned Lucius Clay. She
was shocked by the skin that hung in flaps.

'Don't expect too much,' said Dr Claggart grudgingly. He
was a middle-aged physician with a florid face and sunken eyes.
He'd been somewhat soured by service life. A long experience
of malingerers had taught him to distrust the sick. 'We must
build him up by degrees.'

He prescribed a diet of oatmeal, soft-boiled egg and milk
toast, raw minced beef and onions, with a nightcap of beef
broth.

A succession of sunny days, warm without the sultriness of
August, promised to assist the healing work of Nature.

'Why not sit out,' she urged, and set a chair in the garden.

He couldn't walk far, or stand for very long. He took to
sitting under the apple trees, absorbed in grass, and the greenery

of leaves. Seeing him so frail, muffled up in the greatcoat that no more fitted than the skin which hung from his bones, she felt such tenderness for him. Oh, such tenderness. Or he would fall asleep in the chair. He slept fitfully, dozing during the day, rousing much of the night. The normal rhythms of life seemed quite broken down in him.

Once, at dawn, missing him from her bed, she found him in the garden, gazing out beyond Fort Point, where the rising sun, like melting butter, floated on the waves in flakes of golden light.

'We used to count the days,' he told her. 'Though they weren't days. Not as you understand them.' He came back inside the house, clinging on to her with his bony fingers, as if love too was something he would never again take for granted.

She felt he had plumbed depths of darkness beyond her comprehension. Though he scarcely spoke of it, except in asides.

'You need great patience,' he remarked one day. 'Though it may bring self-control, or it may bring breakdown.'

These musings, fallings from him, troubled her as she turned them over in her mind. She feared he still had miles to travel before he got safe home.

Sometimes he just sat, his hands, all knuckles, lying in his lap, the very image of an exhausted soul. There was a space around him she couldn't enter, though acutely conscious of his presence there, the shifting of his body, the creaking of his chair. Then, sitting at her sewing, she set out to be a loving presence. She thought some revelation must eventually take place.

He had the papers brought round every day, a folly that seemed to fly in the face of the peace and quiet Dr Claggart had prescribed. But he was insistent. She knew, without asking, he *had* to see what was being written.

Now the parade was over, the flags and bunting put away, the post mortem had begun.

The lead was given by no less a person than the president himself, in the pages of the *New York Herald*. Profoundly thankful, of course, that some lives had been saved, he was forced to say he'd never approved of these ventures. He could not believe such advancement of knowledge as they might achieve could in any way make up for such dreadful suffering and loss of life. The *Herald* echoed the president's sentiments in calling for an end to this murderous folly of sending men to certain death.

In other papers, too, there was wide agreement that the game was not worth the candle. It had not gone unobserved that the Secretary for War, in his telegram congratulating the relief squadron on an arduous duty successfully completed, had offered no word to the survivors. It was generally concluded that the expedition had failed in its purpose. No new lands had been discovered. It now appeared that Lieutenant Foxer had improved the British record by a mere four miles. He had not even rounded the tip of Greenland. It was, all the authorities agreed, a small return for such a shameful expense of money and life.

Martha Parish was fiercely, contemptuously angry.

'What do they know,' she said. 'They know nothing.'

The Lieutenant, though, had withdrawn to his room without a door. A space, it seemed, of numbing emptiness.

*

Stirring at last, he began to speak of the tasks before him, the report he must prepare for Congress. There was, too, a mass of paper to get through, putting the expedition's scientific work in order. The Army quartermaster would require an estimate of any chargeable losses to be deducted from the back pay owed to the estates of those who'd died. First, though, he must write to the families. There were wills to execute, possessions to return. Already letters were arriving from families who'd received the bodies of loved ones, and wanted to know what had happened to some watch, or other heirloom.

'I must make a start,' he muttered.

Yet the days passed, and still he'd done nothing. Then, with one of her flashes, she saw he was grieving for his men.

With the sunny weather continuing, she set a table in the garden with the rosewood writing desk that had been a wedding present from Professor Cousins. Thin high bars of cloud stretched to transparency in a sky of blue.

From time to time she glanced through the window where he sat at his work.

A little later, when she went out with his coffee, she found him staring out across the harbour. He'd written not a word.

'What is it?' she asked, though not expecting to be told. And reached out with a hand to his shoulder. Where it lay unregarded. Until at length she had to fetch it back.

Several times Dr Claggart came over from the Navy hospital.

'And how is he today?' The sunken eyes did not quite look at her as he put his question.

'I fear,' she said hesitantly, 'all is not serene within his mind.'

How could she tell him what she didn't know herself?

'No doubt the deaths are weighing heavily with him.'

She felt a spasm of anger.

'If the government had acted promptly,' she flashed back, 'there would have been no deaths.'

Dr Claggart stroked his beard and looked thoughtful. Out of respect, it could have been, for a wife.

One day General Sweetsir came to the cottage, and was closeted alone with William.

She took her work basket out into the garden and began mending an open-work stocking, a finicky task which required all her concentration so that she was but vaguely aware of the murmur of voices from the open window. It was a warm day, tempered by the softest of breezes off the harbour, setting leaves a-stir.

Suddenly she heard William's voice, clearly audible above the whispering leaves.

'It can't be kept quiet for ever. Someone must have seen the bullet holes.'

His note of anguish caught at her throat.

'You did what you had to do,' came the general's gruff rejoinder. 'Besides, it took place beyond any territorial jurisdiction. There's no civil authority on earth can touch you for it.'

The exchange left her trembling. She was suddenly aware she no longer knew what might be required of her, nor by what tortuous paths Necessity would lead her. Only that she must continue to be patient.

She so wished she could have talked to Lucius Clay. But the senator had returned to Washington straight after the parade.

'A good politician is not so very different from a soldier,' he'd quipped. 'He knows when to retire gracefully.'

Though the senator spoke in his usual jesting way, there was a deal of pain behind his voice.

One evening William Parish lit the lamp, and set it on a table by the window. Sitting at his desk he took out the list of names.

As a young lieutenant he'd written his share of letters to the families of dead soldiers. Even at the height of the war it was a duty he'd performed with his usual conscientiousness, and as promptly as circumstances permitted.

Martha Parish had taken up her sewing. It was a still night. There was no wind. No sound came from outside the cottage to disturb their companionable silence, he at his work, she at hers. Now and then she was conscious of the sound of his pen scratching, stopping, scratching again. Between times there was the comforting crackle of the stove.

At ten o'clock, she made his nightcap of beef broth. She would have waited while he drank it, but he shook his head.

'You go,' he said. 'I shall sit a while.'

Sipping at his broth, he stared out at the night. Two miles or more across the water a thin point of light flashed intermittently, a melancholy signal that spoke of loneliness, and the wide sea beyond.

William Parish shrank from the summons. He shrank at the very thought of crawling down that passageway again, and into the stinking hut where the dead lay waiting. Their shrunken faces loomed up at him: Muller, pleading for water he could not provide, poor Rainbird, Asher, the grinning Hanson, Fabius' accusing stare ... *You are responsible ... You ...*

Powerless to restore what he'd taken, the Lieutenant wanted to remember all the good he could. He wanted to give back something to cherish of each son or husband, something distinctive, something that was not a lie. Methodical as ever, he'd jotted down a note against each name: Fromm's ingenuity in making and mending, Hewitt's Christian fortitude, poor Schmidt's unfailing cheerfulness, Diggs, *United we stand ...*

When he'd come to George Reade's name, though, he felt utterly at a loss. What was he to say of George?

 He stared out at the night. All evening clouds had been backing up above the horizon. Now the wind was rising. He could hear it gusting in the branches of the apple orchards. The trees themselves were lost to sight. Only the solitary beam of the Whale Back Light stood firm against the blackness of the night. In contemplating that image of ceaseless watchfulness, steadfast amid the flurries of rain now spattering the window, William Parish was suddenly mindful of all he'd ever wished to be for his men, and had fallen short of.

A yearning swept over him. He took a fresh sheet of paper from his desk. Then, soaring on wings of noble emotion, he began his letter to the mother of George Reade: *To say he was much loved is to do less than justice to the regard in which he was held. All his concern was for others. There were no lengths he wouldn't go to, no trouble he wouldn't take, where it concerned the welfare of the party. He always knew what was needful – more, he was singularly blessed with those qualities which enable a man to do what is needful. He was our rock.*

He died ... he was about to write – then broke off to consider: *... at Camp Resolute* was what he had in mind. It seemed an appropriate name. It pleased him to think it might convey something of the truth of the man. Far better, in any case, than the stark fact: *Your son died no place.*

As if summoned, the desolation assembled itself around him: the ice-field, and a snow-plastered figure, trudging through the storm, trudging endlessly. If you suffer long enough some place, he saw with sudden, panicky certainty, you never leave it. Never. And other men would come with their dream, with their cravings and fixations, to meet with the same blankness, the wind's turmoil, the churning ice. And endlessly the years would come and go. Briefly the sun would circle the summer sky, and sink back to its long absence. And the men would fathom the darkness of the dream.

Then William Parish began to weep, for he had brought those young men to their deaths.

*

One morning a Navy messenger came round with a telegram. The Lieutenant tore it open. He read it, then handed it to his wife. She read:

Please to remember you're still in my safe keeping. No discharge until Dr Claggart gives you a clean bill. In the meantime, continue to regard yourselves as the Navy's honoured guests.

'It seems,' said her husband drily, 'the Navy Secretary wants to keep me under house arrest.'

It was, in fact, a precaution as kindly meant as it was shrewd on the part of the Navy Secretary, whose instinct for self-advancement was sometimes undermined by a quality impossible to characterize unless it were a certain human decency.

Very early that morning he'd been woken in his Fifth Avenue hotel by a private message from the hand of the Navy Surgeon General.

Suggest you get rid of Parish pronto. Send him back to the Army. Hospital staff picking up unpleasant rumours. So Claggart reports. Something very ugly about to break.

Sam Hynes had been expecting something of the sort. He couldn't know when, exactly. Only that it would be very nasty.

He hadn't long to wait. It arrived that very morning, on his breakfast tray. The whole front page of the *New York Sentinel* was given over to the story. The headlines were every bit as bad as he'd anticipated.

A TALE OF HORROR
Dreadful Revelations of Cape Sabine
Secretary Hynes' Secret Memorandum
HOW PRIVATE HANSON DIED
DIRE CONSEQUENCES OF OFFICIAL
BLUNDER

He read on, with sardonic detachment, to learn of written documents in his possession testifying to '*the most shocking catalogue of brutality and savagery*'. It was perfectly true, he'd been privy to the facts for three weeks at least. Stannery had given him a full report. Sure, he'd done everything in his power to keep back the truth. So would they, in his position. *Batten down the hatches, and sit out the storm*, was how Stannery put it. He'd discussed the situation with the Secretary for War. They'd agreed to place a *cordon sanitaire* around Parish and his party, and await developments.

The Navy Secretary had been in the newspaper business himself. He knew very well that what folk might draw the line at in practice, they were eager to read about once it got into the papers. Well, he wasn't about to abandon Parish to the press pack. All the same, he wondered how they'd got the story. Someone at the hospital? One of the rescue squadron? He would have to look into that.

He poured himself another cup of coffee, and turned to the editorial page.

The *Sentinel,* he learned, attached no blame to the unfortunate men, driven by dreadful necessity to their shocking course. The guilt lay with those who'd failed them in their need, more especially with the Secretary for War, who saw no use, as he was said to have put it, 'in throwing any more money after dead men'.

Sam Hynes sucked at a stray fragment of steak stuck in a tooth. He'd thought at the time that remark, if ever it got out, would come home to haunt Elijah.

✳

It was, indeed, a tale of horror: a tale to harrow up the soul, freeze blood, and make the hair stand on end; a tale such as would make the name of Lt Parish's expedition stink for all time in the long and honourable annals of Arctic exploration.

The *Sentinel* told of covert meetings, of conspiracy in high places, of officers and men sworn to secrecy, in an attempt to keep back truth from a public that would be all the more shocked to learn what it was intended they should never know: that men supposedly living on lichens, shrimps and sealskins, had in reality kept themselves alive by feasting on the bodies of their comrades. Many of the men who, it was claimed, had died of starvation, were actually devoured by their ravenous comrades. Medical personnel on board the *Samphire* had been shocked to find that the blankets, used to transport the dead from their shallow graves, contained nothing but heaps of bones, many of them picked clean. An officer, among the first of the rescue party, alerted by the pitiful cries of one survivor, had testified to the man's pleas as, wild with fright, he'd struggled with the navy crewmen attempting to lift him gently from the ground: *O, don't shoot me too. Don't let them eat me as they did poor Hanson. Don't let them do it, sir. Oh, don't … don't …*

As the news spread, copied to every corner of the land, the rotary presses were soon spinning out mutating versions of the story. Many readers, talking over the frightful revelations in stores and parlours, bars and business premises, found themselves at odds as to what had actually happened. Some claimed the party had split into rival camps, one led by Parish, the other following the doctor. The doctor's party, it was said, had been denied their share of the food.

As the allegations were tossed back and forth, the claims of moral principle clashed with those of pragmatism. In his weekly piece for the *Hartfield Republican,* Professor Cousins appealed for sympathy for the beleaguered men. *Which of us*, he pleaded, *can imagine himself enduring what those man had to endure, slowly starving to death?* Was the mortal shell sacrosanct after the spirit had departed, asked the Reverend Dwight. Could it really be wrong to make use of it to sustain the divine spark in those still living?

With fresh revelations coming almost daily, the corridors of the State/War/Navy building were thronged with reporters seeking answers. Did they simply use dead bodies for food? Or did they slaughter the living? And what about Hanson? Was he shot for repeatedly stealing from his comrades? Or was it, as had been shockingly suggested, a case of petty theft on the part of a decent enough fellow being made a pretext for the others to kill and eat him?

The *New York Sentinel* was in no doubt as to whom to hold responsible.

Physically, at least, the Lieutenant was making a recovery. He was growing stronger. He had put on weight. He was able to take exercise, which he did alone, pacing under the apple trees, or along the shore. He was still sensitive to changes in the weather. He felt the cold, while sultry days left him much pros-trated. Even so, he gave no outward sign as, one sticky afternoon, he sat under the trees with General Sweetsir.

'The Secretary wants you to make a statement.' The general mopped his face with a large linen handkerchief. 'Put it whichever way seems best to you. You'll have my full support.'

Martha Parish told herself she would not ask, but watched, and waited, conscious of him struggling with an enormity for which words were wholly inadequate. He could have been racking himself, trying to recall who had been alive and able to move about at times when desecration of the dead might have been possible.

That night, as she took in his cup of beef broth, he reached out a hand towards her.

'I swear to you,' he said, fixing on her a look of utmost desperation, 'I know of no law, human or divine, that was broken at Cape Sabine.'

Her eyes filled with tears. She took his hand and pressed it to her lips.

That same night, under cover of darkness, a grim scene was being enacted in a New Jersey cemetery. The costs of the operation, undertaken for the purpose of setting at rest the minds of a local family, were borne by a leading newspaper. The *New York Planet* was able to report, following investigations carried out in the mortuary chapel, that large pieces of tissue had been cut from the trunk of Private X, whose name was withheld, out of consideration for the relatives. Incisions had been made along the line of the ribs below the shoulder, a section of epidermis lifted, part of the underlying fibrous tissue removed, and the flap of skin replaced. A further examination had revealed that the contents of the large intestine, when scrutinized with the aid of a powerful magnifying glass, contained, as well as scraps of vegetable substance, fragments of tissue. This faecal matter included what appeared to be the fragment of a tendon, evidently severed by some instrument. It seemed very likely that Private X, before becoming food for his comrades, had himself partaken of human flesh.

Not to be outdone, the *New York Sentinel* printed fresh revelations.

ANTHROPOPHAGY
Survivors Acknowledge that
They Consumed Human Flesh

Their correspondent, the ubiquitous naval officer, having described the worn path trodden between the graveyard and the wretches' tent, went on to tell how he'd been held mesmerized by the staring eyes of that same survivor as he recalled his first taste of human flesh. Drawing on memories of cold fowl served by an aunt in Baltimore, young Bitzer spoke of his own continuing nightmares: dreams in which he felt his lips pressing down on bland, flabby meat that must somehow be swallowed if he hoped to live.

Amid the ferment, with amputated limbs thrown daily into the communal pot, little coverage was given to a further statement issued from the Navy Yard.

MAN-EATING TOOK PLACE IN SECRET
Lieut. Parish Denies all Knowledge

Those who knew him recognized in the Lieutenant's repudiation – it would have been, he said, contrary to discipline – something of his stiff, old-fashioned rectitude.

But there was more to come. Fresh speculation surrounded the death of the surgeon, Fabius. One account claimed he took his own life, and was then devoured by the survivors. His body, it was pointed out, had not been returned with the rest. Another version had him done to death by a dissident faction out of favour with the commander, and therefore more famished than the others. Drawing on the seemingly inexhaustible testimony of his informant, the *Sentinel*'s correspondent was able to reveal that the poor man, terrified by the ravening gaze of men waiting for him to expire, had literally died of fright. Then, with the fleeting spirit yet quivering in its passage from the body, the doctor had been dismembered, the dripping fragments, speared on sticks, toasted briefly over a fire by the famished band, and wolfed down. The wilderness had become a screen on which a man might project his bloodiest inventions.

Many readers were by now greatly troubled in their souls. In the First Congregational Church, Hartfield, a visiting preacher, the author of *Apocalypse Fulfilled*, had scoured the Scriptures in vain for a word of healing.

'The prophet Isaiah went naked to foretell a people carried

into captivity; Jeremiah wore the yoke to warn of their enslavement. Now the best and bravest of our young men devour one another. What does that signify?'

His gaze ranged soulfully over the congregation.

'I can't think how Matty can bear him to touch her,' shuddered Cousin Thankful.

The president, uncertain of his party's nomination at the forthcoming convention, was thanking his stars he'd had the foresight to distance himself from the whole enterprise.

'Take it from me, Pliny,' said Amos Potwine, 'that's the last we'll hear of the North Pole.'

Restored now to his desolate corner of Pennsylvania, Rufus Chance gazed from his window at a long procession of trucks clanking past laden with coal and iron ore. As to the eating of human flesh, he had no fixed view on the matter. He could readily perceive where it might be needful. He let his gaze rove contentedly among the heaps of slag and cinders. He was always glad to get back. In the red glow of the furnaces, the perpetual clank and roar, there was a dark grandeur which satisfied his soul.

In the State/War/Navy building the siege continued. Waylaid repeatedly at the doors of their own departments, the two principal officers of state were negotiating the terms of a joint statement.

Attempts at unanimity could not pass without an acid observation from Secretary Crowell.

'*Batten down the hatches, and sit out the storm*. That was how you put it, if I remember rightly.'

The Navy Secretary shrugged. The time for toughing it out was over.

'Let's face it,' he pointed out, 'there may well be other exhumations.'

The following day the double doors of the War Department were opened to members of the press. In they came, their boots clattering over the floor of cherry and white maple, packing into the glowing room. When they were settled, the Secretary for War read out in his grudging voice a succession of brusque sentences.

'Fourteen bodies were recovered from Cape Sabine. They were brought aboard the *Samphire,* where they were stored under a covering of ice. Each body in turn was examined by Navy surgeons. Six were found to have been mutilated. The mutilations had been carried out with some surgical skill. That is all that is known of the matter.'

Dearly would he have had his clerk show them the door and be done with it. But there were questions to be faced. Mostly, his answers were in the negative.

No, there had been no admissions with regard to culpability.

No, he did not believe any more information would be forthcoming.

No, he was holding nothing back.

'My own belief,' he added, 'is that those who died last fed upon the bodies of those who died before.'

It was, as one newspaper man observed, a neat solution: the kind of thing you'd expect from Elijah Crowell.

*

In Washington the first autumn leaves had fallen. Scattered over the grass, they gathered in drifts against the plinth where old Hickory sat on his horse, bringing a touch of colour to the air of gentle melancholy that had begun to take possession of the square.

Squirrels were busy in the buckeye opposite the window, shaded now against the late October sun, where Senator Clay lingered over the final pages of his manuscript. He was reflecting gloomily that a man who has finished his *Memoirs* has come to the end of his life.

He glanced at the yellowing photograph of the boy in the uniform of the Confederacy. That defiant stare awoke a spasm of pain in the old man. Sometimes, in his more despairing moments, he wondered if he wouldn't have done better to have thrown in his hand with Lee, and gone down fighting, since those he loved most had been taken from him. For Lucius Clay the war was the worst thing that could have happened. It had broken him in half.

His gaze shifted to the sweet-faced woman in her crinoline, the ribbon at her throat pinned with the garnet brooch that had been his mother's. That gentle look, at least, held no reproach.

Ah, Sarah … Sarah … She had died so long ago, they might have met and married in another life.

And yet if Time, ordinary destructive Time, offers one dimension of reality, there is another in which all the years and their harsh lessons seem to count for nothing. Though it is the old, mostly, who must endure it. So it appeared to Lucius Clay. For whom things near at hand and things that were far away in time sometimes swam into such close alignment as to bring about a second death.

He was missing Matty: that shared life with the young woman; the nearness of her fears and longings, her trustfulness, the touching need that quickened memories of a deeper, dearer life long missing from his life.

Well, well. He had handed her back to her husband. He did not think it likely he would see her again.

He turned back again to the page. He had written:

Our founding fathers were faced with a profound question: how shall men live most truly from their centre of gravity as human beings? The wisest of them believed a man was best advised to rest content with a 'competence': a plot of land, a useful trade, a worthwhile calling. Yet since the war we have seen that vision of a common life collapsing under the pressure of all it was intended to keep out. Money and big business will put an end to our Republican ideal. Thomas Jefferson believed as much, and so do I.

The old man reflected wryly that of all men engaged in public life, he had become the most pitiable, a political anachronism.

We like to think we were intended for a new creation, somehow dispensed by Providence from the consequences of the Fall. For all that, I fear we may be no different from the rest. Like that deluded youth of ancient Greece we are in love with a reflection. We cling to our myth, our denial of darkness, our insistence that there is no darkness. It is always morning in America.

The Greeks too were a chosen people. They stood apart, with their slaves and helots, surrounded by barbarians. Yet if the Greeks have anything to teach us, it is that noble affirmation can commingle with the blindest folly. In their great tragedies it always calls for the intervention of the gods. Then comes some revelation, some catastrophe, to shatter the tale men tell about themselves, not as they are, but as they dream of being.

For some reason, the words brought to mind the gangling Yankee lieutenant. *The real thing*, Sweetsir called him. Lucius Clay saw him crossing the square, the snow settling on his shoulders, setting off again for an unknown shore. And in the distance, a howling of wolves.

✳

William Parish took the long sick leave he'd promised his wife.

He had spoken privately to each of the survivors. She watched them, arriving singly from the Navy hospital, sitting alone with William under the apple trees, looking out towards the sea. Each man, he said, had given his solemn word. Yet, observing his tensed figure, the long narrow face perpetually shadowed, she was conscious only of his pain and bewilderment. He could not tell whether they spoke the truth or not.

Sometimes the shadows deepened. Sometimes a look would come into his face that left her with a sense of something shut away. Something beyond all telling.

Then she would study the photograph published in

Harper's. It had been taken in the hospital garden. An infinite distance seemed to separate each man. None had any connection with the others. William, a frail figure in a black coat like a deacon's, stood, one hand clasping a Panama. His face wore a gentle, pleading look. His men posed stiffly, clutching the canes they had been given to occupy their hands. One, a little apart from the others, stood with his hand resting on a chair. They did not look at the camera. They looked outwards, at angles, as if searching for escape.

She was comforted by a kind letter from the Rev. Dwight. He had written: *I believe that a single life may experience all the stages of death and resurrection. So come, 'let us return unto the Lord; for he hath torn, and he will heal us; he hath smitten, and he will bind us up' (Hosea 6:i.)*

Thus it was, in the weeks and months that followed, she set herself to binding and restoring, it being given her to heal, if not knowing what.

Mostly they kept to themselves, for the Lieutenant was busy with his report, occasionally going out to attend some military or geographical occasion.

Always she put her arm through his on entering a room. And would hold on to him securely when discovering, on the suddenly deserted shores of conversation, another of the lonely places of the world.